Stephen Alter is the author of eighteen books of fiction and non-fiction. He was born in India and continues to live and write in his hometown, Landour. A recipient of the Kekoo Naoroji Award for Himalayan literature, a Guggenheim fellowship and a Fulbright award, he was also writer-in-residence at MIT and directed the writing programme at the American University in Cairo. He is founding director of the Mussoorie Writers Mountain Festival.

Also by Stephen Alter

NON-FICTION

All the Way to Heaven: An American Boyhood in the Himalayas (1998)

Amritsar to Lahore: A Journey Across the India-Pakistan Border (2000)

Sacred Waters: A Pilgrimage Up the Ganges River to the Source of Hindu Culture (2001)

Elephas Maximus: A Portrait of the Indian Elephant (2004)

Fantasies of a Bollywood Love Thief: Inside the World of Indian Moviemaking (2007)

Becoming a Mountain: Himalayan Journeys in Search of the Sacred and the Sublime (2015)

FICTION

Silk and Steel (1980)

Renuka (1989)

The Rataban Betrayal (2013)

In the Jungles of the Night (2016)

Praise for *The Rataban Betrayal*

'Alter brings to his thriller, set in Mussoorie but focused on Tibet, the same qualities he brings to his other work: impeccable prose, and a deep knowledge of the region, its beautiful but dangerous peaks, its erratic weather, its flora and fauna.' —Eunice de Souza, *Mumbai Mirror*

'Imagine a mix of John Le Carre's slow unspooling spy novels and the vivid time and place descriptions of Wilbur Smith [...] and what you get is a fine espionage thriller that gives a gripping account of murky international politics...' —Vani Mahesh, *Deccan Herald*

'*The Rataban Betrayal* is a fiercely intelligent thriller which maintains a frenetic pace throughout.' —Aditya Mani Jha, *The Sunday Guardian*

GULDAAR

WARLORD OF THE HINDU KUSH

A Novel

STEPHEN ALTER

SPEAKING TIGER

SPEAKING TIGER PUBLISHING PVT. LTD
4381/4, Ansari Road, Daryaganj
New Delhi 110002

First published in the US as *The Dalliance of Leopards* by
Arcade Publishing 2017

Published in India as *Guldaar: Warlord of the Hindu Kush* by
Speaking Tiger 2017

ISBN: 978-93-86702-00-5
eISBN: 978-93-86702-01-2

10 9 8 7 6 5 4 3 2 1

Typeset in Minion Pro by SÜRYA, New Delhi
Printed at Gopsons Papers Ltd

For Kit and Joe Reed

Guldaar. Noun. 1. Common name for leopard or panther (*Panthera pardus*), also known as baghera, cheetah, tendua.
2. The mark of a rose or rosette, which is the repeated pattern of five spots on a leopard's coat.
3. The five petals on a Himalayan musk rose.

—*Naqvi's Urdu-English Dictionary*

Very afraid
I saw the dalliance of leopards.
In the beauty of their coats
They sought each other and embraced.
Had I gone between them then
And pulled them asunder by their manes
I would have run less risk
Than when I passed in my boat
And saw you standing on a dead tree
Ready to dive and kindle the river.

—*Anonymous, fifth century AD*
(Translated from the Sanskrit by E. Powys Mathers)

One

Islamabad

The carpet seller drove an ancient Honda CD 175 cc motorcycle, loaded down with Afghan rugs. Eight of them were folded across the petrol tank in front; ten more were draped over the pillion seat and another dozen tied up in a huge bundle on a carrier at the back. With difficulty, he maneuvered around the potholes in the road, nearly tipping over several times, as the bike whined and fumed, its engine complaining of neglect. When he reached the diplomatic enclave, the surface of the road improved and he picked up speed, though the motorcycle remained unstable under its precarious load. With his wind-tangled beard and unruly turban, the driver could easily have been a Tartar horseman from five hundred years ago, arriving in the city after crossing over the Hindu Kush. He took a corner slowly, one foot stretched out in case he skidded. Twenty meters on ahead, he stopped at a police checkpoint, where two armed constables lifted the carpets cautiously to see if any bombs or weapons were hidden underneath. After a cursory inspection, they waved him through.

Five minutes later, he pulled up at a high steel gate, where another set of guards examined him with greater scrutiny. He produced a wrinkled ID card issued by the United Nations High Commission for Refugees. The card had been laminated, but the plastic was peeling away at the corners. After speaking on their walkie-talkies, the guards frisked the carpet seller, then showed him where to park his motorcycle. He shouldered a load of rugs and carried them through the gate, dropping these on the verandah of the house inside. It was a modern two-story residence, rented out to the US embassy by a senior judge in the Punjab High Court.

Fetching the heaviest bundle of carpets last, the Afghan untied the cloth in which they were wrapped. He spoke to himself, mumbling into his beard…perhaps a prayer, or a curse, or a final calculation of the price.

The diplomat emerged from his house, accompanied by a cook, who would serve as interpreter, though the carpet seller knew enough English to handle any transaction. Greetings were exchanged. *Salaam Alaykum. Wa Alaykum Salaam.* The diplomat had been posted in other Muslim countries and spoke halting Arabic and Farsi, as well as a smattering of Urdu. Tea was offered, and the cook went off to brew it in the kitchen.

'Very old. Three hundred years.' The Afghan tossed a rug on the terrazzo floor.

Knowing nothing of carpets, the diplomat pretended to inspect the texture, his fingers brushing the tasseled border, then feeling the weight of the knotted wool. The first few carpets were traditional Bokhara patterns, with medallions in red and black with hints of indigo. The diplomat had been warned about the wiles of Afghan carpet dealers, but this man came recommended by a Pakistani acquaintance who claimed to know the value of a carpet. He examined several prayer rugs with mihrab designs. They appeared to be well used, with spots where the knees and foreheads of the faithful had worn away the pile.

'This one…beautiful. Two hundred knots per square inch,' said the merchant.

'How old is it?'

'One hundred twenty years. It belonged to my grandfather. I carried it with me when I escaped from Mazar-e-Sharif.'

The cook arrived with cups of tea and remained silent. The

American seemed to like this carpet. It had a floral pattern and more colors than the others, mustard and green, against a background of purples and reds, not a conventional Afghan motif.

'What kind of flower is this?' the diplomat asked.

The carpet seller traced the pattern with his fingers. 'Anaarkali,' he said. 'Pomegranate.'

'How much?'

The Afghan slurped his tea before answering. 'Three thousand.'

'Rupees?'

'Dollars,' the Afghan said with a dismissive laugh. 'Only dollars.'

He drew the carpet aside and removed another from the pile and threw it on the floor.

'Six thousand. This one is two hundred years old, from the time of Shah Shuja.'

The carpet appeared more geometric with hexagonal shapes, a mosaic made of dyed yarns—ochre, red, and yellow, as well as an intricate latticework of patterns along the edges. The American lifted a corner and examined it carefully.

'What's this?' he said.

Knotted into the border was a curious design, repeated every six inches. At first, it looked like a lizard or some kind of locust, until the diplomat recognized what he was looking at: an AK-47. It was unmistakable, a tapered stock and magazine protruding beneath the barrel.

'Two hundred years old? You're kidding me. That's bullshit.' The diplomat shook his head at the carpet seller's deceit. The pattern was like an optical illusion. Each hexagon resolved itself into the fuselage of a helicopter gunship and the floral motifs above them were rotor blades. Either an American Apache or a Russian Mi-24 Hind—the diplomat couldn't make out which. The Afghan remained impassive, as if the provenance of his carpets were immaterial.

The next rug he threw out was the largest in his bundle, six feet wide by nine feet long. It was mostly rust and gold, with a diamond border of blue and red. In the center was the stylized shape of an animal, a large cat with a tail that curled up in a crooked S. The wool had been dyed a pale amber hue. Covering this were the leopard's spots, an irregular pattern of rosettes, like five daubs of ink, or the smudged petals of a rose.

'Tiger,' said the cook with a grin.

'Guldaar,' the carpet seller corrected him, knowing that the diplomat would choose this one. Minutes later, the haggling began. When the Afghan demanded $4,000, the cook intervened, speaking in Urdu and trying to bring down the price by half. After twenty minutes of negotiation, during which the seller extolled the workmanship of the carpet and the rarity of its design, they settled on $2,400.

Telling the cook to bring another cup of tea to seal their transaction, the diplomat counted a wad of hundred dollar bills into the carpet seller's hands. Both men remained silent as the money was handed over, along with a clear plastic case, the size of a thin matchbox, discreetly tucked in amongst the currency notes. After counting the dollars, the carpet seller stuffed them into the pocket of his vest, then examined the plastic case. A memory card lay inside, no bigger than a fingernail. The carpet seller weighed the tiny object in his callused palm before slipping it into an inner pocket of his vest.

Neither man spoke, though their eyes met in the shared knowledge that this transaction was far more valuable than the sale of a carpet. Looking down at the leopard's rampant profile, each of them considered the wild savagery of the beast knotted into the rough fabric of the rug, a cunning predator whose only enemy was man.

Just then, the cook emerged again carrying two cups of tea on a wooden tray. He offered it first to the carpet seller who took his cup by the rim instead of the handle.

A moment later, when the cook turned away, he found an arm around his throat and one hand firmly wedged beneath his jaw. The teacups fell to the verandah floor with a sudden crash. Within seconds the cook's neck had been snapped. The carpet seller performed this fatal maneuver with ease, as if he had done it many times before. Loosening his grip, he let the body slump to the floor and fall across the just-sold carpet. There was no sound beyond a choked whisper and a swift grappling of arms followed by the decisive crack of vertebrae. Immediately, the diplomat reached for a SIG-Sauer P224 that he carried in a shoulder holster under his jacket.

The Afghan seemed unperturbed and looked down at the shattered cups of tea.

'What the fuck is going on?'

'Informer,' the Afghan said in English, looking down at the crumpled figure on the floor.

'How do you know?' the diplomat asked, still holding the handgun ready.

The Afghan shrugged and leaned down to pick up an armful of carpets, before hoisting them onto his shoulder. He showed no fear, and the diplomat slowly lowered his gun.

'Next time, you should be more careful who you hire,' said the rug merchant.

'ISI?' the diplomat asked.

'No, RAW,' the Afghan replied. 'Indian intelligence.'

Two

Ohio

A Winnebago Sightseer drove steadily over the rolling hills of central Ohio, between freshly planted fields of soybean and corn. Farmhouses with barns and silos were set back from the narrow two-lane road. A yellow Mustang was parked beside a mailbox with a For Sale sign taped to its windshield. One of the farmers had erected a billboard advertising pedigreed collies and grooming services. Another had a roadside vegetable stand, which was empty this time of year, too early in spring for anything to ripen. The new leaves on the maples were a bright, translucent green. A dead raccoon lay on the gravel margins of the road, paws reaching toward the sky.

The driver of the mobile home was a ruddy-faced, silver-haired man wearing dark glasses against the glare of the morning sun. Next to him sat a woman with her hair permed and colored, staring out at the passing landscape with a look of boredom in her blue eyes. They could have been anyone, a retired couple driving their RV across the country, along back roads, through the heartland of America. The Winnebago had Maryland plates and a bumper sticker that read ROAD TRIPPERS FOR ROMNEY!

Ahead of them, half a mile farther on, lay a crossroads. Approaching from the right was an Amish carriage, a black buggy drawn by a pair of gray horses. As the two vehicles drove toward the junction, it looked as if they were headed for a collision. Neither showed any indication of stopping. The couple in the buggy rode in silence, the man in his thirties with a black beard and broad brimmed hat, his young wife beside him in her drab blue dress, blond hair pinned up beneath a starched white bonnet. As they approached the crossing, it was like a choreographed moment of anachronism, when springs in clocks explode, calendars fly backward, and the sun reverses direction in the sky.

But none of this happened. Instead, the RV accelerated and the Amishman drew back on his reins. The women waved at each other politely as they drove on. Time and history continued uninterrupted like the ribbon of asphalt stretching across the land.

Another mile on ahead was a sign: WELCOME TO EGGLESTON, OHIO. Population 16,438. The RV passed a couple of churches surrounded by empty parking lots and a strip mall with a JC Penney, and Home Depot. A golf course skirted the north side of town. Beyond it stood a large corporate facility, some kind of factory or warehouse, with a private airfield. A small jet was taking off. By now the road was lined with homes, each on its own parcel of land. The speed limit decreased to thirty miles an hour. Children were playing soccer outside a school. The RV turned left, its red indicator blinking.

BROMFIELD COLLEGE. A large stone plaque set in concrete marked the edge of the campus. The architecture changed from clapboard and aluminum sidings to yellow bricks. Students were passing between classes. Tennis practice was in full swing on the courts beside a horseshoe of dorms. After the library with its Corinthian columns, the RV took a left turn. Fraternity housing lay across the street, a beer keg upended on an uncut apron of grass.

Another right and then a sharp left onto College Lane. The RV was almost too large to negotiate the side street. The driver swung wide to take the turn before coming to a halt beside a split-level home, the kind of place assistant professors own before gaining tenure. It was a tidy, modest house, with clipped yews and a sloping lawn.

The side windows of the RV were small and tinted, like portholes on a yacht. Neither the driver nor the woman beside him made any move to get out. A squirrel was foraging in the rain gutter along one side of the house, but that was the only movement. Seconds later, the rear doors of the Winnebago opened and six uniformed men leaped out, each of them padded with body armor, helmets strapped to their chins. They cradled lightweight HK416C assault rifles in gloved hands. Fanning out across the yard in silence, the team moved with rehearsed efficiency. One of them tested the basement door as a second stealthily entered the screened porch. A third crouched next to the garage. Another two approached the front door. At a signal from the team leader, one of them rang the doorbell. Nobody answered. He rang it again, making the melodic chimes echo inside the house.

After the second try, the two men put their shoulders to the door and broke the lock. At the same instant, the man on the porch entered through the kitchen. A saucepan sat on the stove, half full of oatmeal. There was the smell of burnt toast. In the living room, a television was on with the volume muted, a morning talk show. The assault team moved cautiously, signaling with their hands. Boots were silent on the carpeted floors. A vacuum cleaner sat next to the coffee table, its hose coiled like a python. Two bedrooms lay at the rear, a bathroom in between. One of the pictures in the hall was a photograph of the Gateway of India in Mumbai with a woman standing in the foreground, holding a bouquet of tuberoses in her hands.

The room on the right was empty and looked as if it had never been slept in, with a floral bedcover that matched the drapes. With their rifles covering their teammate, two men watched intently as the third approached a closed door. Instead of kicking it open, the armed man gently twisted the knob and pushed, then flattened himself against the wall.

As the door swung open, they could see a quilt folded loosely at the foot of the bed. A pair of high-heeled shoes lay to one side, along with a blue sweater discarded carelessly on the carpet. The room smelled of cigarettes. As they entered, the assault team saw a woman standing by the window, which was open. She was smoking and staring out across the lawn, toward a bed of crocuses and daffodils. When she turned to face them, the woman exhaled a thin stream of smoke that coiled upward like a question mark from her lips. Though the armed men were trained to disable or kill without hesitation, she froze them with her pale green eyes. Her hair was gray, with wisps of gold. Her fingers held the cigarette in an attitude of unflinching surety, as if she had been expecting their arrival.

Three

Ladakh

Taking off from Leh, sixty seconds after daybreak, the Aerospatiale Lama headed north, leaving the Indus Valley and setting course for the Eastern Karakoram. Nothing else moved. Not even a shadow. Beneath the helicopter everything seemed lifeless. The percussive murmur of its rotors was almost musical.

Colonel Imtiaz Afridi watched the first rays of sunlight tinting the ridges, reflecting off the snow with brassy radiance, spilling over rocks and sand, illuminating the harsh terrain. Afridi was bundled up in a flight suit, over which he wore a down parka. An insulated helmet protected his head and glacier goggles shielded his eyes, yet he felt exposed. The pilot kept low to the ground, no more than a hundred feet above the rocks. At this hour of the morning, the air was perfectly still. Two lakes appeared in the distance, pools of ice that observed their progress with unblinking omniscience.

At first the mountains seemed distant, scattered along the ruffled hem of the horizon, but as they entered the Nubra Valley, ridgelines began to converge and one summit led on to the next, folding and unfolding like an elaborate origami of peaks and passes. Afridi recognized the shape of the land, and the winding course of the river below. He had flown here dozens of times and had studied the topography, from early British survey maps to recent satellite images.

They kept to the eastern slope of the valley, never climbing above the silhouette of the ridge, though the helicopter was equipped with instruments that made it invisible to those who might try to track its flight. Afridi spotted a road below them, an army fuel dump, and farther on, an encampment of fiberglass huts surrounded by disheveled tents.

As they came around a bend in the river, he caught sight of a sheer ice wall, rising almost eight hundred feet and stretching from one side of the valley to the other. Though he had witnessed this scene more times than he could count, the sight of the glacier always pinched a nerve inside Afridi's chest.

Siachen. The highest battlefield in the world. On either side, unyielding mountains were armored in ice and rock. The frozen carapace of the glacier, littered with debris, was an impervious shield, a barren wasteland. Yet men sacrificed their lives to protect this desolate frontier. Hostile armies of India and Pakistan faced off across the shifting surface of Siachen. For every soldier killed by enemy fire, nine others died from altitude and exposure. Here the fault lines of history converged with the tectonic fissures of Asia, an apex of collision and partition. Less than a hundred kilometers farther west lay the northern frontiers of Afghanistan.

For a moment, it seemed as if the helicopter might not clear the ice wall, its engine straining. Afridi's eyes shifted briefly to the pilot, Flight Lieutenant Bhandari, who was intently watching the flickering gauges on the console before him. He coaxed the throttle to give them a fraction more power. At the last minute, they rose above cracked lips of ice and glided over the broad expanse of Lower Siachen. Afridi's hands were gloved in thick down mittens, but he could feel the cold creeping into his fingers. The Lama's propellant was a special blend of aviation fuel, refined for these altitudes. The air above Siachen made everything viscous, blood and oil turning to wax. The helicopter lurched suddenly as a gust of wind came down one of the lateral valleys, out of territory occupied by Pakistan. It almost felt as if an artillery round had passed beneath their skids.

In front of them lay the painted mountains, Rimo I and III. The pilot banked the helicopter in a shallow arc that followed the course of a secondary glacier, Terong Gal. The difficult part now lay ahead. As they turned 160 degrees, Afridi had an unobstructed view of the Rimo peaks, not a smooth feature on their surface. Raddled ice and blistered snow were mangled into a fierce beauty by the early light. Forty years ago, Afridi had attempted to climb the lesser peak and survived an avalanche on its lower slopes only to turn back 800 meters from the summit as daylight waned and temperatures dropped.

He could see the shadow of the helicopter projected on the hard packed snow beneath them, flying parallel to his thoughts. Crossing Terong Col, at 6,000 meters, they dipped into the upper reaches of the Shyok Valley, the so-called 'river of death.' Another glacier spread below them, narrower than Siachen, steeper and more constricted. They were out of range of Pakistani guns, though Chinese intrusions along the Aksai Chin had put this region in dispute.

Bhandari spoke into his microphone. 'Sir, up ahead…should we bear left or right?'

'To the left,' Afridi said, hearing his own voice amplified inside the helmet. 'Beyond that bergschrund, where the glacier bends out of sight.'

His eyes scanned the slopes. For several minutes nothing revealed itself, but as they entered the bowl beneath the northern flank of Rimo's massif, Afridi spotted the wreckage. He raised one hand and gestured. The pilot saw it too.

On a sloping ice field, at the uppermost end of the glacier, lay the fuselage of an aircraft that had broken into three pieces. One of the wings had been sheared off three hundred meters lower down, at the point of impact. The other had fragmented as the twin-engine turboprop ploughed its way uphill. From a distance, it looked as if the plane might have had a chance to land safely, but as they approached, Afridi could see how the glacier fractured and buckled. They were almost above the crash site now, fifty feet off the ground, as the pilot began to circle. A black smear of oil marked the trajectory of the plane. One of the engines lay to the side, its propellers remarkably intact. Afridi noted that it was an Anatov AN 24, not an Illyushin IL 114, as the initial report had indicated.

The crash had occurred barely twenty-four hours earlier, and the first reconnaissance reported no survivors. The plane's markings had been painted over, though Afridi could see an indistinct line of numbers and letters near the tail. It hadn't caught fire, but there was no chance of anyone coming out of this accident alive. Even if they had, they would have frozen to death by now. More than likely, only two or three crew had been on board, no passengers. The helicopter hovered over the largest piece of the fuselage.

'What's that?' Afridi said, as if speaking to himself. His microphone conveyed the question to his pilot, who descended within twenty feet of the glacier. A human hand seemed to beckon for help, its fingers grasping at nothing. Where the plane had been ripped in half, the ice was strewn with body parts, dozens of arms and legs. Torn shreds of cardboard fluttered in the breeze as the rotor blades kicked up snow, making it difficult to see. But the severed limbs were unmistakable, a gruesome tableau, as if dozens of victims had been butchered on the ice.

Afridi heard Bhandari curse, an expression of bewilderment and dismay.

'Put her down over there,' the colonel instructed, waving to a level patch, thirty meters from the crash debris.

Once they were on the glacier, the helicopter's blades came to a halt, though the engine kept running, and Bhandari unbuckled himself from his seat.

'Go and take a look,' Afridi said. He would have got down

too if his legs permitted. The pilot walked cautiously across to the gruesome remains, stopping for a moment, as if he didn't have the courage to go on, then kneeling beside one of the legs, its foot shod in a black leather boot. Reluctantly, he picked it up and also retrieved an arm that lay nearby, cut off below the elbow. A few minutes later, he returned to the helicopter. As Bhandari opened the hatch on his side of the Lama, he handed Afridi the two limbs. Both were artificial. The hard synthetic material was a pinkish hue, like the plastic complexion of a mannequin.

When they lifted off again, Afridi was still holding the prostheses on his lap. The arm was female, tapering to the wrist, fingers open, as if gesturing for something. The leg was a man's, with steel calipers on either side of the knee, a hinged mechanism that made it possible to walk. Below him, Afridi could see many more of these false limbs littering the crash site. The smaller arms and legs were for children, like dismembered dolls lying in the snow, scattered pieces of a human puzzle.

Four

When Luke agreed to accompany the body back to America, it wasn't because of any sentiments for the man who had died. It was a free business class ticket, round trip to Washington DC. He had been told that the casket would be delivered directly to the airport. All he had to do was travel on the same plane as a courier. He also had to carry the dead man's suitcase and sign some papers to verify the identity of the deceased. His name was Carlton Fletcher. Luke had met him once or twice at cocktail parties in Islamabad, an older expatriate in his late fifties. Fletcher had introduced himself as a consultant for a waste water project in Gujranwala, funded by USAID. That was all Luke knew about him.

The only thing they had in common was that they smoked, though Luke had quit since then. A month ago, he and Fletcher had spent five minutes alone together on the balcony of a friend's house off Murree Road, while their cigarettes burned down in the darkness. He remembered that Fletcher talked about hunting wild boar on the outskirts of Islamabad.

'Unbelievably good eating,' he said. 'I'd almost forgotten the taste of fresh pork.'

If he'd met him again on the street, Luke might not have recognized Fletcher. He didn't have distinctive features, a moderately overweight man with a bad complexion and receding hairline. His glasses were tinted, the kind that change color with the light. At the end of their conversation, Fletcher had stubbed out his cigarette in a potted fern. After the two of them went back inside, they didn't speak again. Four weeks later, Luke heard he was dead and the embassy was looking for someone to travel home with the body. One of secretaries in the Commercial Section called Luke and persuaded him to volunteer. He was told that Fletcher had died of a heart attack in the bathroom of a service apartment he shared with another consultant who was away in Sialkot when it happened.

As a journalist, Luke lived on the margins of the expatriate community, but unlike most of the foreign correspondents, he had been born in Pakistan and spoke Urdu. His dark brown hair and beard allowed him to move about unnoticed on the streets of Rawalpindi, where he rented an apartment in a modest, middle-class neighborhood. At the same time, he kept his contacts amongst the embassy crowd in Islamabad, shuttling between the two worlds out of professional necessity but also because it was something he had done for most of his life. He was entirely comfortable sitting around with Pakistani reporters and speaking Urdu or Punjabi over innumerable cups of tea or having dinner with the bureau chief of *The New York Times*, listening to bombastic theories about American foreign policy. Though he didn't completely belong to either world, Luke had learned how to adapt to circumstances.

Once or twice a year, he returned to the United States, not because of any particular need to maintain his tenuous links with the country, though his sister lived there, but because it seemed necessary to keep his professional identity intact. He often traveled for work to other parts of Asia, but when a chance like this came up, Luke was happy enough to accept a free ticket to the US, even if it meant accompanying a dead man halfway round the world.

Repatriation of human remains is a relatively routine process. After a doctor issues a death certificate, the embassy takes over and handles all of the details—informing the family, cancelling the passport, getting clearances from the police, hiring a mortician to embalm the corpse, and booking the coffin on an international flight. The consular official who dealt with Fletcher's case was in his late twenties, a pale, bored-looking man who might as well have been sending a piece of lost luggage back to its original destination. He gave Luke a manila envelope full of papers and explained that someone from the family would meet him when he reached Washington. Representatives from a funeral home would collect the body at the airport. Luke just had to sign a receipt and hand over the suitcase, as simple as that. When the consular official gave him his ticket, he glanced at it for moment.

'You're coming back in a week?' he said, as if it were a mistake. Luke nodded. 'I'm just going to visit family for a few of days.'

'Short trip,' the official said. 'If I were you, I'd stay away from here as long as I could.'

Smiling, Luke said. 'I've lived in Pakistan most of my life. This is home for me.'

'No shit!' the man said, then looked aside, as if it made him uncomfortable.

The flight they'd booked him on was Emirates to Dubai and then United direct to DC. Because the dead man had been working for the US government as a contractor, it had to be an American carrier or a codeshare airline. Even in death, Carlton Fletcher was obliged to comply with the protocols of Washington's bureaucracy. Altogether, it was a twenty-hour journey. But, of course, that didn't matter to the dead man. For Luke, it wasn't so bad either, since he was traveling business class. As a freelance writer, he was used to economy seats and cheap connections.

Leaving Islamabad, everything went smoothly. He didn't even have to see the casket because the people from the embassy took care of that. Fletcher's only piece of luggage was a hard shell

Samsonite case that looked as if it had been around the world a couple of times. Checking it in, along with his own bag, Luke wondered what was inside and whether he would need to declare anything at Customs, but nobody seemed concerned.

The flight took off on time, and he fell asleep almost immediately. At Dubai, he had a two-hour layover. Resisting the urge to buy a carton of Marlboros, he got a bag of Iranian pistachios instead and two bottles of duty free perfume as a gift for his sister and her partner. He didn't know what kind of perfume they would like, but the Filipino salesgirl recommended something with a Scandinavian name and another called Scheherazade. Back on the plane, when he sniffed his wrist where the girl had dabbed the fragrance samplers, he wasn't sure he'd made the right choice.

Once they were in the air again, they left behind the slender spire of the Burj al Khalifa and the stylized outline of the Palm Jumeirah development, its drooping fronds and artificial lagoons protruding into the blue waters of the Persian Gulf. Luke stared out the window, but soon there was nothing but desert stretching in all directions, an ocean of Arabian sand. He tried to watch a movie but fell asleep again, waking up as they were flying over the Mediterranean. He felt an ache between his eyes and an edgy feeling of needing a cigarette. He hadn't smoked for three weeks, but being in an airplane seemed to make the craving worse. As the flight dragged on, Luke found himself getting angry with Carlton Fletcher for having died and making him go on this journey. He wasn't looking forward to meeting the dead man's wife or kids, whatever family he had. He didn't want to offer condolences to strangers, pretending to be sympathetic as he gave them the suitcase. For a moment, Luke began to wonder what it would be like if his corpse were in the hold and Fletcher was taking him back instead.

Better you than me, my friend, he said to himself, shaking off the thought. Hours later they circled Washington and touched down at Dulles. Entering the terminal, Luke walked as quickly as he could, avoiding the escalators and taking the stairs to stretch his legs. The luggage was already going around and around on the carousel when he got there, his own and Fletcher's. At Customs, he handed over the papers for repatriation of human remains. The female officer who flipped through the documents was wearing latex gloves.

'Are you a family member?' she asked.

He started to explain. 'No, just an acquaintance. The embassy—'

'Anything else to declare?'

Luke shook his head.

From there he had to go to a special reception area, wheeling his trolley through an automatic door, where an airline official told him to wait.

A few minutes later, two men in black overcoats walked in. He could tell they were from the funeral home before they introduced themselves. Luke gave them the envelope containing the death certificate and canceled passport. Another door opened, and a baggage handler wheeled in the coffin on a gurney. It was a simple, aluminum box, smaller than he had imagined.

'Is someone from the family here?' Luke asked.

One of the undertakers nodded. 'She's parking her car.'

A minute later, the door opened again and a woman walked in. She was in her mid-thirties, with short brown hair, a year or two younger than Luke. Wearing a gray wool coat over a pleated black dress, she looked as if she were going straight from here to the funeral.

'Ms Holman,' the undertaker introduced them, 'this is Mr McKenzie.'

She glanced across at the casket briefly before shaking Luke's hand. When she turned in his direction, her eyes were dry and her face composed.

'I'm sorry about your father,' Luke said.

There was a trace of a smile on her lips.

'My uncle,' she said.

The airline official seemed to be in a hurry and got them both to sign the papers on his clipboard, then nodded to the men from the funeral home. The coffin was taken outside, and suddenly it was just the woman and Luke. For a moment, he didn't know what to say, before pointing at the suitcase.

'That's his,' he said. 'Would you like me to take it to your car?'

'What about you? Where are you going?' she asked.

Luke mentioned the hotel that the embassy had booked for him, near Farragut Square.

'I'll drop you there,' she said. 'It's the least I can do.'

Five

After a brief halt in Leh for refueling, the helicopter returned to the Himalayan Research Institute in Mussoorie, touching down a few minutes past noon. Situated at the highest point on the ridge in Landour cantonment, overlooking the central range of the Himalayas, HRI was a secluded complex of buildings surrounded by deodar trees. Except for the satellite dishes and the helipad, it might have been a colonial club rather than a state of the art surveillance center. Over the past three decades, Afridi had established HRI as India's primary intelligence facility in the Himalayas, and he directed the institute with the singular purpose of defending the country's northern frontier. Although technically retired from military service, he was acknowledged as the foremost expert on mountain warfare and security, an analytical genius with a fierce sense of national duty.

Tired from the journey but grateful to be home, Afridi's first priority was to examine the evidence they had retrieved. Removing his helmet and hoisting himself out of the Lama and into his wheelchair, the colonel gave instructions that he wanted the artificial limbs taken to the MI room. He would be there in half an hour.

Afridi's office had an attached bathroom, where he washed up and shaved before changing into gray flannel trousers, a fresh white shirt, and a blazer. Injured in a climbing accident years ago, he had overcome his disabilities through careful adherence to routine and physical discipline. Though Afridi would turn seventy next year, his upper body remained strong and agile, even if his lower extremities were immobilized. The irony of having recovered prosthetic limbs above 6,000 meters in the mountains wasn't lost on him. Flying back from Leh, eastward across Zanskar and Spiti, then above the gnarled ranges of Kinnaur into Garhwal, he had wondered what it must be like to walk with artificial legs. Though his left foot had been amputated due to frostbite, Afridi had never considered getting a prosthesis. Over the years he had come to terms with the limitations of his body, the scars he bore, deadened nerves and the atrophy of muscles and sinews that once carried him up and over the highest mountains in the world.

Wheeling himself into the MI room, which also served as a forensics lab, Afridi acknowledged Major Gopinath's salute. Posted to the HRI less than a year ago as medical officer, Gopinath maintained his clinic fastidiously. The artificial arm and leg had been placed on an examining table as if they were being prepared for surgery. The only other person in the room was a nurse named Esther Masih.

'So, tell me, Gopi. What do you make of these?' Afridi said.

'Sir?' The medical officer looked baffled.

'What are they?'

'A leg and an arm, sir,' Gopinath answered. He hadn't been told where they were found or the circumstances of the crash site. Afridi harbored a longstanding distrust of doctors. Most of them, he believed, had no imagination, since the medical profession required them to approach everything with clinical objectivity.

'Yes, of course, I know that,' Afridi said, positioning his wheelchair so he had a better view of the limbs. 'But, please…I want you to tell me something I don't know.'

The doctor seemed unnerved and glanced at the nurse.

'These are crude prostheses, sir. Manufactured in China.' Gopinath picked up the leg and worked the hinged calipers on the knee. 'At least thirty years out of date. The material is some kind of fiberglass. The moving parts are stainless steel and PVC. Inferior quality.'

'But are they functional?' Afridi interjected. 'I mean, could you fit this leg on someone and actually make him walk?'

Gopinath bent and extended the knee a couple of times before answering. He had a maddening habit of analyzing things from every angle before replying. Several weeks ago, Afridi had come to him with a toothache. Before examining his mouth, Gopinath had checked his blood pressure and asked him about the prescription for his reading glasses.

'It's my tooth, damn it, not my eyes,' Afridi had said.

'Yes, sir. I'm just excluding all other sources of pain,' Gopi tried to explain.

Now, the doctor carefully put down the artificial leg as Afridi waited impatiently for an answer.

'Ambulation would be severely restricted. Whoever wears this leg will need to walk with a cane, or crutches. We have much more sophisticated prostheses now, which offer greater mobility.' He glanced at Afridi, unsure of where this conversation was leading.

'Do you suppose it might be suitable for someone who has been injured by a landmine?'

Afridi continued. 'In Afghanistan, for example...hypothetically?'

'Possibly, sir. It's an inexpensive option. Cheaply produced, simple to maintain.'

'And the arm?'

'Purely cosmetic,' Gopi replied. 'Show it to me,' Afridi said. The nurse handed him the arm.

'Hollow?' Afridi said, tapping the upper portion, which had nylon straps and a crude clamp for attaching to a person's elbow.

'Yes, sir,' said Gopinath. 'It reduces the weight.'

'Miss Masih,' Afridi said, handing the prosthesis back to the nurse, 'does anything about this arm strike you as odd?'

She turned it over and shook her head. 'Take a closer look,' said Afridi.

The nurse held the arm up to the light, squinting as she examined the rigid fingers.

'It unscrews at the wrist,' Afridi prompted her.

Cautiously, she twisted the hand, which rotated stiffly at first, then loosened and came apart from the rest of the arm.

'Empty, sir,' she said, peering inside.

'Of course.' Afridi nodded. 'But you could easily fill it with something, couldn't you? Five hundred grams of heroin, for instance.' Esther Masih looked up with alarm, meeting Afridi's gaze. She had worked at the institute for fifteen years, and he trusted her more than most of his staff.

'The leg also comes apart,' he said. 'You could fit a kilo inside, maybe more.'

The colonel smiled at Major Gopinath, who was watching him with a look of incredulity.

'Where did it come from, sir?' Gopi asked.

'From the Eastern Karakoram. These were part of a shipment that was on its way to Afghanistan,' Afridi said, with a grimace. 'These days, Afghanistan has a monopoly on two things: amputees and opium.'

Six

'So, how come you were born in Pakistan?' she asked.

'My parents were missionaries,' Luke replied.

'But you're not a missionary,' she said. Her first name was Tracy. 'No, I'm a journalist,' he replied, 'though I've taken six months off to write a book about Humanitarian Aid projects in the tribal areas of Pakistan.'

'They don't like us much over there, do they?' Tracy said.

'Not exactly,' said Luke. 'Americans haven't made themselves very popular.'

'Do you speak the language?'

'Urdu, some Pashto and Punjabi,' he answered.

'It must be dangerous.'

'Not if you know what you're doing.'

She was driving fast along the highway, heading into the center of Washington. The car was a black Lexus coupe with leather upholstery, certainly more comfortable than taking a taxi. Tracy Holman had thrown her coat in the backseat. The sleeveless dress she wore revealed slim but muscular arms and several inches of well-tanned thighs. She had a severe kind of beauty that her makeup couldn't soften, and Luke sensed a seductive tension in the car.

'Yeah, I suppose you could die of a heart attack anywhere,' she said, changing lanes.

Hesitating, Luke said, 'I'm afraid I didn't know your uncle very well.'

Tracy shook her head, eyes fixed on the traffic.

'Neither did I.'

As they rode in silence for a while, Luke was increasingly self-conscious of how disheveled he looked and of his bloodshot eyes. A subtle fragrance filled the Lexus, a clean yet musky sweetness with a hint of cloves. Twenty minutes later, they pulled up to his hotel.

'Thanks for the ride,' he said. Tracy looked at him and smiled as they shook hands. The doorman opened the car for her, thinking she was getting out.

'She's just dropping me,' Luke said to the doorman, then glanced at her. 'Unless, of course, you'd like to come in for a drink.'

Tracy examined her watch, a Bulova with a gilded strap. 'Thanks, I might,' she said, surprising him by handing the doorman her keys.

More than ever before, Luke wished he hadn't spent the last twenty-four hours in airports and on a plane. As he checked in at Reception, Tracy sat texting in one of the lobby chairs. Luke was about to suggest they meet in the bar, after he'd had a chance to wash up, but she headed straight for the elevator as soon as he was done. His room was on the fifteenth floor. He glanced at Tracy's reflection in the elevator mirror. She returned his look with a suggestive smile.

The bellhop had brought up his bag in the service elevator and met them in the hall. Luke waved the keycard in front of his door and a green light clicked on. The minute he entered, he was aware of another person inside, a man sitting near the window with his legs crossed. Luke realized he'd been set up as soon as Tracy tipped the bellhop, who retreated out the door.

The man in the chair got to his feet and put out his hand. Luke took a step backward, swearing under his breath. 'Shit!'

The tinted glasses were a jaundiced hue. His thinning hair was combed back from a prominent forehead. There was no mistaking Carlton Fletcher. He was alive and well in Washington, DC. Tracy pulled up another chair for Luke and opened the minibar.

'I think you probably need that drink,' she said. 'Scotch or something else?'

Still trying to comprehend what was going on, Luke didn't answer at first, watching her pour two miniatures of Glenfiddich into a single glass.

'What the hell is this?' he finally demanded. 'This isn't why I agreed to fly halfway around the world.'

'I realize we owe you an explanation,' Fletcher said, his voice apologetic but firm.

'Who was in the coffin?' Luke asked. 'Or was it empty?' Working as an investigative journalist in one of the most dangerous parts of the world, Luke had faced his share of ruthless surprises and blatant lies. His instincts told him to remain calm but guarded. 'I'm afraid we can't reveal the victim's identity. But we're grateful that you brought him home,' Fletcher said, gesturing for Luke to sit, as Tracy Holman opened a can of club soda. She topped up the whiskey before handing Luke his drink.

'I should have guessed you were a spook,' he said. 'But why did you have to make this so complicated?'

'Let's just say there were events…circumstances that required us to meet you here.'

'Why do we need to meet at all?' Luke said, furious at having been deceived.

'Cheers,' said Fletcher, holding up his glass, which had an inch of clear fluid at the bottom. It could have been water or vodka.

Luke swallowed hard and sat back in his chair.

'We're interested in a piece you published in *Salon*.' Fletcher spoke quietly, his voice restrained. 'Very well written. Fascinating.'

Tracy Holman sat on the corner of the bed, leaning forward. The article was based on a chapter from the book that Luke was writing, a firsthand account of disaster relief operations in Chitral and Azad Kashmir. He was still getting used to the idea that Fletcher was alive.

'You interviewed a man in Abbottabad named Hakim.' Holman spoke this time.

'That's not his real name, of course,' Luke said, keeping his voice level. He'd played this game before and knew how to protect his sources.

'We know,' Fletcher said. 'It's what he told you that was interesting, the part about rescue operations after the flash floods along the Jhelum.'

Despite his exhaustion and the numbing effect of the scotch, Luke felt a switch go off in his mind, signaling caution.

'What about it?'

'You quoted him as saying that simply doing good for people isn't enough. Altruism has a price.'

'He was speaking Urdu, and I loosely translated what he said,' Luke explained.

'But he goes on to say that even the greatest acts of charity imply some sort of guilt, just as evil can have a moral face.' Holman was quoting the interview word for word.

'What exactly did he mean by that?' Fletcher said.

Luke shrugged. 'Hakim styles himself as a bit of philosopher. I thought it was an interesting paradox, particularly in a part of the world where most people view things as either black or white.'

'But isn't he suggesting that some of the relief efforts are funded by those who might have blood on their hands? The implication is that good deeds balance out the bad—what might be called a Robin Hood effect,' Fletcher looked across at Holman.

'I suppose that's one interpretation,' Luke said. Fletcher drained the liquid in his glass.

'Did he mention any organizations in particular?' Holman asked. 'A specific NGO or charity that might be an example of what he meant?'

Luke shook his head slowly.

'For instance, did he talk about the Sikander-e-Azam Trust?' Fletcher asked.

Luke met his eyes.

'You've heard of it, of course,' Fletcher persisted.

'Sure,' said Luke, understanding now why he was here. 'But I'm not prepared to tell you anything more than that. Journalistic privilege. I can't compromise my sources.'

Fletcher stared at him for fifteen seconds without speaking, then picked at a scab just below his ear.

'So, what are you willing to talk about?' he asked.

Luke shrugged. 'I don't know. Why should I tell you anything?'

'How about explaining what you know about Peregrine?' said Holman. For the second time, Luke felt as if someone had pressed a switch at the base of his spine. He sat up in his chair.

'The company or the bird?' he asked.

'You interviewed Roger Fleischmann, Peregrine's CEO, when he was in Islamabad last month. An unofficial visit.' Fletcher spoke.

'Nice guy, with a lot of Midwestern charm,' Luke said. 'As a kid, Fleischmann grew up flying model airplanes in his grandfather's hayfields in Ohio. Then, after dropping out of college, he turned his hobby into a multi-billion dollar aeronautics and defense technology firm.'

'You asked him a question about Peregrine's links with the CIA, whether they were one of his investors. According to your interview, he laughed it off. You quote him as saying he's a private entrepreneur with no ties to the US government,' said Fletcher.

'Yeah.' Luke took the last sip of whiskey from his glass as if it were medicine.

'Was he lying?'

Luke shook his head again. 'How should I know?'

'Usually you can tell,' said Fletcher. 'A good interviewer knows when he's being sold a load of crap. You can see it in his eyes.'

'Roger Fleischmann seemed like an honest, plainspoken businessman. He said he was just trying to sell his drones and other hardware to the generals in Rawalpindi.'

'Except that he would only be allowed to do that if the CIA and Defense Department okayed the deal,' said Fletcher. Holman had fallen silent. Luke could tell from the way she held her phone that his conversation was being recorded.

'Obviously, he wasn't selling top of the line. These were second generation Peregrine drones, pretty much obsolete,' said Luke. All of this was in the published interview.

'Was anyone with him?'

'No, I met him alone,' said Luke.

'And he didn't mention any of his associates in Pakistan?'

'Not that I can recall,' said Luke. 'I happened to meet him through another journalist, Ali Siddiqui, who was working on a story about private military contractors in the NWFP. It was a last minute thing. We met at the Serena Hotel in Islamabad, then drove to the airport together before Fleischmann caught his flight back to the States.'

'Did he say anything off the record that might have indicated who arranged his visit?'

'No. But if it was off the record, I wouldn't tell you,' Luke replied. 'Somehow, I get a feeling you know exactly what this is about,' said Fletcher.

'Fuck you,' said Luke. 'I don't have any idea what's going on, except that I've been hustled over here to Washington under false pretenses and you're trying to squeeze privileged information out of me.'

'We've traced a charitable donation from Peregrine Corporation to the Sikander-E-Azam Trust. One point five million dollars. Does that ring any bells?' Fletcher's voice had gone completely flat, as if his batteries were running down.

Luke waved the question aside.

'If they did, I never heard about it,' he said.

'Roger Fleischmann didn't mention his philanthropic goals?' asked Fletcher.

'No. We only spoke about his business interests. It's all in the interview.'

'He didn't say anything about the commissions he was paying his representatives in Pakistan, who they were, or what sort of exclusive arrangements he had with them?'

'No,' said Luke. 'He told me that he'd been to Pakistan several times and he liked the food, especially chapli kababs, though he had trouble pronouncing the name.'

Fletcher ignored this. 'What about security? Did he have bodyguards with him?'

Luke shook his head. 'Not that I could see.'

'And didn't that strike you as odd? The CEO of a major American arms manufacturer, visiting a country that's crawling with terrorists, suicide bombers, and armed militants,' said Fletcher, 'and he moved about without any personal security?'

'Maybe he didn't want to draw attention to himself,' said Luke.

'Or maybe he had the kind of protection that doesn't require a security presence,' Fletcher suggested. 'Maybe he was meeting with folks on the other side.'

Seven

The wedding party arrived at the village in a convoy of eight Toyota Landcruisers, throwing up a plume of dust that stretched for almost a kilometer over the dry brown hills. Most of the passengers were men, all of them armed with handguns and automatic rifles. They were welcomed by the bride's father and the elders of the village along with a dozen gunmen, who received their guests with cautious deference and rituals of hospitality. The guests were offered scented water in copper jugs to wash away the dust of the journey. Samovars of tea were waiting in the Jirga Hall, adjacent to the mosque. Unlike the other buildings in the village, which were made of mud, the assembly hall was a recent construction of reinforced concrete with marble cladding. Carpets and cushions had been spread on the floor. Tea was served in china cups, while platters of dried fruit and nuts were passed around.

As the men settled themselves comfortably, the bride's aunts greeted the three women from the groom's family and led them away to a separate building. No men were present, and veils were lifted as the women admired the bride. She was seventeen, a fresh, rose-cheeked girl with golden hair. Compliments were offered on her beauty and the clarity of her features. Though the girl kept her head lowered, one of the women put a hand under her chin and raised her face to examine the youthful profile, rouged lips, and kohl-rimmed eyes with irises of the palest blue. The bride's ornaments were silver and gold, a dozen strands around her neck adorned with amulets and antique coins. Her hair had been carefully braided and her pink ears were pierced with diamond studs, the only modern jewelry she wore. Henna decorated her hands, and her fingers bore an assortment of rings, while her wrists were weighed down with dozens of bracelets.

The father of the groom arrived half an hour after the rest of the marriage party. Under the watchful gaze of two bodyguards, he embraced each of the elders, apologizing for his delay and replying to their courteous questions about the hardships of the journey. The conversations were formal and prescribed by ancient traditions of etiquette. Gifts were exchanged, a pair of Italian pistols for the bride's father, who reciprocated by presenting a Belgian hunting rifle to the father of the groom. Polite inquiries were made about the boy. They were told that he was abroad, unable to attend his own wedding. The marriage would be solemnized in his absence. A distinguished imam had come from Peshawar to preside over the wedding. He confirmed that the nikkah could be performed without the groom being present. Questions were raised by one or two of the older men in the bride's family. But the father of the groom assured them that his son would consummate the marriage within a week.

More guests had arrived by now, for the groom's father was an important man in the region, a prominent tribal leader whose authority extended across the border into Afghanistan. He had a reputation for being ruthless with his enemies but magnanimous with those who offered him their loyalty. The marriage contract had already been negotiated and the walwar, or bride price, was paid in gold.

The ceremony itself was brief, almost perfunctory. After the nikkah had been witnessed and the imam recited verses from the Quran, news was sent to the women who began their songs of celebration. Rifles were fired in the air, crackling like fireworks. By this time more than a hundred male guests were gathered in the Jirga Hall.

When the midday azaan was heard, all of the men went across to the mosque and offered zuhr prayers. Recently rebuilt with bright blue tiles and a marble dome, the mosque had two slender minarets and a new borewell that provided fresh water for ablutions. All of this was due to the beneficence of the groom's father, who was known throughout the region for his wealth and generosity.

Before the feast began, the bride's father proposed a target shooting contest, a traditional part of Pakhtun weddings. Leading his guests to a hillock on the outskirts of the village, the host pointed to a stainless steel saucer, which had been placed on the opposite ridge, five hundred meters away. It glinted in the harsh sunlight, far out of range. Several of the groom's party raised their rifles and fired, kicking up dust on the slope below the target. Even the bodyguards missed the target. Finally, the father of the groom asked for the Belgian rifle with its telescopic sight.

Resting the rifle on the shoulder of one of his kinsmen, the tribal leader took aim and fired. The first bullet went low by six inches. Gauging the distance with his eyes, he worked the bolt action and loaded another shell in the chamber. This time, he aimed above the saucer and instantly found his mark. The sound of the bullet striking metal rang out like a distant bell as the dish clattered down the rocks.

The wedding party returned to the hall for their feast. Sheep and goats had been slaughtered, and only the choicest portions were offered to the guests. The meal consisted of several courses of different kinds of meat from lamb and mutton to chicken and quail. While the men ate heartily and murmured blessings on the couple and their families, a storyteller regaled the audience with tribal myths and legends. The father of the groom had brought him along for entertainment. A toothless old man with a grizzled beard, he recited heroic tales of the Greek conqueror who left his mark on these mountains centuries ago. The raconteur reminded the wedding guests that each of them carried Alexander's blood in their veins. The marriage they were celebrating today would carry on Sikander-e-Azam's lineage.

As the feast concluded with sweetmeats and dates imported from Medina, the old man's stories turned from bloodshed and valor to the romance of Sikander and his beloved Rukhsana. As he regaled the audience with their love story, one of the bodyguards approached the groom's father and handed him a cell phone. The tribal leader took the call. He exchanged a word or two, then reached into the pocket of his vest. Taking out a small plastic case, no more than an inch square, he removed a memory chip and inserted it into his phone. For a moment, the screen lit up and then went blank, except for a blinking icon in the middle, pulsing like a beacon.

Interrupting the storyteller, the father of the groom rose to his feet and thanked his host and the assembled guests for their gifts and good wishes. He expressed regret that the celebrations must be curtailed. They needed to reach home before dark. A few protests were uttered, but the bride's father immediately sent word that his daughter should prepare to depart. While most of the guests remained in the Jirga Hall, the immediate families retreated to the edge of the village and performed a brief leave-taking ritual. Now fully veiled, the bride was led away by female members of the groom's family to one of the vehicles parked nearby. The two fathers embraced, and each of the wedding party said their farewells, climbing behind the wheels of the Landcruisers and driving away in a trail of dust.

Nobody noticed that the phone had been left behind among the cushions in the Jirga Hall.

By this time a Peregrine MV I drone had already crossed the mountains to the north of the Khyber Pass flying a low trajectory, like a raptor intent on its prey. The 233G JetStream engine was virtually silent, and the sleek fuselage, with sweptback wings, glided over the contours of the barren mountains, maintaining a constant height, forty feet above the ground. A CIA programmer at Bagram Air Base had locked in on the signal from the homing device in the phone. The guests at the wedding included several men who carried a price on their heads, local warlords and other persons of interest who supported the Taliban and their foreign allies.

Coming in over the ridge where the shooting competition had taken place, the drone fired two missiles that passed between the minarets of the mosque and rammed the Jirga Hall, bursting into a fireball that decimated the structure and killed most of the guests within. The sound of the explosion echoed across the hills, but the groom's party, now several kilometers away, heard only a muffled crump, like thunder reverberating out of a cloudless sky.

Eight

Afridi was informed of the agent's death by Manav Shinde, associate director of the Research and Analysis Wing, better known as RAW. Manav had called the night before, just as Afridi was about to go to bed. Their conversation was brief and cryptic, though both of them were aware of the emotion in each other's voice. They had been colleagues for almost twenty years, though Afridi worked for military intelligence and Shinde was a civilian. In many ways, they couldn't have been more different from each other in manner or personality, but over time they had developed a trust that was unusual in the intelligence community. Their collaboration went beyond official protocol and hierarchies, a personal bond that arose out of a shared sense of duty.

For the past eight years, Qasim had been one of their most successful undercover operatives in Pakistan. Afridi had recruited him, and Manav provided the funding and logistical support required to keep an agent in the field, including secure channels of communication. One of their brightest and bravest assets, Qasim had very little schooling but all of the survival instincts that made him a natural spy. Educated up to class five at a government primary school in Pahalgam, Kashmir, he was forced to start working as a mess boy at the age of twelve to support his widowed mother and two sisters. Afridi first met him fifteen years ago at the BSF mess in Pahalgam and he was immediately struck by Qasim's intelligence and resourcefulness.

After he had been given training and proved that he was not

only capable but utterly dependable, they sent him across the border into Pakistan. Qasim accepted the assignment without hesitation. His only request was that his family should receive his monthly paychecks. This was done discreetly through an NGO that worked with Kashmiri widows. Meanwhile, Qasim made his way to Rawalpindi and Islamabad. He created a convincing cover for himself with help from Shinde's makeover team, who provided him with documents that identified his birthplace as a village along the Jhelum in Pak Occupied Kashmir. His first job was as a dishwasher at a hotel before he got hired as a houseboy for a consular official at the American embassy. From there, with enthusiastic letters of recommendation, he went on to be employed by three other US embassy officials. Eventually, Qasim found himself working as a cook for the CIA deputy station chief.

As a household servant, he aroused little suspicion among the Pakistanis. In fact, the ISI had tried to recruit him to gather information on the Americans. His greatest value lay in the fact that he could report on the comings and goings of various American officials and their meetings with Pakistani military officers, Taliban informers, and tribal warlords involved in the Afghan conflict. Often used as a translator, Qasim had traveled to Peshawar several times with his employer, and he had been able to provide information on conversations between the CIA and Afghan factions.

The report of his sudden death had been delayed for twenty-four hours because it took the Americans some time to smooth things over with the Pakistan police. All that Manav could gather from his sources was that the cook had fallen from the upper balcony of the diplomat's house and broke his neck on the steps of the verandah below. He was identified by his cover name, Mansoor, and the death had been ruled accidental, though Afridi and Manav both knew that Qasim had been killed in the line of duty. He was twenty-eight years old.

After receiving the news, Afridi was unable to sleep, until he finally dozed off in the early hours of the morning. His grief was compounded by regret at the loss of an invaluable source of information. Of course, if anyone had traced Qasim back to RAW, they would have denied the connection. Even as he mourned the young agent's death, Afridi knew that Qasim's sacrifice would never be recognized. Most Indians thought of Kashmiris as insurgents or traitors, and they would never learn of the heroic actions of men like Qasim who gave their lives as bravely as any soldier. Only three weeks earlier, Qasim had reported on a series of meetings between his employer and a man named Roger Fleischmann, CEO of Peregrine Corporation, an American firm that manufactured aeronautical equipment, remote guidance systems, and drones. It wasn't clear why Fleischmann had come to Islamabad, and Afridi wondered whether there was a connection to Qasim's death. Recently, he had been worried about their communication protocols. Qasim's reports were forwarded directly to Shinde by a secretary in the High Commissioner of India's office in Islamabad. It was possible that some of these messages had been intercepted, despite the strictest precautions.

The next morning, after only a couple hours' sleep, Afridi was in his office studying a map of Kashmir. Seeing Pahalgam marked with a single dot, he felt a pang of remorse. The map showed no roads or physical features, for it was printed in Pakistan. It had been acquired through a Ministry of Health and Family Welfare official who attended a conference in Lahore a year ago. Afridi found the map both amusing and informative because of its inaccuracies.

All of Kashmir was depicted outside the borders of India. The Survey of Pakistan cartographers were engaged in an elaborate fiction of denial. The Line of Actual Control, where the two armies faced off, wasn't even shown on the map. To an uninformed observer it might have seemed that anyone could drive unimpeded from Muzzafarabad to Srinagar. The only hint of ground realities was that east of the Pir Panjal most of Kashmir was blank. Aside from Pahalgam, the towns of Baramullah and Gulmarg were also marked, as well as the Banihal Tunnel and further north the Zoji La Pass, Kargil, and Leh. But these were little more than random specks on a vacant quadrant of the map. Farther west, in those areas of Kashmir occupied by Pakistan, details were more complete, with highways and clustered settlements, airfields, and borders of districts or tribal agencies.

For a few minutes, Afridi's finger strayed northward into the high Karakoram, locating K2, Broad Peak, and Nanga Parbat. As a mountaineer, one of his greatest regrets was that he never had a chance to explore this region. For Indian citizens, these mountains remained forbidden territory. Lower down the map, he could see the Khyber Pass, Torkham, and Jamrud, an area from which his own ancestors originated long before partition. Afridi's great grandfather had accompanied Colonel Algernon Durand on the first survey of the Northwest Frontier, marking the borders of Afghanistan.

Catching himself, Afridi shifted his attention to the question at hand. Throughout the NWFP, including Chitral and the Northern Areas, as well as Afghanistan, the mapmakers had identified the locations of major hospitals. Each of these was marked with a bright red crescent, a sprinkling of medical facilities scattered across the Karakoram and Hindu Kush. Afridi consulted a second map, this one much larger and more detailed, produced by the Indian military, which showed the Siachen Glacier region where the plane had crashed.

Sources in Nepal had been able to establish that the turbo-prop departed Kathmandu soon after dark, an unscheduled flight for which there was no official record. It seemed this aircraft had flown into Nepal from either Guangzhou or Kunming. After refueling, the AN 24 appeared to have crossed back into

Chinese airspace, north of the central range of the Himalayas, until it reached the borders of Ladakh. Here it cut across Indian territory, heading for Afghanistan. Flying under cover of night, the pilot gambled on his route. It would have been a safer option to swing northward beyond the upper reaches of Siachen, but instead, he made a fatal decision to try and save a few minutes. It was a dark, moonless night and he miscalculated the altitude of the mountains that lay in his path.

Afridi traced possible routes the AN 24 might have taken if it had continued westward into Afghanistan. On the Pakistani map, he saw two red crescents clearly marked, one at Faizabad, the other at Kunduz. Both towns had airfields.

At that moment his telephone rang. Distracted, Afridi lifted the receiver and heard a dial tone before realizing it was his personal cell that was ringing. Reaching across his desk to pick it up, he noticed a number he didn't recognize.

'Hello,' he said cautiously.

'Is this Colonel Imtiaz Afridi?' It was a woman's voice with an American accent, though she didn't mispronounce his name.

'Speaking.'

'My name is Daphne Shaw and I'm calling from the United States.'

She paused, and there were several seconds of silence, though Afridi could hear the distant intake of her breath, half a world away. 'I was given your number by a mutual friend, Jehangir Daruwalla. He suggested that I could contact you in an emergency.'

'What sort of emergency?' Afridi asked. Daruwalla represented several European arms manufacturers. They had known each other since 1989, though Afridi hadn't been in touch with him for the past year at least.

The woman coughed gently at the other end of the line. 'I'm being unjustly targeted,' she said, 'by the American government.

This morning six armed men broke into my house and threatened to arrest me. They accused me of harboring terrorists.'

Afridi interrupted her. 'Madam, I don't know who you are or what you imagine I can do to help, but I have no authority or influence in the United States. And as you may be aware, this telephone call is probably being monitored as we speak.'

'No,' she said decisively, her voice taking on a more confident tone. 'I'm calling from Eggleston, Ohio, and this is a secure line.'

'I still don't know how I can help you,' Afridi replied.

The woman's voice was hushed but firm. 'By persuading the Indian government to grant me asylum.'

Nine

Luke knew they hadn't finished with him, though Fletcher and Holman, or whatever their real names were, had finally left his hotel around midnight. Jet-lagged and unsettled by the interrogation, he collapsed into bed, afraid of what he might find when he woke up. Yet for all his exhaustion, he couldn't fall asleep. This wasn't the first time he'd been questioned about the Sikander-e-Azam Trust, which supported a number of NGOs in northern Pakistan and Afghanistan as well as dozens of schools and hospitals. The trust had offices in several major cities, including Peshawar and Kabul, as well as field stations in Gilgit and Chitral. Among the people of Northern Pakistan, SEA had a popular reputation, for it operated without the corruption and bureaucracy of government agencies. The schools they funded were properly built, and their teachers were paid on time. Their hospitals were much better equipped than government clinics and the doctors well trained. For many, SEA's work was a model of the kind of development that could be done in the region, providing direct aid and a sustainable future amid all of the uncertainty, pain, and deprivation.

'Why do you think an American company like Peregrine would give them money?' Fletcher had asked several times.

'I have no idea,' said Luke. 'SEA doesn't publish annual reports.'

'But you must have some sort of hunch,' he insisted. 'Take a wild guess.'

'I really can't begin to speculate,' Luke continued to stonewall them.

Several times during the evening, Fletcher had excused himself and gone out on the balcony to have a smoke. Luke resisted the urge to join him.

The truth was that Peregrine's one-and-a-half-million-dollar donation was only a drop in the bucket. By even the most cautious estimates, Sikander-e-Azam Trust was annually spending half a billion dollars in the border areas. Over the past five years, SEA had become one of the most influential donor agencies in the region. It carried out projects of its own but also funded NGOs, government projects, and even Islamic charities, to make sure that nobody begrudged their presence. The staff members were skilled professionals, most of them with management degrees. Those who received SEA grants were held accountable for achieving specific goals and targets. Unlike many donor agencies, they kept their own costs down and operated efficiently and effectively. The Sikander-e-Azam Trust was often cited as an example of responsible philanthropy in a part of the world where waste, cynicism and corruption were endemic.

'What's their real motivation?' Holman had asked. 'What's the driving force behind their work?'

'I suppose they want to improve the lives of those they serve,' Luke answered.

'You don't suspect some larger political purpose?' Fletcher suggested.

'Maybe.' Luke threw up both hands. 'But, honestly, I don't know what it would be.'

Everyone knew there were troubling questions about the trust, partly because it had grown so quickly. Luke had tried to get information about their board of directors and SEA's decision-making process, but he couldn't even lay hands on an organizational chart. Unlike most agencies, they didn't publish glossy brochures or have an active website. SEA's offices were simple but well equipped, and the people who worked there always had a positive energy and purpose about them. But they became guarded when anyone asked where the money came from or who was controlling their operations. The institutions they funded had few complaints, though some of them privately questioned SEA's priorities.

Fletcher and Holman had tried to get Luke to reveal the identity of the man called Hakim, but he wasn't going to betray his source. In fact, Hakim was a social worker at one of the SEA hospitals in Azad Kashmir. He seemed a sincere and honest man, who had been employed by the trust for a year and a half. Though Hakim praised SEA for the support they gave the hospital, providing everything from generators to CT Scan machines, he had his doubts.

'Sometimes it seems almost like a secret cult,' Hakim had said, speaking off the record, 'as if they're twisting history, using ancient myths to justify current realities.'

Sikander-e-Azam was the Urdu name for Alexander the Great. The trust's primary mission was to provide education, healthcare, and poverty alleviation programs in the Hindu Kush and Karakoram region. Many of the people in this part of the world traced their ancestry to Alexander's army, when Greek satraps once ruled the borderlands of India, around 300 BCE. Among the clans who claimed a Hellenistic heritage were the Kalash, Pathans, and Burusho. Kafiristan was the traditional homeland of the Kalash, where the inhabitants worshipped deities that could be traced back to early Persian and Greek faiths. Under Muslim rule most of the inhabitants had converted to Islam, and Kafiristan was now known as Nuristan, the land of enlightenment, which had been purged of idolatry. Yet even among conservative Muslims like the Pathans, ethnic chauvinism was an appealing agenda, reviving the lost glory of Bactria and Gandhara. Fundamentalists condemned these claims as un-Islamic but the Sikander-e-Azam Trust had a working relationship with even the Taliban, and they weren't seen as a foreign threat.

Luke had researched SEA for the past two years. He had contacts among the NGOs they funded, but very few people were prepared to go on record, fearing that if they talked to journalists the money would dry up. Most grants included a confidentiality clause. Within a feudal society like Pakistan, there was nothing unusual about this or that SEA didn't appear to comply with government regulations. They had never been audited and seemed to avoid any form of official oversight. Part of the reason was that almost all of their funds were disbursed in semi-autonomous tribal agencies, AJK and Chitral. In Afghanistan too, there was little control. The medical and educational work they did was situated in parts of the country where nobody else bothered to build schools or hospitals. Locally, SEA cultivated a level of goodwill and loyalty that protected them from governmental interference. A few months ago, when Luke was in Kabul and asked about the Sikander-e-Azam Trust, one of the government officials told him, 'Why should we stop them? It is God's will that they are doing good.'

'You have to understand,' Fletcher had said, returning from a cigarette break. 'We don't want to interfere with the work they do. It's the people and power behind them that interests us.'

'Maybe it's better not to find out,' said Luke.

'What do you mean by that?' Holman jumped in, as if he were finally opening up.

'I don't know,' said Luke. 'Stir the shit, and you never know what sort of stink you'll discover.'

'Are you suggesting that SEA is a cover for something else?' said Fletcher.

'No, I think you're the one who's suggesting that,' said Luke. 'Come on! We can spin all sorts of conspiracy theories, and half of them might even be true, but in the border areas you never know what the real story is. All you can do is patch together some reasonable approximation of the truth. Everybody is trying to claim a piece of the action, whether it's drug deals or illegal arms, extortion and contract killings. The Taliban, the CIA, the DEA, the Chinese, even the Canadians and Brits have agents on the ground, and none of them know who's working for who.'

'But we're not trying to solve the whole puzzle. We just want to know who's behind SEA and what they're all about.' Fletcher scratched the side of his face where the skin was dry and peeling.

'For all I know, the whole thing could be a CIA scam,' said Luke. 'Some sort of covert trust-building operation. *How to Win Friends and Influence Your Enemies*? You guys probably still use Dale Carnegie as a standard ops manual.'

Fletcher showed no amusement, though Holman gave Luke a tight-lipped smile.

'Actually, we believe that SEA represents a significant threat to American interests in South Asia,' said Fletcher. 'Behind its benevolent facade, there's a serious effort to undermine peace and destabilize the region. We don't know for sure who's running this thing. But we know that it's dangerous, particularly when we've got a nuclear standoff between India and Pakistan.'

There was a pause, and Luke could see Fletcher's eyes fixed on him now.

'If you don't want to talk to us, we can't force you,' Fletcher continued. 'But then maybe you'll have Armageddon on your conscience.'

Luke didn't blink. He was used to this kind of intimidation. Whether it was Americans or Pakistanis, government officials always tried to pressure journalists into revealing hidden truths. The fact that the Sikander-e-Azam Trust attracted the interest of American intelligence agencies wasn't surprising. It seemed suspiciously successful where many other NGOs had failed. Living and working in Pakistan, Luke had been approached several times by spooks who tried to persuade him to work for them. 'Informal cooperation' was the euphemism they used.

Of course, they paid much better than the money he got for articles and interviews he published. But Luke understood that the minute he crossed that line, his position in Pakistan would become untenable. As a journalist, he had a reputation for reporting events without the arrogance and judgmental voice of most foreign correspondents. He was often critical of American interests and policies. The US press attaché in Islamabad once called him a 'Goddamn fucking Jihadi,' to his face, soon after 9/11, when he wrote a story about embittered youth in Pakistan who saw America as a satanic power.

Despite everything, Luke tried not to take sides, though he understood that objective truth was the first casualty of armed conflict, a discredited myth sacrificed on the altar of global security. Often, when asked about his nationality, he lied and said he was Irish or Canadian, not because he was afraid but because it made things far less complicated. His US passport was a liability and more than once he'd thought of applying for Pakistani citizenship. When he mentioned this to journalist friends in Pindi or Lahore, they looked at him as if he'd gone mad. 'I'll tell you what,' Shauqat Ali, a stringer for *The Boston Globe* had said, 'why don't we just trade passports? I'll happily take yours and go back to a nice little apartment in Cambridge, eating Dunkin Donuts for the rest of my life.'

Ten

Daphne emptied the ashtrays and tossed the rest of the cigarettes into a garbage bag before putting her trash on the curb. She hated the smell of stale tobacco smoke, the way it lingered in a room like the dead odor of someone who's never coming back. Long ago, when she was in her twenties, Daphne had smoked—everyone did in those days—but she quit after she got pregnant and hadn't touched a cigarette since. Until yesterday. And only to protect him. They would have asked about the stubs in the ashtrays, evidence of his visit. He had surprised her the night before, arriving at the house without warning, as he always did. A year had gone by since she'd seen him last. Though they spent the night together neither of them slept, sitting in the living room, sharing a bottle of Australian Shiraz, talking, and arguing. Finally, long after midnight, he took her to bed and they lay awake until dawn, not making love but finding solace in each other's arms.

When daylight filtered through the drapes, she made breakfast for him, just as she used to do so many years ago. Before he finished eating, a man in a beige Toyota arrived and the two of them left in a hurry, a rushed goodbye. He warned her that nobody should discover he'd been here. Daphne cleaned up the kitchen, rinsing their plates and bowls before putting them in the dishwasher. A short while later, she saw the Winnebago pulling up and quickly went to the bedroom. Finding the pack of Benson and Hedges he'd forgotten on the dressing table, Daphne panicked for a moment, before taking one and lighting it just as they broke down the door.

While the armed men were searching her house, she pretended to smoke a couple more cigarettes. They had found nothing, except for pictures from Bombay, which she could explain. Daphne knew exactly what to say and kept it simple. If you tried to tell too many lies they got tangled up in knots. Better to stick with an edited version of the truth. She'd known him long ago, back in the eighties. After that, 'he left me and I haven't seen him for fifteen years.' Almost everything was true…almost.

The cellphone she used had been given to her two years ago, a Blackberry that she kept switched off in a toolbox in the basement, tucked behind the boiler, along with the charger and spare valves and wrenches. She only used it when he sent her a signal: a wrong number on her other phone, somebody asking for a man named Bruce, which meant he wanted to talk. He had promised her that nobody could trace their calls but she took her own precautions, driving away from the house and switching on the Blackberry when she was at the mall or supermarket. He always answered after the second ring, though she never knew where he was.

Having put out the trash, Daphne opened the garage and backed her car down the driveway and onto the street. The front door had been nailed shut by a carpenter who said he would replace it next week. Driving past the college, she headed north out of Eggleston. It was a bright spring day, and the fields were turning green. A redtailed hawk hovered over a pasture, ready to drop from the sky onto a mouse or maybe a snake.

She knew this road by heart. It was the only drive she did outside of town, crossing the county line and heading onto the interstate for two exits before turning off at Upfield. Her mind was spinning, afraid and angry, but also calculating what must be done. Before she knew it Daphne was at the Cleveland Clinic's Critical Care and Rehabilitation Centre, a cheerful sign out front, painted yellow, promising hope. The institutional facade of three low buildings hid the tragedies within. Daphne pulled into a parking spot near the entrance. Today she had come earlier than usual.

At the front desk, the nurse on duty greeted her. Daphne waved and smiled, heading down the hall, carrying a bouquet of daffodils.

The door was ajar and another nurse was changing an intravenous bottle.

'Hello, Daphne,' she said, then saw the flowers. 'Aren't those beautiful! Are they from your garden?'

Daphne nodded. Crossing to the bed, she looked down at the expressionless face, then kissed her son's cheek. He hadn't been shaved for a couple of days and she could see grey hairs amid the stubble. Was he really that old? Thirty-two now, almost thirty-three. Daphne brushed her fingers through his hair, noticing how thin it had grown. The skin on his arms was still soft, but it pained her to see the needles in his veins and the tubes that fed into his body as well as those that drained out of him. He was alive but locked away inside a solitary confinement of flesh and bones. She wondered if he ever dreamed. Sometimes his eyelids flickered or his legs twitched under the sheets. These movements had once given her hope, though she knew it was pointless. The instruments that measured his heartbeat and other signs of life displayed a monotonous regularity. When she was alone with him, Daphne sometimes spoke to her son.

'Naseem,' she'd say. 'Can you hear me? Naseem?'

The name on his medical charts was different, part of an elaborate charade that she had been forced to maintain for all these years.

In the beginning, Daphne had come here every day, but now she visited twice a week. The doctors had told her there was no hope of recovery. A persistent vegetative state. Each day, they moved his arms and legs to stimulate circulation and keep his joints and tendons pliable, exercising useless muscles as he lay there like a marionette whose strings had been cut. Yet he looked strangely healthy, as if he might wake up any minute now and open his eyes, unlike the night she'd seen him after the accident, fifteen years ago, his face bruised and swollen. A stupid, senseless accident that had no meaning anymore. It had left him in this coma, lying here unconscious, still breathing, blood pumping through his veins. But Naseem would not answer her, refusing to wake up.

When the nurse finally left, Daphne took the Blackberry out of her purse and stared at it with a surge of anger that brought tears to her eyes. She didn't switch the phone on or put it to her ear, but spoke at it. 'You fucking bastard,' she said. 'You fucking, fucking bastard!'

Eleven

Afridi disliked Delhi, though he had grown up in the city. Too much had changed for the worse. The Delhi he remembered was green and spacious, with broad avenues and verdant lawns. Now, as he crossed over the outskirts of the capital, the sprawling colonies below him looked like a glacier of concrete, extending slowly outward. The disappearing contours of the Aravallis, a range of hills far older than the Himalayas, had been reduced to insignificance by multi-story buildings that jutted above eroded ridgelines. The highest points near Delhi, besides office towers and five-star hotels, were the rubbish heaps in Noida, smoldering mountains of garbage, filth, and discarded rubble from construction sites. As the rotting waste burned out of spontaneous combustion, pariah kites glided through the smoke, scavenging off discarded scraps. Bandicoots and rats infested the stinking mounds of refuse. Having flown down from Mussoorie, Afridi's helicopter circled over this decomposing wasteland before crossing the Yamuna upstream from Okhla. The Ministry of Defense had granted him special permission to land at Safdarjang Aerodrome, in the heart of the city.

A car received Afridi on the tarmac, a white Ambassador with a spacious rear seat that two Sikh soldiers helped him into, lifting him with courteous ease. The April air was warm and dry, the beginnings of a Delhi summer. His suitcase and two folded wheelchairs were placed in the boot. One was a standard model for everyday use. The other was a racing wheelchair he used for exercise. A protocol officer, Major Karamjit Singh, welcomed him and took his place in the front seat of the car. As they left the aerodrome and joined the tide of traffic, Afridi scowled.

'Is there ever any time of day when these streets are empty?' he asked, while they waited at a red light, amid a swarm of vehicles.

The major seemed confused by the question. 'Sir?'

'Never mind,' Afridi said. 'Where are we going first?'

'South Block, sir. The defense secretary has asked to see you immediately.'

'And Shinde?'

'Sir, he's already there.'

Ten minutes later, they turned onto Rajpath and drove toward the Central Secretariat. Here was one part of Lutyens Delhi that still retained its expansive grandeur. Afridi studied the monumental silhouette of the buildings with an appreciative eye. When they entered the sandstone hallways of South Block, he wheeled himself into a lift. He ignored the gestures of assistance from the PA who rushed ahead to open doors.

The defense secretary's office contained most of the original furniture designed by Edwin Lutyens and his team, including a massive teak desk and cabinets with glass fronted doors, filled with books that would never be read. As Afridi entered, the defense secretary and Manav Shinde got to their feet. None of them spoke until they were alone.

'Thank you for coming, Colonel,' the defense secretary said. He was a short, stout man with cropped gray hair and a reputation for losing his temper, especially with his superiors. Afridi liked him better than his predecessor, who had a fawning, diplomatic manner.

Shinde was his usual rumpled self, looking like a politician who just lost an election. His handloom kurta was unironed and his feet splayed out of Kolhapuri chappals. If he were walking down the street, nobody would have taken him for an intelligence officer, one of the best informed and most perceptive minds in the Research and Analysis Wing.

'I'm sure this must be very important,' he said, 'if Colonel Afridi has deigned to leave his hill station hideaway and come down to Dilli at short notice.'

'You received my message?' Afridi said.

'Yes, it made us curious.' The defense secretary nodded, returning to his chair behind a polished expanse of Burma teak. Afridi once calculated that the trees that were felled to make this desk must have been more than five hundred years old, predating the British Empire itself.

'I felt it was better that I brief you in person,' he said. 'Even the most secure forms of communication have a way of springing leaks.' Shinde winced and pulled at a loose thread on the hem of his sleeve. They hadn't spoken again since Qasim's death, but both of them knew it had occurred because security was compromised inside the High Commissioner's office in Islamabad.

Afridi paused to look out the window. He could see the dome of Rashtrapati Bhawan and the sprawling gardens of the Presidential estate. Taking a deep breath, he continued.

'As I wrote to you, we have an unexpected opportunity that may or may not play out in our favor,' he said. 'But it seems quite genuine.'

'You mentioned a woman,' said the defense secretary, impatiently.

'Yes, Daphne Shaw. She used to be an actress in Bombay. By now, she would be in her sixties.'

'She called you?' Manav prompted.

'Yes, from America, on a line she claimed was secure.' Afridi strummed the spokes on his wheelchair, a habit he had when his thoughts were outpacing his words. 'She has offered to cooperate with us in exchange for her protection. She's afraid the Americans, or someone else, are going to kill her. She wants asylum.'

'Is she a US citizen?'

'Naturalized, but she was born in India.'

'Why should we antagonize the Americans?' The defense secretary leaned back in his chair. 'What's in it for us?'

'Because she's willing to lead us to a very important man.'

'And who is that?' the secretary asked, impatiently.

'Guldaar,' Afridi said, pronouncing the name as if it left a bitter taste on his tongue.

Twelve

'Logistics,' said the Bosnian, running a finger across his dented chin where a day's stubble darkened an already shadowy complexion.

'I've never completely understood what that means,' Jehangir Daruwalla replied, watching the drops of condensation roll down his glass, forming a damp ring on the cardboard coaster.

'Getting things from here to there.' The Bosnian looked at him as if he were a fool, then drained his whiskey. 'Like a courier service.'

'Ahh... You mean shipping and handling. That's what we used to call it,' said Jehangir. He wasn't a man who was easily cowed by the derision of others. After all, being a member of one of the smallest minorities on earth thickened your skin, even if it played hell with your genes. Earlier, the Bosnian had asked him if he was Muslim, and what his name meant.

'No. Parsi. Zoroastrian,' he had answered, 'and Jehangir means ruler of the world.'

He could see a sneer of amusement forming on the man's face.

'Repeat?' the waiter asked, glancing down at their empty glasses.

Jehangir was about to put his hand over the mouth of his tumbler in a gesture of refusal, when the Bosnian nodded. 'Double. Large,' he demanded.

The waiter looked confused.

'Do you mean a double large or just a large drink?' said Jehangir.

'Isn't it the same?' his companion said, with an aggressive shrug of his shoulders.

'A large measure is sixty milliliters. A double large would be a hundred and twenty,' Jehangir explained, holding up his glass to demonstrate.

'Sixty,' the Bosnian conceded, giving the waiter a hostile look.

'And I'll have another chhota,' Jehangir added.

He hadn't stayed at the Royal Bombay Yacht Club for at least twenty years. When his cousin Nicky offered to book him a room here, Jehangir thought he'd give it a try for old time's sake. Usually, when he came in from London, he stayed at the Taj, which was next door, also facing the harbor, but that was where comparisons ended. His room in the Yacht Club had a better view than even the best suite in the Taj, looking straight across at the Gateway of India. The club had a shabby gentility, deteriorating slowly into noble decay. His room was big enough to accommodate a badminton court, with high ceilings and furniture that looked as if it had been upholstered before independence. Nevertheless, the Yacht Club was quaintly discreet and the drinks in the bar cost a tenth of what he would have paid at the Taj. Besides, on this trip Jehangir was obliged to keep a low profile—'under the radar,' as Nicky put it.

The Bosnian seemed to have no appreciation for the history or ambience of the club. He eyed the other members with surly indifference: an elderly assortment of Colaba regulars and a noisy table of Sindhis. The top three buttons on his shirt were open, exposing a matted pelt of dark chest hair.

'So, what do you suggest in terms of logistics?' Jehangir asked.

'There's a company in Doha we've used before. They don't ask questions,' said the Bosnian, whose name was unpronounceable. Jehangir had made a point of forgetting it immediately. In this business, it was best to keep things anonymous.

'Where will they deliver?'

'Karachi. F.O.B.'

'F.O.B.?' Jehangir raised an eyebrow.

'Freight On Board,' said the Bosnian, thinking Jehangir didn't understand. 'Customs clearance will be your problem once the ship arrives in port.'

'That wasn't our understanding,' Jehangir replied. 'I was told that everything would be taken care of from your end and we would pay cash on delivery.'

The Bosnian shrugged again as the waiter interrupted them with their drinks. He handed each man a fixed menu, saying the kitchen would be closing in half an hour.

'We'll take our drinks to the table,' Jehangir said, leading the way to the dining room. His companion hauled himself out of the chair, a heavyset, unhealthy man, whose arms were disproportionately short, so that his wrists only reached to his waist. Jehangir noticed circles of perspiration under his sleeves, though the bar was air-conditioned.

The menu was embossed with the Royal Bombay Yacht Club's crest, two anchors crossed behind a flotation ring, topped with a coat of arms and a crown. The Bosnian ordered Chicken Maryland and Okra Provençal, saying he'd eaten too much curry in the last three days. Jehangir decided to have a cucumber and dill salad with mutton cutlets. Only in the colonial clubs of India did recipes of the Raj linger on like the aftertaste of empire.

During the meal, Jehangir negotiated for the consignment to be cleared and delivered all the way to Muzaffarabad by truck. The Bosnian was no match for his bargaining skills and the fact that he was willing to pay cash, in Euros, gave Jehangir the upper hand. By the time he finished his lemon soufflé, the Bosnian looked chastened, maybe even a little unnerved. He excused himself, saying he had a flight to catch at 3:00 a.m.

Jehangir watched him leave, a brutish man with a Mediterranean gait. There were so many others like him in this world—middlemen who worked the margins as best as they could and never earned as much as they hoped. Jehangir disliked this kind of business but his cousin had insisted, and there was always the guilty pleasure of dealing with the dark side of a coin. That was his father's expression. Cyrus Daruwalla would hold up a silver rupee with Victoria's profile clearly visible and explain how it was like the moon. One side was bright and shiny, the other tarnished with shadows. Then he'd flip the coin in the air and catch it on the back of his hand, asking his son to choose, heads or tails.

After ordering a coffee, Jehangir changed his mind and asked for a brandy instead. It tasted like cough syrup mixed with kerosene but the rough warmth cleared his throat as he swallowed it in a single gulp. Signing the bar chits and the bill for dinner, he left a generous tip, though he knew it was against club etiquette. A handful of members still lingered in the bar, reluctant to leave their exclusive sanctuary. Out on the verandah, Jehangir paused to examine a model sailing ship in a glass case and the brass bell of a schooner decommissioned a century ago. Patterned tiles on the floor were worn smooth in places, and the humid darkness was comforting after the cold crosscurrents in the bar and dining room. Though it was past eleven o'clock, animated sounds of the city drifted in, a car horn and voices off the street. He pressed the button for the elevator, debating whether he should walk up the two flights of stairs to his room. For thirty seconds nothing happened, as if the elevator had broken down. Just as Jehangir was about to give up and use the staircase, pulleys creaked and cables moved, with the sound of greased steel and a muttering of gears somewhere deep inside the shaft. The cage rose from the ground floor below, like a giant piston at the heart of an obsolete machine.

When it stopped, Jehangir slid aside the grill. A light was on but the elevator appeared empty. The door seemed to have jammed and he had to force it open. All at once, Jehangir let out a whispered curse. On the floor of the elevator, huddled in a fetal crouch, lay the Bosnian's corpse. His throat had been slit from ear to ear, the fresh wound yawning like a second jaw, blood oozing into the tangled hairs on his chest.

Thirteen

After picking up a rental car, Luke checked out of his hotel. He had been expecting Fletcher or Holman to show up while he was having breakfast, but there was no sign of them. It seemed odd that they had left no contact numbers, no way for him to get in touch. When he asked for his bill, the receptionist checked the computer and told him it had been settled, including the charges for the mini bar. There was no information about who had made the payment. In the brightness of a spring morning, Washington looked deceptively cheerful. The cherry blossoms were just coming out and the white cenotaph of the Washington Memorial rose above the rooftops, like a giant exclamation mark commemorating an American pharaoh.

Luke felt conspicuous driving through the city, as if he were being watched. The GPS guided him to Route 66, a strident female voice that sounded like Tracy Holman. Within half an hour, he was across the Beltway and out of the city, heading toward West Virginia. A couple of times he felt there might be a car on his tail. In the rearview mirror he caught sight of a gray sedan that kept a steady distance, but as soon as he slowed down, the car went past him.

Whitman was a three-hour drive, mostly along country roads. The forests were a dense, monochrome green, and the towns he passed through were small and derelict. He switched off the GPS and turned on the radio to try to distract himself, but between the ranting of talk show hosts and the twang of country music, he couldn't find anything that didn't irritate him. Stopping for a cup of coffee at a gas station, he felt ill at ease, though the woman behind the counter didn't pay him any attention. Luke found a few dollars among the Pakistani rupees in his wallet. Whenever he came to America, he experienced a peculiar sense of reverse alienation. Back in Rawalpindi, he was used to being the only white man on the street, even if his beard provided a disguise. Here, it was disconcerting to find himself blending in, almost invisible, though he felt completely foreign, like his face were a mask.

Luke had driven this route more than a dozen times over the past three years. As he spotted familiar landmarks—a communications tower shaped to look like a pine tree and a billboard that reminded him: JESUS IS THE WAY!—his mind kept going back to Fletcher's questions.

For several years there had been rumors that Pakistan's Inter Services Intelligence Agency, ISI, was using SEA as a cover for activities in Kashmir, sending insurgents across the Line of Actual Control to attack Indian troops and other targets. ISI was also mixed up in the drug trade, providing protection to heroin smugglers and augmenting its budget with a percentage of the profits. One of the SEA hospitals across the Afghan border in Nuristan was discovered to be a laboratory for processing raw opium into heroin, but the British journalist who stumbled upon it was immediately deported and his cameras and notes confiscated.

The ISI had hauled Luke up on more than one occasion, for asking too many questions. Two years ago, when he was doing a story about the Karakoram highway, he had been arrested and spent forty-eight hours in a Hunza jail where a young lieutenant questioned him all night about why he was interviewing student leaders advocating local self-rule. He had been worried that they might cancel his press credentials and ship him out of the country, but in the end the lieutenant let him go with a warning that he should stick to writing about 'all of the good things the Pakistan government has done for these people.'

What Luke hadn't told Fletcher, or anyone else, was that he had been able establish links between SEA and a network of companies that handled the transport of goods and materials between Karachi and Kabul. Since Afghanistan was a landlocked country, there were only two ways in which items could be imported: by air, which was expensive, and by road, which meant a long transit, through either Iran or Pakistan. Karachi was the primary port for shipments to Afghanistan. The arrangement between the two governments was relatively simple, though it was an open invitation to corruption.

Cargo from countries like Japan or Korea was delivered to bonded warehouses in Karachi. These were mostly manufactured items, including everything from refrigerators and kerosene stoves to motorcycles and cell phones. Shipping agents then loaded them onto trucks, which were sealed by Customs authorities and driven across the country until they reached Peshawar. From there the cargo continued over the Khyber Pass, going through Landi Kotal and finally ending up at the Torkham border crossing. At that point, one of two things happened. Either they were delivered to Kabul or they were driven back into Pakistan and offloaded outside Peshawar. Bara Market on the northwestern edge of Peshawar was a huge black market for electronics and other imported goods.

Most of this trade was controlled by a single cartel that included shipping agents in Karachi, warehouses at both ends of the delivery chain, and trucking companies in Sind, Punjab, and the Northwest Frontier Province. Luke had discovered that many of these smaller businesses were owned by a principal holding company known as the Khyber Transport Company, which operated out of Abu Dhabi and Dubai and had a virtual monopoly over billions of dollars in imports to Afghanistan, not to mention illegal profits from the black market on either side of the border. While researching a story on KTC, Luke had also discovered there was a subsidiary called Khyber Transport Ltd. with offices in New York and London. They secured major contracts for supplying American and NATO forces in Afghanistan with food and fuel, as well as other non-lethal military supplies. Though it was impossible to get accurate figures, conservative estimates placed Khyber Transport's annual turnover at 10 billion dollars.

The illegal earnings of the company and its network of smaller agencies and contractors probably added up to twice that amount, which is where most of the Sikander-e-Azam Trust's funding came from. One of Luke's sources in Islamabad was a consultant for the World Health Organization. He had documents proving that payments for constructing SEA's schools and hospitals were always settled in cash. An unregulated slush fund, adding up to hundreds of millions of dollars, supported the philanthropic work of the trust. It was also an efficient way of laundering money, because each of the companies that contracted with SEA for supplying cement and steel rebars was part of the same web of businesses controlled by Khyber Transport.

Of course, the real mystery was who owned KTC and its subsidiaries. More than likely it was the same promoter or partnership that controlled SEA. But they remained hidden behind multiple layers of financial facades, sham companies, and shuffled transactions. The only thing Luke knew for sure was that it was very, very big. So big, in fact, that it was impossible to measure the wealth and influence this person or persons exerted in the region, all of which was politically patronized and protected.

The link with Peregrine Corporation was something Luke hadn't figured out. When Fletcher brought up the company last night, it had taken him by surprise. During his interview with

Roger Fleischmann there was no mention of the Sikander-e-Azam Trust or Khyber Transport, but Luke had learned, after covering the war in Afghanistan for almost ten years, the more dots you connected the more patterns they revealed.

By the time Luke reached Whitman, he had decided that Fletcher probably had a good idea who controlled KTC and SEA. He and Holman were just hoping to confirm their suspicions. Under the circumstances, Luke was beginning to feel more and more vulnerable, but if there was one place on earth where nobody would find him, it was Whitman, West Virginia. The town had only two streets and four stop signs. Luke braked at the crossing of Main and Jefferson, turning right at Alden's Market. The house stood at the end of a winding drive, built on the slope of a hill with lawns that merged into hayfields. A pretentious Victorian, it was out of place among the smaller homes in the town.

He could hear the gnashing of gravel under his tires as he pulled in beside a pickup truck that didn't look as if it had moved since his last visit, six months ago. Roscoe, the dog, got up slowly from his favorite spot on the porch, sniffed the air and barked. A minute later, Luke's sister Ruth opened the door, waving. Having just turned thirty, she was five years younger than him. They hugged each other before Ruth led her brother into the kitchen.

'Poonam!' she called out. 'Luke's here.'

He could see that Ruth had lunch ready on the table: pumpkin soup and a fresh loaf of bread, with an arugula salad on the counter. Just then, he heard footsteps coming downstairs and Poonam entered. She grinned at Luke and they embraced.

'You're thin again!' he said.

She rolled her eyes and moved toward Ruth. 'Where is she?' Luke asked.

'Asleep,' Poonam said.

'Hey, what is this?' Ruth pretended to be hurt. 'The only person you want to see is Nina, not us?'

'Come on upstairs,' Poonam said.

Luke went first and the two women followed. At the landing, he stopped, letting Poonam go ahead and open the door. The shades were drawn, but there was enough light coming into the room for him to see the crib. He hesitated, not sure if he should go any closer, but Ruth took his hand and led him forward. The baby was asleep, her face pinched into an innocent frown. For a few brief moments, Luke forgot everything that had happened over the past two days, the flight from Pakistan, the anonymous body in the casket, Carlton Fletcher coming back to life, and the inquisition last night.

~

'My parents still haven't figured things out,' said Poonam. 'They came to visit last week, and it was like…okay, so you've got a baby. How did this happen?'

She poured Luke another glass of wine, laughing.

'To family.' Luke raised his glass. 'Whatever that means.' Poonam and Ruth had been partners for almost eight years.

They'd met in graduate school in New York. Back then, Luke didn't have much to do with his sister, because of their age difference. He was in Pakistan most of the time, working for Reuters. When their father died of a stroke soon after retirement, shared loss had brought them closer. Yet Luke would never have guessed his sister was a lesbian until she phoned him in Rawalpindi one morning, a long distance call with a disturbing echo. 'I wanted you to be the first person to know,' she said. 'I've got a girlfriend. She's from India. Her name is Poonam.' On the phone, Luke had tried to be supportive, letting Ruth do most of the talking.

'So, Nina's almost a month old?' Luke asked, glancing across the table at Poonam.

'Three weeks and two days,' Ruth said.

'Was it an easy birth?'

'Eight hours of labor. Poonam was awesome. The midwife couldn't believe this was her first delivery.' Ruth blew on her soup-spoon to cool it down.

'What's it like being parents?' said Luke. 'Has she turned your lives upside down?'

'Not yet,' said Poonam. 'We're lucky. Nina sleeps most of the time. A very calm baby. Even when she cries it's only a whimper.'

She and Ruth both worked from home, running an online business they started as soon as they got out of graduate school. Luke had never completely understood what they actually did. It was some kind of computerized accounting system for insurance claims that made them enough money to buy this house and live comfortably together. Being self-employed gave them the flexibility to live in the country, a cheaper, cleaner, simpler way of life than being in New York or Washington. Earlier, he'd been worried about them moving to West Virginia.

'Aren't those rednecks going to lynch you?' he'd asked.

'No, everybody's pretty cool about it,' Ruth said. 'And those that don't approve, they just ignore us.'

Sometimes Luke wished he had his sister's optimism. He was always looking at things from a negative perspective while she seemed to approach things positively and get whatever she wanted out of life. 'So, here's to our service provider!' Ruth said, lifting her glass. It was a joke between the three of them.

Luke shook his head and Poonam laughed, self-conscious for a moment. Paternity wasn't something he had prepared himself for, though Ruth had persuaded him to become the biological father of their child.

'I know I'm asking a lot,' she'd said. 'But it would mean so much to me and Poonam, if you agree. Please, Luke, it's a whole lot better than finding some anonymous donor. And, besides, it gives me a genetic link.'

At first he refused, unwilling to get tangled up in his sister's relationship, but then he realized this was the only family he had. His own brief marriage had ended three years ago, partly because his ex-wife had wanted children and he didn't. The contradictions in his life were overwhelming. Last May, when he was in the US on work, Luke had visited Whitman for a week, having finally agreed to the plan. There was a fertility clinic in a town ten miles from where Ruth and Poonam lived. They had made the arrangements, and all he had to do was go there, fill out a lengthy questionnaire, sign consent forms, and then deposit his semen, as if it were some kind of research experiment. At first he felt strangely detached and a little embarrassed by the whole process but in the end Luke was surprised how pleased he'd been when he got an email six weeks later saying Poonam was pregnant.

Sitting at the kitchen table, Luke heard the baby start to cry. Ruth went upstairs as Poonam began to clear the dishes. When Luke stood up to help her, she put a hand on his shoulder and shook her head.

'Don't worry, I'll do it.'

A few minutes later, Ruth came down with Nina. The baby's eyes were wide open, and she stared at Luke with a dazed expression. Until now, she had been just a name and a few photographs attached to emails, but seeing Nina in his sister's arms startled him. She had honey blond hair, and her skin was a caramel color.

'Do you want to hold her?' Ruth asked.

'Not just yet,' Luke said. 'Let me get used to this.'

~

By that evening, however, he was sitting in the living room with Nina nestled in his lap. Poonam and Ruth were working in their office next door, with an array of computer screens and wires snaking across a hardwood floor. The jet lag and a comfortable hominess made him sleepy. Several of the pictures on the walls had belonged to his parents, watercolors of the Salt Range by a Pakistani artist. He also recognized the Afghan carpets on the floors from their home in Taxila, some of the few things his father had brought to the US from Pakistan when he retired. Their mother had died in a car crash on the road from Murree to Islamabad, back in 1989.

Hearing a phone ring, Luke was shaken out of his reverie. Poonam answered in the other room. A minute later, she came in with the cordless handset.

'For you,' she said with a puzzled frown.

Outside the windows it was already dark. Luke handed Nina to her mother and took the phone cautiously.

'Hello, this is Luke.'

Fletcher's voice shook him awake. He wondered how they knew where to find him but didn't ask.

'Are you near a TV?' Fletcher asked.

'Yeah.'

'Go to the news. CNN or any channel with international coverage.'

Luke found the remote and pressed the power button. Switching channels, he could hear Fletcher chewing, eating something on the other end of the line. Finally, he found the news. The first image he saw was barren mountains, somewhere in the Hindu Kush, and a house in a village that seemed to have collapsed. Somebody was lifting rocks and throwing them aside. Across the bottom of the screen was the breaking news:

EARTHQUAKE IN NORTHERN PAKISTAN,
HUNDREDS FEARED DEAD.

Fourteen

The unmarked bungalow on Aurangzeb Lane was hidden behind high walls topped with razor wire. Afridi stayed here often enough that one of the suites was specially equipped to give him the independence he required. The older he got, the more he resented leaving home. Between the pollution and politics in Delhi there wasn't much that you could see or breathe or hear that didn't compromise a person's physical and mental health. At least his suite opened onto an enclosed garden of cana lilies and a bougainvillea vine that was coming into bloom. By the time he settled in and ate a light lunch, it was mid-afternoon, much too warm to go outdoors.

Manav Shinde had sent across the files he had requested. Two sealed boxes contained the relevant documents up until 1989, after which almost everything had been digitized. Afridi looked skeptically at the single CD with the more recent correspondence and reports. Ordinarily, none of this information would have been permitted to leave RAW's archives, but exceptions were always made for Afridi.

After their meeting with the defense secretary, Shinde had accompanied him back to the guesthouse. Afridi noticed that Manav was unusually silent.

'Something's bothering you,' Afridi said when they were alone in the suite, with the doors closed.

Manav had removed his glasses, wiping the perpetual bleariness from his eyes.

'Are you sure about this?' he finally said. 'We're not just chasing some fictitious phantom who exists only in the minds of paranoid analysts?'

'You're suggesting I'm paranoid?' Afridi smiled.

'No,' said Shinde, obviously uncomfortable, as if he were betraying the trust between them by questioning Afridi's judgement. 'I'm just saying we have no proof that Guldaar represents the kind of threat you're suggesting. He's more of a myth than a man.'

'If we knew all about him,' said Afridi, 'he wouldn't be as dangerous as he is.'

'Still, the evidence is very thin, if nonexistent,' said Shinde. 'More rumors than hard facts.'

'Unfortunately, we're in a business that operates on rumors and guesswork,' Afridi replied. 'Our job is to uncover the truth, no matter how obscure it may be, especially if it's hidden beneath a web of lies.'

Manav shook his head. 'This woman, Daphne Shaw. She called you out of the blue. It doesn't make you suspicious?'

'Of course it does,' said Afridi. 'But that's exactly why I'm curious. Coincidence almost always indicates conspiracy.'

'Imtiaz, I'll be honest with you. This time, I think your instincts are wrong,' said Shinde. He was one of the few people that used the colonel's first name. 'But, frankly, that's less of an issue. What worries me more is that there are those who might turn this against you. Several of our senior colleagues would like to shut down the Himalayan Research Institute. If they could embarrass you—'

'Very little embarrasses me,' said Afridi.

'I know,' said Shinde. 'But if we antagonize the Americans and if it comes out in the press that you are pursuing a target who doesn't exist, HRI will have its budget cut in half, if it isn't closed down completely.'

'I'm aware that some of our colleagues would like to see me fail,' Afridi answered, 'but that isn't sufficient reason to give up an opportunity to uncover the greatest threat to peace in South Asia since Pakistan tested its nuclear bomb.'

'You're exaggerating,' Manav replied. 'It isn't like you to jump to conclusions when you haven't got the facts in front of you.'

Afridi laughed. 'It's a process of deduction, like establishing a scientific proof. First you begin with a hypothesis and then you develop a theory. It requires patience and disciplined reasoning but you have to visualize the big picture, even if it isn't there in front of you.'

'But you're suggesting a conspiracy on a scale that defies logic,' said Manav. 'How is it possible for one man to wield so much influence?'

'I'll give you an example,' said Afridi, turning his wheelchair toward the window, as if he could see something outside in the garden. 'The houbara bustard.'

Shinde looked baffled and shook his head. 'I beg your pardon?'

'Last year, thirty-three permits were issued by the Pakistan government for hunting houbara bustards in Punjab, Sindh, and Baluchistan provinces. The list of foreign hunters in whose name these licenses were granted includes virtually every Arab head of state, from the Emirs of Kuwait, Qatar, and Dubai to the Saudi crown prince. Of the thirty-three permits, twenty-eight were facilitated and organized through one company, Shikar Outfitters and Associates, which has its registered office in Dubai. This company handles all of the necessary formalities in Pakistan, where bustard licenses are issued by a special desk in the prime minister's office. SOA also organizes the hunts, supplying everything from air-conditioned luxury tents to reconnaissance aircraft and special radar facilities to locate the birds.'

'What's so special about a houbara bustard?'

'The Arabs believe their meat is an aphrodisiac, particularly the liver of a male houbara. It can sell for as much as ten thousand dollars an ounce. The birds are severely threatened, in danger of extinction. They've been virtually wiped out in Arabia. Every winter, flocks of houbara migrate from Central Asia to Pakistan. The sheikhs are permitted to set up their hunting camps and licensed to kill a hundred birds each year.'

'Do they shoot them?'

'No, they use falcons. Theoretically, the hunters aren't permitted to use firearms, though it's hard to believe they don't resort to shotguns or rifles once in a while. Each expedition has a liaison officer who's supposed to oversee the hunt, but it doesn't take much to buy them off and you can be sure the Arabs kill more than their quota. The politicians are all in their pockets. Many of the sheikhs have refrigerated containers that are flown back home every day with the dressed carcasses of birds. It's like a factory, and Shikar Outfitters makes it all happen.'

'For a fee?'

'Of course. But who can put a price on an emir's libido?'

'Who owns Shikar Outfitters?'

'That's the billion dollar question. It's difficult to get details on any business registered in Dubai because there's usually an Emirati promoter along with other investors whose identities are discreetly obscured. Whatever names appear on the official documents are usually fictitious. But we have been able to trace things down to a holding company called Khyber Transport, which handles imports into Afghanistan, one of the major logistics companies in the region. Our intelligence confirms that Guldaar started this company twelve years ago, and he built it up with a complex structure of subsidiaries and diversified interests that keep his identity concealed. Shikar Outfitters is just one of dozens of companies that are part of his empire.'

'So, a rare bird is going to become extinct because of the sexual inadequacies of Arab sheikhs? It's unfortunate,' said Shinde, 'but that doesn't add up to a threat to world peace.'

'Shikar Outfitter's profits are secondary to the influence they wield. The hunting licenses are diplomatic favors, and those who arrange them seek other kinds of rewards. Access to those sheikhs is priceless. The cost of these hunting expeditions run into millions of dollars. Special planes carry the falcons, flying them in from the Gulf. You can't imagine the extravagance of these hunts. Last year, one Emirati royal had a dozen Porsche Cayenne SUVs flown in for ten days, just so he could race around the countryside searching for the birds. They use satellite telemetry to track the migration. More time and effort is expended on finding houbara bustards than the Americans spent searching for weapons of mass destruction in Iraq.'

Shinde still looked unconvinced. Afridi wheeled himself across the room and produced an envelope from a pile of papers on his desk. Opening it, he handed over a sheaf of photographs.

'These were taken this winter, about three months ago, 22nd January, in central Punjab near the Khushab Nuclear Facility. It's a popular hunting area for bustards and attracts several thousand birds each year. The hunting permit was issued to one of the senior members of the royal family of Qatar, but as you can see from these photographs the guest list included a number of other dignitaries, all of whom seem delighted to be posing with falcons on their wrists. We can assume that they weren't just hunting at Khushab. The dignitaries were taken on a tour of the uranium enrichment facility. Of course, we couldn't get any pictures from inside, but you can be sure the Pakistanis took good care of them.'

'Is Guldaar in any of these pictures?' Shinde asked.

'No. We have no recognizable images of him, and he isn't likely to have been there. He prefers to remain out of sight.'

'Who's this?' said Manav, picking up a photograph of a blond-haired man grinning at the camera, with a falcon perched on his arm. He was standing between the CIA director and Pakistan's chief of army staff.

'Roger Fleischmann. CEO of Peregrine,' said Afridi.

Manav registered the name. 'The same Peregrine that manufactures the drones?'

Afridi nodded. 'Standing behind him is Jehangir Daruwalla.' Again, Manav recognized the name.

'How is Peregrine mixed up in this?'

'Guldaar seems to have been negotiating on their behalf, part of a CIA arms deal with Pakistan. He often uses Daruwalla as a go-between, his personal emissary and troubleshooter. Peregrine is hoping to get a contract to equip Ghazni missiles with an updated remote guidance system, but the Pentagon has been dragging its feet because the Pakistanis haven't been cooperative on other fronts.'

Manav's eyes shifted behind his glasses, and Afridi could tell that he was beginning to understand the consequences

'Where did you get this information? These photographs?' Shinde demanded. 'Why wasn't I informed?'

'Qasim sent them to me three weeks ago, from Islamabad,' said Afridi.

'Why didn't they come through our regular courier?'

'Because I asked him to send them to me directly.' Afridi's voice revealed no emotion, but his hands were clenched on the arms of his wheelchair.

'Without informing me?'

Afridi nodded. 'I didn't trust your delivery systems. There was a security breach at the High Commission. I don't know who it was or how it happened, but for several months I'd been suspecting something. Qasim was betrayed, and he paid for it with his life.'

Manav looked down at his hands, studying his knuckles.

'Do you think the Americans knew about him?' he asked, without looking up.

'Probably not,' said Afridi. 'But if I had to guess who arranged to have him killed, more than likely it was Guldaar.'

'Our best agent,' said Manav looking up to meet Afridi's gaze. 'Such a pity. Such a waste.'

'Qasim's life won't have been wasted,' said Afridi, 'if we can catch Guldaar.'

~

After Shinde left, Afridi turned his attention to the boxes of files. Cutting the seals with a pen knife, he rooted through the first carton, most of which seemed irrelevant. It was only in the second box that he found what he was looking for: a thin dossier marked 'Daphne Shah.' The papers smelled faintly of Gamexene, which protected the documents from worms and silverfish.

Inside were a series of studio photographs of a beautiful woman. Afridi recognized her face from pictures in magazines many years ago, when Daphne was a model and actress. She had toffee-blond hair with a natural wave. The unblemished contours of her face seemed to be lit up by an inner radiance rather than the harsh glare of studio lamps. She looked as if she might be European, perhaps Spanish or Italian. For a while, the film magazines had referred to her as a Greek goddess or nymph because of her name, ethereal beauty, and statuesque figure.

Each of the photographs was slightly different, though all of them were glamorously posed, the kind of publicity shots that film producers hold up for review when casting a suitable female face to go with the hero of their latest movie. Though Daphne made a successful debut as an actress, she had one fatal flaw. At five eleven she was five inches taller than most of the male stars in Bombay, who felt intimidated by her height.

Flipping through the dossier, Afridi skimmed over clippings from gossip columns reporting rumored affairs with industrialists and erstwhile maharajahs. A few of these were confirmed by intelligence reports, including her relationship with a Russian diplomat who was deported because of a bribery case. Daphne was innocent, and the confidential report exonerated her, though it raised questions about her nationality. Toward the end of the file, there was a reference to her relationship with a man named Jasbir Bakshi. Afridi recalled that Bakshi had gained brief notoriety in the Bombay underworld during the eighties as a smuggler and conman who partied with film stars. Later, after an income tax raid on his flat in Worli, he disappeared abroad, one of those flamboyant criminals whose fortunes flared up and flamed out on the society pages. Another document in the file was a passport application with a photograph of Daphne, looking far less glamorous but still beautiful. She gave her name as Laila Shah, daughter of Mohammed Aslam Shah, with a permanent address in Kalbadevi, undoubtedly false. There was no indication whether the passport had been issued or not. Afridi glanced at the accompanying CD and decided he would save that question for later.

Daphne's file contained a copy of an Interpol Red Corner Notice for Jasbir Bakshi. No recent photographs were available, but as Afridi worked his way through the dossier, moving backward in history, he found pasted to a police report two pictures of a man in his early thirties with a fair complexion, a prominent nose, and long hair, looking like a drugged-out rock star. He had been arrested for smuggling gold from Dubai, but the police closed the case due to insufficient evidence. The original report recorded twenty-five kilos of gold in his possession, but later documents reduced the amount to twenty-five ounces. The man in the photograph was identified as Jasbir, and his address was a flat in Bandra. Afridi studied the picture, unable to recognize the face. He knew this photograph was of an imposter, part of an elaborate shell game of identities.

The dossier also contained several photographs of Jehangir Daruwalla as a young man, though he was identified as Jamshed Baksh, alias Javed Irani. Afridi had to smile at the rakish pose and cigarette tucked into a surly smile. There were several telexes in the dossier between Jamshed Baksh and someone in London about a shipment that was delayed. None of it added up to anything more than a business transaction that may or may not have been illegal. The photograph that caught Afridi's eye was a candid shot taken at a party in which Daruwalla and Daphne Shah were seated together in front of a plaster mural of mermaids. A mirror behind them caught the camera's flash. Both were laughing at a joke. On the back of the photograph, someone had written their initials. 'DS and JD. New Year 1982.'

Reaching for his phone, Afridi searched through a list of contacts, then made a call.

'Miss Tagore,' he said, when a woman's voice answered. 'How have you been? All well, I hope?'

Afridi listened for a moment and then replied.

'Actually, I'm in Delhi. I flew down from Mussoorie this morning.'

He flipped through the file distractedly as the woman responded. 'Business, of course,' Afridi said. 'I was wondering if we could meet. I wanted to discuss something with you. Perhaps this evening? Humayun's Tomb. 18:00 hours?'

Fifteen

By the time Luke reached Dulles airport, his ticket had already been rebooked. After returning the rental car, he took a shuttle to Departures and checked in. Though he was officially on leave, his editors were already clamoring for him to file reports on the earthquake. Going back to Pakistan was the only choice he had. Luke figured if he made it to Islamabad within the next twenty-four hours, he'd be able to reach the affected areas by the following day, provided he could hitch a ride on a helicopter. From what little he had learned, the epicenter of the quake was northwest of Chitral, in a valley that wasn't heavily populated, though surrounding areas had been badly damaged. He had called a couple of contacts, who claimed that whole villages had been buried and most of the roads destroyed.

Ruth was upset with him for leaving so abruptly, though he tried to make her understand. When he left the house, Nina was awake. Luke had kissed her on the forehead, promising he would come back in the summer.

'Be careful,' Ruth said. 'Don't take any stupid risks.'

'No worries,' he said.

Poonam hugged him before he got in the car. 'You didn't even get a chance to change her diapers,' she said.

'Next time, for sure,' he said, as he drove off. Though he sounded confident and waved at the three of them, he felt an ache of remorse, the familiar insecurity of leaving and never knowing when he'd be back. Sudden departures had always been a part of his life, constantly traveling to cover the next story, unable to settle down. He envied his sister the contentment and security of her home, a lover who was there each morning when she woke up, and now a child to raise together.

After passing through security, Luke still had an hour until his flight. With his business class ticket, he was able to go to the executive lounge, where he got himself a cup of coffee, picked up copies of *The Wall Street Journal* and *The New York Times*, and found a quiet corner in which to browse the news. Ten minutes later, he saw Carlton Fletcher enter the lounge. Despite a momentary urge to hide, Luke raised his hand. Fletcher came across and sat down beside him.

'Are you on this flight?' Luke asked.

'No,' said Fletcher. 'I just came by to wish you bon voyage.'

'That's kind of you. For a minute I thought you might not let me go back,' said Luke. 'Keep me here for questioning.'

Fletcher gave a tentative smile. 'You'll be a lot more help to us over there.'

'You know,' said Luke, 'I don't want to sound ungrateful, but I told you already, I'm not interested in working for the CIA.'

When Fletcher took his glasses off for a moment, his eyes looked tired and vulnerable.

'I'm not with the CIA,' he said. Luke fell silent for a moment.

'What about Tracy Holman?' he asked. Fletcher shook his head.

'All right, so who do you work for?' Luke asked.

'Let's just say we're part of the NSA,' said Fletcher, 'and leave it at that.'

'Okay, but you're still wasting your time,' Luke replied. 'I'm not going to work for the US government.'

'Of course,' said Fletcher. 'I understand.'

For several seconds he remained silent as one of the other passengers in the lounge walked by on his way to the men's room.

'We don't want you to work for us,' said Fletcher.

'I thought that was the whole point?' said Luke. 'All that bullshit about repatriation of human remains, flying me here. The only thing you didn't plan on was the earthquake. I'm sorry to disappoint you.'

'The truth is, you haven't disappointed us,' said Fletcher. 'You've done exactly as we asked. Mission accomplished.'

Luke reached for his coffee and took a sip. 'Really?'

'Yes, the body you brought back was extremely important to us, along with the contents of the suitcase. Fortunately, everything came through intact and nothing got into the wrong hands.' Fletcher paused and cracked his knuckles. 'There are times we can't even trust our own people, and it becomes necessary to operate through alternate channels.'

'What was in the suitcase?' Luke said.

'Evidence,' said Fletcher, with an enigmatic smile.

'And if they'd opened it at Customs?' Luke said. 'What would have happened?'

'You would have gone to jail for the next ten years,' Fletcher replied. 'Of course, if they'd opened the coffin, it could have been a whole lot worse.'

'I don't believe you,' Luke said with a laugh.

'You don't have to,' said Fletcher. 'It's a moot point. You successfully made the delivery, and we're genuinely grateful to you.'

Luke found his irritation growing. 'Then why all the questions about the Sikander-e-Azam Trust, all that crap about ethics and morality?'

'We just wanted to make sure you're the kind of person you say you are,' said Fletcher.

'What is this?' Luke was angry now. 'Why are you jerking me around?'

'Calm down,' said Fletcher.

'I'm a US citizen,' said Luke, 'and an accredited journalist. You can't fuck around with me like this.'

'Nobody's fucking with you,' said Fletcher. 'Take it easy. I'm just telling you the truth, so you'll understand how important this is.'

'You haven't told me anything, goddamn it,' said Luke. 'I don't know who you are or what you're after.'

'How was your visit with your sister?' Fletcher inquired. 'None of your business,' said Luke.

'And the baby's well? She's almost a month old, isn't she?'

Luke felt his mouth going dry. Fletcher's voice had changed almost imperceptibly, though the warning in his words was loud and clear.

'What do you know about her?' Luke said.

'Everything,' said Fletcher. 'We know that you're the father. We know that Ruth and her partner have a successful business and a pretty good life in the country—clean air, no traffic, no commute, fields, and forest all around.'

'So what?' said Luke.

'We also know that they've been cheating on their taxes, claiming deductions with phony receipts. The IRS could make things very difficult for them.'

'You're threatening me,' said Luke.

'Let me finish,' said Fletcher. 'Your sister's partner...Her name is Poonam Tewari. She came to the US from India on a student visa, which she overstayed. An immigration lawyer, Kent Brookes, did some fancy footwork to keep her here, but the fact is, she doesn't have a green card or a valid visa. She's an illegal alien, and we could deport her within twenty-four hours because she's broken half a dozen laws. Even her smartass lawyer wouldn't be able to save her.'

Luke kept quiet, staring at the folded papers on his lap. 'I'm only trying to be persuasive,' said Fletcher.

'What is it you want?' Luke demanded.

'We need you to do your job as a journalist, that's all,' said Fletcher. 'But in the course of your investigations, if you turn up the kind of information we're looking for regarding the Sikander-e-Azam Trust and Peregrine, I'd be grateful if you shared it with us.'

'Jesus!' Luke said.

Fletcher leaned in a little closer.

'The dead man you brought back was one of our assets, an independent contractor taken hostage in Azad Kashmir, three weeks ago. He was severely tortured before they killed him. The body shows signs of everything from electric shocks to broken fingers and a whole lot of things you can't imagine a human being could endure. They wanted him to talk but, unfortunately for him, he didn't have the information they wanted. We recovered what was left of the body from a ditch outside Muzzafarabad.'

'Who did it?' said Luke.

'That's the disturbing question.' Fletcher looked toward the window, where a British Airways 747 was pulling into its parking bay. 'Because it might have been some people we thought we could trust.'

'And what makes you think I can help?' Luke asked, feeling an uncomfortable itch between his shoulder blades.

'Because you have contacts with SEA. We suspect they had something to do with this.' Fletcher sat back in his seat. 'And just in case you're thinking about alerting them, please keep in mind that the suitcase you were carrying contained five kilos of heroin. The baggage tag with your name on it is still attached.'

Sixteen

Humayun's Tomb had been recently renovated and restored by the Aga Khan Foundation and the Archeaological Survey of India, who did extensive repairs and cleaning and replanted lawns and gardens. Anna hadn't been here for at least ten years. She remembered her last visit, with a group of college friends. They all got stoned near the Barber's Tomb, one of the peripheral mausoleums, with intricate sandstone screens. Anna recalled taking hits from a joint and watching the carved patterns turn into a fluid tapestry of light and shadow until she couldn't tell the solid geometric shapes from the spaces in between.

Arriving early, she sat under one of the arches inside the main gate and waited for Colonel Afridi to show up. His call had surprised her in the middle of an audio surveillance project, tapping phones at the Bangladesh High Commission. Manav had warned her that someone would be in touch, but he hadn't told her who it might be. The last time she and Afridi had spoken was almost nine months ago, though she recognized his voice immediately.

Now she saw him appear at the far corner of the gardens, entering through the southern archway instead of the main gate, to avoid the steps. He hadn't spotted her yet, as she approached along the water channels, passing under the matted branches of a ficus tree. Afridi paused by a fountain, and after finally catching sight of Anna, he raised one hand in greeting. He was alone, but she knew that his escorts must be close by. When Anna reached him, she began to put out her hand, then leaned forward and lightly kissed his cheek.

Afridi was not easily flustered, but he looked startled for a moment, embarrassed by her impulsive gesture of affection. Ever since Anna joined the intelligence service, she had been in awe of him. When they worked together on the last operation, she had found him a generous mentor as well as a strict and demanding case officer.

'How have you been, sir?' she asked, taking a step back. Though the sun was descending beyond the western walls of the garden, it was warm, and she could see a trickle of perspiration on the side of Afridi's face as he turned his wheelchair.

'Very well, thank you,' he said, with quiet formality.

'I was surprised when you said you were in Delhi,' Anna continued.

Afridi smiled.

'As you know, I avoid this city as much as I can, but whenever I'm here, I like to visit the few places that remind me what Delhi used to be like. These gardens have been brought back to life,' he said. 'Do you come here often?'

Anna shook her head, deciding there wasn't any point in telling Afridi about her last visit.

'I've always found this tomb more impressive than any other Mughal monument,' said Afridi. 'A perfect blend of architectural aesthetics and natural beauty.'

She nodded, knowing that he would eventually get around to telling her why they were here, but only after he'd finished musing on the mausoleum.

'It is spectacular,' she said, glancing up at the enormous marble dome and the red sandstone facade. Afridi lifted a hand and seemed to trace the outline with his finger.

'Humayun's tomb was built by a woman in memory of her husband, whereas Shah Jehan was commemorating the death of one of his queens. You can see the difference, can't you?' Afridi said. 'This is a truer, more powerful statement, whereas the Taj Mahal is romantic hyperbole, a lot of semi-precious stones and marble along with superfluous minarets that take away from the grandeur of the dome. The emotions expressed are much deeper and more passionate. Humayun's widow walked through these gardens every day, mourning her husband until she finally followed him into death. I much prefer this mausoleum to the Taj.'

'There are people who would disagree with you, sir,' Anna said with a laugh.

'To hell with them,' Afridi replied, setting off in a counterclockwise direction. For a while he continued to spin architectural theories, drawing her attention to the five pointed stars that appeared at each corner of the tomb.

Anna wanted to interrupt, but she knew better than to try and change the topic. After a while, they stopped under a tamarind tree. She could hear the prolonged whistle of a train leaving Nizamuddin Station nearby. The sun was dropping below the crenelated walls, gilding the white dome with a burnished aura.

'It's like the last light on the mountains,' Anna said, remembering the view of the high Himalayas from Afridi's cottage in Mussoorie.

'Alpenglow,' he said. 'The same effect, whether it's marble or snow.'

As the blush of color began to fade, Afridi turned toward Anna. 'Miss Tagore, I need your help,' he said. 'We have an urgent situation that requires somebody I can trust.'

'You're inviting me back to Mussoorie?' Anna asked.

Afridi smiled. 'No. Not just yet,' he said. 'I want you to go somewhere else. Somewhere you'd never imagine.'

Anna looked at him with a puzzled expression as he fell silent. 'Where?' she finally demanded.

'Am'rika,' said Afridi, teasing her with the pronunciation.

She broke into a laugh, knowing how much he disliked the United States.

'You're joking,' she said.

'No,' he replied, setting off along the path again, both hands working the wheels on his chair.

'Sir, why would you send me there?' she asked, catching up with him.

'To do some research,' said Afridi. 'You'll be studying the archived papers of a Sanskrit scholar and philologist named Dennis Shelton. He was an accomplished translator who produced the first English rendition of Bilhana's lesser known verses.' Afridi was moving faster now, as if to escape her questions.

'Bilhana?'

'The twelfth-century bard of Kashmir,' he replied.

'I don't know anything about poetry,' she said.

He let his palms slide along the steel rims of the wheels for a moment, slowing down as they came abreast of the northeast corner of Humayun's tomb, where the shadow of the dome extended across the grass.

'You'll have to do your homework,' said Afridi. 'But I can assure you that Shelton was an interesting man. He gave Bilhana's lyrics a modern voice. His own poems weren't bad, either, though the American idiom has never appealed to me.'

Anna now fixed him with her eyes, unwilling to play this game any longer.

'Sir—' she began, but he interrupted her.

'It's your cover, Anna, nothing more than that. The collected papers of Dennis Shelton are stored in a library at Bromfield College in Eggleston, Ohio, his alma mater. We'll arrange for you to travel there, as a scholar of Sanskrit poetry, working on her PhD in comparative literature. All of that will be explained to you, along with your alias and the necessary documentation.

However, the real purpose is to put you in a position where you can befriend a woman who is, for us, a person of extreme interest.'

'What's her name?' Anna asked.

'Daphne Shaw. You've probably never heard of her. But she's the former mistress of a man named Guldaar.'

'Guldaar?'

'Literally, the mark of a rose but also a common name for leopards, because of the rosettes on their fur. Guldaar is the nom de guerre of a particularly ruthless and elusive warlord in the tribal areas of Pakistan, who controls a multinational syndicate of crime and corruption,' said Afridi. 'Unfortunately, we don't know his true identity.'

'I've heard rumors,' said Anna.

'Yes, that's all we've had for a long time…rumors. There's no concrete proof that Guldaar or anyone like him exists, except for circumstantial evidence of his power and influence.' Afridi began to wheel himself forward again.

'This woman, Daphne. She must know him, if she was his lover.'

'Yes, she even had a son by him, named Naseem. He's Guldaar's only child,' said Afridi. 'They lived in Mumbai until the boy was severely injured in a motorcycle accident on Marine Drive.'

'He's alive?'

'Yes, but in a coma,' Afridi explained. 'Brain dead, though he's been kept on life support for fifteen years. Daphne moved with him to the United States. He's in a critical care facility near Eggleston, Ohio. She's been there with him all this time. Certainly not a happy way to spend your life, but perhaps she doesn't have a choice.'

'How did you make contact with her?' Anna asked.

'She's a friend of a man I've known for years. Jehangir Daruwalla. He's an arms trader based in London but originally from Bombay. Daruwalla is mixed up in some of Guldaar's businesses. He gave Daphne my private number to use in an emergency.'

'Why did she call?'

'Guldaar visited her a few days ago, and it seems some agency in the US government, possibly Homeland Security, is trying to track him down. They raided Daphne's house, hoping to find him, but by that time he had disappeared.'

'Sir, with all due respect, it sounds as if we're chasing ghosts,' Anna said.

'Exactly, but the analogy I would offer comes from astrophysics instead of the paranormal,' Afridi continued. 'You've heard of black holes and dark matter, I assume? Scientists suspected their existence long before they could prove that they were really there, the collapsed residue of stars, an invisible sinkhole of cosmic gravity. The presence of dark matter was only inferred by the responses of other phenomena that could be observed.'

Anna shook her head impatiently, thinking Afridi was wandering off track again, but he turned to face her, with a deft U-turn of his wheelchair.

'It's the same with Guldaar,' he said. 'For a number of years, we've known that someone was controlling most of the criminal activity in Afghanistan and Pakistan—the drug trade, hawala transactions, smuggling of arms, commissions from military contracts, almost every facet of the illegal economy. All of this could only be possible with the collusion of the CIA, Pakistan's military and the ISI, not to mention some of our own politicians and generals. If Guldaar exists, as I'm sure he does, then he's far more dangerous than all of the underworld dons combined. We've been following the trail of money, murder, and extortion, which points to a central figure whose reach extends across South Asia and the Middle East.'

'And you're sure this woman can lead us to him?' Anna said.
'I'm sure of nothing,' said Afridi. 'What I believe is largely a

matter of conjecture and faith, arrived at through a process of elimination. Guldaar may be a leopard who changes his spots. But I have to accept that he's there, hiding in the borderlands of Afghanistan, like dark matter, because otherwise nothing else makes sense.'

'So, you're sending me off to America to study Sanskrit poetry but actually to find a man who may or may not exist?' Anna stared at Afridi with a look of disbelief.

'Something like that,' he said, 'though it's bound to be much more complicated, and a good deal more dangerous than either philology or astrophysics.'

Seventeen

The Pakistan Army helicopter dropped them at a point where the valley broadened, next to a dusty village with a few apricot trees and barking dogs. All of the houses had been damaged by the earthquake, but most were still standing. Only one person had died here, unlike in the settlements farther on, which had suffered many more casualties. The epicenter lay somewhere to the north, but the devastation radiated down the valleys.

A crowd of curious children followed Luke along the path but turned back after he reached a spring, where water spattered onto the rocks. Here he could see beyond the barren profiles of the nearest ridges to the snowy peaks higher up. The river below them was gray with snowmelt and writhed in an angry current. Ahead of him were three porters carrying medical supplies, stooped under their burdens. They had demanded twice the usual rate to carry the loads. Dr Ibrahim Qureshi and his assistant, Mushtaq, both of whom worked for the Sikander-E-Azam Trust's Emergency Relief Team, had shouldered loads as well. Luke carried his own backpack, which he had pulled together a few hours after landing in Islamabad. At this altitude, he could feel his lungs ache with the effort of sucking oxygen out of the meager air. Strung out along the path, they looked like explorers setting off on an expedition to survey terra incognita, a small band of men walking single file into nowhere. In fact, they were trekking twelve kilometers up the valley, to the highest village in the region, which had been completely destroyed.

After an hour they came to a wrecked bridge over a stream. The porters showed them where to ford, and the freezing water gnawed at Luke's calves. The remains of the bridge, a narrow span of steel, looked as if it had been twisted by monstrous hands, the flimsy girders wrenched apart. Other than the bridge there was little evidence of a quake, until they came to a second village. Here, six of the fifteen houses had collapsed. The survivors were living in tents, which had been dropped from the air, along with blankets and food supplies. Ibrahim stopped to treat a man with an injured leg. The shinbone was broken below his knee, and an infection had set in. Luke helped by holding the man's shoulders as he moaned softly, a muted prayer of pain.

Half an hour later, leaving the village and heading on, Luke saw a pair of vultures feeding on the remains of a horse, its ribcage stripped of flesh. Feeling a wave of disgust, he averted his eyes but then, forced himself to watch the huge birds tearing at the rotting entrails with their beaks.

Taking out his camera, he snapped several pictures of the flattened homes. By now, he could see a broad delta of ice filling a valley to their left. In the midday light, this glacier had a stark whiteness, contrasting with the browns and tans of the ridges on either side.

Ibrahim dropped back to keep Luke company. They spoke in Urdu.

'During winter this river freezes over and men can walk on it, like a paved road,' he said, pointing into the valley.

Luke tried to picture the tumbling rapids congealing into ice, the surface of the river slowly freezing until the flow of water finally stopped.

'Nobody comes here in winter,' Ibrahim continued. 'The passes are closed with snow. For eight months of the year these mountains are cut off. It's so cold your tongue will freeze if you talk too much. When a child is born during winter, they kill a lamb and make a sack out of its fleece. They sew the baby up inside to keep it warm, with only its head sticking out.'

Farther on they spotted a herd of markhor, wild goats, that dislodged stones as they clambered up the cliffs. Luke couldn't see any grass for them to feed on, and it seemed impossible that even the hardiest creatures could survive in this harsh environment.

'There are wolves up here,' said Ibrahim, 'and snow leopards. *Shaan*.'

'Have you ever seen one?'

'No.' He shook his head. 'But I've seen the skin of a leopard the villagers shot. As soft as rabbit's fur, with gray markings, like petals of soot.'

The markhor had moved on up the ridge and out of sight. Luke could imagine an invisible predator stalking them across the cliffs.

'What about jihadis?' he asked. 'Are there any here?'

Ibrahim looked away.

'Perhaps,' hc said, under his breath. 'These days jihadis are everywhere. But many of the people in this region are originally Kalash, who came across from Bashgal in Afghanistan, during the 1930s. Most of them have converted, but they still hold onto their traditions and don't trust the Taliban at all.'

Several times, they heard choppers passing overhead, ferrying relief supplies. One hovered above a ridge to the east like a giant wasp. Luke wondered what he might be able to offer these people. Ibrahim was a doctor, but what could a journalist do? He was supposed to report on the earthquake and make others understand the extent of the damage and suffering. Perhaps his stories might pierce the conscience of the outside world, inured to catastrophes around the globe, but Luke felt impotent in the face of disaster. At this moment, he could report nothing at all. There was no signal on his cellphone, no internet connection to send an email. He thought of Carlton Fletcher and their conversation in the executive lounge at Dulles, the threat in his voice, a tone of menacing insistence.

Luke envied Ibrahim the altruistic purpose of his medical work. They had known each other for three years, and Luke had seen him operating in other crises. Calm and efficient, Ibrahim comforted his patients with assured detachment. Luke wished he had his skills and focus. Even in the face of the worst calamities, Ibrahim remained dispassionate, while Luke's emotions surfaced at the slightest suggestion of human anguish.

The final two kilometers of their trek were a steep ascent up the twisted spine of a ridge. Though he could hear the roar of the river, it was now hidden within a gorge. The only sign of life was a lammergeyer wheeling overhead, the vulture's wings outstretched against the clouds. Luke ate a chocolate bar to give himself energy but also because he knew that once they reached the third village, he wouldn't want to eat. Coming down the path toward him was a flock of long haired goats, herding themselves.

When he finally crested the highest spur on the ridge, Luke collapsed onto a flat stone and gazed back down the valley. Tresses of smoke rose above the village they'd left behind, where the bright orange and blue tents looked almost festive amid the bleak terrain. He was afraid to look ahead, but as he turned and stumbled to his feet again, he could see their porters had reached the mounds of rubble.

It looked as if a bomb had exploded. A two-story building, which might have been a school made of reinforced concrete, had snapped in the center and fallen in upon itself. Nothing was left but tangled steel and chunks of concrete. The trail approaching the village had sheared off and part of the hill above had slid down over a row of houses. It was like coming upon the ancient ruins of a historical site, except that all of this had happened less than three days ago, in the space of sixty seconds, the earth shifting of its own volition.

Flying into the valley, the helicopter pilots had told them that they had counted fourteen survivors in this village. When the choppers came in low enough to drop food and blankets, the villagers had gestured frantically for them to land, their cries drowned by the drumbeat of engines. But the pilots had been instructed not to carry out the injured. Already, there were too many victims to treat at government hospitals down the valley.

Ibrahim had climbed ahead of Luke and stood atop the debris. He was talking to an old man, who was gesturing wildly with both arms. Only five of the original fourteen survivors were still alive. The other bodies were piled together in a macabre embrace. A noisy flock of magpies were squabbling over the remains. Turning aside, Luke began to retch but stopped himself, tasting the sour saliva at the back of his tongue. The old man had dug a shallow trench beside the bodies. He pleaded with them to help him bury his neighbors.

Two women were huddled beneath a lean-to shelter, wrapped in chadors and blankets that covered them from head to foot. When Ibrahim kneeled to see if they had been hurt, both of them drew back as if he were a threat. A few feet from them lay an unconscious man, his face a mask of crusted blood. The only sign of life was his right hand, which slowly opened and closed. A boy of eight or nine crouched beside him. Luke guessed it was his son. The child was unhurt but his eyes were blank. As Ibrahim examined the injured man, the ground shuddered with an aftershock, and the boy hid his face and wept.

After treating the victim as best he could, Ibrahim shook his head and said there was little he could do. The man's skull was badly cracked. Moving him would do more harm than good, so they covered him with blankets and turned their attention to the dead. The porters helped finish excavating a grave. Ibrahim, Mushtaq, and Luke put on gloves before shifting the remains to the trough, which looked like a broad furrow ready to be planted. This had been a village of thirty-five homes, the porters said, more than a hundred people altogether. By the time they piled the last stones on the grave, shadows were ascending the ridges. It was only then that Luke remembered to take photographs in the fading light, framing the grim tumuli between darkening profiles of the mountains and a vacant sky.

Nothing more could be done for the survivors, and it was too late to go back down the valley, so they descended to a knoll below the village to pitch their tents. Any other time, this would have been a spectacular campsite, with a view of the river and a ring of snow peaks. But they were exhausted and depressed. Ibrahim persuaded the porters to spend the night and gave them a tent, while he and Luke shared the second tent with Mushtaq.

'The old man said there were voices coming from the rubble until last night,' Luke said. 'He claimed they were ghosts, but it must have been people buried underneath.'

Ibrahim expelled his breath, as if he were angry with himself. 'We couldn't dig them out even if we tried,' he said.

Eighteen

At dawn, Afridi was driven across to Lodhi Gardens, where he completed his morning workout. The racing wheelchair he used was manufactured in Switzerland and designed for para-athletes. It had a lightweight titanium frame with three wheels, a low-slung seat and mesh cradle to support Afridi's legs. Every day in Mussoorie, he did three laps of the Chukkar Road near his home, a distance of ten kilometers. Lodhi Gardens had a number of paths that circled through the trees, past ancient mausoleums. He completed five circuits of the garden, arms pumping with a steady, relentless rhythm. By the time he finished, the park was full of morning walkers, joggers, as well as people doing yoga and calisthenics on the lawns. At that hour of the morning, there was still a hint of coolness in the air.

Back at the guesthouse on Aurangzeb Lane, he finished off with a series of stretching exercises that kept him limber, moving his arms as if he were climbing a rock face, clutching at invisible handholds.

By the time he'd bathed and eaten breakfast, it was half past nine. Several minutes later, he heard voices coming down the hall. Major Karamjit Singh, the protocol officer from MOD, knocked and entered the library, followed by Jehangir Daruwalla, who reached out to shake Afridi's hand.

'Colonel, my apologies. The flight from Bombay was delayed. I've come straight from the airport.' Nothing in Jehangir's manner suggested that he was under arrest.

Major Singh asked if anything more was required. 'Tea or coffee?' Afridi asked his guest.

'Coffee, please. Black. No sugar,' Jehangir replied, taking a seat and glancing around. As soon as the major had left, he asked. 'What is this place?'

'A government guest house,' said Afridi.

'Very nice for a sarkari setup,' Jehangir said. 'Tastefully furnished.'

'I insisted on the decor,' said Afridi. The library was wood paneled, with a flat-screen television on a wall alongside watercolor sketches of Delhi monuments. The chairs were upholstered in pale leather and the tables and bookcases had been lightly stained, so the natural grain of the wood was visible. A fan was slowly oscillating above their heads, enough to stir the air without disturbing conversation. Afridi avoided air-conditioning. He could see that Daruwalla was perspiring.

'You're keeping well, I hope?' Jehangir asked, wiping his face with a handkerchief, and trying to act as if nothing was wrong.

Instead of answering him, Afridi cut straight to the point. 'I hear there was some trouble at the Yacht Club.'

Daruwalla rubbed his knuckles thoughtfully. 'Very nasty. I wasn't particularly fond of the man, but nobody deserves to have his throat slit.'

'Why was he killed?' Afridi said.

'I really don't know.'

'You had dinner with him. What was that all about?'

'Logistics,' said Daruwalla with an evasive wave. Afridi kept his eyes on him but said nothing.

'He was arranging a shipment for us,' Jehangir continued, reluctantly.

'Weapons?'

'Small arms.'

'And where was it going?' Afridi demanded.

There was a long pause.

'Muzaffarabad,' said Daruwalla. He knew better than to lie to Afridi.

'P.O.K.,' said Afridi. 'Pak Occupied Kashmir.'

Jehangir gave a tentative smile as the coffee arrived. The bearer set the tray down on the table between them, and Afridi gestured for him to leave. Neither of them spoke as Afridi poured Daruwalla's coffee.

'You realize, of course, I could have you thrown in jail,' Afridi said. 'For aiding our enemies and supporting the insurgency in Kashmir. It would be a clear case of abetting terrorism.'

'It's not what you think,' Jehangir protested, the coffee cup unsteady as he raised it to his lips.

'Whatever I may think will be irrelevant once they lock you up,' said Afridi. 'The dead Bosnian only complicates things. Your passport has been impounded, hasn't it?'

Jehangir nodded.

Despite himself, Afridi felt genuinely sorry for Daruwalla. He was a likeable man, articulate, urbane. But Afridi could read the desperation in his eyes, despite his attempts to make casual conversation. For the past two days he had endured interrogation by the Intelligence Bureau in Mumbai.

'Shipping arms to terrorists is a serious crime,' Afridi said.

'Please, Colonel…'

Afridi scowled at the flavor of the coffee, too much chicory, though he found Daruwalla's pleading even more distasteful. The last time they'd met was in Mussoorie. Afridi had invited him to spend the weekend, hoping to extract information about an arms deal between an Italian company that was negotiating with Pakistan to supply lightweight artillery for mountain warfare. Jehangir wasn't particularly forthcoming but they discovered that they shared a number of common interests, including the novels of Graham Greene and well-blended Scotch. Though he hadn't been able to get the information he wanted, Afridi had enjoyed Daruwalla's company.

'You gave my telephone number to a woman named Daphne Shaw,' he said.

Jehangir's expression changed abruptly, a furtive look in his eyes. 'Yes.'

'She called me a couple days ago,' said Afridi. 'Did you know about that?'

Daruwalla shook his head.

'Why did you give her my number?'

'I thought it might be useful,' Jehangir said with a pensive smile. 'For her…for you, perhaps.'

'In what way?' Afridi demanded.

'I'm not sure. Maybe she can assist you—'

'In Eggleston, Ohio? Why would I need anything from her?'

Jehangir slowly put his cup and saucer on the table, his hand still shaking.

'Perhaps she knows someone.'

'Guldaar?'

'Possibly…though she probably knows him by another name, one of his many aliases.'

'But you know him as Guldaar.'

'I don't really know him,' Jehangir began. We've never met and—'

'How could that be possible?' Afridi interrupted him. 'You've represented Guldaar on more than one occasion.'

'Yes, I have, but he likes to keep himself aloof,' Daruwalla explained. 'We speak on the telephone whenever it's necessary. But he's always insisted that we should never meet face to face. I suppose it's safer that way, for both of us.'

Afridi studied him for a moment, as if he wasn't convinced. 'But Daphne Shaw has met him, hasn't she?' he asked.

'Of course.'

'And how do you know her?'

'From long ago, when she lived in Bombay and worked as an actress. We've been friends since then.' Jehangir replied.

'Were you lovers?' Afridi asked.

'No,' said Jehangir with a choked laugh. 'Of course not.'

'I still don't understand why you gave her my telephone number,' Afridi said. 'Or why you told her that I could help in an emergency.'

'Insurance,' said Daruwalla. 'What's known these days as risk management.'

This time Afridi laughed, though his face showed little amusement.

'What do you mean, exactly?'

'You see, it's the only way I can protect myself from Guldaar, because I really don't know who he is or what he looks like. But Daphne does.'

Afridi could see the furtive tension in Daruwalla's eyes, as if he had played the only card he had. Reaching into his pocket, he took out Daruwalla's passport.

'Jehangir, I'll give you a choice,' he said, holding out the passport. 'We can keep you here in protective custody. Nobody will find you. It's safe and comfortable, though you'll have no access to any form of communication. Cold storage. Or, you can tell me everything you know about Guldaar, and I'll give you back your passport. You can walk out of here, take your chances, and catch the next flight home to London.'

He could see Daruwalla calculating the odds.

'What about the dead Bosnian and the shipment?' he asked.

'Nobody will stop you from leaving the country,' Afridi assured him.

'And if I stay?'

'I can't guarantee how long we'll have to keep you here.' Afridi still held the passport in his hand. 'Either way, you'll tell me what I need to know.'

'Where do you want me to begin?' Jehangir asked.

'I want to know everything about Guldaar,' said Afridi. 'What sort of business you conducted, your mutual contacts...But before we go there, I'm curious about his connections with the Americans.'

Daruwalla moistened his lips with his tongue and glanced aside.

He understood that Afridi knew enough to recognize if he was lying. 'As I said before, I've never met him. All of my contacts were through third parties. Several times we spoke on the phone. At least, I think I spoke to him. I don't know how he got started with the Americans, but he handled major arms shipments to the mujahideen back in the eighties, when they were fighting the Soviets. Later, he brokered significant deals with the Pakistan army, taking kickbacks from both sides.'

'What kind of deals?' Afridi asked.

'The upgrading of Abrams tanks, a whole new guidance and navigation system,' said Daruwalla. 'After that it was a contract for supplying Raytheon anti-missile batteries. A hundred and twenty million dollars, of which he got twenty percent. There were other deals too, but these are the only ones I know for sure. The CIA supports him and turns a blind eye to his other activities because of his connections in the tribal areas. Though I'm told he provided critical information on Al Qaeda hideouts, I didn't have much to do with that side of things. Most of my contact with him was related to the arms trade, though I know he made a good deal of money off the Americans by taking a percentage on the political payoffs to various Afghan factions. As you know, in the Hindu Kush, the only thing that talks is money.'

'Is he involved in the drug trade?'

'Not directly, but he facilitates shipments between Afghanistan and India, as well as Tajikistan, Iran, and Europe. More than the drugs, it's part of a complicated money laundering operation, using kickbacks from NATO contracts, mostly fuel and cement, to finance the purchase of heroin and cover the cost of smuggling it abroad. Then he takes the profits and channels them into political donations in cash, for which he and his partners receive everything from a stake in major development projects to shares in public sector companies that are being privatized. Guldaar doesn't touch any of it himself, but he has links to every government in South Asia and the Middle East. If he needs a billion dollars in Kathmandu tomorrow, he can source it from banks in Dubai or Oman without anyone being able to trace the transactions, because it's broken down into payments of less than $10,000 to fictitious accounts, under the guise of foreign workers sending remittances back home. Some of it is channeled through his charities, particularly the Sikander-e-Azam Trust. The whole thing is like a huge pyramid scheme with only one investor. It's all based on trust…and fear.'

Daruwalla paused and looked around, as if he expected a bullet to come at him through the window.

'Go on,' said Afridi. 'Keep talking.'

For the next two hours, Daruwalla explained whatever he knew of Guldaar's contacts and operations. At points, when he seemed to be avoiding details, Afridi insisted on names. There were questions that he couldn't answer, and some of his information was questionable at best, but within a couple of hours, he'd revealed almost everything he knew.

When they finally finished, it was ten minutes past noon. Afridi held out the passport.

'Why would you let me go?' Daruwalla asked. 'Risk management,' said Afridi.

With the slow, deliberate gesture of a gambler wagering everything he possessed, Daruwalla reached out and took the passport before rising to his feet.

'Before you leave,' said Afridi, as if it were an afterthought. 'I have one more question.'

Jehangir nodded, his fingers stroking the British lions on the passport cover.

'You haven't told me about Peregrine.'

Afridi could see the alarm in Daruwalla's eyes, even as he tried to control the muscles in his face.

'What about Peregrine?' he said.

'Guldaar is their agent, isn't he? Or is he a silent partner?'

'I'm not totally sure.'

Afridi shook his head. 'Come on, Jehangir. I don't believe you.'

'He's heavily invested in the company, if that's what you mean,' said Daruwalla. 'I don't know how much, but it's a significant share.'

'The Pakistanis are interested in drones that Peregrine manufactures, aren't they?'

'Yes, of course.' Daruwalla put his passport in his pocket, as if afraid it would be taken away from him again.

'So are we,' said Afridi. 'Both countries are in the bidding.'

Jehangir raised both palms in a helpless gesture of confirmation.

Afridi nodded. 'Major Karamjit Singh can call you a taxi.'

'Colonel...' Jehangir began to speak, then stopped himself before they shook hands. For several moments their eyes were fixed on each other. Then Daruwalla left the room without saying another word. Afridi admired his courage and composure, though he knew that Jehangir might as well have put a pistol to his own head. Inevitably, Guldaar would learn of their conversation through his informants in the ministry and put two and two together. He would know that Daruwalla had not only confessed to him but was his link to Daphne.

Nineteen

The following morning, when Luke and Ibrahim woke up, the porters were gone. Though they had been paid only half their money, the men had left before daybreak. Mushtaq, who got up earlier, claimed he had tried to reason with them, but they wouldn't listen, saying they had homes to rebuild and families to care for after the earthquake. The boxes of medical supplies they left behind—cartons of syringes, vials, splints, tablets, bandages and bottles of antiseptic—were much too heavy for the three of them to carry. Here it would go to waste.

After brewing some tea, once the sun had reached their tent, they went back up to the ruined village and found the survivors were gone as well, except for the man with the fractured skull, who was dead. His fingers no longer opened and closed but were frozen into a fist. There was no sign of the others. Ibrahim and Mushtaq called out, but no one replied and Luke felt a sudden, overwhelming loneliness. The magpies had returned, perched on the rocks above the communal grave. A stench of death still hovered over the site. The sky was a deep blue, and the clouds had vanished. Above them, the arid slopes were strewn with boulders, and Luke could see cliffs higher up. When he asked Ibrahim what he thought had happened, the doctor said nothing and scanned the ridges anxiously.

'Maybe they left with the porters,' Luke suggested.

'No,' said Mushtaq. 'I saw those men crossing the ridge below. There were only three of them.'

'Could the others have left on their own?'

'Where would they go?'

Just then, Luke saw a movement on the slope above, higher up the ridge. He thought it might be wild sheep, but after a minute he could make out two human figures. The sun was in his eyes, and the glare made it difficult to see.

'There's someone,' he said, pointing. The men were about two hundred yards away, descending a goat path between the rocks.

When he glanced at Ibrahim, Luke could see fear in his eyes. The doctor reached out, as if to pull Luke aside. In that instant, there was a shot. The bullet caught Ibrahim in the chest and his body twisted backward as he fell to the ground. For a few seconds, Luke didn't understand what was going on. Then he saw Mushtaq running toward one of the shattered walls, trying to take shelter. Two more gunshots rang out and Mushtaq fell, turning over once then lying still. Luke knew that he was next, but his feet wouldn't move. The figures were still far away. He couldn't tell who they were. The bullets had come from higher up, a sniper hidden among the rocks. Luke stood waiting for the shot that would kill him as he watched the two men approach. They were dressed in salwar kameez and sheepskin coats, with turbans on their heads. One of the men carried an AK-47, which he pointed in Luke's direction. The other held a pistol. They said nothing as they approached, and it seemed to take forever before they reached him. Luke didn't try to run. There was nowhere for him to go, and the shock of seeing Ibrahim and Mushtaq die had left him unable to move or speak.

With the butt of his pistol, one man clubbed Luke across the face. He fell sideways and tried to crawl away but felt another blow at the back of his head. The next thing he saw were scuffed boots in front of his face and blood in the dust. They tied his hands behind his back and hit him once again, knocking him unconscious. When he came to, his eyes had been covered with a blindfold, and someone held him by the arm, hauling him to his feet. Luke's head throbbed with pain, and he could taste blood in his mouth. They dragged him forward until he began to walk on his own. He heard voices but couldn't understand their words. The path they took must have been the same one the attackers came down, heading up the valley. They walked for several hours. Luke's mouth and throat were dry. He asked for water. Immediately, he felt a stab of pain in his side as the muzzle of a gun prodded him below the ribs.

At one point, he heard a helicopter pulsing overhead. His captors threw him to the ground, and Luke could sense that they were hiding, probably behind a boulder. When Luke could no longer hear the chopper, he was hauled to his feet and they started walking again. Twice he tripped and fell, landing heavily on one shoulder because his arms were tied. When they finally stopped, he was aware of being taken inside some kind of shelter. It could have been a house or a cave. The sun was no longer on his back. Someone yanked the blindfold from his face. As his eyes adjusted, he could make out the contours of a dark, windowless space. Before he knew it, a flash went off. His captors took two photographs of him. Luke wondered if they were using his camera. Blinded by the harsh light, he couldn't see anything except shadows moving in front of him. They tied the blindfold across his eyes again and pressed a steel cup to his lips. He drank the water eagerly, spilling it in a rush to swallow. The cold liquid stung the cuts on his face.

After this, they pushed him forward until he fell through a hole in the ground, scraping his arm as he dropped eight or ten feet, landing heavily. His right leg hurt badly, but he could still move it. Luke guessed they had thrown him into a well or some kind of underground chamber. He could feel cold walls on either side. Overhead, someone was dragging a heavy stone to seal the exit. His hands had been freed. Luke waited, until he felt sure he was alone. Reaching up to uncover his eyes, he stared into the darkness. A slit of light entered through a narrow gap above. The walls were made of rough concrete. One section of the ceiling had collapsed, probably during the earthquake.

Trapped inside this vault, he could hear no other sounds but the rasping of his own breath. He locked his fingers together, trying to calm his nerves. Though it looked as if he was praying, no words could express the fear and desperation he felt. In his mind, Luke pictured his sister Ruth holding the baby, smiling at him with a curious look of concern. He recalled Fletcher's threat and wished he'd stayed with them, worried about what might happen to them now. The cell in which he crouched was cold and empty as a tomb. Drawing his knees up against his chest, Luke remembered Ibrahim's story—a newborn child sewn up inside the skin of a slaughtered lamb.

Twenty

An auto-rickshaw dropped Anna near one of the side gates of the US embassy in Delhi. After haggling with the driver, she joined a queue in front of the reception window. Ten years ago, she'd gone through the same process to get a student visa for graduate school. That was soon after 9/11, and security was at the highest level. This time it wasn't any different. A long line of anxious applicants waited to enter the holding area where the visa process began.

Originally, the diplomatic enclave in Chanakyapuri had been designed with broad, tree-lined boulevards and spacious embassy compounds encircled by gardens. With the threat of terrorist attacks, each of these had become a fortified citadel, surrounded by razor wire, security cameras, concrete barriers and blast-proof walls. Two blocks from Roosevelt House, the US ambassador's palatial residence, stood the Russian embassy with its stolid socialist architecture, formerly a bastion of the Soviet Union. Across Shanti Path, the Avenue of Peace, lay Pakistan's High Commission, its blue dome the color of lapis lazuli.

When Anna's turn came at the bulletproof window, she showed her passport and the letter inviting her for an interview. Her name had been changed to Sheetal Khanna. She knew that Manav Shinde was to blame for that. It was the name of a joint secretary in the Home Ministry, a woman they both despised. Through connections at Fulbright House, Manav had been able to get Anna's interview expedited. The clear plastic folder she carried contained letters of invitation from Bromfield College along with false documents, including a State Bank of India passbook showing sufficient funds and certificates of fixed deposit, the title deed to a flat in Kalkaji, and affidavits to the effect that she had an elderly mother who depended on her, all of which was supposed to convince the Americans that she wouldn't overstay her visa. A packet of forged testimonials from the Department of Sanskrit at Delhi University identified Sheetal Khanna as a linguist pursuing her PhD. Anna had studied the documents this morning to make sure she could answer any questions that arose.

After passing through the gate and surrendering her cell phone, she was given a number and told to wait. At least a hundred other applicants were seated in the outdoor enclosure under whirring fans. As she glanced around her, she saw elderly couples who were hoping to visit children in America, young men who looked as if they had just come off a farm in Haryana, wearing Harvard or Cornell teeshirts, and IT professionals clutching files that would win them an H-1B visa. Everyone seemed to want a better life.

Two armed marines in camouflage patrolled the area along with Indian guards employed by a private security company. There was tension and fear in the air. Whenever a number was called, everyone's eyes followed the applicant through the door and into the room where the consular officials would decide his or her fate.

Three hours later, when it was over and Anna had answered a few questions through another pane of bulletproof glass, she stepped back outside onto the street. The interviewer had been a distracted woman who didn't seem to care if Anna knew anything about Sanskrit poetry or whether her aged mother needed her to come home. The only question she asked was whether Anna had bought her round trip ticket. After studying the airline printout, she told Anna to come back after 4:00 p.m. to collect her passport.

It was hot outside, and no auto-rickshaws or taxis were in sight. As Anna headed down the access road, her phone rang.

'Sheetalji, may I give you a lift?'

'Where are you?' she demanded.

'Parked at the corner, next to the silk cotton tree.'

Anna spotted a white Honda standing in the shade. The driver pulled onto the street and came toward her. Anna got into the backseat beside Manav who greeted her with a polite namaskar.

'So?' he said.

'So what?' said Anna, tossing the transparent folder between them.

'Are the Americans going to let you visit their country?'

Anna rolled her eyes. 'Why did you have to choose Sheetal Khanna as an alias?'

'Why not?' said Manav with a wounded smile. 'Would you have rather been Pooja? Or Kunti? Or Akanksha? I'm glad I don't have children…I'd never be able to decide on a name. So many to choose from. A sweet Bangalee girl like you. Would you have preferred Bipasha?'

'Anything but Sheetal,' she said.

'You're cross with me. And hungry too, I'm sure. It's almost two.' Manav leaned forward and spoke to the driver. 'Malcha Marg Market. Fujiya.' Then he glanced at her. 'I know you like Chinese.'

'Fujiya is Japanese.'

'Same thing,' said Manav. 'Here in Dilli, it's all the same.'

The restaurant was a five minute drive away and they were soon seated in a dimly lit booth. Anna and Manav had eaten at Fujiya more times than she could remember. A year ago, they were eavesdropping on a Chinese diplomat who was blackmailing a Member of Parliament. Under Manav's direction they had set up a listening post in a rooftop barsati apartment on Malcha Marg, not far from the Chinese embassy. It had been a futile exercise but they'd picked up a lot of chatter in the area, including some awkward phone sex between a Canadian consular official and a priest at the Papal Nuncio. Anna's estimation of the international diplomatic corps had fallen several rungs after listening in on hours of gossip and hearing the German plenipotentiary's ringtone, the theme song from *Skyfall*. He also liked to place bets on European League matches with a bookie in Paris, at 2:00 in the morning.

Once the waiter had taken their order, Anna asked if Afridi was still in town.

'No. He flew back up to Mussoorie yesterday,' said Manav.

'He hates Delhi, doesn't he?' said Anna.

'But he's very fond of you,' said Manav. 'Insisted that he wanted you for this job. Nobody else would do.'

'Should I be flattered?'

Shinde was her superior, but they had established a working relationship that dispensed with rank and formality. Anna knew her place, of course, but she also felt she could speak her mind with Manav. He was one of the few men in RAW who didn't see her as a threat or an opportunity to ogle.

'I really can't explain Colonel Afridi's mind,' said Manav. 'Frankly, he's a bigger puzzle than even our honorable home minister.'

They shared a dislike of politicians, though Manav was a master at dealing with cabinet ministers, employing a combination of obsequious guile and subtle deceit.

'Now, tell me what's wrong?' Anna asked. 'You weren't just parked outside the US embassy for no reason, were you?'

'Of course not.' He shook his head and tapped his fingers on the chopsticks, as if he were typing a text message. 'Actually, I'm concerned about this operation. It's not like Afridi to act impulsively on unconfirmed reports. He's usually far more cautious than I am, but this time, he seems to be operating on instinct alone.'

Anna kept silent, studying the chopped green chillies in vinegar, next to a bottle of soy sauce. Shinde seemed reluctant to continue, then lowered his voice.

'Anna, what I'm going to say is totally unofficial. You can take it or leave it. But please understand that I am not trying to undermine Afridi's authority. Nobody is a genius in our line of work, but he comes as close to it as possible. I have complete respect for his commitment to national security....' The tapping on the chopsticks continued. 'However, this time I have serious doubts about his judgment. We know that someone called Guldaar exists, though he's not as dangerous as Afridi believes. A local warlord in the Khyber Agency, he's got connections throughout northeastern Afghanistan and the tribal areas, but he isn't any more powerful or wealthy than a dozen other men in that region. We know that Pakistan is a failed state with rampant corruption throughout the tribal region. The drug trade has raised the stakes considerably. Hawala transactions take place in the billions. The Gulf States and the Saudis are involved. No question about that. The laundering of funds adds up to more than the total GDP of Afghanistan. But to imagine that all of this is being controlled by just one man doesn't make sense. Of course, there are filthy rich smugglers and arms traders, but nobody comes close to what Afridi imagines Guldaar to be.'

Anna could see it was painful for Manav to criticize his friend and colleague.

'I think he's making a huge mistake, and I feel, somehow, he's being trapped. Afridi is so fixed on catching Guldaar, he hasn't understood that he himself might be the target. It's very possible the Pakistanis are trying to lure him into a compromising situation to destroy his credibility. I tried to warn him, but he won't listen.'

'So, what are you suggesting I do?' Anna asked.

'Follow his instructions, of course,' said Manav. 'I'm not

overruling him just yet. But keep an ear out for trouble, especially from the Americans. This whole operation just doesn't seem right. If at any point you sense a trap, please contact me at once.'

As if on cue, the spring rolls arrived. Using his chopsticks, Manav placed one on Anna's plate, then deliberately changed the subject.

Twenty-One

Afridi knew that Shinde would warn Anna about the unsubstantiated nature of his suspicions, but he also knew that she was capable of making judgments on her own. He wasn't surprised that his interest in Guldaar had been met with skepticism in Delhi. Both the defense secretary and Manav had humored him by allowing Anna to go to Ohio and meet with Daphne Shaw. However, she was under strict instructions not to take any direct action or break any US laws— no weapons, no audio surveillance, no forcible extraction. They also made it clear that asylum would not be given by any of India's diplomatic missions. If Daphne left the country and came to India on her own, that was another matter, but under no circumstances should it to appear that RAW or Military Intelligence facilitated her departure. Relations with the Americans were already prickly, and there was no need to make things worse.

Seated in his office at the Himalayan Research Institute, the morning after he returned from Delhi, Afridi let his gaze travel over the knotted patterns in the wood paneling. Most of the pictures on the wall were from his earlier days, when he had climbed almost every major peak in India, standing on some of the highest Himalayan summits—Kamet, Nanda Devi, Trishul, and Kangchenjunga. His office window overlooked the mountains, but his eyes remained fixed on a framed map from 1840 that hung between two book-cases. It was a military relic from the first Anglo-Afghan War, with troop placements and routes of advance and retreat marked in a neat hand by an anonymous East India Company officer, long since dead. Reflecting on the creased and yellowed paper pasted to a gauze backing, Afridi considered the map an elaborate maze of contour lines as complex and puzzling as the spiral grains of wood. It charted the fatal retreat from Kabul, in which every officer and soldier would lose his life, except for a lone survivor...one of Britain's greatest colonial defeats. It seemed as if the contours of the Hindu Kush were inscribed with tragedy, the fatal cartography of futile campaigns.

Almost 175 years later, India and the United States both recognized the strategic importance of the tribal belt that ran along the borders of Afghanistan, though they had different reasons for their interest in this region. The Americans saw it as a no man's land in which the last survivors of Al Qaeda were still hiding out, where they could launch their drones with impunity and claim to have successfully killed another enemy of the free world. India was more practical, for it provided a porous frontier with Pakistan through which they could infiltrate enemy terrain. Having cultivated an alliance with the current regime in Kabul, Delhi's spymasters were able to support insurgent groups in Baluchistan, Waziristan, and other border areas, in retaliation for Pakistan's covert activities in Kashmir.

Though he had never visited the Hindu Kush, Afridi knew that his ancestral homeland had a deceptive heritage of lore and legends about mythical races and ancient peoples. The colonel gave scant credence to claims of ethnic legacies and lost Aryan tribes like the Kalash and Nuristanis. Linguists had tried to trace their origins to early invaders who had settled here along the margins of history. Others believed they were descendants of Greek armies under the command of Alexander the Great. The Hindu Kush was a region of perpetual uncertainty yet people clung to ambiguous truths with absolute conviction.

Guldaar was part of that riddle.

Afridi wheeled himself across to a bookcase and carefully removed a four-volume set of Neville Murchison's *Survey of the Karakoram and Hindu Kush.* The heavy, leather-bound books had belonged to his grandfather. Though he was tempted to flip through the pages, he carefully set the volumes aside. Built into the wall behind the books was a small safe. Afridi turned the dial to the right, then back to the left and right again before stopping at the final digit in the combination. The door swung open and revealed the contents: a stack of files, several flash drives, and a yellow envelope, which the colonel removed.

Shaking the envelope's contents into the palm of his hand, he studied the gold chain and pendant, about an inch long, in the shape of a miniature horse's head. A single diamond formed the stallion's eye and a ring of smaller stones studded the halter. According to an archeologist Afridi had consulted, it was a recent copy of an older piece of Bactrian gold that was in the Victoria & Albert Museum in London. The archeologist had told him the horse was probably an image of Bucephalus, Alexander's favorite steed. Beautifully rendered with a flowing mane and flared nostrils, the tiny animal had a wild, untamed expression. A tag attached to the chain bore the stamp and signature of the military comptroller. This chain and pendant were now the property of the government of India, though Afridi held onto it as evidence, from an incident in August 1994.

~

He had gone to Srinagar for a meeting with regional intelligence officers. They were preparing for the long winter in Ladakh by recruiting Changpa nomads in the northern plateaus beyond Pangong Lake to keep an eye on the Chinese. For once, Pakistan was not on the agenda. Aside from occasional border skirmishes and minor ceasefire violations, conditions were relatively calm along the Line of Actual Control. Afridi recalled his first evening at the Officers' Mess. Phunsok, a young captain in the Ladakh Scouts, argued that the greatest threat to Kashmir was China, not Pakistan. Nine months later, he was killed in a firefight with insurgents near Baramullah.

On the second day, Afridi was having lunch with the corps commander, when Phunsok arrived just as they were tasting the general's tsampa halwa. Proud of his culinary skills, the corps commander boasted about having invented this recipe while stationed at an observation point on Siachen Glacier as a junior officer. It was a mixture of toasted barley flour and condensed milk, along with a fistful of raisins. The general also suggested pouring a large peg of Hercules XXX rum over the halwa as a final touch. Afridi was grateful for Phunsok's interruption, which spared him from finishing the bowl of thick, over-sweetened gruel drowned in defense services alcohol.

Phunsok reported that three Greek tourists had been arrested following a road accident near Dha and Hanu, a pair of villages 120 kilometers southwest of Leh. Their vehicle had collided with an army truck. While the Greeks were being taken to the military hospital in Kargil, it was discovered that they were carrying a satellite phone and $35,000 in cash. Trekkers were forbidden from entering Dha and Hanu, and the villagers themselves discouraged visitors. The people of this region were known as Drogpas, a unique tribe with unusually fair skin, Caucasian features, and a culture distinctly different from the majority population of Muslims and Buddhists. By some accounts, they were related to the Kalash people of Kafiristan. A few years earlier, two German girls had been arrested because they had gone to Dha, Hanu and the neighboring village of Darchik, hoping to get pregnant with pure Aryan sperm. Afridi knew it was a delicate issue. The people of Dha and Hanu practiced open marriages. Both men and women had a reputation for promiscuity. Of course, much of it was exaggeration and cultural prejudices spread by outsiders. The Drogpa habit of kissing in public scandalized Indian army officers and made them declare the region off limits to civilians.

From time to time, parties of tourists had wandered into the valley, and there had been an unpleasant episode with a Spanish photographer who was badly beaten up. Usually, the trekkers were escorted back to Kargil or Leh and spent the night in a police lockup before being sent on their way. But this time, the authorities in Kargil had grown suspicious about the Greeks because of the sat phone and currency. The villagers reported that the foreigners spoke Urdu among themselves. Captain Phunsok summoned them to Srinagar by jeep, guarded by military police.

Ordinarily, Afridi wouldn't have wasted his time on a routine interrogation, but the story intrigued him. If they were Pakistanis, it might be useful to learn how they had crossed the border and what they were doing in Dha and Hanu. He was also looking for any excuse to leave the general's tsampa pudding unfinished.

When they reached a military intelligence facility near Nishat Bagh, Afridi wheeled himself into a low, windowless room, where the three men were seated. It was immediately clear which of them was the leader, though most of his face was hidden by a bandage, with only one eye visible. The military doctors who administered first aid had reported superficial wounds on the left side of the man's head but they'd wrapped him up with so much gauze and cotton wool it looked as if he'd had brain surgery. One of the two other men had an injured arm.

The man with the bandaged head appeared to be Afridi's age. Though it was difficult to see his features, he could easily have been Greek. His passport looked real enough and his name was given as Theodore Amanatidis, with a permanent address in London. His one visible eye was a dull blue, the color of slate. His skin had a pale complexion except where the bruises had spread beyond the bandage. They studied each other for several seconds.

'Is there anything you require?' Afridi asked in English.

'A cigarette, perhaps,' was the immediate reply, though the man's voice betrayed no anxiety. His English was fluent, with an Oxbridge accent. Afridi gestured for the guards to grant them this request. A pack of Charminar was brought in, and all three men lit up at once. The unventilated room was soon clouded in smoke.

'Where in Greece are you from?'

'Thessalonika. But I am based in London,' said the man, who was the only one to speak.

'And why are you here?'

'Tourism. We have been visiting monasteries. Lama Yuru. Thiksey. Hemis.'

'Do you know why you've been arrested?' Afridi continued. The man shook his head as he took a long drag from the cigarette. His one eye remained fixed on Afridi, and he seemed entirely unconcerned, as if the two of them were carrying on a casual conversation between strangers. The bandage was like a mask, making it difficult to read his expression.

Seeing that one of the others had a splint on his arm, Afridi addressed him in Urdu, asking if the bone was broken. For a brief second, the prisoner looked as if he might reply, before glancing down at his arm in silence.

'He doesn't understand what you said,' the other man replied. 'Do you?' Afridi asked.

'Yes,' he said with a confident smile. 'This is my sixth visit to India. I lived in Bombay for a year.'

Something in the man's attitude puzzled and disturbed Afridi. Despite his injuries and having spent three nights in a police lockup, there was a note of arrogance in the man's voice that made him suspicious. If he wasn't who he said he was, then it was going to take a long time to break him. Afridi turned his wheelchair around and excused himself, telling Phunsok to continue with the questioning. As he was about to leave the room, the man spoke up.

'Colonel, I'd like a word alone with you, if possible.'

Afridi glanced back over his shoulder, meeting the same untroubled gaze.

'Why?'

'I have a personal request.' He glanced at his companions, hinting that he preferred they didn't hear what he had to say.

Afridi nodded toward Phunsok. The military policemen took the two silent men by their arms and led them outside.

'May I?' said the man, helping himself to another cigarette and lighting up.

Giving the prisoner a moment to fill his lungs, Afridi spoke in a level voice. 'Mr Amanatidis, I don't know who you are or what you're doing here, but I can assure you that once we're through with you, there will be nothing left for you to hide.'

'All of this is an unfortunate mistake,' the man replied. 'And, of course, avoidable.'

'Tell me what you were doing in Dha and Hanu with a sat phone and more dollars than anyone can spend in a year up there.'

'I was looking for a bride,' the man said with a confident smile. 'The purest of genes.'

Afridi studied him with a skeptical look and said nothing, wondering how serious his injuries really were and whether the bandage was just a disguise.

'Come now, Colonel,' the man said. 'Both of us are Pakhtun. We value our history. You're an Afridi. I'm also from the Hindu Kush. We understand each other.'

'So, you admit you're not Greek?' Afridi said. 'You're Pakistani.' The bandaged man laughed. 'Does it matter? I have no nationality other than my tribe. Like you, I am a man who lives outside the borders others create.'

'In case you have any doubts, I am an officer of the Indian Army. A citizen of this country,' said Afridi.

'I admire your patriotism,' said the man, 'but tell me, Colonel.

What has your country done for you, except promise you a paltry pension at the end of your career—certainly not enough to support a comfortable lifestyle?'

The cigarette fumes encircled the bandaged prisoner like snares of smoke. Reaching between the unbuttoned collars of his shirt, he withdrew a gold pendant, shaped like a horse, that hung from his neck on a heavy chain. Without removing the pendant, he stroked it between his fingers. Afridi could see that the gold was embedded with diamonds.

'I can assure you Colonel, I will make it worth your while if you arrange to have us released. This pendant is worth two hundred thousand Euros…more than you've earned in a lifetime. Take it, and when I've left your country, another hundred thousand will be deposited in any bank account you choose.'

Afridi did not move, but the man edged forward in his seat until he was less than a foot away, his fingers fondling the links on the chain while the cigarette smoldered between his lips. The gauze and sticking plaster made him look as sinister as he sounded.

The blow that Afridi delivered with the knuckles of his right hand caught the man on the side of his face not covered by the bandage, sending his cigarette spinning to the floor, drawing blood from his nose, and splitting his lip. For several moments, the prisoner leaned aside in shock and pain, holding a hand to his face. When he turned to look at Afridi, his smile turned into a venomous sneer.

'You're a pathetic, crippled man,' he said, as he spat blood on the floor. 'Believe me, Colonel. Someday, I'll put you out of your misery.'

Afridi rang the buzzer to signal that he was done. Captain Phunsok entered immediately.

'Keep him separate from the other two. No more questions—I'll speak with Delhi,' said Afridi. 'And take away the gold chain and pendant around his neck. Make sure it's weighed and recorded as evidence.'

Afridi didn't look back as he left the room. His right hand hurt from the blow, but he was grateful for the pain. A few minutes later, he called Army Intelligence headquarters and explained the situation, telling the director that the prisoner had tried to bribe him and urging his superior to make arrangements to have him securely guarded.

~

More than twenty years later, Afridi held up the same gold chain. Bucephalus's eye glittered in the sunlight coming through his office window. One of the colonel's greatest regrets was that he hadn't personally ensured the prisoners were properly locked up, instead entrusting them to the military police. That same evening, Afridi was informed that the Greeks had escaped without a trace. He could never be sure of the man's identity. Nobody had thought to take photographs of the prisoners when they were arrested. Yet the more he learned about Guldaar, the more Afridi was convinced that this had been the same man.

Twenty-Two

Hunched against the wall, arms wrapped about his knees, Luke couldn't sleep. The glimmer of light overhead had disappeared. He felt invisible in the darkness, unable to see his own fingers, even when he held them an inch away from his eyes. He still had his watch but couldn't read what time it was. They had taken his camera, wallet, and cellphone. One of the guards had thrown a torn blanket into his cell, which he'd wrapped around himself. His down parka and boots kept him from freezing, though his face and hands were cold.

Unable to think with any clarity, he kept remembering how Ibrahim had died, folding up beside him without a sound. He could still see Mushtaq running and then being shot, lying spread-eagled in the dirt. Luke had wept for them as he was walking, the blindfold absorbing his tears, but now his grief had receded deep inside like a bullet lodged against his heart. More than anything he wanted a cigarette, though he knew it was impossible and absurd.

The room where he was imprisoned had a dry, earthy odor. A short while ago, he'd felt an aftershock. The walls trembled and flakes of concrete fell from the ceiling. He needed to urinate and finally forced himself to stand, stumbling into the far corner of the cell. In the darkness, he had only a vague sense of the space, no more than eight or ten feet across. He emptied his bladder in a painful, pleasurable stream. Inhaling the sour stench of urine was strangely comforting, proving that he was alive.

Just as he settled down again, Luke heard the grating sound of the rock being removed from the opening overhead. Two men with lights peered in at him and shouted, though he didn't understand their words. Extending their arms for him to grab, they dragged him out of the chamber, then roughly pushed him ahead as they walked along a dirt track toward the silhouette of a building, some kind of village home. This time, they didn't cover his eyes. He ducked his head to enter a low doorway. A lantern sat on a table. Six or seven men were gathered in a loose circle, all of them armed. The flickering light cast tall shadows against the walls. He was pushed forward onto the floor. Kneeling, with his face lowered, he heard a voice speaking to him in Urdu, with a heavy accent.

'Are you a doctor?' the man asked.

Luke raised his head and saw a weathered face. The man had a pained yet gentle expression and tangled beard. His right arm was in a sling. Luke could see that his fingers had been crushed.

'No,' Luke said, softly. 'You killed our doctor.'

He felt a blow against the back of his skull, and for a minute or two he was knocked senseless, until someone dragged him up onto his knees again. The boxes of medicines lay on the floor in front of him.

'Do you know what these are?' the man asked. Luke nodded.

'What is this?' One of the men picked up a strip of pills but Luke couldn't read the label in the shadows, his eyes still blurred by the blow to his head.

The man shone a light on the tablets.

'Cipro,' Luke said. 'For infections. There are other antibiotics too.'

Another strip of tablets was thrust in front of him. 'Paracetamol. Painkillers.'

One by one they took the packets and bottles from the boxes, forcing him to identify each of the medicines. Most of these he knew, for he had helped Ibrahim repack them before they started up the valley. One box contained packets of IV fluid; another, plastic splints of different sizes. Though the room they sat in hadn't been damaged and only one or two of the men appeared to have been hurt, he realized that his captors had suffered in the earthquake like everyone else. Some of them had probably been killed.

After he identified vials of codeine, the man with the injured hand gestured to one of his lieutenants, who removed a syringe from a box and handed it to Luke. He knew what to do, having helped Ibrahim in the past. Unsheathing the needle and piercing the seal on the vial, Luke filled the syringe. It was difficult because his hands were shaking. When the dose of codeine was ready, he glanced up at his captor.

'Inject yourself first,' the man said.

He watched carefully as Luke opened his parka and slipped one arm out of its sleeve.

'Go on,' he said. 'Are you lying?'

'No. This will ease your pain.' Luke's eyes shifted to the swollen hand in the sling, fingers blackened and caked in blood. The wrist was turned at an awkward angle, obviously broken.

'Go on. First you inject the medicine. Then, I will see…'

Without rolling up his sleeve, Luke jabbed the needle into his arm through the flannel fabric, six inches below his shoulder. It was easier than he'd thought, and there was a dull ache as he pressed the plunger. For several minutes they watched him.

'You are American?' the man asked.

There was no point in denying it. They would have found his passport if they searched the tents. 'Yes,' he said. The codeine was already working its magic. The pain in his head was gone, and he felt lighter, almost at ease.

'You work for the CIA?' the injured man asked.

'No,' he said. 'I'm a journalist. The other men with me were a doctor and his assistant.'

'Don't lie to me,' said the man.

'I'm not lying,' Luke said.

'How did you learn Urdu?'

'I was born in Pakistan, in Murree. Most of my life I've lived here.'

The injured man gestured to one of the fighters, who handed him a second vial of codeine and another syringe. Luke prepared the injection as his captor continued to speak.

'There are men I know in the CIA. Brad Foster. Davis. Tom Ruggles. Do you know them?'

'No,' said Luke, piercing the sealed vial with the needle.

'They came here when we were fighting the Russians, but I knew that someday we would have to fight them as well. Why do you Americans always interfere?'

'I'm only here to report on the earthquake.'

'What good will that do?' The man laughed as one of his fighters rolled up the sleeve on his injured arm. Luke's hand was shaking as he raised the syringe. Quickly, he gave the injection, and when he withdrew the needle a tiny bead of blood appeared.

The codeine had brought on a weird kind of calm that took Luke outside himself, as if his nerves had separated from his flesh. The chemical solace eased more than just his injuries. He began to laugh at the absurdity of those names: Brad Foster. Davis. Tom Ruggles. Who were these men and what did they hope to achieve? A short while later, they hauled Luke to his feet. He felt like a drunk being carried home from a bar. When they pushed him through the hole in the roof of his cell, he felt no pain as he fell to the floor. The hard surfaces seemed softer now, and minutes after they drew the stone across the opening Luke swam effortlessly into sleep.

Twenty-Three

'India's mid-range nuclear missiles, capable of striking targets at a distance of 1,200 kilometers, are named Agni, after the Vedic god of fire, who has been worshipped in sacred rituals of sacrifice for more than three millennia.'

Anna watched the slides on the screen advance while the professor spoke, moving from an image of the Agni missile to another weapon of mass destruction.

'On the other side of the acrimonious border and so-called 'Line of Actual Control,' Pakistan too has developed missiles equipped with nuclear warheads. These are named Ghazni, after the first Muslim invader to cross the mountains of Afghanistan and conquer areas of northern India, penetrating as far as the Somnath Temple in Gujarat. Here in South Asia, mythology and history, as well as faith and national destiny, converge in a conflict that could reduce the subcontinent to an anarchic wasteland.'

The students sat in bored silence as the power point lecture continued. Professor Satish Verma clicked forward to a political map of South Asia.

'The deployment and location of these missiles is one of the best kept national secrets in both countries, which have maintained a nuclear standoff for more than a decade. Today, the question before us is whether the deadly force of these armaments is real or symbolic, freighted as they are with metaphors that have nothing to do with the volatility of enriched uranium but carry a coded message of religious antagonism, suspicion, and hatred.

I ask you, are these Agni and Ghazni missiles simply quaint names, arising out of the imaginations of military scientists and engineers, or are they contemporary avatars of an ancient yet enduring conflict?'

The concluding slide was a newspaper cartoon of the Taj Mahal, its minarets replaced by missiles. Anna sat near the back, having slipped into the lecture hall a few minutes late, though she could tell Professor Verma was aware of her presence. As the students began stuffing notebooks into backpacks, he reminded them that their mid-term papers were due next week. Anna watched from a distance, irritated by the short, animated figure in his sweater vest and tweed jacket over jeans. He looked every bit the postmodern academic. Though Verma retained a Kanpur accent, he had acquired hints of a Midwestern drawl. He was intelligent and articulate. Anna wondered whether he was dissatisfied teaching political science to undergraduates at Bromfield College and if he yearned for the Ivy League.

They had met the day before. After introducing himself, Verma invited her to his lecture, suggesting that he had important insights to impart. Anna knew that he was hitting on her, though she also knew he was married and had an infant child. Verma had helped facilitate her research fellowship at the college. He was head of the Political Science department and ensured approval from the dean, all of which Afridi had orchestrated through the consulate in Chicago. Despite his theories about nuclear standoffs, Verma had no idea that he was being played like a pawn in the larger game of geopolitics.

Coming up the aisle of the lecture hall, he greeted her with a cheerful twitch of his mustache. Verma was three inches shorter than Anna, and his eyes were level with her chin but drifted lower to her chest.

'So, what do you think, Sheetal?' he demanded. 'Did I pose the question properly?'

She laughed and shook her head.

'I have no idea, professor,' she replied. 'Politics and military standoffs aren't my thing. You know I'm only interested in poetry.'

'But that's exactly the point I was trying to make: the poetics of power and conflict!' Verma's voice became more excited the longer he stared at her breasts. 'As a scholar of comparative literature I was hoping you might interpret Indo-Pak relations through Spivakian tropes that we must unlearn. After all, these missiles are nothing but subaltern texts....'

'With explosive devices attached,' Anna replied.

Verma sniggered. 'How about a coffee? We can discuss this further. I'd like to know your views...There are so few people here with whom I can have an informed conversation.'

'Thank you, professor, but I have to get back to my research.'

'Please call me Satish,' he said with an ingratiating grin.

Anna dislodged herself from his gaze and left him standing outside the lecture hall with a laptop under his arm and a briefcase dangling from his shoulder. Yesterday, she had arrived at the college and settled into a guestroom on campus, where a note from Verma had greeted her, giving his cell number. The college was smaller than she had expected, and the town of Eggleston more provincial. Anna's last visit to the US had been on a Fulbright, ten years ago, when she did her master's at Texas A&M in acoustical engineering. The only literature she read was detective novels.

With Verma's help, she'd gotten her library card and was assigned a study carrel in the basement of the stacks, a quiet space where she could pretend to read the papers of Dr Shelton. The librarian had shown her where the boxes of documents lay, in a vault at one end of the basement—six cardboard cartons full of loose-leaf notebooks and typed drafts of translations. These old papers held no more interest for Anna than Verma's lecture on nuclear deterrence.

Heading toward the library, she decided she couldn't face the documents right now. Jet lag made her drowsy and she felt better being outdoors. It was twenty degrees cooler than Delhi, but the sun was out and the campus had a leafy charm. Turning away from the library, Anna headed down a side street, past a couple of dorms. Students lounged on the grass while others rushed between classes. An elderly couple walked their dachshund, and a red-haired girl went by on a mountain bike. Every hundred feet, attached to lampposts, were emergency call boxes that connected to campus security. It seemed an idyllic place, safe and uncluttered, so far removed from Delhi it could have been another planet. As Anna strolled along the sidewalk, she saw a sign for College Lane ahead of her.

The houses stood close together, separated by strips of lawn. Several cars were parked by the curb. Nobody was on the street. She walked as if she knew where she was headed, though this was the first time Anna had wandered away from campus. Her eyes picked up the numbers of the homes. 33 College Lane: Afridi had given her the address, and she quickly spotted the split-level house with evergreens growing along the foundations. A carpenter was working on the front door, repairing the hinges, his van parked in the driveway. Anna slowed her steps and glanced at the windows. Nobody was looking out, but she knew that the woman she had come to meet, Daphne Shaw, must be inside.

Across the street, Anna noticed a black Lexus coupe with tinted windows. Her instincts kicked in immediately. Without breaking stride, she continued to the end of the block, where College Lane ran into Shiloh Street. Turning left at the stop sign, Anna kept walking slowly. The neighborhood changed almost immediately. Instead of well-groomed lawns and the privileged spaces of the college campus, there were older houses falling into disrepair. A Doberman was barking behind a chain-link fence, and two boys on skateboards came down the sidewalk toward Anna, swerving past her with fixed expressions of bored insolence. Several of the homes were flying American flags, and one yard was full of plastic Easter bunnies, most of which had toppled over. An obese couple sat on a porch with two Siamese cats on their knees. At the next crossing, Anna took another left and headed back around the block until she reached the end of College Lane again. The Lexus was still there. Taking out her phone, as if to read a text message, Anna clicked three pictures of the car.

~

The day before, arriving at Cleveland's Hopkington International Airport, Anna had noticed the John Glenn NASA complex at one end of the runway. From Delhi, she had flown Air India, direct to New York, and then connected to an American Airlines flight into Cleveland. As they taxied toward the terminal, Anna saw several hangers with PEREGRINE painted on the side. The corporate logo combined a stylized falcon and an arrow, streaking toward the earth. Afridi had briefed her before she left Delhi, explaining that he believed there was a connection between the aeronautical company and Guldaar. The founder and CEO of Peregrine was a man named Roger Fleischmann, whose company was based in Ohio. One of Peregrine's main facilities was located in Eggleston, on the outskirts of town. Fleischmann himself was born here and attended Bromfield College before dropping out in his junior year. Having founded Peregrine in his parents' barn twenty years ago, he was now the single largest employer in Eggleston. Though Fleischmann never graduated from Bromfield, he was a major donor for the college. One wing of the library was named after his mother and the new Peregrine Science and Engineering Block was fully funded by him. Professor Verma held the Isabel Fleischmann chair in Political Science, which was named after Roger Fleischmann's wife.

Driving in from the airport yesterday, Anna had been struck by the pastoral beauty of the rolling farmland—freshly plowed fields patched together with stands of oak and maple. She tried to imagine what this landscape must have been like before any settlers arrived, but it was impossible to picture Ohio except under cultivation. Approaching the outskirts of Eggleston, she saw a couple of signs for the Peregrine facility. On one of the billboards was a photograph of Roger Fleischmann, with a boyish, toothy grin, and a tousled mop of blond hair. In red, white, and blue letters was the corporate slogan: Defending America Abroad, Rebuilding America at Home. Off in the distance, a corporate jet was coming in to land at the company's airstrip. A minute later, Anna saw another aircraft, flying low to the ground, thirty feet above the trees. It took her a moment to realize it was a drone. The sleek, aerodynamic shape, with sweptback wings and an engine at the rear, came sailing overhead like some sort of UFO. As Anna leaned against the taxi window, trying to keep the drone in sight, it passed above them without a sound. Though she knew it must be a test flight, Anna couldn't help but brace for impact.

~

Returning to College Lane in the afternoon, Anna confirmed that the Lexus was still there, parked in the same place across the street from Daphne Shaw's house. Anna retraced her steps until she came to a lamppost with an emergency call box and pressed the red button. After a couple of seconds, a man's voice answered.

'Campus security. How can I help you?'

'There's a fire on College Lane,' Anna shouted into the speaker, putting on an American accent.

By the time she'd made it halfway around the block, Anna could hear the sirens. Turning onto Shiloh Street, she could see the same couple, with their two cats, still sitting on the porch, though the Doberman had stopped barking and there were no skateboarders on the sidewalk. A police car raced past Anna, blue lights flashing as it turned at the stop sign. Slowing down, Anna listened as more sirens converged, howling in a chorus of alarm. When she reached the corner of College Lane, she could see two fire engines at the opposite end of the street with red lights flashing. Several people had come out of their homes and were watching from the sidewalk as the firemen went through their emergency routines. By now, they probably knew it was a false alarm, another college student acting up.

Anna could see the driver-side door of the Lexus open. A woman got out. She was about Anna's height, with short brown hair, wearing a tan jacket and jeans. One of the firemen came over and asked her to move the car. The carpenter had finished repairing the door at number 33, but there was no sign of Daphne Shaw. When the woman from the Lexus turned around, Anna pretended to check her phone and was able to get a couple of pictures. The woman was arguing with the firemen but finally turned around and got back in her Lexus. A minute later, she drove off.

Twenty-Four

'Unlock the ocean.' Four letters. Starting with 'q' and ending with 'y.' Daphne studied the cryptic clue for a minute then penciled in the letters to spell 'quay.'

Through the plate-glass window, she could see a man riding a lawnmower in circles. The sound of the engine droned softly but steadily like the purring of a mechanical cat. Facing the window, she sat in a chair next to her son's bed. For the fifteen years he had lain in this room, Naseem had never once looked out the window. The few times his eyes opened they stared straight up at the ceiling, vacant and without recognition. Whenever Daphne had looked into his eyes it frightened her. According to the doctors his retinas and optic nerves no longer functioned. The eyelids opening and closing was a reflex action, nothing more. Occasionally, a tear slid down his cheek but there were no emotions, no sadness or anger, regret or love. His soul had died but his body remained alive.

While she sat with him, Daphne usually did *The New York Times* crossword puzzle, which she carried with her to the clinic. Assyrian Sun God. 23 Down. Seven Letters. Second Letter 'H.' How was she supposed to know that? Daphne was sure that 15 Across was 'Potash.' Alkaline Compound Containing Potassium. She remembered this from her high school chemistry class, though she couldn't recall what it was used for. Why did some things stick in your mind and others evaporate instantly? 12 Across looked as if it should be easy to figure out. It might even give her a clue to the Assyrian deity, a dead god whom nobody worshipped any more. Colonial Shipping Line. Six Letters. Cunard. Yes, that was it! She filled in the squares with her pencil and looked across at Naseem. His lips were moving, though he did not speak, as if he were trying to help her solve the puzzle.

Just then, the nurse came in, a young African American woman named Grace who greeted her with a familiar wave.

'How are you, Daphne?' she asked, a casual question that required no answer.

'Okay,' she lied. 'Just fine, thank you.'

The nurse began to check the monitors and typed something on a keypad. In the beginning, when Naseem was first admitted to the clinic, Daphne had wanted to know everything they did, but over the years she had learned to let the machines do their work of keeping her son alive, without asking too many questions. A doctor would arrive later in the afternoon and read the daily report before examining the patient. Nobody at the clinic expected progress or recovery. When the nurse finished keying in the data, she talked for a few minutes about a wedding she'd attended in Cincinnati, her cousin's marriage. It was the kind of disconnected conversation that fulfilled a need to share moments of happiness amid the lifeless sorrows of the clinic.

When the nurse left, Daphne was aware that someone else was standing at the door. For a moment she thought it might be the doctor but when she turned to look, it was a man she'd never seen before.

'Ms Shaw?' he said.

She acknowledged him with her eyes but didn't speak.

'Sorry to disturb you. I was wondering if I could have a word.' The glasses he wore were the kind that changed color with the light. 'My name is Carlton Fletcher.'

'What's this about?' Daphne asked.

'I've just driven up from Washington, and I had a few questions.'

He glanced at Naseem, and she could see his eyes studying her son.

'Is it important?' she said.

'I'm afraid it is.' He came around the end of the bed and sat down in the chair across from her. Looking into his face, she remembered a description from a novel that compared a man's complexion to Stilton cheese, blue veins showing through the skin on his nose and cheeks.

'Does this have anything to do with the men who broke down my door last week?'

'Could be,' said Fletcher.

'Then I don't have anything more to say. I told them all they wanted to know.'

'We were wondering if you'd heard anything from your husband?'

'I don't have a husband,' she said.

'The father of your son,' said Fletcher, gesturing toward Naseem.

Daphne looked away and realized that the lawnmower was gone and there was silence.

'I haven't seen him for fifteen years,' Daphne said.

'We have reason to believe he came to your house last week.' Fletcher sat forward in his chair, as if his back was sore.

'You can believe whatever you choose to believe,' she said. 'But I haven't seen him since I lived in Bombay, more than fifteen years ago.'

'After your son had his accident,' said Fletcher. She nodded.

'The US government paid for him to come here for his treatment. Every year, it costs three quarters of a million dollars to take care of your son in this facility.' Fletcher paused for a moment, leaning back stiffly in his chair. 'Do you have any idea why American taxpayers should foot the bill for his medical expenses?'

'Mr Fletcher,' she said, 'you're from Washington, aren't you?'

He gestured with one hand, an affirmative wave.

'Then why are you asking me?'

'I spoke with Senator McHale. I believe you know him. He's taken a special interest in your son's case. According to him, it's a matter of national security but he wouldn't tell me anything more than that.'

'Senator McHale has been very helpful,' said Daphne.

'He's retiring this year,' said Fletcher. 'Do you think that might affect the care your son receives?'

'I don't know,' said Daphne. His questions troubled her, but she tried not to let it show.

'Ms Shaw, let me honest with you,' said Fletcher. 'We believe that Senator McHale has used his influence on the Senate Foreign Relations and Intelligence Committees to look after your son. Furthermore, we believe your son's father visited this country last week and met with Senator McHale at his home in Virginia, then spent a night with you here in Eggleston before leaving the country on a flight from Chicago. We would have arrested him at your home, but somebody tipped him off. Do you know who that might have been?'

'No,' she said. 'The only thing I know, Mr Fletcher, is that you should ask your questions in Washington, not here. This is my son. I am his mother. Beyond that, frankly, I don't give a damn.'

Picking up the folded newspaper, she studied it intently. The veins in the man's face had turned from blue to red and he looked as if he was about to lose his temper. One of his hands reached up to touch the box of cigarettes in his shirt pocket, but he withdrew it self-consciously. A monitor attached to the comatose patient beeped softly twice, but that was the only sound. Finally, Carlton Fletcher rose to his feet and headed toward the door.

'Mr Fletcher,' Daphne said, just as he was about to leave. 'I have a question for you.'

He stopped, a look of expectation behind the amber lenses.

'Yes?' he said.

'Would you happen to know the name of the Assyrian sun god?'

Fletcher glanced across at the crossword puzzle in her lap.

'Shamash,' he said and left the room.

Daphne's lips moved to form the words, 'Thank you,' but it was left unsaid.

Twenty-Five

Luke was awakened by the sound of the rock being dragged aside. A flood of daylight entered the chamber. He had been lying with his back to the wall, and his eyes were blinded by the brightness, though he could see the shapes of men above him, peering down. One of them lowered a dented plastic bottle full of water and a bowl of greasy broth with two flat cakes of bread. The water was murky and the bottle filthy, but he drank a little and ate the food. Though the soup smelled faintly of mutton, it was tasteless except for the salt.

The men left the hole open, and there was enough light for him to see the contours of the vault in which he sat. It was rectangular in shape, about twice as long as it was wide. The walls were made of rough concrete, and two cracks converged in one corner. A fine layer of silt covered the floor. He realized that it was an old water tank, which had probably been damaged by the earthquake, useless now, except as a prison. Above his head was a small aperture, like a large bullet hole, through which a half-inch pipe must have entered, filling the cistern from a nearby stream or spring.

Remembering the events of the night before, the lantern-lit room full of armed men, he wondered if this was a village or shepherd's camp, though he couldn't remember seeing anything on Ibrahim's map to indicate settlements farther up the valley. He had no idea who these men were. Jihadis, of course, but there was no way of knowing which faction they supported, or where their loyalties lay. Some of them seemed to be foreign fighters. The leader, with the injured arm, looked like an Afghan. It was hard to tell from his accent. His Dari sounded like a dialect from the north. Luke wondered if anyone beyond this valley knew that he had been taken hostage, or that Ibrahim and Mushtaq were dead. It would take several days before someone came to search for them. Without any form of communication, it could be a week or more before the rest of the world realized that they were missing.

A little later, the men came back and took the bowl, handing him a rusted canister to use as a toilet. The chamber was sealed again with the stone. Luke was too disoriented to be afraid, focusing on his immediate circumstances rather than worrying about what would happen next. His watch showed that it was 8:22 a.m. and Tuesday, only forty-eight hours since he was captured, but he felt as if much more time had elapsed. The cistern was dry but cold. After eating, he huddled himself into a corner and closed his eyes. Every time he made a noise, coughing or scraping his boot on the floor, the sound echoed inside the cistern. Luke wondered, would anyone hear him outside if he shouted?

His mind began to drift into random thoughts and memories, recalling incidents from his childhood in Murree, disjointed images of games he'd played as a boy, pretending to be a soldier, creeping up a hillside to capture a flag. He thought of Ruth and Poonam in West Virginia, with the baby. They didn't know that he was here, trapped inside a concrete tomb. Nina's face appeared in his mind, a look of innocence and fragility. And then, he thought of Fletcher in the airport lounge at Dulles, the menacing tone of voice, a man he'd thought was dead, the threat to his sister and her family. There were times when Fletcher seemed like a malevolent ghost, an ominous, invisible presence. He would probably be the first to learn that Luke had been abducted. Maybe he already knew. When would they find his corpse? He would be like the anonymous man in the coffin that he'd accompanied back to Washington. Would his tortured, mutilated body be shipped to America or would they bury him in Pakistan, maybe in the graveyard in Murree next to his mother? Perhaps he'd never be found and this concrete cistern would serve as his grave.

For several minutes, Luke drifted into sleep but woke almost immediately with a suffocating sense of desperation. He imagined the tank filling with water, a clear, cold stream trickling through the inlet overhead, then pooling at his feet and slowly rising up the walls, until he finally drowned. The sudden panic woke him out of this dream. Sweating, he shivered inside his coat. The codeine from the night before still blurred the lines between waking and sleep.

On the wall across from him, Luke saw a disc of light, eight or ten inches across. In his disoriented state, he thought it was a window, for he could see the profile of a mountain with snow on top and faint ridgelines, as well as clouds. The window was circular, like a luminous portal into another world where everything was upside down. For almost a minute, he stared at this vision, thinking it was part of his dream, like the icy water rising to his throat. But the shapes seemed real, even if the mountain was inverted. His mind struggled to comprehend the image until he finally realized what it was.

A beam of light was projected through the aperture above his head, casting the image on the wall, like a giant camera obscura. Looking up, he could see where the sunlight flowed through the pipe hole, shining against the opposite wall and creating an image of the mountains. Luke crawled closer and saw the layered shapes of clouds, the play of light and shadow on the ridges. It made him remember science experiments when he was a child, pinhole cameras made out of shoeboxes. There was a simple magic to the optical illusion that appeared in front of him. He watched it for almost half an hour, the bright circle moving slowly up the wall before it faded into darkness. A phenomenon so simple, yet so utterly real, it gave him hope.

Twenty-Six

Pushing her grocery cart down the aisle of the supermarket, Anna kept the woman in sight while choosing a box of granola from the shelf. She already had a carton of 2 percent milk, some blueberry yoghurt, and half a dozen bananas, which was all she needed. The woman she was following had grabbed some fruit and was heading for the bakery section. Gauging the time it would take her to round the aisle, Anna circled back and approached from the other side. As they maneuvered their carts past each other, Anna smiled at the woman and greeted her.

'Good morning, Ms Shaw,' she said.

The woman looked startled, then fixed her with a questioning gaze.

'How do you know my name?' she said. 'Have we met before?'

'No,' said Anna. 'I'm Sheetal Khanna. Colonel Afridi sent me to meet you.'

'Ah,' said Daphne with a relieved toss of her head. 'It's taken you a while.'

'I got here day before yesterday, but I didn't want to come to your house. I'm sure it's being watched.'

'Probably,' said Daphne. 'They may have followed me here as well.'

'Is there any place we can meet, discreetly?' Anna said.

'Where are you staying?' Daphne asked, leaning across to choose a loaf of bread from the shelf in front of her.

'At the college. I'm supposed to be doing research in the library.'

'I could meet you there,' said Daphne. 'I have a guest membership at the library.'

'My carrel is in the basement, level C of the stacks.'

'I'll be there in an hour,' said Daphne, pushing her cart past Anna with a nod of her head, as if they'd been discussing the comparative merits of whole-grain versus multi-grain bread.

~

The supermarket was a thirty-minute walk from campus, and Anna had to drop her groceries back in her room. Taking the elevator down into the stacks, she switched on the lights. Nobody else was around. Very few students or faculty seemed to use the stacks. Waiting for Daphne to arrive, Anna picked up a sheaf of papers from one of the boxes, photocopies of Sanskrit verses, on which Dennis Shelton had jotted notes in English. The original, from which the copy had been made, was an old edition, and she could see that the pages were coming apart at the binding. Shelton's handwriting was neat and precise. He often crossed out a word and replaced it with another. His personal copy of Monier-Williams' Sanskrit-English dictionary, with his notes in the margins, was also in the box. Anna remembered taking a class in Sanskrit once, as a girl, and thinking how pointless it was to try and pronounce words she would never use.

Just then, she heard the elevator door open. Daphne entered the stacks. Though she was in her early sixties, there was a youthfulness to her walk that suggested a woman half her age. Anna pulled up a second chair.

'Thank you,' Daphne said. 'I've never been to this part of the library before.'

'I don't think anybody comes down here,' said Anna. 'They're all doing research online instead.'

'It's like catacombs,' said Daphne.

Anna laughed. 'I have to apologize. I hope I didn't startle you in the supermarket.'

'That's all right,' said Daphne. 'I've been startled several times this week. Where in India are you from?'

'Delhi.'

'Sheetal Khanna. That's a Punjabi name,' said Daphne. 'You don't look Punjabi.'

Anna shrugged and smiled. 'My mother's Bengali.'

'I hope I can trust you,' Daphne continued. 'Colonel Afridi assured me that he would do whatever he could to help.'

'What is the problem, exactly?' Anna asked.

'I've lived like a hostage in this town for fifteen years,' said Daphne, 'and I hardly know a single person beyond saying hello in passing, not even my neighbors or my hairdresser.'

'I would have thought it was a friendlier place than that.'

'Maybe it is, but I've been forced to be discreet…and because of my circumstances, I just haven't made the effort. I don't belong to any of the churches in town or the women's clubs.'

'Do you work?' Anna asked.

Daphne shook her head. 'For a while I had a job, the first two years I was here, but then I quit. Writing up purchase orders for the US military isn't exactly the most stimulating form of employment, even if it's in the national interest.'

'You worked for Peregrine?'

'Almost everybody in Eggleston does,' said Daphne. 'They practically own this town.'

'What about the college?'

'Sure,' said Daphne. 'The company has given almost $50 million to Bromfield—buildings, laboratories, scholarships, named chairs. Even this library is endowed by Peregrine. Roger Fleischmann was a student here, and he's made it his mission to revive the town and support the college.'

'Isn't that a good thing?' said Anna.

'Maybe. But he controls both the board of trustees and the Eggleston town council. Nothing happens here without his blessing and his money,' said Daphne. 'There's a company airport and test facility just beyond the golf course. They send up UAVs all the time, supposedly for testing but often I think they must be watching us, every move we make.'

'I saw one,' Anna said.

'On the surface, Eggleston looks like a picture-perfect Midwestern town—red barns and silos, cornfields and kids bicycling down a sidewalk—but when you realize it's all supported by an industry that builds weapons that destroy people's lives in other parts of the world, things look different.' Daphne stopped herself with a flick of her wrist, as if erasing all she'd said. 'Of course, I should be grateful. Even after I quit my job, they've kept me on the payroll thanks to some powerful connections.'

'It must get lonely,' Anna began, 'being on your own….'

'No, no,' said Daphne. 'I'm not complaining. And, please, don't feel sorry for me. I like to be alone, most of the time.'

'But your son—'

'He's been in a coma since 1998, at a critical care facility in a town nearby. I visit him two or three times a week, but he doesn't know it. The doctors say he can't see or hear or feel or think. He might as well be dead.'

'I'm sorry,' said Anna.

'His father came to see me eight days ago, on the sixth of April. He and I split up soon after our son was born, but when Naseem had his accident, he made arrangements to have him brought here to America and receive the best treatment in the world.' She paused and looked away. 'Not that it does any good. But he takes care of me as well, I suppose.'

'Guldaar?'

Daphne laughed. 'I've never called him that. It sounds too melodramatic. Guldaar Khan! Like something out of Kipling or the movies.'

'What do you call him?'

'A fucking bastard, most of the time,' said Daphne.

'Why did he come to see you? Colonel Afridi said it had to do with your son.'

Daphne looked away for a moment at the shadowy spines of books on the shelves. The surrounding darkness of the stacks was claustrophobic but also gave them a sense of security— that nobody was listening.

'Let me ask you first,' said Daphne. 'What is Afridi like? I've only heard his voice on the phone. He sounds like an interesting man.'

'He is,' said Anna. 'He's a mountaineer, or used to be. When you meet him, you'll find him gracious and old fashioned, but he's one of the smartest men I know. A true officer and a gentleman.'

'You sound as if you're in love with him,' said Daphne.

Anna laughed. 'No, he's almost seventy. Older than my father.'

'That's no reason not to fall in love,' said Daphne.

'He's in a wheelchair,' said Anna. 'His legs were paralyzed in a climbing accident forty years ago.'

'Ah,' said Daphne. 'Why didn't you tell me that first?'

'Because it's not the first thing that comes to mind,' Anna said, feeling uncomfortable. 'His disability doesn't slow him down.'

'You're very loyal to him, I can tell,' said Daphne, 'but I'm still wondering if I can trust you. I have to be sure.'

'What would convince you?' Anna replied.

Daphne turned the ring on her finger around, so that Anna could see an emerald set in gold, almost as big as a sparrow's egg.

'If you tell me your real name,' said Daphne. 'It isn't Sheetal, is it?'

Anna met her eyes with a deliberate stare.

'No,' she said. 'Annapurna Tagore. Most people call me Anna.'

Daphne extended her hand to shake. 'Thank you, Anna. Now we can start again. You asked me the name I use for my son's father. It's Jimmy, but I'm the only one who calls him that.'

Letting go of Anna's hand, she laughed again, as if to reassure her.

'Why did he come to see you last week?' Anna asked. 'Did it have something to do with Peregrine?'

'I don't know, honestly. Jimmy hardly ever talks about that side of things, but I know, of course, he's close to them…Probably owns a stake in the company too. That's why they've supported me all these years.'

'What did you talk about?' Anna asked.

'He had a proposition,' said Daphne, her face now drained of humor and looking older. 'He's found a wife for our son.'

Anna looked at her, confused.

'Yes, it is absurd, isn't it?' said Daphne. 'He even brought a picture of the girl, a pretty young thing straight out of a village in the Mohmand Agency—blue eyes, pink cheeks.'

'But your son—'

'Common sense and logic have never been Jimmy's strengths. Of course, women in that part of the world get married over the telephone all the time. They're known as mobile brides. You can even perform a nikkah on Twitter, I'm told.'

Anna studied Daphne's face in the half-light of the library bulbs. For the first time she saw a trace of sadness in her eyes. Half her face was in shadow, and her profile was as perfect as in the publicity photos Afridi had shared with her, a look of tragic beauty.

'Jimmy wants a grandson,' said Daphne.

'He has no other children?'

'No,' said Daphne. 'But it's not for lack of trying. Even before Naseem's accident he wanted to father another child. For a while, Jimmy thought I might get pregnant again, but nothing came of it and he moved on to other women. At first, I was hurt and jealous when he told me that he'd married some girl from Hyderabad. Then he divorced her and found another bride, and after a while I realized it was desperation on his part and denial. He hardly seemed to care about the women. All he wanted was to produce an heir, but it wasn't happening. So now he's come up with another plan, to take sperm from our son and have the bride artificially inseminated to carry on his name, his lineage.'

'Is that even possible?' Anna said.

'Jimmy seems to think so. Modern medicine performs all kinds of miracles these days. Some doctor in Chicago has assured him that it can be done, the same way they collect sperm from stud bulls—a rectal probe ejaculation.'

She said it softly but with suppressed anger in her voice. Anna could see that her hands were trembling.

'Of course, he needs my permission for the procedure,' Daphne continued. 'And I'll tell you, Anna, with God as my witness, I will not let Jimmy have his way with him.'

Twenty-Seven

The website *www.martyrsofamudarya.com* was crudely designed, with a stock image of pink roses growing out of twisted stems of barbed wire and *Bismillah al Rahman al Rahim* written in Arabic and English at the top. On the homepage were two links. The first led to a page with photographs of martyrs, most of them young men from Afghanistan who had died fighting the Russians and Americans over the past twenty years. The images were disturbing in their stark simplicity, mostly black and white snapshots of men holding rifles and landmines, looking straight into the camera. None of the martyrs appeared to be more than thirty years old, and some were in their teens. Death gave them an ageless quality of eternal youth. Reading the names, Afridi felt dismay and anger, the senseless violence and enmity in a part of the world that had so little humanity to spare. The second link took him to a blog, with a Facebook account under the name of ShabeerAli91. The most recent picture posted was of an American journalist taken hostage somewhere near Chitral.

Afridi studied the photograph, comparing it in his mind to the images of martyrs. The American was slightly older, in his early thirties. He had a wound on his forehead and his face was bearded. The message on the site suggested he was still alive. A splinter group of the Martyrs of Amu Darya, operating in Nuristan, along the border between Afghanistan and Chitral, claimed responsibility for the kidnapping. They demanded a ransom of two million dollars, along with the release of several of their fighters who had been taken prisoner by NATO forces. Afridi had been alerted to the post by one of his analysts, who was keeping an eye on the borderlands of Afghanistan and Northern Pakistan following the air crash near Siachen. Because of the recent earthquake, there had been a lot of activity by Pakistan Air Force helicopters, mostly relief work, but some of which strayed suspiciously close to the LOAC, and seemed more opportunistic than humanitarian.

Afridi read through the hostage demands, which were written in Urdu on the website. It was clear that the Martyrs of Amu Darya were allied with Pakistani Taliban fighters. Though they did not disclose where the prisoner was being held, there was a reference to the earthquake and demands for increased medical supplies in the region.

'Excuse me, sir.'

Narender Rawat, one of HRI's senior analysts, was standing at Afridi's door.

'Yes, what is it?' Afridi replied, still distracted by the website.

'The flight from Kabul has landed, sir. You asked me to call you.'

'Yes, of course,' said Afridi.

He glanced at the photograph of the hostage one more time, the dazed blue eyes, dusty brown hair, and dark beard. His name, according to the website, was Luke McKenzie. Afridi moved his hand to the mouse attached to his laptop and closed the tab, revealing a clutter of icons on his desktop and a photograph of a mountain at sunset, tinged a reddish hue.

Wheeling himself away from his desk, he passed through a set of automatic doors onto the verandah of the Himalayan Research Institute. It was just after dusk, and the snow peaks were faintly visible through a cross-hatching of deodar needles. The air was crisp, and the wisteria vines that trailed along the verandah roof were in full bloom, pendant purple blossoms emitting a faint perfume. Reluctantly, Afridi returned inside, passing through another set of automatic doors and entering a large room alive with an array of digital technology—more than a dozen screens relaying satellite images and live feeds from observation posts in every part of the Indian Himalayas. One of the larger screens displayed a Chinese airfield in the trans-Himalayan region, with fighter jets landing like flies.

Narender Rawat directed Afridi toward a monitor at the far side of the room, connected to a CCTV feed at Indira Gandhi International Airport Terminal 3. A single CISF constable was on duty at the gate, which opened off a jetway.

'When did the flight arrive?' Afridi asked.

'Ten minutes ago,' said Rawat. 'They've just opened the doors.' Seconds later, passengers began to stream out of the gate and pass down the hall toward Immigration and Baggage Claim. The quality of the image was remarkably clear. Unlike most CCTV feeds, the new cameras installed at the airport were high definition, with a facility to focus on specific objects and faces. Afridi recalled that when the Dutch surveillance company had demonstrated the cameras, they showed how you could read the visa number in a passport from fifty feet away. He watched in silence as Air India Flight 244 from Kabul disembarked. Most of the passengers appeared to be Afghans, though there were plenty of Indians among them—contract laborers, diplomatic personnel and Sikh traders with shops in Kabul. It was only a two-hour flight.

'There. That's one of them,' Afridi pointed at the screen, as a man leaning on a cane with an exaggerated limp came through the gate. 'Take a closer look.'

Rawat keyed in a command, and the camera closed in on the passenger as he made his way slowly down the hall. His left leg was stiff and dragging at the toe as he hobbled forward. When he reached an escalator, they could see him bracing himself and using both hands to climb onto the moving staircase.

Rawat switched to another camera at Passport Control, where passengers had formed a queue.

They picked up the Afghan at Immigration. Afridi could see his face more clearly now, a man in his fifties with a graying beard and a karakul hat. He kept his balance as he waited in the line, though he favored his right leg.

'Show me the rest of the passengers,' Afridi demanded.

The camera pulled back, and they could see a line of immigration booths, with more people arriving from the flight and waiting their turn.

'Those two women at counter number six,' Afridi said.

Both of them had their heads covered and their arms were hidden beneath long, loose sleeves. They approached an immigration officer together, and one of them handed him their passports and landing cards. Rawat zoomed in to take a look at the papers, but they were hidden from view as the officer checked the documents.

'Can you get a closer shot of her other hand?' Afridi said.

The camera panned to the right, where the woman's arm hung by her side inside folds of layered clothing. Only the fingers were visible, emerging from the hem of her sleeve. As Rawat adjusted the magnification, they could see the forefinger and thumb. For a minute they watched to see if there was any movement, but the hand remained rigid. Eventually, when the woman lifted her arm and the cloth fell away below her wrist, the smooth plastic skin on the prosthesis was unmistakable.

Shifting the camera back and forth between the women and the man in the karakul hat, Afridi and Rawat watched them collect their bags and move separately toward the Green Channel at Customs. One of the officers, in a white uniform, stopped the two women and asked them to X-ray their bags. Afridi could see the man hesitating, then circling back toward the Duty Free shops, where he pretended to sort through his documents, marking time a short distance away. Eventually, the women were let through and he quickly followed them out the door, having been waved past by the Customs officer.

'Sir, shouldn't we have them detained?' Rawat asked, as the trio moved out into the reception area, where another camera picked them up.

'No, not yet,' said Afridi. 'I want two cars following their vehicle. We need to know where they go and whom they meet. Make sure we don't lose them. I want an hourly report and call me immediately if anything unusual occurs.'

Turning away from the screen, he wheeled himself outdoors again, where it had grown completely dark. The fragrance of the wisteria blossoms seemed stronger, almost cloying. A thin crescent moon was rising above the Himalayas like an eyelash of gold.

Twenty-Eight

For the past three hours they had been climbing over scree and moraine, broad slopes of loose shingle and boulder fields that seemed to go on forever. The jihadis hadn't covered Luke's eyes, but his wrists were loosely tied behind his back. It hardly mattered, for he had no idea where they were going, except that it seemed his captors were headed toward the crest of the ridge on the western side of the valley. Three men accompanied him. At first, he thought they were taking him out to be executed. Each of them had a rifle slung across his shoulder.

Finally, they reached a snow bridge over a swift stream, which they traversed cautiously, hearing the ice creaking under their feet. Luke could see the pass above them, a narrow gap in the rocks with a funnel of snow extending down to the stream. Clouds had come in and covered the sun. As they started to climb, the snow was soft in places, and his boots sank up to his knees. At other places there was a glaze of ice, and they had to kick steps into the slope. When they finally reached the pass, daylight was fading, and they hurried down the opposite side, a more gradual descent. At nightfall they took shelter amid a cluster of boulders. Luke's head ached from the altitude. When the men gave him a handful of dried apricots to eat, he had trouble chewing and swallowing them down. The rocks protected them from the wind, but the cold was severe and they lay together for warmth.

Luke had no idea where they were taking him or why. The next morning, they continued down off the pass and stopped near a patch of juniper to boil some water for tea and warm themselves by the fire. After this, they wrapped a cloth across Luke's eyes and made him walk between them for an hour until they came to a settlement where he could hear voices and animals. A few minutes later, he was lifted onto a horse and they continued on their way. At one point someone untied the ropes and put a flat piece of bread in his hand. He ate it slowly, the dry doughy texture making him gag. As he finished eating, he heard a diesel engine, and they hustled him into the back of a truck which set off along a rough, winding road. The second night was spent in the truck parked somewhere in the darkness. His blindfold was removed and he was allowed to get down to relieve himself and drink water. Overhead, the sky was brilliantly clear and the stars had a phosphorescent clarity, like glowing creatures at the bottom of the sea.

The next day, Luke was blindfolded again and shifted to another vehicle, a smaller SUV. They drove for hours. At places, he could hear sounds of traffic and felt as if they were passing through towns. The only roads in this region, as far as Luke knew, converged on Peshawar, and he wondered if that was where they were headed, approaching the city from the north. For a while, the winding road seemed to straighten out, and his ears popped several times as they lost altitude.

Finally, the vehicle came to a halt, and he could hear men shouting and the sound of a gate being opened. He had lost all track of time and any sense of direction. Rough hands took hold of his legs and dragged him out of the vehicle, and he found himself standing unsteadily, eyes still covered. Luke expected the worst, but when the blindfold was removed he was startled to find himself in a garden, standing amid beds of larkspur, snapdragons and poppies. A small fishpond was full of golden carp and pink water lilies. To his right was a large ranch-style house that could have been somewhere in California, with picture windows and gently sloping roofs. Plush green lawns spread between the flowerbeds. Two pink oleanders were in bloom, as well as a pomegranate tree laden with fruit. Only when he looked up at the sky did he feel he was still in Pakistan, a concave dome of turquoise set amid a distant circle of dusty hills.

His captors had driven off, and a different set of guards surrounded him, four men in dark green uniforms. Their assault rifles and black berets made them look like paratroopers, though they wore no insignia. Luke glanced down at his soiled jeans and muddy boots. His parka was ripped, and feathers were spilling out of the torn fabric. One of his hands was bleeding where it had scraped against the tailgate of the SUV. His eyes hurt, and his mouth felt as if it were full of sand.

The guards gestured for him to go up the steps to the house, but at that moment the front door opened and a middle-aged man walked out. He was neatly groomed and dressed in a linen bush shirt with pale gray trousers. His black wingtip shoes were polished to a perfect gleam. Luke had never seen him before, but he looked like one of the patrons of the Rawalpindi Polo Club, a member of Pakistan's feudal elite.

'Welcome, Mr McKenzie, welcome,' he said. 'Please come inside. We'll get you a bath and something to eat.'

Luke stared at him with a dazed expression of disbelief as the man extended his hand to introduce himself.

'My name is Jehangir Daruwalla.'

Twenty-Nine

At the southeastern corner of Jahanpanah Forest in South Delhi lies a small octagonal tomb made of brick and sandstone, with a band of broken blue tiles encircling the drum of its dome. Awkwardly positioned between the barrier wall of the forest and an electric substation, the tomb faces a crossing where the main road continues on toward Tuqlakabad Industrial Area and a side lane winds its way into Greater Kailash Part II. Most people who drive along this road never notice the tomb, for it is hidden behind a line of fruit vendors and a spider's web of electric wires, poles, and fuse boxes. A miniature version of the famous Rukn-i-Alam tomb in Multan, this fourteenth-century mausoleum is believed to contain the bones of a sufi named Hafiz Jamaluddin, popularly known as Kanra Pir, the one-eyed saint. The Archeological Survey of India has erected a small sign that declares it to be the grave of one of Ghiyasuddin Tuglaq's generals, but for the faithful who gather here each day it remains Kanra Pir's tomb and nobody can convince them otherwise. They offer prayers and green muslin chadors to cover the gravestone, burning incense while invoking the sufi's blessings and his healing touch.

Most of the people who visit this tomb are crippled in some way, missing limbs or suffering from withered arms or congenital disfigurements. Some have lost a hand in accidents; others can no longer walk. The legend of Kanra Pir goes back to the time of Mohammed Bin Tuglaq. Originally from the mountains of

Afghanistan, the sufi wandered into India, as mystics have a way of doing, and crossed paths with Tuglaq's army just after they had subdued a marauding force. One of the officers had been badly wounded, his hand severed at the wrist by an enemy sword. When the saint came upon him in the aftermath of battle, he offered the injured man water to drink, after which the officer discovered that his hand was healed. As recompense for this miracle, however, the sufi had lost his left eye. Farsi verses attributed to Kanra Pir declare that 'a soldier without a hand can no longer defend the faithful, but a true believer needs only one eye to see the path to paradise.'

Afridi had known about the tomb for some time. One of his colleagues had even suggested that he go and pray to the saint, in the hope that his legs might be restored. The colonel had told him off politely and made it clear that he had no time for superstition. Now, as he studied the queue of supplicants lining up on the pavement, he felt irritated and depressed by the desperation that drove so many people to believe in the curative powers of a mendicant who may or may not have died six hundred years ago.

Rawat and his technicians at HRI had tried to get a satellite image of Kanra Pir's tomb, but it was impossible because of Delhi's polluted air, which reduced visibility to a dirty haze. As an alternative, a mobile surveillance unit had been deployed across the street, where its cameras could follow the comings and goings. As Afridi had predicted, the three passengers who arrived from Kabul the day before were standing in the queue at Kanra Pir's tomb, waiting to receive whatever miracles a dead sufi might bestow upon their missing limbs. As soon as Rawat recognized them on the screen, he informed the colonel.

Watching the chaotic traffic around the tomb, with people who could barely hobble trying to negotiate the broken pavement and mounds of rubbish tossed near the fruit vendors' carts, Afridi felt grateful to be far away from Delhi.

'Sir, do you think they know they are carrying heroin?' asked Rawat.

'That's a good question,' Afridi replied. 'The fact that they've come here this morning makes me think they have no idea what's going on. They are simple, god-fearing pilgrims, as they said they were.'

The Afghans had gone straight from the airport to a guesthouse in Lajpat Nagar. Through discreet inquiries Afridi's team had learned that the man was the father of one of the women, who was accompanying her widowed friend on a visit to the tomb of Kanra Pir. They had heard that many people like them had been healed and for three years now they had been saving up for this journey. Both women had lost an arm when a landmine exploded under a bus they were traveling in. The father's leg had been amputated eighteen years earlier after it was shredded by a Russian artillery shell. When asked about their artificial limbs, they said they had recently been fitted with new prostheses at a hospital in Jalalabad, run by the Sikander-e-Azam Trust. None of them spoke English, but the one woman knew enough Urdu to answer questions, saying how grateful they were to have these new limbs and the opportunity to visit the sufi's tomb. The trust had even provided them air tickets for their journey to Delhi.

Despite the HD cameras in the surveillance van, it was difficult to see what was going on. Afridi waited until the supplicants entered the crowded courtyard in front of the mausoleum before returning to his office.

'Excuse me, sir,' Rawat asked. 'Shouldn't we alert Narcotics?'

Afridi smiled. 'Why are you always so impatient?' he said.

'But if they are carrying heroin—'

'If they are,' said Afridi, 'we'll get one kilo, maybe two at the most, which is a sizeable amount, of course…but if they aren't carrying anything, then we'll have tipped Guldaar's people off, and they'll find some other way to smuggle it in next time.'

Rawat began to protest, but Afridi raised his hand.

'Patience, Rawatji, please. This is a dry run, to test things out and make sure nobody's watching. There's no reason for us to act in haste. Next week, when the death celebration of the so-called Kanra Pir takes place, on 23 April, hundreds of pilgrims will be coming, many of them from Afghanistan. You can be sure that, when Narcotics conducts its raid that night, they'll seize twenty or thirty kilos of heroin, not just three or four.'

Rawat seemed unconvinced.

'Besides,' Afridi added, 'heroin is the least of our concerns.'

Thirty

The annual Laurel Day Parade began at the far end of Bromfield campus, near the new Fleischmann Student Center, and followed a route along Main Street, through the center of Eggleston. Three flag bearers led the way, each of them a veteran in uniform, carrying the stars and stripes, the Ohio state flag, and a banner honoring soldiers missing in action. After them came the captain of the local high school football team, wearing a Roman helmet and breastplate, with a sword and shield. The school's mascot was a gladiator. He was followed by six twirlers, who looked as if they had just stepped out of a frieze in Pompeii, throwing batons in the air. Behind them was the high school marching band, also in faux Roman uniforms, a raucous phalanx of trumpets and trombones, along with saxophones and clarinets. Two bass drums brought up the rear, thudding loudly to the beat of a John Philip Souza march. Everyone wore a laurel wreath on his or her head, even the town councilors, who followed the band in Cadillac convertibles, waving to the crowd. They were accompanied by members of the Rotary, Lions, Elks, and Kiwanis clubs. Next came another group of veterans on motorcycles, mostly Harleys, decorated with red, white, and blue regalia. Several floats had been made by local organizations, each pulled by a tractor. One had a tableau of Roman deities, including an obese Bacchus with a red beard, holding up a handful of plastic grapes. Another was shaped to look like a huge siege engine, with a blond nymph in the catapult, who looked as if she were about to be launched into outer space.

Anna had seen posters for the parade as soon as she arrived in Eggleston, and Professor Verma had encouraged her to attend, saying, 'It's the town festival. You'll get to observe the natives performing ancient martial rites.'

Verma offered to accompany her but Anna had avoided him and gone down to the corner of Main and Buckeye, near the First Presbyterian church, where she could watch the parade on her own. The street was decorated with bunting and streamers, all red, white and blue. An annual celebration of spring that began years ago, the Laurel Day Parade had recently been revived as a way of building community morale and helping restore Eggleston's town pride. Roger Fleischmann had a lot to do with it, Verma had explained, and Peregrine sponsored a couple of floats that showed off their military hardware. People cheered and clapped as a huge display with the company's logo went by, the falcon and arrow fashioned from rosebuds and laurel blossoms.

A few seconds later, Anna saw the first drone go overhead. It was flying about forty feet above the crowd, down Main Street, and passed over the floats and marching band without a sound. This was followed by a dozen more in a loose formation, like a flock of geese, skimming over the rooftops and trailing plumes of colored smoke. Then Anna heard a roar that sounded like all of the Harleys revving their engines at once. It seemed to be coming from the far end of Main Street. Suddenly, a vintage fighter jet appeared above the rooftops, a World War Two Curtiss P40 Warhawk, with a single propeller and a snarl of teeth painted on the lower half of the fuselage below the cockpit. Dipping its wings, the plane buzzed the crowd, then did a barrel roll above the Town Hall before climbing steeply, as if searching for a dogfight.

Anna caught the eye of a young man beside her, holding his son on his shoulders.

'What was that?' she asked.

The man laughed. 'Roger Fleischmann in his latest toy. He collects antique planes. Every year, he flies a different one.'

The Warhawk circled back and came around for a second pass, so close that Anna could see the pilot waving to the cheering crowd as he roared above the parade. Seconds later, he pulled up again and veered away from the town, heading south. The sound of the engine had diminished but Anna heard a distinct sputtering noise and saw the vintage fighter bank sharply at an awkward angle before it plunged to the ground. As the crowd now screamed with terror instead of excitement, there was the sound of an explosion followed by a rising column of black smoke.

~

Daphne and Anna had planned to meet again in the library the day after the parade, but following the crash almost everything in town remained closed. Classes were canceled at the college, and all of the flags were lowered to half-staff. Even the library shut down as a mark of respect for its benefactor. A sense of shock and mourning settled over the campus. The Eggleston Tribune carried a full-page photograph of Roger Fleischmann accompanying a lengthy obituary and tributes from the state senators and representatives as well as the secretary of defense. According to the police reports, the crash was being treated as a tragic accident. Flying a seventy-year-old fighter jet, even if it was carefully restored and maintained by a team of expert mechanics, was a risky business. But Fleischmann was a man who enjoyed taking risks, as the newspapers suggested, the more dangerous and bigger, the better. He had built his company out of a fearless sense of entrepreneurship and patriotism. As the defense secretary remarked, Peregrine represented America's willingness to take on the most desperate threats around the world. After 9/11, many had questioned how the country could respond to terrorist groups like Al Qaeda. Peregrine's drones were the answer. American innovation and technology would triumph over the regressive forces of evil, ignorance, and hatred.

Eggleston's tragedy became a national cause for mourning. In her room, Anna watched the story play out on all of the television networks—a small-town hero and businessman, self-made and determined to stick to his roots. That he had been flying a World War II fighter plane made Fleischmann's death all the more poignant. One commentator after the other compared him to ace pilots who shot down German Messerschmitts and Japanese Zeros. Anna was amazed how quickly history got muddled with the present as dozens of posts celebrating American warplanes produced in the 1930s and 40s swept through social media. All kinds of photographs were posted, with technical data and nostalgic reminiscences by the last few living pilots of that era. The way they reported the accident, it seemed as if Fleischmann's Curtiss P40 had been on a mission against the enemy, rather than showing off at small town parade. A cartoon in *The Eggleston Tribune* depicted the gladiator in tears.

The funeral was scheduled for three days after the crash. Before the event, the White House issued a statement, saying that 'Roger Fleischmann was a true American hero. Not only did he build weapons of stealth that saved hundreds of military casualties on the ground but he was a courageous captain of industry who manufactured drones in the American heartland, with American grit and determination, creating jobs for American workers.' The barrage of hyperbole made Anna switch off the TV.

When the library opened again, two days after the accident, Anna went back to her study carrel and waited. She had no way to contact Daphne. She didn't want to use a phone for fear that it was tapped. Security on campus was tighter, and two armed policemen were posted outside the library building. With the memorial service planned for the college chapel, everyone seemed on edge.

By now the news cycle had turned. After an initial outpouring of grief and praise for Roger Fleischmann, there were suggestions of a possible conspiracy. The FAA was investigating the crash. Nobody was suggesting sabotage or terrorism yet, but there were reports that Peregrine's CEO had received death threats. His drones were killing Taliban commanders in Afghanistan and Pakistan. It stood to reason that they might want to take revenge. From one newscast to the next, Anna could see the paranoia building in the media.

Sitting at her desk in the library, pretending to leaf through a manuscript of Sanskrit verse, Anna saw the elevator open, and a woman stepped into the stacks. She was wearing a tan jacket, and Anna recalled her short brown hair. She'd shown this woman's photograph to Daphne, who said she didn't recognize her and didn't remember noticing the Lexus outside her house. After surveying the dimly lit stacks, the woman came toward her.

'Sheetal Khanna?' she asked, with a severe look on her face.

'Yes,' said Anna.

'I'd like to ask you a few questions, please.'

'What for?' Anna said.

The woman reached into the pocket of her jacket and flashed an official-looking ID, holding it up so briefly that Anna could see only the photograph and crest but no name.

'My name is Tracy Holman. I'm a federal agent,' said the woman, glancing around and pulling up a chair. 'Are you a foreign national?'

Anna nodded.

'We're checking on illegal aliens here in Eggleston, and I was wondering if you could tell me why you're here?'

'I'm a visiting scholar,' Anna said, 'researching the papers of a philologist named Dennis Shelton. He translated—'

'Can I see your passport, please?' Holman interjected before she could finish.

Reaching for her backpack, Anna unzipped an inner pocket and took out the passport with the three Ashokan lions on the cover. She wasn't sure whether this was routine or something else was going on. The fact that this woman had been keeping Daphne under surveillance two days before Roger Fleischmann's crash made her suspicious.

Holman flipped through the passport and, when she found the visa, scrutinized entry and exit stamps. Most of the pages were blank.

'You don't travel very much,' she said. Anna shook her head.

'How many days have you been here?'

'Five, I think,' said Anna. 'I arrived last Thursday.'

'Where are you staying?'

'In one of the college guestrooms in Judson Hall.'

'And who have you met?'

'Excuse me?'

'People,' said Holman impatiently. 'Who have you been talking with?'

'Really, only Dr Satish Verma. He's a professor of political science at the college, who helped arrange my fellowship.'

'Is he Indian too?'

'I think he's an American citizen but originally from India, yes.' Anna restrained an impulse to say something more pointed.

'Are you Muslim?'

Anna began to laugh, taken aback. 'No, I'm Hindu by birth.'

'And this guy Verma? What's his religion?'

'I'm afraid I don't know what he believes in,' said Anna. 'And, honestly, Agent Holman, I don't understand what religion has to do with this.'

The woman stared back at Anna, accusation in her eyes. 'Have you heard of Peregrine?' she asked.

'The company? Yes, of course, it's in the news because of the crash,' said Anna. 'I was at the parade and saw it happen.'

'Why did you attend the parade?' Holman's questions had an edge of hostility that suggested she knew more than she was letting on.

'I went out of curiosity,' said Anna.

'You've got a three-month visa. When are you planning to go back to India?' said Holman.

'I'm not sure. It depends how quickly I finish my work,' Anna said, pointing to the boxes of papers beside her desk.

'And you have no other knowledge about the death of Roger Fleischmann?'

Anna shook her head as Holman returned the passport and stood up. For a moment, they stared at each other in silence.

'Thank you,' said Holman, 'and have a good day.'

Thirty-One

Wheeling himself home along the Chukkar Road, which circled the top of the ridge near the Himalayan Research Institute in Mussoorie, Afridi paused several times to stop and consider the events of the past few days. He hadn't heard anything from Anna, though the news of the crash in Ohio had reached him. Afridi knew she would be keeping a low profile, and he didn't expect any communication, unless there was a problem. He guessed that by now she must have met Daphne Shaw.

The distance from HRI to Ivanhoe, Afridi's cottage, was a kilometer and a half. He usually went home by himself without a guard, though he carried his service revolver in a shoulder holster beneath his blazer. It was a necessary precaution, even if most of the people he passed on the Chukkar didn't know who he was. The Himalayan Research Institute was hidden discreetly behind fences and walls that kept curious tourists from trespassing but did not announce its importance as a key Military Intelligence facility. Technically, Afridi was a retired army officer with a cottage on the north side of the hill. He kept to himself as much as possible, though from time to time he had a few neighbors and friends over for dinner or dropped in at the mess for a drink. Afridi knew that the best form of security was to keep a low profile rather than move around with bodyguards or ride in jeeps with beacons flashing.

As he came to the south side of the ridge, he paused to look down at the Dehradun Valley spread out below him. It was early evening, and lights were just coming on. He could clearly see the sprawling colonies of the city and patches of forest and fields. In the foreground lay the main ridge that ran from Mussoorie to Rajpur, along which the old walking road used to ascend in the days before cars and buses could reach the town. When the British first settled these hills, they rode ponies up the rough track. Early visitors exclaimed over the views from Landour and the precipitous drops at the side of the trail.

Directly below him, on the main ridge, lay Bala Hissar, now part of Wynberg Allen School. It was here in the 1840s that Dost Mohammad Khan, Amir of Afghanistan, was imprisoned in a hilltop bungalow named after his fort in Kabul. The British East India Company Forces had brought Dost Mohammad here into exile while they tried to secure Afghanistan against Russian imperial ambitions. It was a fatal campaign, by the end of which only one Englishman survived out of a force of 12,000 troops. Eventually, the East India Company released Dost Mohammad from imprisonment. Looking down at Bala Hissar now—the old bungalow had been razed to the ground, and a new building stood in its place—Afridi often wondered what Dost Mohammad thought of Mussoorie and his exile in these forested hills. He had been held captive with members of his retinue, while a cordon of secrecy surrounded his incarceration. British troops guarded the ridge, and spies lurked along the road from Rajpur to make sure that nobody tried to assassinate Dost Mohammed or free him from Bala Hissar. Sometimes, it seemed to Afridi that history was a wheel that kept turning without ever moving forward.

He continued along the Chukkar, his mind travelling to the mountainous borders of Afghanistan, much drier, browner hills than these, and the Khyber Pass over which so many armies had crossed to face inevitable defeat. The recent news that Peregrine's CEO had died in an air crash in Ohio seemed as if it might be connected to the drone attacks in the tribal belt that claimed dozens of lives every week, though it was hard to tell if it was just an accident or somehow linked to Guldaar. A few days ago in Delhi, Manav Shinde had suggested he was being paranoid. The thought amused Afridi, for he knew that irrational fears had led to some of the most devastating debacles in the past. While defending India from outside forces, both real and imagined, many lives had been lost in the borderlands of Afghanistan. History was not kind to those who meddled in affairs of the Hindu Kush. Everyone from Alexander the Great to British imperialists had paid a harsh price in the region, and now, more recently, the Russians and the Americans had learned this lesson the hard way.

Turning a corner, where he could see the Garhwal Himalayas, bastions of snow and ice, arrayed to the north, he wondered if his suspicions were getting the better of him. These mountains were a great deal higher and more formidable than the Hindu Kush but far less treacherous when it came to politics and warfare. At least it was clear who the enemy was across the border in Tibet, while you never knew whom to trust in the tribal areas of Pakistan. The Great Game had been set in motion by British ambitions and fears of Czarist expansion, most of which were exaggerated. In the end, after losing an entire army, the East India Company reinstated Dost Mohammad on the Afghan throne, another inevitable turn of the wheel. Afridi's hands propelled his chair forward. While he knew that his instincts were correct, it was difficult to keep his doubts at bay.

Twenty seconds later, as if to confirm that the game was as dangerous as he believed, a speeding vehicle came around the corner behind him. Hearing the roar of the engine and glancing back, he saw a white SUV accelerating in his direction. Earlier, he'd noticed the Scorpio parked at Sister's Bazaar where the Chukkar bifurcated, but he hadn't paid any attention. The road was barely fifteen feet across, with a steel fence along the outside made of two galvanized pipes with a gap in between and supporting posts every twelve feet. Afridi's reflexes made him swerve toward the fence. Throwing himself out of the wheelchair, he lunged for the upper pipe and swung himself clear of the vehicle, between the pipes and down the steep hillside. The SUV collided with the chair just as Afridi tumbled down the slope, crashing through a tangle of barberry bushes and sliding thirty meters until he came to a stop against an oak. By this time, he had been able to rotate his body so that he was facing upward, the pistol ready in his hand.

Above him, he could just make out the side windows and roof of the SUV, which had stopped after hitting his chair. The driver side window opened and a man looked out. It was impossible to get a clear view of his face. Afridi resisted the urge to fire, though his finger tightened on the trigger just as the Scorpio drove off with a shriek of tires. Lowering his gun and searching through his pockets, Afridi found his cell phone and called the head of security at HRI. By the time the guards arrived, he had hauled himself back up to the road, clutching at roots and rocks. Aside from a few scrapes and scratches from barberry thorns, he wasn't hurt, though the wheelchair had been mangled beyond repair.

Thirty-Two

For several minutes Luke stood in the bathroom staring at his reflection in the mirror. He looked a wreck, which was understandable after everything he'd been through, but part of his mind refused to accept that he was actually here. He kept expecting the figure in the mirror to disappear like the image projected on the cistern wall. His room was like a luxurious hotel suite, with a king-size bed. Everything in the house seemed to have been made in the USA, from the Ralph Lauren towels and American Standard porcelain fittings to the bar of Dove soap by the sink.

The hot shower, which stung the gash on his hand and other injuries he hadn't noticed until now, helped convince him that he was alive and conscious. A fresh set of clothes had been laid out on the bed, a kameez and salwar that were almost the right size, along with a pair of Peshawari chappals. Jehangir Daruwalla had told him to wash up then join him in the dining room for lunch. Luke was hungry but he still felt dazed after riding blindfolded, a lingering nausea from the winding roads.

Pushing open the bedroom door, he stepped into the hall. Nobody was in sight, though Luke felt sure the armed guards were close at hand. As he entered the living room, Daruwalla got up from the sofa.

'How do you feel?' he asked. 'Any better now?'

Luke nodded and tried to smile.

'Please come and have a seat. The cook is going to put lunch on in a minute, but would you like something to drink, a beer?'

Luke nodded, still disoriented. A servant had appeared in the doorway, and Jehangir told him to bring a Heineken, which arrived a minute after Luke sat down.

'Where are we?' Luke asked.

'About twenty kilometers northwest of Jamrud,' said Daruwalla. 'In the Khyber Agency, just off the main road to Landi Kotal.'

'And why am I here?'

Jehangir laughed. 'Don't worry, everything will be explained to you shortly.'

Luke picked up the glass of beer and drank two-thirds of it, the cold liquid flowing down his throat as if he'd swallowed an icicle. He tasted the bittersweet flavor only after putting down his glass.

'Is this your house?' he asked.

'No, unfortunately not,' said Jehangir. 'Like you, I'm only a guest.'

'Whose is it?'

'I'm sure you'll meet our host soon enough.'

'Mr Daruwalla,' said Luke, irritated by the evasive answers. 'Let's cut the bullshit.... For the past week and a half, I've been kept prisoner in an empty water tank with nothing but a torn blanket and one meal a day. Now suddenly, I feel like I'm in a hotel in Beverly Hills. I need to know what's going on.'

'Sorry,' said Jehangir, with an apologetic nod. 'You've been through a lot. I'm sure it was traumatic.'

Luke swallowed the rest of his beer as the servant appeared and gestured toward the table, which was now laden with food. A large platter of pullao, garnished with nuts and raisins, lay next to a dish of mutton curry, a plate full of grilled chicken, salads, and yoghurt. The smell of the food was impossible to resist.

They served themselves in silence, and Luke took a couple of mouthfuls before he spoke.

'Don't get me wrong. This is a whole lot better than where I've been,' he said. 'But I want to know how I got here. And why?'

Jehangir helped himself to the mutton curry as he spoke.

'The men who were holding you captive are members of a militia that operates in the borderlands of northern Afghanistan. They call themselves the Martyrs of Amu Darya, and they've been allied to certain factions of the Tehrik-e-Taliban in Pakistan. When our host heard that you'd been taken hostage and they were demanding a ransom, he negotiated with them. I'm not sure what he paid in the end, but he bought them off and they delivered you here.' Jehangir spoke quietly, as if he were taking Luke into confidence.

The chicken was perfectly cooked, with a marinade that penetrated the meat and made it so moist that Luke barely had to chew the tender flesh, as it separated from the bones.

'Why would he have done that?'

'Honestly, I don't know,' said Jehangir. 'But I'm sure he feels that he can use you in some way. He certainly didn't do it out of pity.'

'And why are you here?' Luke asked, tasting the saffron in the rice.

Jehangir laughed, as he sucked marrow from a lamb shank.

'I'm not sure I'm of any use to anyone anywhere at the moment.'

'Daruwalla is a Parsi name,' said Luke. 'Are you Pakistani or Indian?'

'Neither,' said Jehangir, wiping his fingers on a napkin. 'I'm a British subject, though I was born in Bombay.'

'You're a long way from home, wherever it is,' said Luke.

'Indeed.'

They ate in silence for a while, and Luke was aware how quiet it was in the house. Nothing made a sound, except for their forks and spoons.

'So, how long have you been here?' he asked.

'About a week,' Jehangir replied.

'And do we get to use a phone or email?'

'No. I'm afraid not.'

Luke nodded. 'Does anyone outside this house know that we're here?'

Jehangir shook his head.

'And the person who owns this place, where is he?'

'I really don't know. He comes and goes.'

As Luke tried to process everything he'd learned, as well as the things he knew he hadn't been told, he realized there was no less danger here than in the mountains, though the food and accommodation were certainly better. He pushed his plate aside as a sudden sense of anxiety gripped him. The servant entered on silent feet and removed their plates without a word. When he returned, he was carrying another bowl and two plates.

'Dessert?' said Daruwalla. 'The cook makes an excellent firni.'

Though the fear had dampened Luke's appetite, he helped himself to a couple of spoonfuls of rice pudding.

'Is there any way to get out of here?' Luke asked.

'I wouldn't try if I were you,' said Jehangir. 'This compound is a fortress, guarded on all sides with the latest security equipment. It would be easier to escape from Guantanamo Bay. I suggest you get accustomed to being here and enjoy the generous hospitality for what it is.'

Thirty-Three

The memorial service and funeral for Roger Fleischmann was held on Tuesday morning. Anna could hear the governor of Ohio's helicopter arriving on the college green at exactly 10:00 a.m. From the window of her room, she watched a procession of cars approach the chapel and listened as the bells tolled melancholy chimes. She had decided to stay indoors, to avoid drawing attention to herself or meeting Tracy Holman again. The service was broadcast on TV. It was strange to see the buildings of Bromfield College and the town of Eggleston on the screen, as if she wasn't really here and it was all happening somewhere far away. Suddenly, this quiet corner of Ohio was the center of attention. One of the spectators at the parade had filmed a twenty-second video of the fighter jet going down. They kept playing the clip on TV, between reports of the governor's visit. Anna could remember exactly how the plane had wavered and twisted to one side before it went down. She knew that Afridi and Manav would be watching the same broadcasts, wondering where she was.

By now, more and more of the television channels were suggesting that the accident might actually have been a terrorist attack, though there was virtually no evidence to support this theory. Several commentators pointed out the way the Warhawk had veered suddenly, speculating that maybe someone had fired a missile at the plane. The news stories seemed absurd to Anna, but the frenzy of voices on TV grew louder and the film clip was repeatedly shown in slow motion.

In his eulogy, the governor extolled Fleischmann's vision of America, 'a secure and prosperous homeland that defends our nation's values both within our borders and abroad.' By that evening, reporters in Afghanistan had picked up the story and were interviewing American servicemen and women stationed there, who spoke about the strike capabilities of Peregrine drones and how these weapons gave them a significant edge over guerrilla fighters. Even as Roger Fleischmann's burnt and mangled body was being lowered into the fertile soil of Ohio, the drone attacks continued. CNN reported that two Taliban commanders in the Mohmand agency had been killed and there were hints of retaliation. As night fell over Eggleston, the sun was just coming up in the Hindu Kush. Anna watched scenes from a village where the drones had destroyed several mud houses and a building identified as a 'madrassa,' where Taliban terrorists were supposedly trained.

Falling asleep to the late night news and talk shows, Anna kept thinking of Agent Holman and her questions. America no longer seemed a safe and civilized country, despite its cultivated lawns and rolling farmland. She could hear the anxiety and anger in the voices on TV and finally turned the volume off. This war had nothing to do with Roman gladiators or vintage fighter planes. It took place in a different kind of arena, the adversarial medium of images and words. As she fell asleep, Anna dreamt of the parade, a combination of memories and TV clips that blurred together in a weird hallucination. She could see Afridi in his wheelchair, with a laurel wreath on his head, leading the marching band, and Manav Shinde riding in a Cadillac, but the face that haunted her most was a man she didn't recognize, though she knew it must be Guldaar.

By the next morning, most of the dream had been erased, leaving only a fragmentary sense of unease. Anna reluctantly turned on the TV for a few minutes to get the headlines. Nothing had changed, though there were other stories now, besides Fleischmann's death. Debating when it would be safe to go out, Anna ate breakfast in her room, spooning granola out of a mug and finishing off the last two bananas she'd bought.

At 9:30, the doorbell rang. Looking through the peephole, she saw a young man wearing a Cleveland Indians tee-shirt and baseball cap. She opened the door cautiously, not sure what to expect.

'Are you Sheetal?' he asked. She nodded.

'There's a note for you. A woman at the library asked me to give you this.'

'Thanks. Are you a student here?' Anna asked, taking the note.

'Yeah,' he said, turning away without looking her in the eye. 'Work-study.'

The note was in a sealed envelope with her name written on the front in a woman's hand. When she tore it open, there was only one scribbled line: *Come to Level B Visitor Parking next to the library.*

Collecting her backpack and switching off the lights in her room, Anna decided to take the stairs instead of the elevator. Her guestroom in Judson Hall was a five-minute walk from the library, and she went directly to the parking garage. When she reached Level B, the headlights on a car flashed briefly.

'Get into the backseat and lie down,' Daphne said, through the window.

'Are you sure this is a good idea?' Anna said.

'Yes, hurry. Keep your head low, so nobody can see you.'

'Where are we going?' Anna asked, as she reluctantly got into the car.

'Home,' said Daphne, starting the engine and pulling out of the parking slot before Anna had got herself settled.

The drive took less than three minutes. Anna could hear the garage door opening, as Daphne pulled into her driveway. Only when the door shut behind them, did she raise her head.

'I'm sorry about that,' said Daphne. 'But I was being followed. A red pickup. I've seen it before. Everything's been so crazy these last few days.'

She seemed flustered and anxious. A narrow staircase from the garage led up to her kitchen. Venetian blinds on the street side of the house had been lowered, so that nobody could look in. The kitchen smelled of coffee and the citrus scent of dishwashing liquid.

'Are you okay?' Anna asked, as Daphne stood by the sink for a moment, catching her breath and clutching the kitchen counter.

'I don't know,' she said. 'I really don't know.'

When she turned to look up, her eyes were full of tears.

Going across to her, Anna put out a hand, unsure of what to do as Daphne broke down. Drawing her close, she held the older woman for several minutes, feeling her shaking in her arms as she wept. After a while, Daphne broke free, took tissues from a box on the kitchen counter and dried her eyes.

'I'm sorry,' she said, collecting herself. Though Daphne's eyes were red from crying, Anna could see that she had recovered her composure. Her mouth was set in a determined frown.

'What happened?' Anna asked.

'Naseem died last night. On Friday, I signed the papers to take him off life support. For a long time, I'd been thinking of doing it, but I finally made up my mind. He won't suffer any more. We had the burial this morning.'

Her voice quavered with emotion, but Anna could see she was steeling herself.

'As soon as Jimmy finds out what I've done, someone will be at this door,' she said. 'We need to get out of here right away.'

'Are you sure?' Anna asked.

'Yes,' said Daphne. 'I need your help.'

Anna hesitated. 'I've been given orders not to involve myself in any illegal or covert activities. I can't break the law.'

Daphne shook her head. 'Colonel Afridi promised that he would protect me. You need to get me to India.'

Anna could hear Manav's warning echoing in her mind, but she could also see the desperation in Daphne's eyes.

'There's a lot of security around with the crash and Roger Fleischmann's death, as well as the governor's visit. I was questioned by a woman who was watching your house, the one in the Lexus. She claims she's from the NSA. I don't know if they've made the connection between us or not, but I'm worried they might come after you.'

'I don't care,' said Daphne looking as if she were going to break down again. 'I'm just afraid of what Jimmy will do. You've got to get me out of here!'

Daphne's voice was muted with a suppressed sense of terror.

'I'll do my best,' Anna said, knowing that Afridi would expect this of her. 'But I'll have to go back to my room and collect my things.'

'I'm already packed. My suitcase is in the trunk of the car. I've also got eight thousand dollars in cash, a present from Jimmy. He told me to buy myself whatever I wanted.'

'Okay. Let's go.'

'Wait,' Daphne said. 'I've also got something for you.'

As she spoke, she opened a drawer in the kitchen and took out a Beretta 92A1 with an extra clip of ammunition.

'You know how to use this, I hope,' she said.

Anna took the handgun and nodded, slipping it into the outer pocket of her backpack.

Thirty-Four

Afridi was applying disinfectant to a scratch on the side of his face when Manav Shinde called him. The injury looked worse than it was but made it difficult for him to shave. Glancing down at the buzzing cell phone beside the sink, he saw Shinde's private number.

'Afridi Sahib, how are you?' Manav said, with his usual blend of bluster and bonhomie. 'I was sorry to hear what happened. Very sorry! I hope you weren't badly hurt.'

'I'm all right, thank you. Nothing serious,' Afridi replied. 'If the traffic in Mussoorie is getting so dangerous, maybe you should think of moving back to Dilli,' Manav continued. 'Has anyone been able to trace the vehicle?'

'No,' said Afridi. 'I wasn't able to read the license number. The police say they couldn't track the Scorpio, though they informed all of the checkposts on the roads out of town. I suspect some constable is richer by a few thousand rupees.'

Manav made a sound of disapproval. 'Disgraceful,' he said. 'Do you have any idea who it might have been?'

'There are plenty of people who would like to see me dead,' Afridi answered. 'Who knows which of them it is?'

'I'm sending two of my men up to Mussoorie to investigate,' Manav said.

'Don't bother,' Afridi replied.

'No, we have to take this seriously. I'm going to speak with the defense secretary. You need proper security up there…not your fauji chowkidars.'

'Our security is perfectly adequate,' Afridi insisted. 'And I certainly don't want your black cat commandoes prowling around. The last thing we want to do is draw attention to ourselves.'

'Let's see what the secretary says,' Manav replied, then he paused before continuing. 'On another matter, there's someone I'd like you to meet. He's on his way up to Mussoorie as we speak, along with two of my inspectors. They should reach there by three in the afternoon. Would you mind giving him a cup of tea at your house and having a discreet chat?'

'Who is he?' Afridi turned away from the bathroom mirror. With his free hand, he wheeled himself into the other room. Dr Gopinath had provided a spare wheelchair to replace the one that was destroyed.

'He goes by the name of Harsh Advani, a security analyst…'

'Manav, I told you, I don't need anyone to assess our security up here, and why would he come to my house?' The irritation in Afridi's voice was clearly audible. 'Why not send him to my office?'

There was a pause on the other end of the line, and immediately Afridi knew that Shinde was covering up and didn't want to explain too much. The fact that he was using his private line added to his suspicions.

'Just meet him, please,' said Manav. 'He'll explain everything.… And for my sake, Imtiaz, please don't lose your temper until you've heard him out.'

~

The business card gave nothing away:

HARSH ADVANI
TOTAL SECURITY SERVICES
245 TILAK ROAD, PUNE
9832765123 h.advani@tss.net

Afridi set the card on the coffee table, next to a book of photographs by Cartier Bresson he had been looking at the evening before. Without speaking, he poured a splash of milk into his guest's cup before serving the tea.

'How much sugar do you take?' he asked.

The man across from him was observing every move with a watchful eye.

'Sir, three cubes, please,' he said.

Afridi was doing the best he could to hide his annoyance. Performing the gestures of hospitality, he offered his visitor a plate of sweets, which one of the HRI technicians had sent across to celebrate the birth of a daughter.

'Try one of these. It's bal mithai, a local specialty.'

'Thank you, sir.' The man was in his early forties, with gentle features and thinning hair that made him look like a junior lecturer in management. Perhaps that was what security analysts did these days, assess the risks and calculate variables, reducing everything to algorithms and spreadsheets. Afridi was sure all of the details on the business card were false.

'So, tell me, Advaniji,' Afridi said. 'I'm curious. You've come all the way here to meet me. Mr Shinde insisted that it was important, but he wouldn't explain any further.'

The man held his teacup steady, as if he had been well schooled in simple etiquette.

'Thank you for seeing me, sir,' he began, with formality, carefully placing the cup and saucer on the table. 'I've always been a great admirer of yours, and I've read most of the papers you've written, especially your most recent assessment of the Kashmir situation in the *Journal of Security Studies*. It is an honor to meet you, and I'm grateful that you've taken the time out of a busy schedule, particularly after—'

'What exactly does your company do?' Afridi cut him short, setting his cup on the table and picking up the card with irritation.

'Actually, that's irrelevant.'

Afridi bristled, leaning forward in his chair and brushing his fingers over the bandage on his right hand. 'What do you mean?'

'Sir, I'm not Harsh Adva—'

'I guessed as much.'

'Major Yaqub Hussein. ISI. I've been operating undercover in Delhi for the past six months. The Pakistan embassy doesn't even know I'm in India.'

For a moment Afridi's face froze with a look of disbelief that slowly resolved itself into anger. He didn't know whether to shoot the man in front of him or Manav Shinde for sending him here. Reaching under his tweed jacket he took out his pistol for the second time in less than twenty-four hours.

'And what the hell are you doing here?' Afridi said.

Yaqub Hussein smiled weakly, though his eyes seemed to harden.

'I'll explain.'

'Yes, you will,' said Afridi. 'And if you move at all, there will be a bullet in your chest. Are you the ones who tried to kill me yesterday?'

'No,' said the major. 'Those must have been contract killers working for someone else.'

'Does Shinde know who you are?' Afridi's mind was racing, trying to comprehend the situation. If anyone in Delhi learned that he was serving tea and sweets to a Pakistani agent, it would compromise everything

'Yes, I introduced myself to him, just as I've done with you—'

'And why didn't he have you locked up or deported?' Afridi demanded.

'Because, for once, perhaps, we have an issue of mutual concern,' said Major Yaqub. 'A problem we might solve together.'

'I don't think that's possible.'

'Sir, everything I said earlier about my admiration for you

is completely true. You may not believe this, but at the Centre for Strategic Studies in Islamabad they teach a course on counterintelligence, and we studied several of your cases.'

'I don't care what you've studied,' said Afridi. 'I want to know why you're here.'

'Please, I will tell you everything, I promise,' said the Major. 'But I want you to understand that I'm not here as your enemy. When I was a cadet in the academy, one of my instructors suggested that Colonel Imtiaz Afridi had to prove himself to be an exceptionally patriotic Indian, more dedicated to the nation than any of his colleagues, because he was a Muslim. I argued with him, sir, saying that belief in one's country is an absolute choice. Our decision to defend our nation has nothing to do with our religion.'

'What did your instructor tell you?' Afridi's voice escaped between clenched teeth.

'He laughed and called me a naive fool,' said Yaqub Hussein.

Afridi kept the pistol raised though the tension in his shoulders eased.

'I would have done the same,' he said. 'Now, tell me why you're here. Quickly.'

'Because I believe you are interested in a man known as Guldaar,' said the major. 'So are we. He has close links with the ISI, but also with the Americans. There are some of us who feel he enjoys too much influence in our country.'

'Explain,' said Afridi.

'Sir, I want to assure you that I'm not here on a fool's errand, or lying to you.' Major Yaqub moved his hands for the first time since Afridi had produced the gun, reaching across to pick up his tea. 'May I?' he asked.

Afridi realized that he was dealing with a professional, someone who understood the gestures of trust, even in the most desperate circumstances.

'Last week, you released a man named Jehangir Daruwalla and allowed him to leave the country. He caught an Emirates flight out of Delhi to London. Unfortunately for him, the flight stopped over in Dubai, where he disappeared from the transit lounge. We have a confirmed report that Daruwalla was taken into custody by immigration authorities in Dubai and handed over to Guldaar's men, who flew him to Kabul, from where he was brought to a safe house in the Khyber Agency. We expect Guldaar to visit the safe house within the next two days.'

'Then why can't you just go in and arrest him when he shows up?' Afridi said.

'With all due respect, I believe you know the answer to that, sir, better than I,' said Yaqub. 'The Khyber Agency is part of Pakistan, but those who live in that region operate outside the laws of our land. They are supported by certain members of our government and military, including the ISI, who believe that feudal anarchy in the border regions serves our national interests. Not all of us agree. We do not want foreigners operating with impunity inside the borders of Pakistan, whether they are Arabs, Americans, or anyone else.

'Guldaar is protected by a complex but unshakeable scaffolding of connections with men in power around the globe. All of them owe him something, or hope to gain from him. He plays them off each other whenever he chooses. Even here in India, I'm sure you're aware that he has ties that reach very close to the top, in politics and in the military, as well as the corporate sector. The Americans have set up a special desk at Langley to support and protect him—Project Keystone. He is virtually untouchable, immune to any investigation. In Pakistan we dare not question his influence. There are men in the ISI who would start a war for him.'

Afridi listened to Yaqub without interrupting. Whether this man was telling the truth or not was hard to guess, but the integrity in his voice was convincing, as well as the facts he revealed.

'Who sent you here?' Afridi asked.

Yaqub smiled. 'I was expecting you to ask me. Unfortunately, that's the one question I cannot answer.'

'Why not?'

'Because if his identity is revealed, or even hinted at, our colleagues in the ISI would have him executed immediately, provided Guldaar doesn't kill him first. I can only tell you that he is a senior brigadier who shares my sense of loyalty to Pakistan.'

'But you are betraying your country, aren't you, coming here like this?'

'As I told Mr Shinde, my mission is very clear, no matter what means or methods I must use. A group of us in the ISI have decided to destroy Guldaar and those who support him. More than likely it will be impossible for me to go back to Pakistan, even if we succeed. Right now, nobody suspects what we are trying to do, but as you saw yesterday, Guldaar has people everywhere.'

Afridi finally lowered the pistol, though he kept his finger on the trigger.

'Either you're very brave or very foolish,' Afridi said. 'So, you want to work for us?'

'No, sir. I'm not a double agent. My loyalty is to Pakistan, not India. But I will work *with* you,' said Yaqub. 'I believe in my country as strongly as you do in yours. Guldaar has helped turn Pakistan into a corrupt and violent state where nobody feels safe. Only a few of us believe that we can destroy this evil, the cynicism and fear that rots our nation to the core.'

Afridi recited in Urdu under his breath: '*Once I had a two-edged sword. It turned into the chains that shackle me now.*'

The line was from Mohammad Iqbal's famous 'Mu'tamid's Lament in Prison.'

Yaqub replied with the concluding verse: '*How whimsical and indifferent is the author of our fates.*'

Afridi nodded in appreciation.

'Major Yaqub,' he said, 'you weren't by any chance at the Royal Bombay Yacht Club a week ago?'

The man in front of him no longer had the demeanor of a management specialist and now seemed capable of violence.

'Why do you ask?'

'A Bosnian arms broker was found dead in the lift.'

Major Yaqub showed no reaction but spoke in a quiet, controlled voice, 'I was the one who cut his throat. He was too clever for his own good.'

Afridi nodded. 'I thought as much.'

Thirty-Five

According to the GPS unit, the distance from Eggleston to JFK Airport was 548 miles. Approximate travel time worked out to eight hours and forty-five minutes. The route was relatively simple, 71 North toward Cleveland, then across to Akron on 76, joining up with Route 80 as soon as they crossed the state line, after which it was a straight shot across Pennsylvania to New York City. On the map display it looked straightforward.

Before packing her suitcase and leaving the guestroom, which took less than fifteen minutes, Anna sent Afridi a brief message through an encrypted email, explaining that she was helping Daphne leave the US. She also checked on the Air India flight they hoped to catch, nonstop from New York to Delhi. According to the airline's website, plenty of seats were available. They would purchase their tickets immediately before check-in to avoid raising alarms. Anna had also switched on an emergency tracking device concealed in her backpack. Though she had her cell phone, she would use it only in an extreme emergency, for fear the Americans might be listening in. As an audio surveillance expert, Anna knew that the sole means of avoiding eavesdropping was not to have any conversations at all. She didn't inform Shinde about what was going on because he would certainly disapprove. More importantly, if he was aware that Anna was assisting Daphne to escape, it would be difficult for him to deny any knowledge later on, should it become a diplomatic or political issue. In any case, Anna realized that her job was on the line.

As they drove away from the college campus, Daphne seemed more anxious than before, convinced that they were being followed. When they stopped to fill up gas at a Sunoco station, Anna offered to drive.

'Thank you,' said Daphne. 'I'd feel a lot better if you did.'

The car was a 2006 Ford Taurus sedan with only 25,000 miles on it. Anna adjusted the seat and started off slowly, getting a feel for the car. She wasn't used to driving an automatic or being on the righthand side of the road. The Ford felt sluggish, though it had plenty of power. Two blocks from the gas station, she caught sight of a red pickup behind her. Guided by the GPS and Daphne's instructions, they made their way out of town, along a two-lane road over rolling farmland. The interstate was eight miles on ahead.

Behind them, the red truck followed close enough for Anna to see two men in the cabin. She slowed down to five miles below the speed limit, but the distance between the two vehicles didn't change. Nobody else was behind them, and only a couple of cars were coming from the opposite direction. As she crested a low hill, the road flattened out and the double yellow lines down the middle gave way to a passing zone. Anna was relieved when she saw the truck move over into the left lane. As they went by, the men didn't look at her and she told herself it was all Daphne's imagination. The truck continued to pick up speed until it was almost fifty yards ahead, when it suddenly braked. Anna could see the rear end of the pickup skidding sideways. She had just enough time to stamp on the brakes. The Taurus began to fishtail.

'Hold on,' Anna said.

The next thirty seconds went by in a blur, as if time had stretched like a rubber band and then snapped back upon itself. Both vehicles appeared to be out of control, but the driver of the truck knew what he was doing, spinning 360 degrees and then coming to a stop broadside, blocking the road. Anna wished she had a gearshift, which would have made things easier. Calculating the distance, she let the Taurus swing around, as if it were going to crash into the pickup. At the last moment, she accelerated out of the skid and was able to gain traction on the unpaved shoulder of the road, just missing the tailgate of the truck. Once she was past them, her right foot pressed the accelerator to the floor and she could hear the tires screaming.

The men in the pickup hadn't expected a trained driver, especially not one who had received a commendation for topping her class at the Israeli Defense Forces Training School in Haifa. They took another thirty seconds to get turned around. By then, Anna was almost a mile ahead. As soon as they passed over the next hill, she spotted a crossing in front of them.

'Do you know where that road goes?' Anna asked. 'No idea,' said Daphne.

The choice was to try to reach the interstate, where it would be harder for the pickup to stop them because there would be more traffic, or attempt to escape along country roads.

'Did you recognize either of those men?' Anna asked.

Daphne shook her head. 'I hardly saw them.'

'Who do you think they work for?' said Anna. 'Peregrine?'

'Probably,' said Daphne. 'They have a whole security operation, with undercover agents guarding the plant.'

Letting her instincts guide her, Anna took a right turn at the intersection, ignoring the GPS. Ahead lay a patch of forest, which might have hidden them from view, but before they reached it, she saw the truck appear again and she knew they would spot the Taurus.

Less than a minute later, the road took a gradual turn to the left toward a bridge across a small river. Up ahead was a state park, with a sign for canoe rides and tubing. A dozen cars stood in the main parking lot. Farther on was a second lot with a picnic area. Anna pulled in behind a lilac hedge that was just coming into bloom. If they were lucky the men in the pickup wouldn't see them and drive on.

A few seconds later, she heard the roar of the pickup as it crossed the bridge. The vehicle seemed to slow down but Anna didn't have a clear view of the road. A minute went by and then another. Anna kept looking at her watch. If the pickup didn't appear in three more minutes, they would get back on the road, reverse direction, and head for the interstate. She waited four minutes, just to be safe. Before starting the engine, Anna reached into her backpack and took out the Beretta, checking to make sure it was loaded.

Slowly, she pulled forward. A family was getting into a canoe on the river, the children wearing life vests. Another group was splashing about in the shallow water as they got ready to float downstream on inner tubes. There was no sign of the truck as Anna headed for the exit.

'Where are they?' Daphne asked.

'I think we've lost them,' Anna replied.

Seconds later, she heard an engine start and the pickup pulled out from behind a line of vending machines. It edged forward, parallel to them and fifty feet away. Anna stopped. For several moments, nothing seemed to move, except her right hand as she raised the pistol. Rolling down her window, she took aim and fired twice.

The sound of tires exploding was louder than the gunshots.

'Stay down,' Anna shouted, as she accelerated past the truck and headed out onto the road. The driver of the pickup tried to follow, but his vehicle lurched forward on flat tires.

'They're tracking us. It could be this,' Anna said, reaching for the GPS unit and tossing it out of her window, as they hurtled along the country road, heading back the way they'd come, toward the interstate.

For a couple of miles nothing happened, and it seemed as if

they were clear. The country roads and barns had a picturesque simplicity. Ahead of them, Anna saw an Amish horse and buggy, rolling along the road, as if it were a century ago. Without slowing down, she swung wide to pass the black carriage, which was driven by an elderly man with a white beard and in a black hat. He looked up at them with an indifferent expression, as if he had no interest in going faster than ten miles an hour. There was nothing for him to escape.

As soon as Anna moved back into her lane after passing the buggy, she was aware of a shadow on the fields to her left, keeping pace with the car. At first she didn't know what it was, but then she understood. Lowering her window, she put her head out in the rush of air and glanced overhead. Silhouetted against the blue sky was a small surveillance drone, about the size of a skateboard with wings, flying directly above them.

Thirty-Six

The Urs of Kanra Pir drew pilgrims from across North India, most of whom prayed at his tomb for the restoration of injured limbs. Some had suffered strokes that paralyzed an arm or a leg, and others were victims of accidents, war wounds, or birth defects. Each of them harbored the fervent hope of becoming whole again. Islamic charities organized free kitchens, feeding the destitute in a park near the tomb, which attracted a number of street dwellers as well as the poorer pilgrims. A detachment of Delhi Police stood by as the line of supplicants queued up at the tomb to pray and light incense at the dargah, invoking the saint's name and receiving his posthumous blessings. These celebrations went off peacefully, and the police blotter for the day recorded, 'no untoward incidents.' Only a few local 'mischief makers' were rounded up ahead of time to ensure that nothing got out of hand.

In the newspapers, however, there was a story about a narcotics raid at a guesthouse in Lajpat Nagar, where some of the pilgrims from Afghanistan were staying. Thirty-five kilos of high-grade heroin was seized from a gang of drug smugglers, three of whom were arrested. Street value of the heroin was estimated at 200 crore rupees, approximately 50 million dollars. Photographs appeared in some of the papers, showing the narcotics team posing with plastic bags full of heroin and the artificial limbs in which they were hidden. Though it was the largest heroin haul in years, the story was pushed back to the inner pages of most of the papers, on account of the engagement of an industrialist's daughter to an up-and-coming Bollywood hero, which captured front page headlines.

Afridi was relieved that the narcotics raid had gone smoothly and didn't draw too much media attention. The gang members who had been arrested were minor figures, but the investors financing the smuggling would certainly feel the loss. Most important, from Afridi's perspective, Guldaar's key contacts were likely to react and that would provide confirmation on his network in the capital. According to information he had gleaned from Jehangir Daruwalla, there were three key individuals who worked for Guldaar, and Afridi had them each put under surveillance. One was a retired brigadier who worked as a consultant for foreign arms companies. He was already under investigation by the CBI in a disproportionate assets case. The second was a real estate baron, who had made a fortune buying agricultural land in Haryana, which was then converted to commercial use and sold at fifty times its original value. The third person was a well-known socialite in Delhi, cousin of a former chief minister from Rajasthan, who was often seen at polo matches and celebrity book launches. Afridi was curious to see how each of them reacted to the raid.

He didn't have to wait long. By ten o'clock that morning, the supervisor of the surveillance team gave him a call. The brigadier and the socialite had arrived at the India International Centre within five minutes of each other. They were now having coffee in the main dining room on the first floor. Both appeared agitated, and their conversation seemed heated, though it was impossible to monitor what they said because of the noise level from surrounding tables.

Afridi could easily imagine the situation. Though a life member of the IIC, he found the place pretentious, full of garrulous intellectuals who seemed to have nothing better to do than sit around and discuss the collective woes of their country.

He avoided the dining hall as much as possible because of the decibel level, though he occasionally attended talks at the center, most recently a lecture on the political situation in Arunachal Pradesh.

Ordering the team to maintain discreet surveillance, he told the supervisor to report back at 19:00 hours with an update. In the meantime, Afridi instructed his analysts at HRI to screen any cell phone calls or SMS transmissions using software that identified encrypted messages. The program ignored ordinary phone calls and text messages but would identify anything unusual that might contain a coded reference to the heroin seizure. On top of this, a high priority watchlist was sent to every airport in the country with instructions to keep an eye out for specific individuals who might be trying to leave the country. The list had been compiled in consultation with two of Shinde's analysts and Interpol's narcotics specialists in Delhi. Though Afridi didn't hold out much hope of catching anyone significant, it was necessary to cast the net as wide as possible.

Meanwhile, a handler had relayed a message from Major Yaqub that Guldaar was at his home in the Khyber Agency after arriving on a private flight from the Gulf. Yaqub probably realized that he needed to establish his credibility. Afridi remained distrustful of him, and he had put one of his analysts on the job of researching his career and compiling a dossier on his past. It turned out that he had passed out of the military academy in Abbottabad at the top of his batch and had been presented with a ceremonial sabre. His father had been a paratrooper and rose to the rank of lieutenant colonel. The son had been expected to join the same regiment, but according to a classified report there was a note in his file that indicated he was 'too bright to jump out of airplanes,' and had been picked as an ISI prospect. Yaqub impressed his superiors but exhibited an independent streak and had written a report that was critical of the Kargil debacle.

This had not gone down well with the top brass and he had been passed over for promotion, though he seemed to remain a loyal officer with a fierce commitment to his country.

According to his handler, Yaqub had rented a barsati apartment in Nizamuddin and continued to maintain his cover as a security analyst. As a further test of his integrity, Afridi had sent word to Yaqub that he wanted to confirm the identity of Guldaar's associates in Delhi. Within six hours, he sent the names, which tallied with Jehangir Daruwalla's information. After a phone call from Afridi to Shinde, the three of them were taken into custody. The brigadier was picked up from his office in Hauz Khaz, and the developer was arrested as he was trying to board a plane for Singapore. It took a little longer to locate the socialite, but she was eventually traced to a hotel suite in the Taj Mansingh, which she was sharing with a young polo player from the royal family of Jaisalmer. All three were placed under arrest at the safe house on Aurangzeb Lane, which served as a lockup whenever discreet detainments were required. It would take a few days for their lawyers to intervene. By then, Afridi suspected that they would agree to betray Guldaar in exchange for some level of immunity.

Thirty-Seven

Luke held the shotgun in his hands, admiring the ornate engraving and the blue luster of the steel barrels side-by-side, as well as the subtle grain of the walnut stock. The trigger guard and safety catch were made with functional precision yet, they also reflected aesthetic design. The gun seemed more like a work of art than a lethal weapon.

The man who had handed him the shotgun held another, identical weapon in his hands.

'Can you tell me which one is genuine?' Guldaar inquired, exchanging weapons with Luke, who weighed the second gun in his hands and pressed the lever to open the breach. The mechanism was smooth, and the catch released with a decisive click. Holding the barrels up to the sky, Luke could see two parallel tunnels of polished steel tapering toward the muzzle.

'One of these was made by James Purdey and Sons in 1912. The other is a copy produced last year, fifteen miles from here in Dara, by a local gunsmith named Abdul Haq. You've been to Dara, I'm sure?'

Luke nodded. He had passed through the village dozens of times on his way to Kohat and other tribal agencies to the south. In the mud huts nearby were crude workshops, where village gunsmiths produced everything from Uzis to RPGs. These homemade weapons were on sale at a roadside bazaar. Most customers lived in the tribal areas where the guns were legal. But the quality of the workmanship was far less refined than this shotgun—cheap knockoffs of AK-47s or Smith & Wesson .32s. The gun in his hands, and its perfectly matched pair, were clearly the handiwork of master artisans.

'I don't know much about shotguns,' said Luke, 'but they look identical.'

'Watch this,' said Guldaar, gesturing to one of his guards who had accompanied them to a low hill beyond the house, outside the limits of the garden. The guard loaded the gun and handed it to Guldaar who took his stance, then called out, 'Khol!'

Where the hill fell away into a shallow depression stood a concrete structure, barely visible and well camouflaged in the dusty soil. From out of this bunker, a pair of chukar partridges erupted in a flurry of wings. With the shotgun wedged comfortably against his right shoulder, Guldaar fired twice, no more than a couple of seconds between each shot. Both birds fell to the ground in a spindrift of feathers.

At the sound of the gunshot, Luke heard dogs begin to bark. A minute later, he saw a pair of mastiffs bounding toward them. They were barrel chested and short-haired, with their tails and ears docked. Luke stood still as they sniffed his legs, sensing their suppressed aggression.

Guldaar had arrived sometime the night before. When Luke got up soon after dawn, his host had introduced himself, suggesting they take a walk around the estate before breakfast.

'Would you like to try?' Guldaar inquired, offering Luke the shotgun.

'No thanks. I'm sure I'll miss,' he said.

Handing both guns to the guards, Guldaar led Luke along a path to a nearby ridge on which a single stunted tree had taken root. The landscape was typical of this region, a harsh and barren beauty. The dogs followed them, tongues lolling out.

'Mr McKenzie, you're a writer, aren't you?' Guldaar asked, lighting another cigarette. His hair was combed back from a wrinkled brow. He was a healthy-looking man, approaching seventy, with the pale features of a Pathan and a prominent nose. But it was his eyes that caught Luke's attention, the pupils a dull shade of blue, almost gray, fastening his gaze with unblinking intensity.

'A journalist,' said Luke. 'I'm working on a book.'

'About NGOs in Pakistan. You've been researching the Sikandar-e-Azam Trust,' Guldaar said.

Luke had guessed there was a connection, but the openness with which Guldaar mentioned the trust surprised him.

'The book is about development work and disaster relief, mostly in Azad Kashmir and Chitral.'

Guldaar let the smoke trickle out from his lips as a precursor to his words. 'I've read a couple of your articles,' he said. 'Very perceptive. A Pakistani couldn't have written them, neither could a Westerner. You're somewhere in between.'

Luke made a noncommittal gesture with one hand, as if waving off a fly.

'My only complaint with your writing,' said Guldaar, 'is that you seem to believe in right and wrong. There's a strong ethical prejudice to your words…a judgmental voice that doesn't suit a journalist.'

'I've never believed in complete objectivity, if that's what you mean,' said Luke, surprised by Guldaar's tone. He sounded more like an editor than a warlord.

'I studied philosophy at Cambridge for a year,' said Guldaar, as if he'd read Luke's mind, 'before I was sent down for breaking my tutor's nose. University was a complete waste of time for me. But it allowed me read a lot and to develop my own views on morality.'

They had reached the far end of the ridge, from where Luke could see up a valley to a small settlement, half-hidden amid the hills.

'My village,' said Guldaar, pointing. 'The old railway line to

Landi Kotal runs to the west, and the main highway over the Khyber is a kilometer to the east. You might be interested that instead of a footpath, there used to be a six-foot-deep trench from the main road to our home. A necessary precaution, because you never knew when your neighbors might take a potshot at you.'

The dogs began barking at something on the opposite hill, though Luke couldn't tell what it was, until he saw a jackal slinking between the rocks. Looking back in the other direction, he could see the luxurious house and the high mud walls that enclosed Guldaar's estate.

'Was all of this your family property?' Luke asked.

Guldaar shook his head. 'I acquired this land a few years ago, and my American friends built the house for me. It's not exactly what I wanted but comfortable enough.'

'Do you stay here often?' Luke asked.

'No, it isn't particularly safe,' Guldaar said with a thoughtful smile. 'I'm sure you've heard about me, Mr McKenzie…May I call you Luke?'

'Sure.'

'If you were to judge me, just as you have judged others in your articles, you would probably suggest that my ethics are tainted, my values corrupt…perhaps you would even suggest that I'm evil.'

Luke said nothing, though Guldaar paused. The guards followed at a discreet distance, carrying the shotguns and their automatic weapons. For a moment, Luke felt as if he were on the set of a TV western, somewhere in the badlands of New Mexico or Arizona, held captive by a gang of desperadoes, the kind of villains he used to watch on television when he was a boy.

'Luke was one of the Christian apostles, wasn't he?' Guldaar asked.

'Yes. He's known as the evangelist, but I haven't lived up to my name,' said Luke.

'I'm not a religious man,' said Guldaar. 'Whatever faith I might have had in my youth was wrung out of me at Cambridge. I'm lucky they didn't convert me to Communism. But you see, I've never believed that human beings are inherently 'good' or 'evil.' Instead, I hold to the view that we, as a species, are interested in only one thing: survival. Human instincts are not colored by morality. We are simply driven to be stronger and more aggressive than others of our kind. Questions of right and wrong, good and evil, don't arise, except in the minds of idle, weak-hearted men who have nothing better to do than judge each other. Ethics have no meaning in a place like this, where the only path home is a trench that protects you from an enemy bullet.'

He paused a moment and surveyed the hills, which were now flooded with sunlight. From the direction of the house, Luke could see three men walking toward them. One he recognized as Jehangir Daruwalla.

'I know you don't agree,' said Guldaar with a shake of his head. 'Someone like you would say that what makes us human is the fact that we can choose between right and wrong, unlike a jackal or a hawk. You would probably argue that there is something called 'free will,' which gives us the ability and the license to make ethical decisions, independent of our natural instincts or the greater will of God.'

Snapping his finger, Guldaar called one of the dogs to his side, the larger male whose face and neck were badly scarred. He stroked the dog's head.

'But, frankly, we're no better than these animals,' he said. 'They are fighting mastiffs, bred to kill. If they see another dog, they have only one instinct—to rip its throat apart. Don't worry, they won't attack you, as long as I'm here. I got them when they were pups, from a breeder in Herat. At six months, we cut off their ears and tails so they wouldn't be ripped off in a fight. Then we fed these to the dogs. If they devour their own flesh, it's a sure sign of how ruthless they'll be when they mature. You should have seen these two, they ate their ears and tails in a couple of minutes, as if they were rawhide treats.'

He laughed when Luke made a face. Guldaar had stopped near the lone tree and glanced back to see the approaching men, who were only a hundred meters away. The dogs began to growl, but fell silent at a command from their master. He then gestured to the nearer guard and took a shotgun from his hands.

'This is the gun I fired,' he said, snapping open the breach. 'It is a perfect copy of the Purdey, exactly the same in every way, except for one small detail that I asked the gunsmith to add, so that I could tell them apart.'

He showed it to Luke, who could see where the ornamental arabesques in the engraving had been formed into a small but distinctly visible rosette with five petals, a flower etched in steel. Guldaar took two cartridges from his pocket and loaded the gun.

'Each of us is said to have been made in the image of God, which suggests that we contain trace elements of divine goodness in our blood. But I would argue that we are like one of these guns, or these dogs, merely copies of our ancestors. There is nothing inherently admirable or false about us. We are what we are… nothing more, nothing less.'

Jehangir Daruwalla arrived on the ridge and stopped to wipe his forehead.

'Good morning,' he called out with a wave of his hand.

Before he could say anything more, Guldaar emptied both barrels into his chest.

Deafened by the explosions, Luke watched in horror as the linen shirt and Jehangir's torso were shredded by the spray of lead pellets. The blast threw Daruwalla backward and spattered the dusty soil with his blood.

Thirty-Eight

When Anna slowed down, the UAV immediately reduced speed, its guidance systems locked in on their car. Pulling over, she stopped near a fenced pasture where a dozen horses were grazing. The drone hovered overhead like a red-tailed hawk. In addition to the engine that propelled it forward, it had two auxiliary rotors under each wing to keep it steady. Anna knew the drone was unarmed, but she could see the camera in a spherical pod at the front, like a single eye watching them from the air. The UAV was thirty feet above her, close enough for her to see a blinking red light at the base of the nose cone. Raising the Beretta quickly, Anna fired once. The bullet struck the drone somewhere near the tail. The gunshot sent the horses galloping across the pasture. By that time, Anna had accelerated down the road. The last she saw of the drone, in the rearview mirror, it was performing an awkward spiral far behind them.

Five minutes later, they reached the on-ramp to the interstate. No other drones were following. Daphne had a map of Ohio in the car, but it covered only the first few miles of their route. As soon as they crossed into Pennsylvania, Anna stopped at a rest area to get another map, which showed Route 80 cutting across the middle of the state, through sections of the Alleghany National Forest. It looked less populated than Ohio, with fewer towns.

Leaving the rest area, they weren't aware of being tailed, but after slowing down in a construction zone, Anna spotted two vehicles that seemed to be keeping pace with her. One was a gray Toyota and the other a yellow Buick. For a while, the Toyota stayed ahead and the Buick was behind her, but every three or four miles they switched places. When Anna overtook the Toyota, she could see the Buick change lanes and speed up. Both cars had tinted windows, so she couldn't see the drivers. Daphne seemed unaware that they were being followed.

Up ahead was an exit, with signs for food and fuel. Crossing under the highway was a narrow, two-lane road. Anna decided to test her instincts and switched on her turn signal. A few seconds later, she saw both cars signaling too. As they approached the exit, she slowed down and let the Buick turn off onto the exit ramp ahead of her. At the last minute, she put her foot on the gas and swerved back onto the highway. In her rearview mirror, she could see the Toyota swing back behind her. Off to her right, the Buick continued along the exit ramp, which circled down to the two lane road, where a couple of gas stations stood next to a McDonalds. The interstate was busy, but there wasn't any traffic on the crossroad.

'What's wrong?' Daphne asked, as they picked up speed.

'This is going to be rough,' Anna said.

The on-ramp was a hundred yards ahead. Anna kept her foot on the gas. The Toyota was following close behind. At the last minute, Anna pulled hard on the hand brake. Their car shuddered, then began to spin. Releasing the handbrake, she touched the accelerator gently to control the skid. The Ford was heavy enough and low to the ground, so it didn't flip over, but they overshot the on-ramp as Anna did a U-turn and drove onto the grass-covered berm. Someone blew a horn. Without losing momentum, Anna pulled the car around and headed down the on-ramp, ignoring a Wrong Way sign. The driver of the Toyota tried to brake but didn't react fast enough, and there were too many cars behind him. Seconds later, Anna saw the yellow Buick coming at her, trying to get back onto the highway. She aimed straight for him and caught sight of the driver's face for the first time through the windshield. Hitting her horn, she swung around the oncoming vehicle as he crashed into the railing on his side of the ramp.

Hoping there weren't state troopers nearby, Anna continued down the on-ramp in the wrong direction. From what she'd seen, the Buick wasn't going anywhere soon, and the Toyota would have to turn around at the next exit, fifteen miles ahead.

'Where did you learn to drive?' said Daphne.

'Delhi,' Anna replied with a grin.

'How did those cars find us?'

'There must be another tracking device in here,' Anna said.

'Could be,' said Daphne. 'Jimmy bought this car for me three years ago.'

The road they were on didn't look promising, a poorly paved rural road through forested hills, with an occasional farm on either side. The terrain was more rugged and the land looked less productive than in Ohio. Several of the farms had oil rigs, pumping up and down like giant seesaws. Anna hoped they'd come to a turning before too long, but there were no crossroads for several miles, and the road seemed to grow narrower and was full of potholes.

'This doesn't look as if it's going anywhere,' said Daphne. 'Maybe we should turn around.'

'That's not an option,' said Anna.

Just then, she saw something that caught her eye, as they came around a corner. Up ahead was a farm wedged into the hollow of the hill, with a gray, unpainted barn and several tractors in the yard. Three oil wells stood in the fields in front of the house, but only one of them was pumping. Halfway up the driveway sat a Jeep Wrangler with a For Sale sign under one of its windshield wipers. Anna turned in, drove the Taurus up to the house, and parked behind a tractor. Stepping out of the car, she saw a woman watching her through the screen door at the back of the house. The Beretta was in Anna's pocket.

She waved as Daphne undid her seatbelt. When they started toward the house, the woman came out of the door, followed by a dog that barked but wagged its tail.

'What can I do for you girls?' the woman asked. She was wearing jeans and a green sweater, her dusty blond hair pulled up in an untidy bun.

'We'd like to buy your Jeep,' Anna said.

The woman smiled and looked across at the Taurus.

'Something wrong with your car?' she said.

'It's been giving us trouble,' said Anna. 'Does yours run all right?'

The woman looked away, down the drive to where the Wrangler was parked.

'It's not mine,' she said.

'Whose is it?' Anna asked.

'My son's,' said the woman, brushing back a stray strand of hair that blew into her eyes. The dog was sniffing at Daphne's shoes.

'Where is he?' Anna said, worried they were wasting time.

'Afghanistan,' said the woman. 'This is his third tour. I told him not to go, but you know how it is. They never listen.'

'But the Jeep's for sale, isn't it?' Daphne asked, petting the dog and looking up.

'I guess,' the woman replied, in no hurry to answer them. 'He loved that Jeep, but his credit cards maxed out and he couldn't make the payments anymore.'

'How much do you want for it?' Anna said.

'Joey bought it used,' the woman said, 'for three thousand dollars. There's about fifteen hundred still owing on it. I'd have to get the papers from the bank.'

'I'll give you two thousand. Cash,' said Daphne, reaching into her purse and taking out a handful of hundred dollar bills.

Anna glanced across at her and nodded.

'He said he hoped he'd get twenty-five hundred. That's the Blue Book price.'

'You're sure it runs okay?'

'Yeah, I drove it down to Meadville last week.'

'Here's twenty-five,' said Daphne. 'We'll come back and do the paperwork later.'

The woman studied her for a moment, before taking the money. 'You're not from around here, are you?'

'No, but we'll be back,' Anna said.

'Where are you from?' the woman asked.

'Mexico,' Anna lied. 'Do you have the keys?'

The woman counted the money and shook her head. 'I don't know,' she said. 'He loved this Jeep.'

'Where in Afghanistan is your son?' Daphne asked.

'He's not allowed to tell me, but it's somewhere in the mountains. Last time he was there, he was in Gela…something. Gelela.'

'Jalalabad,' said Daphne. 'I've been there.'

'Whoa!' the woman said. 'No shit! That's further away than Mexico.'

She looked as if she didn't trust Anna, but Daphne seemed to win her over.

'Let's see, there's two sets of keys,' she said, turning back into the kitchen. 'I know I put them somewhere.'

'We just need one set,' Anna called after her. We'll get the other when we come back.'

Two minutes later, she returned.

'You girls are sure in a hurry,' she said, holding out the keys. 'I could make some coffee.'

'No thanks. We're running late,' said Anna.

'The registration and insurance are in the glovebox, and it's got about a quarter tank of gas.'

Daphne smiled and put out a hand to shake.

'Thank you,' she said. 'I hope your son comes back safely.'

'Yeah, so do I,' the woman said. 'Thirty-three more days until his tour is up, but I don't know, he seems to like it over there. Or maybe it's just an excuse to get away from home.'

As they walked back to the car, Anna handed Daphne the keys to the Taurus. The keychain the woman had given them had an empty rifle shell attached. When Anna started the Jeep, she could see the boy's mother still watching from the porch.

Getting into the Wrangler, Anna noticed it had a bumper sticker on the back, with the American Flag and the motto THESE COLORS DON'T RUN. Hanging from the rearview mirror was a GI-Joe figure. The Jeep started on the first try, though the muffler sounded as if it needed repair. Anna didn't have time to worry about that as she headed back along the road. Less than two miles from the farm they came to a crossing and turned right toward a town called Quinton. Three minutes later, Anna noticed a sign for a cemetery and turned in. There didn't seem to be anyone around, and the granite headstones were scattered down the hill. At least a dozen American flags were planted near the graves of veterans. They parked behind a grove of evergreens. Anna took their luggage out from the Taurus and put it in the backseat of the Wrangler. Locking the Taurus, she tossed the keys behind one of the headstones. It was a quiet, secluded spot. On a bright, spring day, this seemed as good a place as any to be buried.

Abandoning Daphne's car, they got back in the Wrangler and continued on into Quinton, where they filled up with gas. Heading out of town, Anna spotted a sign for Route 80. So far the Toyota hadn't shown up, and by the time they were on the interstate again Anna began to relax.

Thirty-Nine

Luke felt as if he was going to throw up, watching the guards drag the body off the trail and roll it down the side of the hill into a barren gulley. The two mastiffs sniffed at Daruwalla's shoes and then moved away, sensing something was wrong. From a distance of thirty feet, the sudden brutality of the killing seemed almost worse than watching Ibrahim and Mushtaq die two weeks ago. The gunshots still rang in his ears. Guldaar's twelve-gauge snapped open and two empty cartridges were ejected, falling to the ground. Luke could smell the acrid odor of gunpowder, mingling with the smoke of a freshly lit cigarette.

'Why did you kill him?' he asked, finding it hard to speak.

'He betrayed me badly,' said Guldaar. 'It wasn't just business…a personal matter. This was the first time we met, but he knew I had to kill him.'

As they walked slowly back to the house, Guldaar kept his hand on Luke's shoulder. Maybe it was supposed to be a gesture of reassurance, but Luke felt he was being restrained. The surrounding hills seemed even more desolate, and Luke wondered if they would eventually bury the body or leave it to be eaten by jackals and vultures.

When they reached the house, Guldaar allowed Luke to go to his room, where he lay on his bed for a while, shaken by the killing. An hour later, there was a knock at his door, and a servant gestured for him to follow. Reluctantly, Luke got up and passed through the deserted living room. The artworks on the walls were abstract oils, but the shapes and colors seemed grotesque. Everything about this house disturbed him now, its American furnishings like photographs in a Williams Sonoma catalogue, completely out of place in this world. Even the flowerbeds outside the bay windows, a flurry of pinks and blues, seemed cruel and corrupted.

The servant led him to a staircase that descended into the basement, then down another level, two stories beneath the earth. When they reached the bottom, a guard was stationed by a heavy steel door and ushered Luke inside. The first room they came to was a windowless lounge with mismatched chairs and a coffee table strewn with newspapers in Urdu and Farsi. The second door took them into a large office, where Guldaar was seated behind an empty desk. He had a cigarette in one hand. Smoke hung like cobwebs from the ceiling.

'Luke. Come in,' he said, with a generous smile. 'I'm afraid I upset you this morning, but you have to understand I had no choice. Because of Jehangir, my only son is dead.'

He gestured for Luke to take a seat, and for several moments they just stared at each other. The office felt like a crypt. Luke could see vents near the ceiling where the air circulated, but there was no sound of fans or air-conditioning.

'I've brought you here because I want to offer you a commission,' said Guldaar. 'You work freelance, don't you? This is a writing assignment that might interest you.'

Luke was slowly taking in his surroundings, the carpets on the floors and a glass cabinet along one wall, filled with artifacts that looked as if they belonged in a museum. Several sculptures stood on either side of the room, lit up by gallery lights from the ceiling. A Buddha figure presided over one corner, while a crudely carved wooden chair, like a throne, sat against the wall.

'First of all, however, I want to tell you something about myself, so you understand the motives behind my actions, the truth beyond the lies.'

Guldaar gestured toward the ceiling.

'As I said, the Americans built this house for me, but I don't stay up above. It's safer down here. Even if they dropped a bomb directly on the house, we would survive.'

'Why would they target the house, if they built it for you?' said Luke.

'You can never trust anyone,' said Guldaar. 'It's sad but true. All of us are expendable. The only thing that protects me is that I know much more about them than they know about me.'

There was another pause, while Guldaar got to his feet and came around the other side of the desk, directly in front of Luke. He lit another cigarette before he spoke.

'People call me Guldaar Khan out of respect. It's not my name, but I accept it as an honorific. Everyone fears a leopard. Most people assume that I'm a Pathan, Pakhtun. I do not deny it, of course, because it suits me, but my family were originally Kati Kafirs, Red Kafirs, from the Bashgal Valley. In the 1930s, when my father was a boy, his family escaped persecution by crossing the border near Chitral. Our people used to worship ancient gods, idols with the features of Greek and Iranian deities, and names that no one can pronounce today. You've heard of Kafiristan, of course. Nuristan. The land of enlightenment?'

Luke nodded, aware of the history and mythology of this region.

'Then you understand the cruel ironies of our people,' Guldaar laughed. 'We are accused of ignorance and heresy for preserving traditions that go back to a time before the Prophet Mohammed, before Jesus Christ. For a while, my family took refuge among the Kalash tribe, the Black Kafirs, as they are known, in Birir and Bumburet, across the Durand Line. British rule protected us. When my father came of age, he married a Kalash, my mother. She was the most beautiful girl in the valley, with hair like corn silk and cheeks the color of wild roses and eyes as blue as glacial ice.'

Waving his cigarette, Guldaar circled his desk.

'Forgive me, I'm not a poet, and my metaphors are rustic analogies from peasant life. But there is nothing romantic about being a refugee. Our people suffered in exile. They were shepherds, a hard life in an unforgiving land. When the British left in 1947, we were threatened by some of the tribesmen, not the Chitralis but others who disapproved of our gods and our customs. They called us immoral, licentious, corrupt.

'By this time, my father had given up the pastoral life and started a small business, transporting goods and produce from Peshawar to Chitral. He converted to Islam out of expediency but also because he saw what the future held. In 1951 we moved to the village I showed you this morning and started our lives again. The Pakhtun headman was a close friend of my father's and we were adopted into their family. My father accepted the name Salim Khan, and he made my mother convert to Islam too, though she still prayed to her gods in secret and taught me the language of my ancestors, the names of Bulumain and other deities who are worshipped in fire rituals, ancient heroes like Budulak, the shepherd king, progenitor of the Kalash people. My father permitted her this much, though he prayed at the mosque every day. My name was changed to Jamshed Khan, and I was circumcised at the age of nine, which is an experience you never forget.'

Luke knew that the story he was hearing could easily be true, or at least as true as anything might be in this part of the world. Guldaar spoke with little emotion, except when he mentioned his mother.

'My mother came from a well-respected Kalash family, and her grandfather had been a tribal shaman, Rustom Jan. Even when I was very young, I remember she used to tell me how our family traced their ancestry to Sikander-e-Azam. We were the descendants of Alexander and Rukhsana, Roxanne, the daughter of Porus, or Puru, as my mother used to pronounce it. These were stories handed down from her grandmother. She said our family were ancient warriors who became shepherds when there were no wars to fight. Our fair complexion and the pale color of our eyes come from our Greek ancestors. Our blood is like the waters of the Indus, which is fed by many streams but remains pure until it flows into the sea. These were the heroic stories I heard as a boy. My mother recounted these legends until the day she died, ten years ago. After her death I founded the Sikander-e-Azam Trust, to honor her memory.'

Luke watched him light another cigarette, as if the smoke sustained the stories.

'Come here,' said Guldaar, waving toward the display cases on the wall. 'I'll show you something.'

He waited until Luke joined him, then opened one of the glass panels, taking out a chunk of stone the size of a cricket ball. At first, there didn't seem to be anything special about it, until Luke held it in his hands and saw that part of it was delicately carved with the cherubic features of a human face, one eye and an ear, as well as curls of hair.

'I collect Gandhara sculptures. This piece would have been carved in the first century, BC. It was broken off a statue by Muslim zealots—fragments of idolatry.'

From a jeweled box on another shelf, Guldaar took a couple of old coins.

'These are gold and silver coins from the time of Alexander. That's his face on them, wearing a lion headdress,' he said. Seeing the skepticism in Luke's eyes, he added. 'You can buy cheap imitations in Kabul, but I can assure you these are real.'

Luke felt the weight of the coin in his palm. He could just make out the Macedonian features embossed in dull silver and a similar emblem on a brighter, untarnished piece of gold. His eyes traveled over the glass case, seeing shards of pottery and clay figurines, metal clasps, and rusted blades of daggers. Nothing was labeled, but Luke could tell every object had its story.

'This is only a small part of my collection,' said Guldaar. 'I have a great deal more I can show you, but first I want to know if you're willing to accept my commission.'

Luke turned to him. 'Do I have a choice?'

'Not if you wish to remain alive.' Guldaar's eyes hardened.

'What do you want me to write?' Luke asked. 'A history of the Kalash people?'

'No,' Guldaar smiled. 'Perhaps later. That could be another project. But for the moment, I only want you to write about the present…a series of investigative articles, which we will publish online.'

'Investigative?'

'Don't worry, I'll give you all the material you need. No other research is required,' said Guldaar. 'I've got an extensive archive of documents, video and audio recordings, transcripts, tapes, and photographs.'

'And what are these about?'

'Evidence of greed and treason—bribes, kickbacks, hawala payments. I've kept a careful record of all of my transactions: recordings of telephone calls, photographs of money changing hands, CCTV footage, bank statements, incriminating emails, and text messages. These include details about heads of state, ministers of different countries, World Bank, NATO, EU and UN officials, businessmen, spies and military officers, presidents of banks, and managing directors of corporations. It's all carefully filed away but needs to be narrated in a convincing way, telling these stories of corruption, the hidden weaknesses of powerful men. I would do it myself, but I'm not a writer. That's why I need you. Believe me, Luke, the material I have is more explosive than any nuclear warhead. I'm not asking you to make up these stories, only to tell the truth. Any journalist would stake his career on it.'

'You're planning to use it as blackmail?' Luke said.

'Perhaps,' said Guldaar. 'But I would call it protection. I'll release the articles selectively, and only if necessary, along with supporting evidence.'

Luke felt the nausea returning, a sour-sick taste at the back of his throat.

Guldaar opened one of the drawers beside him and took out a newspaper, which he tossed across the desk.

'Here's your first assignment,' he said.

On the front page of *The New York Times* was a photograph of Roger Fleischmann, with a headline about his death.

'You interviewed him, didn't you?' said Guldaar.

Luke nodded as he skimmed the story of the air crash in Eggleston, Ohio. It was the first news report he'd seen in almost two weeks, since he'd been abducted.

'There are rumors,' said Guldaar, 'that the CEO of Peregrine was killed by terrorists. All kinds of conspiracy theories are circulating. Some people probably think I killed him, by sabotaging his plane.'

'Did you?' Luke asked.

Guldaar shook his head as he took a plastic file from the drawer. 'In a way, I suppose, I did. But it wasn't an accident, nor was it murder. Suicide, plain and simple. There was nothing wrong with the plane. Roger Fleischmann killed himself by flying it into the ground.'

Luke stared at the photograph of the man he'd met a month ago, recalling his easygoing laugh and their conversation about military contracts and international relations.

'Why would he have done that?' Luke asked.

'Because I showed him this,' said Guldaar, opening the file and passing it across to Luke, 'a little over a week ago, when I visited Ohio. It's unfortunate that he took his life. I had hoped he would stay on as CEO, but Roger lost his nerve.'

Guldaar winced, as if it was painful for him to recount what happened.

'Once you read the documents and see what's on the DVDs, you'll understand how the company secured illegal contracts and bought influence in Pakistan and neighboring countries. Peregrine is like any other corporation. They depend on sales and marketing, which is a dirty business, no matter where you go in the world. I suppose the most damning part is that some of the investments in Peregrine came from the heroin trade, indirectly of course, but there's a paper trail. Roger Fleischmann is dead, but I want you to write the truth about him, based on these documents. Today, he's an American martyr and hero. But when they learn the facts, it'll be a different story.'

Forty

Afridi watched their progress on the satellite map as the vehicle moved slowly across Pennsylvania toward New York, like an iridescent beetle drawn to the light. He could picture Anna behind the wheel of the car. Beside her, Afridi imagined Daphne Shaw. He wondered what they were talking about, how much Daphne had revealed about her relationship with Guldaar. He assumed that she would trust a woman more than a man with her secrets. Beyond the factual details of her life and the elaborate charade Guldaar had created for her, Afridi was interested in the subtle intimacies between them. Not the sexual encounters but those moments in which their masks fell away. Was he cruel to her? Did he spoil her with gifts and endearments? It was impossible to know what kind of man Guldaar was, except in abstract terms, the money he extorted and embezzled, the murders he committed or commissioned, the debts he collected as favors from the rich and powerful, because he was richer and more powerful than the rest.

Watching the blinking icon moving imperceptibly forward along the highway, Afridi could almost hear the sound of Daphne's voice telling her story, though the tracking device wasn't equipped with a microphone.

~

They had stopped only once, to get coffee. Anna was still worried that they were being followed. Daphne seemed exhausted by the emotions of the past few days. For a while, she talked about her son, remembering him as only a mother could, his childhood tantrums.

'Naseem inherited his father's temper,' she said. 'Though he could be as gentle and timid as a kitten sometimes, even as a teenager.'

'Did he know his father well?' Anna asked.

'No, not really,' said Daphne. 'Jimmy was always traveling, and we weren't married. He had several homes and several other women. Sometimes he'd come and visit, bringing extravagant gifts. But I could tell that Naseem distrusted him from an early age. Sometimes he'd say to me, "I'm going to kill him, mamma. I'm going to kill him."'

Anna could hear the sorrow in her laugh. 'Why would he say that?' she asked.

'It was my fault, maybe. I'd complain about Jimmy, or we'd have arguments when he came over. Naseem would hear us shouting. It didn't happen very often, but when Jimmy lost his temper—'

'Did he hit you?'

'No. It was only words,' said Daphne. 'Though several times, he threatened me with a pistol, and once he put the muzzle right against my forehead. I knew he'd shot other people, but I wasn't afraid, at least not in that moment. I said, "Do it! Go on, do it!"'

'Was Naseem there?' Anna asked.

'He was watching from the bedroom door, but he was only three or four. I don't think he would have remembered.' Daphne stared out at the passing rooftops of a town along the highway. There were more trees than houses, and parts of the town looked derelict, empty factories and desolate streets.

'You never thought of leaving him?'

'I tried several times but I couldn't hide from him. He always seemed to be able to track me down. And whenever we met, he was charming, full of apologies and promises. At least in the beginning I believed him.'

'Later, when your son had the accident, what did Guldaar do?' Anna was almost afraid to ask but Daphne seemed willing to talk.

'He came to the hospital in Breach Candy, near the club where we used to go swimming. There was a pool shaped like the map of India...' Daphne stopped herself for a moment, as if realizing her memories were wandering. 'Jimmy spoke with the doctors, and I remember thinking, *This is something he can't fix*. Naseem was in the operating theater. The doctors said he had a thirty percent chance of survival, which sounded absurd to me, because how do you calculate something like that? The next thing I knew there were people from the US embassy asking me about my passport and somebody from an air ambulance company who made me sign some papers. Once they had Naseem stabilized, we flew to the US. Jimmy said he was going to be on the flight with us but, as usual, he changed his plans just before we took off. There was just Naseem and me and a doctor. I kept thinking none of this is real. We had different names and American passports.'

The bitterness in her voice was like the aftertaste of their unsweetened coffee in Styrofoam cups. Anna listened, though her eyes remained on the road, checking the rearview mirror from time to time. A lot of trucks were on the highway, and every time they passed an eighteen-wheeler, the Jeep shuddered in its wake. She was driving ten miles above the speed limit, as fast as she dared.

By the time they reached New York, Daphne had told her almost everything about her life. For the first few years, she had waited for Naseem to wake up out of the coma. She had waited for Jimmy to come and visit her. She had waited for some kind of release from the fictional world in which she lived, false identities and the watchful presence of men who kept her under surveillance from the day she reached America. Were they there for her protection or were they making sure she didn't escape? Daphne had never been sure.

'Who was watching you?' Anna asked.

'Peregrine's security has always been there, but maybe Jimmy hired his own guards to keep an eye on me. Maybe it's all tied in with the CIA, private contractors, and corporate agents. The lines get blurred. All I know is that ever since I got here, someone's been keeping me under surveillance, tapping my phones, keeping track of when I come and go. No privacy. It's like being an actor,' she said with a bitter laugh. 'But without the celebrity.'

'The men who broke down your door two weeks ago?'

'I don't know who they were. They had no IDs or insignia on their uniforms, but they must have worked for the government…I just don't know which branch or agency.'

'Did you report it to the police?'

Daphne shook her head. 'There wasn't much point. I'm sure they learned about it but nobody ever came around. The local police have a close working relationship with Peregrine.'

'But the men who stormed your house were federal agents?'

'I have no idea. They threatened me with arrest and said they could lock me up without a warrant, but in the end they got back in their RV and went away.'

'They were after Guldaar?'

'Of course,' said Daphne. 'They said they knew he'd been with me. I denied it, and there wasn't any proof he'd been to the house. Then three days ago, someone from Washington came up to see me at the clinic. He didn't identify himself but said he worked for the government and he wanted to know about Jimmy.'

'Homeland Security?' Anna asked. 'FBI?'

'NSA? There are plenty of acronyms for dangerous people who claim to be protecting our freedom. Who knows?'

'Did this man give you any indication why they were after Guldaar?'

'Because of Jimmy's connections, I suppose. He knows a couple of senators and congressmen, as well as some of the top military intelligence officers working in Afghanistan. They use him and he uses them. It all started when the Russians invaded and he made himself invaluable.'

'Did Guldaar tell you this?'

'In a roundabout way,' said Daphne. 'He talked with me about certain things, but I always knew there were secrets he would never share.'

By seven in the evening, they finally reached the airport. It was growing dark as they drove up the ramp into long-term parking. Daphne's suitcase felt almost empty when Anna put it on the cart, as if she had left everything behind. Pushing the luggage into an elevator, she pressed the button for Ticketing and Departures. Daphne seemed restless and uneasy, looking into every face they passed without meeting anyone's eye. The flight was scheduled for 10:30 p.m. Anna debated whether she should wait another hour before buying their tickets but decided to go ahead. She used the credit card Manav had given her, signing her name as Sheetal Khanna. They went straight from there to Check-in, where they got their boarding passes. Before going through security, Anna went to the washroom and dropped the Beretta and the extra clip of ammunition in a trash bin, after wiping them clean of her prints.

Passing through the scanners, she felt a sense of relief, as if everything was going to be all right. She watched Daphne retrieving her handbag from the X-ray machine and putting on her shoes, admiring the courage that lay beneath her beauty and grace.

At that moment, she heard a voice behind her. 'Excuse me, are you Sheetal Khanna?'

Looking up, Anna shook her head, more in surprise than denial. Two men were standing close behind her.

By this time, Daphne had also turned to face them, a look of resignation in her eyes.

'Please come with us.'

Forty-One

They had left the house at quarter past six in the morning and were driving along a military road that cut off the main highway out of Peshawar, heading south. The land was uncultivated and desolate, scarified with ravines. Already they had passed through a couple of checkpoints. Ahead of them was a high fence, and Luke could see an airfield beyond, with a control tower and radar dishes.

Guldaar was in a talkative mood.

'This airfield was built in the 1950s by the Americans,' he said. 'It has a runway big enough to land a 747. In those days the U2 spy planes used to operate from this base. Francis Gary Powers. You've heard his name?'

Luke nodded.

'He took off from here before he was shot down by the Soviets.' Guldaar laughed. 'This part of the world has seen all kinds of conflicts.'

When they reached the gate, two military guards blocked their way, but recognizing the officer escorting the car, they backed off quickly and let them through. In the distance, Luke could see a squadron of fighter jets and fortified hangers. Two C-130 cargo planes and a swarm of helicopters were parked nearby. Their SUV headed onto the tarmac and made a straight line for an executive jet that stood at the edge of the concrete apron. Luke tried to imagine what a U2 must have looked like—a sleek black silhouette. He'd been told stories about the Cold War missions launched from Peshawar, when Ayub Khan and his generals allowed the Americans to build airbases in Pakistan. A couple of years ago, he'd done a series of interviews with retired army officers who enjoyed talking about the good old days. Things hadn't changed very much, except for enemies and allies.

Their plane was a Falcon 2000, a nine-seater twin engine jet, with a private suite in front. The pilot was an American named Craig. He greeted Guldaar and Luke with laconic deference and a hint of flyboy swagger. As they boarded the jet, their Pakistani escort stiffened but did not salute. Guldaar thanked him, putting a hand to his heart. Nobody had checked their passports or conducted any departure formalities.

As they settled into their seats, which faced each other, Guldaar lit a cigarette. The jet began to taxi toward the runway. The engines had a wasp-like whine underscored by a resonant growl. Within five minutes they were airborne, climbing steeply. Through the window, Luke could see snow-capped peaks in the distance.

'How long will it take you to write the article about Peregrine?' Guldaar asked.

There was only one other passenger, a bodyguard who sat behind Luke with a machine pistol resting across his thighs. The plane banked steeply as it turned to the southwest, flying parallel to the mountains.

'A week, at least,' said Luke.

'Really? Why would it take so long?' Guldaar seemed disappointed. 'All the research has been done for you.'

'I'll need to write and revise three or four drafts. With all of the material you've given me, it'll be about three thousand words.'

Guldaar tapped his cigarette into an ashtray next to him. Luke had fastened his seatbelt out of habit, but Guldaar left his open and seemed unconcerned, as if his safety were assured.

'Of course, I won't rush you,' he said. 'We want this to be a good piece of reporting, something that makes people question their assumptions and see the world for what it is.'

Luke hadn't forgotten the shotgun going off and Jehangir Daruwalla toppling backward from the blast. The interior of the jet seemed absurdly comfortable after his confinement in the empty cistern, though he knew that he remained a hostage.

'We'll have to come up with an appropriate pseudonym for you,' Guldaar said. 'Unfortunately, this article can't appear under your name.'

'Where will you have it published?'

'I was thinking *The Military and Foreign Policy Review*, their online edition. Are you familiar with it?' Guldaar asked, staring out the window at the cloud formations below.

'No,' said Luke.

'It's published by a conservative think tank in England, the Hoath Centre for Security Affairs. The director, a former Tory MP, owes me a favor or two,' said Guldaar. 'It has a relatively small circulation, but once the story is out there, I'm sure it will be picked up by others. What do they call it? Going viral?'

The plane shuddered with sudden turbulence, but Guldaar didn't seem to notice.

'Of course,' he said. 'The truth is, I may not have to publish anything at all.'

Luke studied him without looking straight into his eyes, keeping Guldaar in his peripheral vision. He wondered what he could tell Carlton Fletcher about this man, how he might describe him— arrogant and vicious, certainly, but with a cultivated sensibility. The Oxbridge accent was deceptive but he could hear another voice within the voice that echoed a rough, unsettled past, a bullying boy from the badlands of the Hindu Kush, with a crude sense of self-importance.

As soon as they reached their cruising altitude, a male attendant entered from the galley and asked what they would like to drink.

'Tea,' said Guldaar. 'But maybe you'll have a whiskey...'

'No thank you,' Luke said. 'Tea is good.'

As the attendant excused himself, Luke asked, 'Can I ask where we're going?'

'Dubai,' said Guldaar, without hesitation, though Luke could tell he was not prepared to say any more.

They continued to speak about the article. Guldaar said that he would only read it once Luke was satisfied with what he'd written.

'I don't plan to do much editing,' he said. 'The facts will speak for themselves. All you need to do is structure it carefully and make sure it's a compelling narrative.'

Luke didn't argue with him, though he wondered if the article would ever get published. What worried him more was that Guldaar had been as candid as he was, revealing details about his contacts and his relationship with Peregrine. Luke knew this meant that he had no intention of ever letting him go free.

'What about your role in the story?' he asked.

Guldaar seemed puzzled for a moment. The tea had arrived, a cup for each of them and one for the bodyguard, who sat silent as an armed Buddha in his seat.

'What do you mean?' said Guldaar.

'There must be things that you don't want me to put in the article,' said Luke, awkwardly. 'Because it might incriminate you...'

Guldaar laughed. 'Of course,' he said. 'Like you, I must remain anonymous. But as you'll see in the files, I don't leave fingerprints.'

'Won't the CIA or ISI realize who's leaking this information? They'll trace the story back to you, won't they?'

Guldaar's smile tightened. 'So what if they do? It sends a message, doesn't it? And there are plenty of other stories where this one came from. You see what I mean...'

Luke met his captor's gaze for a moment, realizing that the more he learned about Guldaar, the less likely he was to get out of this alive.

Forty-Two

Anna and Daphne were taken from the security screening area to a door behind a kiosk in the departures concourse. One of the men who accompanied them punched in a code and ushered them inside. They passed through a long corridor with fluorescent lighting. Anna noticed signs for the Immigration and Naturalization Service, as well as Customs and the Department of Agriculture. The room into which they were led was unmarked, except for a NO ENTRY sign.

It was a small conference room with an oval table and uncomfortable chairs. A window looked out onto a line of aircraft parked at their departure gates. Most of these were international carriers— Lufthansa, Swissair, Qatar Airways, Air India. Anna guessed this last one was their plane, and she could imagine the passengers lining up at the departure gate inside.

'May I see your passports please?' The man who asked was middle-aged, with receding hair, a curdled complexion, and tinted glasses. Daphne had already recognized him from his visit to the clinic last week, though she said nothing as she handed over her passport.

'Sheetal Khanna,' Fletcher said, glancing at Anna's passport first.

'Is there a problem?' she asked.

The man looked up at her with a tired expression that suggested so many problems he didn't know where to begin.

'You're flying to India, right?' he asked. 'New Delhi.'

'Yes,' said Anna, glancing at her watch. 'Our flight leaves in forty-five minutes.'

He didn't react.

'What's the big rush?' he said, picking up Daphne's passport and riffling through the pages. 'You only bought your tickets half an hour ago. Is this some kind of emergency?'

'Yes,' said Anna. 'A family crisis.'

'So, are you related to each other?'

'Just friends,' said Anna. Daphne remained silent.

'Ms Khanna, you arrived in this country a week ago,' said the man.

Anna nodded.

'And you, Ms Shaw, what takes you out of the country?' he said, catching Daphne's eye. They looked at each other for a moment.

'It's Mr Fletcher, isn't it?' she said. 'My son passed away, a couple of days after you came to see me.'

He nodded. 'I'm sorry for your loss.'

The second man sat to one side, saying nothing. After a prolonged silence, there was a knock at the door and Tracy Holman came in. She was wearing a dark gray suit and glanced at Anna with recognition but said nothing.

'Ms Khanna. Ms Shaw,' Fletcher introduced them, as if this were a business meeting. 'My colleague, Agent Holman.'

'Are all of you with the National Security Agency?' Anna asked. Fletcher smiled for the first time.

'We'll answer that question later on. Right now, we want to know why you ladies are in such a hurry to leave the United States,' he said.

Daphne looked across at Anna.

'We haven't broken any laws, if that's what you're suggesting,' Anna said. 'There's nothing illegal about our departure.'

'Except that this morning you shot out the tires on a pickup truck in Ohio,' said Holman, her red lipstick forming each word.

'And your reckless driving caused another vehicle to crash on Route 80 in Pennsylvania, endangering several lives.'

'We were being followed and threatened,' Daphne said. 'It was self-defense. Those men were trying to stop us.'

'Why do you think they were doing that?' said Fletcher.

'Ms Shaw's life is in danger, ever since her son passed away,' Anna said.

'You mean, once she took him off life support,' Fletcher replied. Daphne maintained her composure. 'Yes, that was my decision.'

'And you donated his organs to be transplanted, am I right? Your son's heart, his kidneys, cornea, and liver?'

Anna glanced across at Daphne who closed her eyes for a moment. 'It seemed the right thing to do, giving someone else a second chance at life,' she said.

'Yes, of course. A generous and admirable choice,' said Fletcher. 'And your son's father knew about this?'

'No,' she said. 'I suppose he does now. That's why you've stopped us, isn't it?'

Tracy Holman shook her head. 'Actually, we'd like to help you.' Anna could tell that she was attempting to sound sympathetic, though her eyes were cold and unemotional and her voice sounded as if it were a recording—digitized words and inflections.

'How could you help us?' Anna asked.

'We'd like to protect you from whoever it is that's trying to kill you,' said Fletcher. 'But first we need to know who it is.'

Daphne's hands were folded on the table and she turned the ring on her finger slowly, so that the emerald glinted in the fluorescent light.

'We're going to miss our flight,' she said.

Fletcher shook his head. 'Don't worry. We've arranged for it to be delayed. A minor technical snag.'

Anna looked across at the Air India 777, which was being loaded with baggage. A Sky Gourmet flight kitchen van was parked next to the plane.

'Mr Fletcher,' said Daphne. 'When you came to see me at the clinic in Ohio, you explained that the men who broke down the door of my house were looking for someone, the father of my son. He goes by the name Jamshed Khan, but most people call him Guldaar. I'm sure you know who I mean.'

'Do you know where Guldaar is right now?' Holman asked.

'I have no idea,' said Daphne.

'But probably not in India,' said Fletcher. 'Am I right?'

'Not that I know,' Daphne replied.

'And Ms Khanna, you work for the Indian government?' said Fletcher.

'I'm a researcher—'

'Bullshit,' said Fletcher.

'Excuse me?' Anna replied, her eyes level with his.

'You can cut the crap,' he said. 'We know you're not interested in Sanskrit poetry.'

Holman interjected, 'As I said before, we'd like to help, but we need your cooperation.'

Fletcher fell silent and nodded.

'We'll be happy to let you board your plane, provided we can establish some sort of working relationship,' said Holman.

'Such as?' Anna asked.

So far, all of Holman's remarks had been directed toward Daphne. She now looked at Anna with a patronizing smile that gave nothing away.

'I know that Ms Shaw's safety is your primary concern,' she said. 'And I appreciate the fact that you were able to successfully bring her here to New York, but you need to understand, Ms Khanna, that if we identify you as a foreign intelligence agent, operating within the borders of the United States, we are authorized to detain you for as long as necessary without a trial. And I suspect your government would deny involvement. Am I right?'

Anna remained calm, as if there were no threat in Holman's words.

'I was asking what kind of working relationship you were suggesting,' she said.

This time Fletcher answered, after clearing his throat.

'Okay. So, we're going to let you get on your flight to Delhi, but Agent Holman will accompany you. She's got her boarding pass, same row, the seat across the aisle. Once you get to Delhi, we'd like you to keep her informed about where Ms Shaw is staying and if anyone tries to contact her, especially Guldaar or his people. We would also expect that your government, or whatever agency you work for, will extend assistance and any diplomatic courtesies that Agent Holman might require.'

'I can't promise that,' said Anna.

'You can't, or you won't?' said Fletcher.

'I don't have the authority to promise what you're asking for,' said Anna.

Fletcher and Holman looked across at each other.

'Then call someone who does,' said Fletcher, glancing down at his watch. 'It's 9:45 p.m. right now. If I'm not mistaken, it's 11:15 in the morning in India. Whoever you need to talk to should be at work.'

Anna took a moment to collect her thoughts, then reached into her backpack and found the cell phone, which she hadn't used until now. Switching it on, she scrolled through her list of contacts, most of whom were identified by code names. When she came to 'Ivanhoe,' Anna made the call.

Forty-Three

Afridi had silenced his cell phone while attending a briefing about recent border incursions in Ladakh. A young intelligence officer, Captain Sachdev, was conducting the briefing for a group of HRI analysts, to help them interpret satellite images. While the terrain in Ladakh was unforested and relatively easy to monitor, parts of the region appeared deceptively bare of physical features. Sachdev was explaining how the Chinese were able to move into Indian territory without being detected. Afridi's phone vibrated. When he saw it was Anna, he excused himself and went outside.

In a tense but muted voice, Anna outlined the situation. Afridi could tell she wasn't alone. Others were listening to her side of the conversation, and he was sure that his responses were also being monitored. For that reason, he kept his questions brief and to the point.

'You're not injured or in any physical danger?' he asked.

'No, sir. We've been detained at Kennedy airport,' she said.

'By whom?'

'I'm not sure,' said Anna. 'They want to send one of their agents to Delhi with us and are asking for our cooperation.'

'What sort of cooperation? How are we supposed to cooperate if we don't know who they are?' Afridi spoke softly, but his voice was full of anger. 'Tell them I want to know who we're dealing with.'

There was a long pause, after which Anna reported: 'They are part of a counterintelligence unit in the National Security Agency. That's all they're going to say.'

'And what do they want from us?' Afridi asked.

Anna explained that the Americans were interested in locating Guldaar and wanted to share intelligence on his operations and his whereabouts. They requested that Tracy Holman, one of their agents, be permitted entry into India with full immunity from arrest or prosecution. Anna paused, as someone in the room with her dictated what she should say.

'They want access to whatever information we have on Guldaar. If he's captured, they would like to have an opportunity to question him. Agent Holman will need to know where Daphne Shaw is staying.' Anna paused as she was given further instructions. 'The US embassy should not be informed of Agent Holman's presence. She will need a handgun for her protection.'

'Damn it, I'm not going to arm a foreign agent,' Afridi said, unable to control his temper.

He could hear Anna relaying his message.

'In that case, they are asking that she be permitted to carry a firearm with her, which will not be confiscated upon arrival.'

'I'll have to speak to the Home Ministry,' he said.

'We don't have time for that, sir,' Anna replied.

'I know,' said Afridi. 'Tell them I'll arrange for the three of you to enter the country without going through immigration or customs. But they must understand that my authority is limited and Agent Holman will have to operate with complete discretion. If she goes around shooting people, I can't protect her.'

'Thank you, sir,' Anna said, as she hung up.

Though he could hear the dial tone and knew that Anna was no longer on the line, he added in a whisper, 'Good luck.'

Instead of returning to the briefing, Afridi wheeled himself to the edge of the verandah and let himself roll down into the yard. He made his way along a gravel path, under the shadowy branches of the deodar trees. At the far end of the compound, facing southeast toward the Tehri Hills, lay a rockery that he had started years ago, when HRI was first established. Over time, he had collected a variety of high altitude species, which had been replanted on the slopes below the institute. At this time of year, most plants were just beginning to bud—several kinds of rhododendrons, as well as primulas and fritillaries. Several times, he had gone himself by helicopter, to supervise the gathering of seeds and bulbs. HRI employed three gardeners to take care of these plants. Afridi had built a greenhouse too, for the more delicate species that required regulated temperature and humidity.

He knew that his staff found it amusing that someone who was charged with the nation's security should spend his spare time cultivating wildflowers. But Afridi found solace in his rock garden, and he often retreated here when he needed to think clearly. The involvement of the Americans unsettled him, almost as much as the visit from Major Yaqub. He had hoped to stalk Guldaar alone, with stealth and secrecy, carefully laying a trap into which his adversary would walk unsuspecting. Now, Afridi's plans were being complicated by others who had sensed an opportunity to join the hunt. Yet the Americans' interest in Guldaar confirmed his importance. Afridi knew that a country's security agencies were often at odds with each other, particularly in the United States, where they approached everything as an adversarial process. Being a creation of the CIA, Guldaar probably raised the specter of fear and loathing in the hearts of other agencies. He wondered if the people who had detained Anna and Daphne were actually working for the NSA. It was a risk he had to take. Perhaps Afridi could turn those competitive jealousies to his advantage, just as he hoped to undermine the ISI by involving dissident elements of their organization. But nobody understood the risks of this strategy better than Afridi. No amount of technological hardware or satellite telemetry could insure against the possibilities of betrayal and counterintelligence that might undermine this project. He could only fall back on his instincts and a conviction that Guldaar represented immeasurable danger to peace and security in South Asia.

When he reached the edge of the garden, Afridi spotted a bed of wild irises lifting their heads among the rocks. They were a dark purple color, far more intense than their hybrid cousins, but also smaller and more delicate. One of the gardeners was adding fertilizer and moss. Afridi spoke with him, urging him not to overwater the irises. Some of the rocks in this garden were from mountains that he had climbed and had been carefully collected and brought here over the years. Amid the irises was a pale chunk of granite taken from the glacial moraine at the head of the Bhyunder Valley, a piece of a mountain called Rataban. Afridi brushed his fingers over the rock, then plucked an iris. Its labial petals revealed a natural symmetry even as the flower looked like a ruffled cockade. For Afridi, the pure purple color and bright exuberance of the iris represented the antithesis of human treachery and greed.

Forty-Four

As the elevator climbed to the 133rd floor, Luke felt his stomach drop. Its interior was decorated like a Louis XIV boudoir, with gilt-framed mirrors and painted cherubs on the ceiling. A sofa, upholstered in satin with gold embroidery, was set against one wall for those who found it tiring to stand while ascending two thousand feet above sea level. Luke's ears popped, though the elevator was so precisely engineered, it was impossible to tell that they were climbing fifty feet per second. Only two other people were with him: the Pakhtun who had accompanied them from Pakistan and another guard who had received them in the parking garage, who was either Ethiopian or Somali.

Guldaar had traveled separately from the airport. Instead of landing at the international terminal, their jet had touched down at an air force base in the desert, about fifteen miles outside the city. They had driven straight from the tarmac to Burj al Khalifa, the tallest building in the world. Luke had been to Dubai often enough to recognize where they were. Once again, he felt as if his life had taken a wrong turn into some kind of lavish nightmare.

There was no possibility of escape, particularly now that he was trapped in the Burj al Khalifa. The floor numbers were ticking over like a time bomb on fast-forward. His guards were silent, but he knew that neither of them would hesitate to put a bullet through his skull. When they finally reached the 133rd floor, the polished brass doors, engraved with unicorns against a field of fleur-de-lis, opened without a sound. Luke stepped into a semicircular lobby with white leather chairs and sofas, a modern, minimalist interior. Two geometric Mondrian paintings hung on the wall—most likely reproductions, but Luke had to wonder if they might be genuine. The only other furnishings were six birdcages of different sizes suspended from the ceiling. Instead of cockatoos or canaries, they were full of tropical fish. Each birdcage enclosed an aquarium and the fish swam about as if they were flying from perch to perch. The largest of these cages was five feet tall and three feet in diameter. It contained a colorful pair of trigger-fish and a miniature shark that circled with a flick of its tail.

One of the doors opened, and a Filipina woman dressed as a French maid greeted him. She spoke English and gestured with attentive hospitality, leading him into a suite with huge windows looking out over the desert. He had little time to take in the rest of his surroundings, for the maid darted ahead of him and he had to rush to keep up. They passed through several drawing rooms and finally came to a hallway with doors on either side. His room was the third on the left. When he stepped inside, Luke was immediately drawn to the window. Dubai spread below him like a giant diorama: highways feeding in from the desert, clustered towers, the Creek full of dhows, the Burj al Arab with its sail-like architecture, and, beyond that, the Persian Gulf. Oceans of sand contrasted with the still, blue water. Luke imagined that he could see all the way to Iran. The maid asked if he wanted something to drink. He shook his head, overcome by a breathless sense of vertigo.

~

For the first twenty-four hours, there was no sign of Guldaar, and Luke ate his meals by himself. The maid, whose name was Gloria, brought him a change of clothes. This time, instead of salwar kameez, he was given jeans and a polo shirt. Next morning, a technician came to his room and set up a laptop and a printer. When he tried the Internet, the computer denied him access. There was no phone in his room, and he remained cut off from the world. Luke imagined that everyone still assumed he was a hostage somewhere in the Karakoram, guarded by jihadis, instead of being a prisoner in the most luxurious skyscraper in the Middle East. He wished he could reassure Ruth that he was all right, at least for now.

On the second evening, Guldaar summoned him to the floor above, connected by an internal elevator that opened onto a similar suite.

'I hope you're comfortable,' he said.

'Thank you. I've never been this high up in a building before,' said Luke.

'You're not afraid of heights, are you?' Guldaar laughed. 'I want you to make yourself at home. Ask for whatever you require. It's important that you concentrate on your writing. How's the article coming along?'

'I've finished the first draft,' said Luke. 'And I should be able to show it to you by tomorrow.'

'What do you think of our late friend, Roger Fleischmann, now that you've read the files and put his story together?'

Luke shrugged. 'He was a hard-nosed entrepreneur, whose only real interest was the bottomline. You can't blame him for that. Of course, the fact that he bought and cheated his way to success doesn't cast him in an admirable light. But the thing that really incriminates him is that he used drug money to finance his research and development, then hired assassins to kill off the competition, including an American contractor in Muzaffarabad. Once that's been exposed, nobody will hail him as a hero.'

Guldaar was seated in an armchair beside a blue porcelain vase, decorated with white egrets. He took a cigarette from the marquetry box on the coffee table and lit it with a match that he dropped into a crystal ashtray.

'This is why I needed a writer,' said Guldaar, with a look of satisfaction. 'Of course, I could have released the information online, but then there's no way of controlling the message. Someone has to organize the specific details into a logical account, with a beginning, middle, and an end. Others would have misinterpreted the facts and manipulated the story. Luke, I can tell you understand my motives, even if you disapprove of me.'

'It's not a question of disapproval,' said Luke. 'I'm just an ordinary hack, putting words on a page and doing what I'm told.'

Guldaar's face broke into a smile, but his eyes retained their cynical glare.

'You're underestimating yourself,' said Guldaar. 'Language is a sacred art. Not everyone has the gift of storytelling, but those who do are able to persuade even the most prejudiced minds.'

'What's my next assignment?' Luke asked.

'I haven't decided yet, but I have a couple of ideas in mind,' said Guldaar. 'Don't worry, there are plenty of stories. As soon as this one's finished, I'll give you another file.'

'I'm beginning to feel a bit like Scheherazade in the Arabian Nights,' said Luke. 'As soon as the story is finished, you'll have me killed.'

Guldaar's laugh had little humor in it, and he got to his feet, picking up a remote control from beside his chair.

'Come. I want to show you my library,' he said. 'It contains several books you might appreciate.'

With the cigarette between his lips, he beckoned for Luke to follow. Crossing a large Bukhara carpet that looked as if it were made of infinite knots, Guldaar pressed the remote control and a pair of sliding doors opened, revealing a large room with bookshelves on two walls. He went across and pulled out a volume at random, handing it to Luke. The book was a history of Central Asia titled *Swords in the Wind*, published in 1865.

Luke noticed that the third wall of the room was a gallery with artifacts.

'This is my real collection,' said Guldaar. 'Not the knickknacks I showed you in the other house. I keep my most valuable pieces here.'

Several Buddha heads were on display as well as a marble bas-relief panel depicting an army marching into battle. Two antique swords with corroded blades hung on the wall, along with arrowheads and daggers.

'Are these from the time of Alexander?' Luke asked.

'Mostly,' said Guldaar. 'But also from two or three centuries following, up until the beginning of the Christian era, when Greek satraps still ruled Bactria. It was a remarkable period of history, with refinement of art and culture. Have a look at this.'

He opened a cabinet in the wall. After entering a code on a keypad, he pulled out a shallow drawer that was covered in beveled glass. The interior was lined with purple velvet, on which ornate pieces of gold were arranged. Luke could see that some of these were amulets and bracelets in the shape of coiled serpents or tendril vines. Several seemed to be fragments from a ceremonial breastplate of gold armor, decorated with images of lions and elephants. Winged angels rode upon gilded griffons, and delicate links of chain mail shone like knitted gold. Guldaar opened a second drawer that contained more of the same, including a dagger with a solid gold hilt. In the third drawer was a girdle with a buckle in the shape of a woman's head, some sort of goddess or nymph.

'Where did all this come from?' said Luke.

'It was dug up by a Russian archeologist in 1984, from a Bactrian tomb in northeastern Afghanistan. Part of the collection was taken to Moscow. The rest was put in the national museum in Kabul. When the Taliban took over, after the Russians retreated, they looted and destroyed most of what the museum contained. Through my connections, I salvaged whatever I could. After that, I made contact with the Russian archeologist and recovered the rest. It cost me a fortune, but it's worth it, don't you think?'

'Incredible,' Luke said.

'Popularly, this is known as the dowry of Alexander, but of course the dates don't correspond. It was probably the burial treasure of a Seleucid satrap from the first century BC.'

As he said this, there was a polite cough behind them. Gloria, the maid, was standing next to a young woman in her teens. Her hair was covered, but her face was unveiled, revealing pale pink cheeks and downcast blue eyes. She was dressed in a long, loose kameez and pleated salwar, made of embroidered silk, with a scarf edged with cowrie shells wrapped around her shoulders and over her head.

'Allow me to introduce my daughter-in-law,' said Guldaar, putting a hand to his heart.

Luke said nothing, and the girl kept her eyes fixed on the floor as Guldaar picked up a gold necklace from the drawer and carefully draped it around her neck, fastening the clasp. He then took a matching girdle from another drawer and, with Gloria's help, wrapped it about the girl's waist. Piece by piece, he adorned his daughter-in-law with the dowry of Alexander, as if she were a mannequin. As he did this, Guldaar seemed to be speaking to himself.

'My most precious possessions,' he said. 'Doesn't she look like a princess?'

With one hand, he lifted her chin as the maid fastened earrings to the girl's pink lobes. The girl was blushing, but Luke could see the sadness and humiliation in her features.

'She speaks no English,' said Guldaar. 'No Urdu, only an obscure dialect of Pashto.'

Guldaar now picked up a gold tiara, with floral designs, petals and leaves formed into a circlet. He brushed the scarf aside, so that the girl's light blond hair was exposed, plaited in a single braid. With a gentle, fatherly gesture, he placed the delicate crown on her head and took a step back to admire the result.

He lit another cigarette as he studied the girl. She held her head up but her eyes remained fixed on the carpet at her feet, and Luke saw tears begin to trickle down her cheeks.

'Such a pity. Widowed five days after she became a bride,' Guldaar said, his voice filled with sudden bitterness. 'Such a beautiful thing. She would have borne me a dozen grandchildren. Such a waste…'

His voice broke off, and Luke was astonished to see that Guldaar was weeping as well.

Forty-Five

Air India Flight 102 was scheduled to reach Indira Gandhi Airport at 15:00 hours, but because of a departure delay in New York, the ETA was now 4:00 p.m. Afridi had been following the 777's progress. When he arrived at his office, they were somewhere over the Caucasus, still in darkness. He could see the flight path on his computer screen, the white icon like a moth crawling across a windowpane, inching its way toward Delhi.

When the aircraft finally touched down, Afridi watched it taxi to the gate. The CCTV cameras picked up the passengers leaving the jetway. Anna and Daphne were among the first to disembark, along with the American agent, Tracy Holman. Afridi could see two army intelligence officers meet them and escort them to a VIP elevator that took them down to the ground floor. Though his cameras couldn't follow them beyond this point, Afridi knew the women would be boarding a jeep to drive them directly to Palam Air Force Station, adjacent to the commercial airfield. Instead of sending his Aerospatial Lama to pick them up, he had arranged a larger Sikorsky S-76 chopper, operated by the National Security Guard. Checking his watch, Afridi estimated they would arrive in Mussoorie within the hour, ten minutes past 5:00 p.m. He rang for his personal assistant and made sure that preparations were in order. For Agent Holman, his PA had arranged a room at Rokeby Manor, a nearby hotel. Anna and Daphne each had a suite in the HRI annex. He knew they would be tired, and he ordered an early dinner to be served in their rooms.

While he waited for his guests, Afridi tried to distract himself by reading a recent report on the melting of Himalayan glaciers that suggested that the effects of climate change had been seriously underestimated. Many of the major glaciers were receding at an alarming rate. Since the 1960s, when he was climbing, most glaciers had shifted as much as a kilometer or two upstream. But at this moment, Afridi found it difficult to focus on the calculations of glaciologists. Impatiently, he set the report aside.

Daphne Shaw's safe arrival in Mussoorie was the first stage of a plan that he had worked out in his mind as carefully as he might have organized an assault on a mountain. He knew that Guldaar would attempt to kill her now. Reluctantly, he had accepted Manav's offer of upgrading security at HRI. A detachment of NSG 'black cat' commandoes had arrived the day before. Their commanding officer established a security perimeter to ensure that any threat on the ground was neutralized immediately. In particular, the annex where Daphne was to stay was protected by both an inner security cordon and an outer ring of NSG guards. Even Afridi himself had agreed to travel back and forth from his cottage with an armed escort. He also had to forgo his daily workouts on the Chukkar, which always made him irritable.

From here on in, it was likely to be a waiting game. Hunting a leopard took patience and perseverance. Afridi tried to lay his doubts to rest, but one piece of information that Major Yaqub had passed on troubled his conscience: the news that Jehangir Daruwalla had been shot. He had liked the man, despite his business associates, and felt responsible for his death.

Though nobody but Afridi and Manav Shinde knew that Daphne was being flown to Mussoorie, it was obvious that word of her presence at HRI would leak out. The Americans would learn of it through Holman, while Major Yaqub would probably connect the dots. Guldaar himself had plenty of informers in place. None of this worried Afridi, for he knew that whatever happened next, it would all be over soon enough.

Just then, there was a sharp knock on the office door, which opened before Afridi could respond. HRI's chief analyst, Narender Rawat, stepped inside. His anxious features showed even more strain than usual.

'Sir,' he said. 'The helicopter took off from Delhi at 17:23. We received confirmation from Air Traffic Control, but thirty-eight minutes into the flight, they lost all contact.'

'What do you mean?' Afridi snapped, both hands instinctively reaching for the wheels on his chair.

'It's gone from radar, sir. Disappeared.'

Forty-Six

Fletcher was not a prejudiced man, but there were certain things that annoyed him to the point of bias and discrimination. One of these was Starbucks. Their coffee was okay, but the elaborate vocabulary they used seemed unnecessarily confusing. All he wanted was a regular cup of coffee with cream and sugar, but instead he had to ask for a grande Kenyan Double Roast. The guy ahead of him in line had his formula worked out, a 'cinnamon dolce latte with an extra shot of Blonde Roast Madagascar.' Usually, Fletcher bought his coffee from a newsstand at the Virginia Square metro station near his office. It had a bitter-sour flavor, suggesting it was brewed the day before, but he could drown it in cream and take the edge off with three packets of sugar. His doctor had tried to get him to switch to artificial sweeteners, but this morning, he didn't care if he lived beyond today.

The woman he was meeting had suggested a Starbucks in Georgetown, because she was familiar with that area. Reluctantly, he had agreed. Fletcher considered getting a blueberry scone with his coffee but abstained, remembering his doctor's warning. Blood pressure, cholesterol, sugar—none of the numbers were looking good.

He was just sitting down, when he saw her coming through the door. There was a family resemblance. She looked around, trying to get her bearings. Fletcher raised a hand and stood up.

'Ms McKenzie. I'm Carlton Fletcher,' he said, shaking her hand.

'Ruth,' she said, with a tense sort of smile.

'Would you like some coffee? I'm afraid I went ahead and got mine.'

'I'll join you in a minute.'

He watched her as she went across and ordered. It was hard to know what she was thinking. Her brother had been abducted two weeks ago, and there was no word if he was alive or dead. She had been contacting everyone she could think of in the government, including her congressman and senator, as well as the embassy in Islamabad. Fletcher wasn't sure if she had any information that might prove useful, but he'd decided to give her a call. On the phone, Fletcher had warned her that he didn't have any updates to share with her, but that didn't stop Ruth McKenzie from driving down to Washington from West Virginia. To keep things simple, he told her that he worked for the State Department, Citizens' Services.

'Thank you for meeting me,' she said, bringing a cup of tea to the table.

'I wish I had some good news for you,' Fletcher said. 'But there's been no communication in the last six days. We've been in touch with the Pakistanis, and they're not telling us much, except that your brother's captors seem to be some Taliban splinter group.'

'What demands have they made?' she asked.

'They want money, of course, two million dollars, and the release of some of their men who are prisoners in Afghan jails.'

'I read that in the papers,' said Ruth, impatiently. 'But somebody must be in touch with them through unofficial channels.'

'As a policy, the US government doesn't negotiate with terrorists,' said Fletcher. 'Nevertheless, we're trying our best to get him out of there.'

'Mr Fletcher, honestly,' she said, 'I don't think anyone's trying hard enough.'

'If we had a better idea where he was—'

'We know he went up into one of the valleys beyond Garam Chashma, north of Chitral. They found the bodies of his companions. How difficult is it to send in helicopters?' Ruth's voice was breaking.

'If he's a hostage, they'd shoot him as soon as the choppers arrived,' said Fletcher. 'These guys are ruthless. Besides, we don't know if they've moved him out of there. It's like a labyrinth in that region. With the earthquake, nobody knows what's going on.'

She sat silent for a moment, staring at her tea. He waited thirty seconds.

'Ruth,' he said, putting his hand on her arm. 'I can promise you, we're doing all we can, but if there's anything you know that would help us out, I'd be grateful...'

Her eyes were tearing up and she took a napkin to wipe her nose. 'What would I be able to tell you?' she said.

'Luke visited you and your partner just before he went back to Pakistan.'

She nodded.

'Did he say anything unusual before he left?'

'No. We hardly saw him. He was going to stay with us for a week, but then the earthquake happened and he rushed back to Pakistan.'

'Did your brother ever talk about his contacts in that part of the world, people he might have known?'

'Not really. He had a lot of friends who were journalists, mostly.'

'You were born in Pakistan, weren't you?'

'Yes. In Murree, like Luke.'

'But you didn't go back, did you? He seemed to think of it as home.'

'Sure, but it's different for a woman, and I didn't have the same kind of ties that he maintained in Pakistan.'

'What kind of ties?' said Fletcher.

'I don't know. Luke loves it there. He always says it's the only place on earth where he can be himself.'

'He doesn't like America?'

'Not really,' said Ruth. 'He only comes here to visit me, and for work.'

'He's the father of your daughter, isn't he?' said Fletcher. 'I mean, your partner's daughter.'

Ruth looked up defensively.

'How do you know that?' she said. 'He told me,' said Fletcher.

'When?'

'In Islamabad. I met him there a month ago.'

'Okay,' said Ruth. She wrapped both hands around her cup of tea, as if to keep it warm. Fletcher could see the uncertainty and suspicion in her eyes.

'So, there's nothing more that you can tell me about your brother that might help us find him…any details about his personal or professional life?'

She shook her head. Fletcher took the plastic cover off his cup and drank a third of his coffee before he spoke.

'Did Luke tell you that on his last visit, he was accompanying a dead body on the plane from Pakistan?'

Ruth reacted with confusion. 'No way,' she said.

'It's true,' said Fletcher. 'He volunteered to travel back with the coffin. The dead man was an undercover NSA operative who was tortured and killed because he discovered an illegal arms deal between an American company and the Pakistanis.'

'Why are you telling me this?' said Ruth.

'Because Luke might have said something to you,' said Fletcher. 'You see, we're really not sure how much he knows or what he's hiding.'

'Luke didn't say anything to me about it,' Ruth replied. 'Are you suggesting that he was involved?'

'We've been keeping an eye on your brother for a while,' said Fletcher. 'You see, we really don't know what he's got himself into. Some of the people he associated with in Rawalpindi were extremists, jihadis. They seemed to have an influence on him.'

'What are you saying?' Ruth demanded.

'Ms McKenzie, we have to consider the possibility that your brother may not have been abducted. He could be working with the Taliban. It's possible that he shot the two men who were with him and made it look like he was taken hostage.'

Forty-Seven

The last known location of the helicopter was 180 kilometers north of Delhi along the Yamuna River, which was the standard flight path to Dehradun. Ambala was the closest airbase, and two IAF helicopters had been dispatched from there for search and rescue. The Sikorsky was likely to have gone down within a radius of a hundred kilometers, much of which was farmland and forest. There had been no distress signal or any communication from the pilots, nothing but a sudden silence followed by no transmissions of any kind. Without hesitating, Afridi ordered Captain Bhandari to get the Lama ready. Fifteen minutes later they were airborne, heading southwest across the Doon Valley. It was just past six in the evening, only an hour of daylight left. The fact that nobody on the ground had reported a crash made Afridi think the chopper might have landed somewhere in the Shivalik hills, a low range of forested mountains that ran parallel to the Himalayas. Most of this area was part of Rajaji National Park, a tiger reserve that straddled the eroded ridgelines of the Shivaliks.

Afridi remained in constant contact with his team at HRI, who were monitoring Air Force communications, as well as wireless reports from the police and forest department, all of whom had been alerted. After crossing over the outskirts of Dehradun, the Lama descended from seven thousand feet to just over three thousand feet above sea level, and less than a hundred feet above the ground. A dense sal forest lay beneath them as they approached the first line of hills. Southward stretched a series of dry riverbeds, which flooded during the monsoon. Afridi kept his eyes fixed on these boulder-strewn ribbons of sand, hoping that the Sikorsky had been able to make a safe landing.

For twenty minutes the Lama zigzagged back and forth over the forest. At one point Afridi saw a herd of deer running for cover as they passed over one of the ridges. A few minutes later they spotted a column of smoke rising from the edge of the jungle, but when they flew in low to investigate, they could see it was just a farmer burning grass along the margins of his fields.

'How much fuel do we have?' Afridi asked the pilot, through the radio in his helmet.

'Another forty minutes, sir, then we'll have to turn back,' Flight Lieutenant Bhandari replied.

In the distance, they spotted one of the Air Force Mi-17 choppers, circling over sugarcane fields near Saharanpur. The sun was slipping toward the horizon.

'Cut across to the Yamuna,' said Afridi, 'downstream from Paonta Sahib.'

The pilot took a sharply banked turn then straightened out, following the furrowed ridges westward. Within five minutes they could see the river, and Afridi caught sight of Timli forest rest house. To their right, he could see where the Asan barrage emptied into a canal. The main river flowed out of the mountains, its water level low this time of year. When they reached the Yamuna, the pilot turned south, and they passed the confluence of the Giri. The white domes of the gurdwara at Paonta Sahib stood to their right, but soon they were over forest again.

'The last signal was thirty kilometers south of here. If they had any chance to land, it could be somewhere in this vicinity.' Afridi's voice sounded hoarse inside his helmet, as if someone else were speaking.

The riverbank was almost a kilometer wide, with the main current flowing along the western shore, right up against the forest. On the other side, beyond the sand, lay elephant grass and scrub jungle. In the fading light, it was difficult to make out any distinct shapes.

'Sir, something over there,' the pilot said, pointing with his left hand.

They were flying directly into the setting sun. The glare made it difficult to see. For ten or fifteen seconds, Afridi was blinded, but as the pilot circled southward, he caught sight of a reflection, a bright flash of light. They were now no more than fifty feet above the ground. As they angled away from the sun, Afridi caught sight of something near the edge of the riverbank. He recognized the tail and rotor of a helicopter rising out of the tall grass.

'It's them,' he shouted.

Bhandari informed the Air Force choppers by radio that the crash site had been located. As they approached, coming in low over the sandbanks littered with river rocks, Afridi stared hard ahead of him for any movement or sign of life. It seemed to take forever before they reached the elephant grass, but as they did, two figures emerged, waving their arms. One of them was Anna.

The rotors kicked up sand as they descended. Afridi could see that the Sikorsky had come in at an angle and tipped over on one side, though the helicopter seemed to be intact. As Bhandari cut the Lama's engine, Afridi removed his helmet and opened his hatch. Once the rotor blades had stopped, Anna came running across.

From the expression on her face, Afridi knew that everyone was safe.

'We're all alive,' she shouted. 'One of the pilots broke his collarbone. Agent Holman fractured her leg and cracked some ribs.'

'What about Daphne?' Afridi asked.

'She's fine. Shaken up a little, but no injuries at all. She and I were sitting at the back. It was a hard landing but not a serious crash. Fortunately, the chopper didn't catch fire.'

'Thank God for that,' Afridi said. 'And you're not hurt?'

'Nothing serious,' said Anna, breaking into a smile. 'I sprained my shoulder, but other than that, I'm fine. We would have called you but there's no signal here.'

'What happened?' said Afridi.

'No idea,' said Anna. 'Suddenly, everything shut down, the avionics, radio, all of the computerized navigation systems. It was like someone threw a switch. Fortunately, the engines kept running, but the pilot was afraid they would shut off too. That's why he brought us down as quickly as he could. Didn't want to take any chances.'

'And you had no warning?'

'Nothing,' said Anna. 'We were flying along normally, at about ten thousand feet. The pilot told us that we had another fifteen minutes to go, when all at once his voice cut out. Even the communication system inside the chopper shut down.'

By now, Bhandari had unstrapped himself. He went across with Anna to see where the others were waiting with the injured. Within five minutes, the two Air Force helicopters arrived with a deafening roar of engines, kicking up a sandstorm on the riverbank. They had a medical team on board, who quickly took over, carrying stretchers and first aid equipment. Afridi spoke to the squadron leader who was piloting one of the rescue choppers. They agreed that the casualties would be taken to the nearest hospital in Dehradun. Two Air Force personnel would stay with the chopper until the police arrived. A short distance from the crash site was a Gujjar settlement, and several boys from there had gathered. They had been herding buffaloes nearby. Squatting on their haunches, they studied the scene with nonchalant curiosity, as if this sort of thing happened all the time.

Afridi watched the injured pilot and the American agent being carried onto the chopper. They were lucky the Sikorsky had gone down where it did. Another hundred yards to the west, and they would have crashed into a jungle of kikar trees. Minutes later, Anna led Daphne over to the Lama. Afridi recognized her immediately. He was surprised how calm she appeared. Her clothes were barely rumpled, and it looked as if she'd even combed her hair. When Anna introduced them, Daphne held out her hand.

'I'm sorry you've had such a terrible experience,' said Afridi. 'I hope you're all right.'

She gazed at him with a look of relief.

'I'm fine, thank you,' she said. 'Colonel Afridi, it's good to meet you at last.'

'My pleasure. I only wish it was under different circumstances.' He began to explain that the second Air Force chopper would ferry them to Dehradun, where HRI vehicles would pick them up and drive them to Mussoorie, but Daphne interrupted. 'I was hoping you'd offer me a lift,' she said.

'Of course,' he said. 'There's room for just one passenger at the back. It's a little cramped but the flight takes only twenty minutes.'

'Don't worry. I'll manage,' she said, as Anna helped her climb into the jump seat. A few minutes later, they were airborne. Though the noise from the engine was too loud for them to have a conversation, Afridi pointed out the town of Mussoorie spread along the top of the ridge, the profiles of the higher Himalayas in the background catching the last rays of sunlight in a magenta glow.

Forty-Eight

Every Thursday at 8:00 a.m. a barber arrived at Ivanhoe to give Afridi a haircut and shave. It was a ritual that his father had instilled in him from an early age. As a boy, Afridi had never enjoyed getting his hair cut, but he was always fascinated by the way the barber performed a rapid-fire scalp massage with all sorts of sound effects, the snapping of knuckles and vertebrae, the clap of palms after kneading shoulders and neck. Now, years later, it was still part of his weekly ritual. The head massage lasted ten minutes, with the grand finale of a double karate chop that sounded as if Afridi's skull had cracked, leaving him blinking with momentary amnesia. The barber, Iqbal, trekked all the way up from New Bombay Hair Dressing Salon in town. He understood that Afridi was a punctual man, and he always arrived a few minutes early, carrying an attaché case with the tools of his trade.

Afridi shaved himself most days, but Thursday mornings he enjoyed the luxury of sitting back and letting Iqbal lather his cheeks. It was also a chance to catch up on gossip from the town, the latest scandals, which Iqbal related with relish—whose daughter had run off with whom and which court case was coming up for a hearing. Iqbal was critical of every politician in town, from the ward representatives to the local member of the state legislative assembly. He had stories of bribes being paid and contracts awarded to cousins and nephews. All of this was recounted as the straight razor stroked Afridi's throat, its sharp blade scraping away lather and beard with lethal delicacy. Afridi closed his eyes and threw back his head as if surrendering to an executioner's blade.

He often thought how a small town like Mussoorie mirrored the country at large, with its corruption, ineptitude, cronyism, and lack of civic norms. Sometimes he despaired, as when he heard from Iqbal how an engineer in the electricity department had filched all the light bulbs from streetlamps or about the contractor who paved the same road every other year, mixing ten times as much sand as cement so that it washed away in the monsoon. Exactly the same things happened in Delhi but on a larger scale, whether it was kickbacks on defense procurements or tainted political donations. He often wondered if there was any hope for the country when everyone took corruption for granted. Afridi's determination to bring Guldaar to justice was fueled by a conviction that if the source of corruption, the motivating evil, was uprooted, it might be possible to destroy the parasitic culture supported by cynicism and greed. But if he did succeed in capturing Guldaar, would it really make any difference?

After the shave was finished, the barber rinsed Afridi's face in a basin of warm water and offered to trim his mustache. This was a weekly argument between them. Afridi insisted that any man who let someone else trim his mustache didn't deserve to grow one. The other debate they had each week was whether Iqbal would be allowed to color Afridi's hair. The colonel refused to give in. He was content with natural gray, though it had been slowly getting whiter. Afridi also insisted on using his own aftershave, a subtle scent he got from a perfumer in France that bore a hint of citron and bergamot, unlike the attar of jasmine and roses that Iqbal doused on the faces of most of his clients.

As the barber began to snip his hair, Afridi wondered if Daphne was awake. Yesterday, she had retired to her suite soon after they landed at HRI. The two of them had agreed to meet this morning at 10:00 a.m. in his office. Anna had come up by jeep the evening before to brief him. Though it was unfortunate that the American agent had been injured—she was still in the hospital—Afridi felt relieved not to have her around.

The haircut itself never took more than five minutes. Iqbal worked quickly with a comb in his left hand, scissors in the right, taking off a centimeter each week. He held up a mirror for Afridi's approval, showing him the back first, then the sideburns and front. With the sheet draped around his neck and covering the wheelchair to his knees, Afridi thought for a moment he looked the same as he did when he was a boy, trussed up in a chair and squirming to get free. But now the massage began. Iqbal's steady stream of stories ended as he cracked his knuckles and gripped Afridi's head, like a potter centering a lump of clay.

Closing his eyes, the colonel tried to forget Guldaar, though it seemed impossible. In his mind he could see the bandaged face from thirty years ago, the bruised eye watching him. Over time, he had researched and uncovered so many details about this man. Yet Guldaar remained a disturbing enigma, more of a 'metaphor than a man,' as Afridi had described him to Anna. That was the worrying part. He couldn't be sure his assumptions were true, whether Guldaar was motivated by criminal instincts or something larger and more sinister.

The barber was now working his way up either side of Afridi's cranium, kneading his hair at the roots. A head massage stimulated blood flow, and Iqbal swore that his weekly champi was the only reason Afridi hadn't gone bald.

Iqbal's deft fingers unknotted his anxieties and doubts, loosening the tangled calculations in Afridi's mind. The barber was now gently pinching both eyebrows between forefinger and thumb, which made Afridi's eyes water. Soon a furious drum tattoo was performed on every hemisphere of his scalp, beaten with an expert touch. With a final flourish, the percussionist accelerated the tempo. For the next three minutes, his mind went blank and the menacing specter of Guldaar was completely erased by the pulsing rhythm of the barber's hands.

Forty-Nine

'How many of these mountains have you climbed?'

'Only three that we can see from here.'

'Which are they?'

'That first one to the west, shaped like the dorsal fin of a fish. It's called Swargrohini, which means light of heaven.'

'A beautiful shape, more like a wave than a fin.'

'If you go across to the right, moving eastward, there's a sharp peak called Sri Kantha and beside it a cluster of summits in the Gangotri group. One of those is Rudragaira. That was the first peak I climbed, back in 1961. That was a lucky year for me. I'd just joined the army and climbed four major peaks in one season, including Trishul. Of course, the next year we went to war with China and everything changed after that. The Himalayas lost their innocence and became a strategic battleground instead of a place of unspoiled beauty and romantic myths.'

'Can you see Trishul from here?'

'No, it's farther to the east, hidden behind that lower range of hills.'

'Which was the third mountain you climbed?'

'Chaukhamba. It's over there, in among those peaks to the east beyond Kedarnath. 7,138 meters above sea level.'

'Seeing them from here, it's hard to imagine anyone climbing to the top.'

'The closer you get, the more complex and challenging they appear, until you're on the mountain itself, and then you just keep going because it's too late to turn back.'

They were outside, on the terrace of the main building at HRI, looking out upon the Garhwal Himalayas. It was a clear morning for this time of year, though a haze of dust, rising from the plains, obscured the farthest peaks. Daphne seemed rested and at ease, despite the events of the day before. Armed commandoes were standing guard, two of them at the gate and another positioned at the edge of the verandah.

'I'm sorry, I didn't mean to keep you standing out here. Please come inside.' Afridi gestured toward his office and wheeled himself up a ramp as she followed.

'It's nice to be outdoors,' she said. 'I've never been to Mussoorie before. Back in the seventies I visited Simla once, and every summer when I was a girl we'd spend a month in Darjeeling, riding the train up from Siliguri with my father. He was in the Railways.'

Afridi opened the door for her. He was glad to escape the attentive gaze of the NSG commandoes. Instead of wheeling himself behind his desk, he offered Daphne one of the chairs near the bookshelves and positioned himself so he was facing her.

'Your father was with the Eastern Railways?'

'Yes, he was posted in Cal for years as a freight inspector at Howrah Station. That's where I grew up, mostly. Later, we moved to Jamshedpur for a while. But originally, our family is from Mughal Sarai.'

'So, you're not Greek, are you?' he said with a knowing smile.

She laughed, tossing back her head and brushing a hand through her hair.

'No,' she said. 'Cent percent Anglo-Indian. But my mother used to enjoy Greek mythology, which is probably why she named me Daphne. It was only when I got to Bombay that people suggested I might be Greek, part of the fiction they create in films.'

'Nobody is ever who they say they are.'

She looked at him with mischief in her eyes.

'I suppose that applies to you as well,' said Daphne.

'Perhaps,' said Afridi. 'But I'm too old to wear a disguise.'

'Who knows?' she said.

There was a pause in their conversation, and Daphne looked around the office, noticing the mountaineering pictures on the walls and a framed map of the Himalayas, stretching from Kashmir to NEFA, as it used to be called. She could tell it was an old Survey of India map, printed long before independence.

'I'm afraid I have some sad news,' Afridi said, in a muted voice.

She looked at him with a pensive expression, ready to hear the worst.

'We've received a report that Jehangir Daruwalla has been killed.'

He could see her wince, though she tried not to show it.

'When? How did it happen?'

'About a week ago. Of course, it's still not confirmed, but I have no reason to doubt our sources. From what we've learned, it seems he was shot by Guldaar himself.'

Daphne looked away, her lips tightening and the color draining from her face.

'I'm sorry,' Afridi said.

She shook her head but kept silent.

'The truth is, I'm probably to blame for it,' Afridi continued. 'I offered to protect him, and we could have forced him to stay in India.'

'No,' she said. 'It's my fault completely.'

'He was a close friend of yours.'

'Yes,' she said, her voice shaking. 'The only person I could trust.'

'Jehangir was involved in a very dangerous game.'

'Maybe. But that wasn't the reason he was killed,' she whispered.

Afridi reached toward his desk and offered her a box of tissues.

Daphne took two and dabbed the corners of her eyes, then blew her nose.

'Jehangir told me that you were being forced to keep your son alive,' Afridi said.

'Nothing is ever as simple as it seems,' she replied. 'But yes, it wasn't my choice. Sometimes you realize it's better to let go of life.'

'Did Guldaar come to see you often?'

'Once or twice a year,' she said. 'It was always a surprise.'

'How did he travel to the United States?'

'The government helped him, the CIA. He once showed me that he had a US passport. He was always boasting about the people he knew in Washington and how he could enter the country without anyone knowing he was there. He'd even been to the White House for some dinner in honor of a Saudi prince. Jimmy always made it seem as if nobody could touch him.'

'You call him Jimmy?'

She glanced at her nails for a moment, and Afridi could see they were cut short but painted a pale salmon color.

'Yes, that was a nickname I gave him when we first met in Bombay. Jamshed Khan sounded too formal. I'm the only one who called him Jimmy.'

'It's not a name that suits him,' said Afridi.

'What's in a name?' she said. 'Bombay. They call it Mumbai now. It seems so silly.'

'And you became Daphne Shaw, with a 'w' instead of an 'h'.'

'Yes, but 'Shah' wasn't the name I was born with,' she said.

'Really?' Afridi was surprised.

'No. It was Murphy. When I came to Bombay, the first producer to cast me in a picture told me that nobody would go to see a Hindi film in which the heroine was called 'Daphne Murphy.' He said it sounded like a transistor radio, and people would make a joke of it.'

'What made you choose Shah?'

'It seemed a neutral choice. Could be Hindu, Muslim, or Christian, and I didn't feel like explaining too much about myself. The producer wanted me to change my first name too, but I refused. I hope you haven't watched any of my films,' she said, the tissues still clutched in one hand. 'They're all so dreadful. Jehangir used to tease me, calling me a vamp because of the dresses they put me in with cleavage showing and slits up the thighs. I can't tell you how awful the costumes were.'

'You don't miss acting?' he asked.

'Not at all. I didn't like the celebrity or the innuendoes, either,' she said. 'But I loved Bombay, particularly when Jehangir would take me out for dinner at a seafood place in Juhu. We'd eat crab curry and laugh all night.'

'I asked him if you were lovers,' Afridi said.

She paused for a moment and caught her breath.

'Forgive me,' Afridi said. 'That was tactless.'

'No,' she said with a shake of her head. 'I'm curious. What was his answer?'

'He laughed at me and said you were close friends, that was all.'

'A true gentleman,' said Daphne, 'to the end.'

'How did you meet Guldaar?'

'He came on the sets of one of my films. I didn't know who he was. Later, he invited me to dinner. It took a while for me to fall under his spell,' said Daphne, her voice echoing a note of regret. 'He can be charming and generous when he wants. Even now, if you meet him, he's personable and witty, a very likeable man. It's only when you realize the things he's done that you understand how cruel and ruthless he actually is. In fact, it makes it worse, because he puts on such a civilized mask.'

'What about the Sikander-e-Azam Trust?'

'I don't know much about that,' said Daphne. 'Jimmy started it while I was in America. It sounds as if they do good work. He's very proud of it, and when he'd come to see me, he'd talk about the schools and medical centers he was opening. To be honest, I found it odd, because he isn't a charitable man, but it seems as if he really wants to help develop that region and improve the lives of those who live there. Maybe it's just guilt, a form of atonement.'

'Do you have any photographs of him?' Afridi asked.

Daphne shook her head. 'He was always camera shy,' she said. 'After a while it became an obsession for him. Jimmy guards his anonymity. Even Jehangir never met him, though he worked for him for almost twenty years.'

'You kept in touch with Jehangir, after you moved to the United States?'

'Yes. As I said, he was the only person I could trust,' Daphne replied. 'We would talk on the phone once a week. Jimmy often used him to send me messages or money, when I needed it.'

'What exactly was his relationship with Guldaar?'

'Jehangir was a go-between, his personal emissary, and they often spoke on the phone. Jimmy used to say sometimes that you need to keep a distance from those you trust, hiding your identity to protect each other. Quite often, if there was a business meeting, he sent Jehangir in his place, as his double or stand-in. Of course, nobody knew it wasn't Jimmy. This was after he'd left Bombay and moved to Dubai, then back to Pakistan, when he began to really earn his fortune. He happened to be at the right place at the right time when the Russians invaded Afghanistan. I remember, I was worried about him being so close to the border, but Jehangir told me that Jimmy was probably the safest man on earth because everybody needed him. He was like a croupier at a roulette table, who was taking all the winnings for himself.'

'Did you visit Guldaar in Pakistan?' Afridi wondered how much of what she said was true, or whether these were lines she'd rehearsed, a scripted version of her life.

'Several times. Before Naseem's accident. I used to fly from Bombay to the Gulf, then catch another flight to Islamabad, switching passports along the way. But I didn't like it there. Boring. I couldn't go outside on my own. He had a beautiful home in the mountains that the CIA built for him, like some kind of suburban American dream house set down in the Hindu Kush. It was a bizarre place, surrounded by fortified walls, razor wire, and landmines, but inside it was very peaceful, a quiet, comfortable home.'

Afridi listened to her talk with a detached sense of curiosity. He already knew most of what she was telling him, and it confirmed what Daruwalla had said. When she paused for a moment, he watched her for any sign of nervousness or discomfort, but she seemed to be telling the truth, clouded by sadness.

'When we spoke on the telephone the first time,' Afridi said, 'you told me that you could positively identify Guldaar.'

Daphne seemed to study him for a moment.

'Is this when my interrogation begins?' she asked, with a disarming smile.

'Perhaps.' Afridi folded his hands together. 'But I didn't mean to make it sound that way. Forgive me.'

'Please don't misunderstand,' said Daphne. 'I'm grateful to be here, and I appreciate your help and hospitality, but I want to be completely clear about what happens next, before I begin to answer questions.'

'What happens next?' Afridi said, with a quizzical glance.

'I mean, am I going to live here in Mussoorie for the rest of my life, guarded by armed men in monkey caps and combat gear, or do you have some clever plan to give me a new identity so I can disappear into the anonymous void of India's great middle class?'

'Which option do you prefer?' Afridi asked.

'Neither,' she said, holding up one hand and counting with her fingers…one, two, three. 'I want to be safe. I want to be free. I want to be myself. For most of my life I've lived according to somebody else's plan. I'm tired of that, and I'm tired of being watched and followed all the time. Colonel Afridi, I'm sixty-one years old, and I've gone through a lot of uncertainty and sadness in my life. Now I just want to be happy from here on in.'

'That sounds like the script for a Bollywood movie,' Afridi said.

'Maybe it is,' she answered him with sincerity in her eyes. 'But I'm ready to buy a ticket to watch that movie and you better make sure it has a happy ending.'

'I offered you safe asylum. That's all. What happens next depends on whether Guldaar is killed or captured. You'll never be safe or happy until he's out of the way.'

'And you're ready to hunt him down?' Daphne said. 'I have to believe that you won't let him get away, because I know how easily he can manipulate a situation or buy his way out of trouble. If I am going to betray him any further, I need to be convinced that you will eliminate him once and for all.'

This time, it was Afridi's turn to glance aside, his eyes studying a photograph from 1961, when he stood on the summit of Chaukhamba. After a moment he looked back to meet her gaze.

'I can promise you that I will do everything I can to destroy Guldaar. Nothing will stop me from achieving that end, unless he kills me first. He may have money and influence, but I stand firmly behind my convictions,' Afridi's voice was level. 'That's all I can say.'

Daphne nodded. 'That's all I needed to hear.'

Without hesitation, Afridi continued, 'Then I'll ask you to start looking at some photographs and see if you can identify him for us.'

Fifty

Anna realized that Afridi would want to meet Daphne alone. She decided to stay in her room until she was called, glad to have an excuse to sleep in. Her left shoulder hurt, and she stretched it gingerly to ease the pain. The night before, she had briefed Afridi for half an hour, after which she called Manav Shinde and explained the circumstances of their departure from the United States. He was not happy to learn that she had taken an active role in Daphne's escape, nor was he pleased to hear that an American agent had accompanied them to India. Anna could sense his disapproval over the phone, his humor muted and noticeable silences between his words. But she also knew he understood why she hadn't contacted him. It allowed Shinde a margin for denial and room to maneuver if things got out of hand.

Right now, the only awkward element was Tracy Holman, who had been admitted to a hospital in Dehradun. Anna had helped her check in. She could see that Holman was in a lot of pain, with cracked ribs and a fractured leg. The doctor put her on painkillers and said she would be fine but required bed rest for at least a week. Manav indicated that as soon as she was fit to travel, he would coordinate with the US embassy to have her medevac'd out of the country. Of course, it would require a creative explanation and some delicate diplomacy to make the Americans understand how she entered the country without a visa and why she was on a helicopter with a fugitive, who was now under the protection of the Himalayan Research Institute in Mussoorie.

'I hope Colonel Afridi is finally satisfied,' said Manav, with curt impatience. 'He got what he wanted, but whether it will lead him to Guldaar remains to be seen. If you learn anything more, please keep me informed.'

'Yes, sir,' she said, with conscious formality, as they ended the call.

Now, as she lay in bed staring out the window at the sunlit slopes of the mountains, Anna wondered why a woman like Daphne would get involved with someone like Guldaar. He was obviously abusive, though she had described him as generous and charming when he wanted to be, even calling him a 'gentleman' more than once. Anna herself had known men like that, and she understood the dangerous attraction, though she had never allowed herself to get into a relationship she couldn't control. Daphne seemed strong-willed, but at times there was a hint of vulnerability about her. Anna wondered how the conversation with Afridi was going and whether Daphne would describe things differently to a man.

It was almost twelve o'clock when the phone finally rang and Afridi asked if she could come across to his office. Anna hurried to get dressed. She couldn't remember how long it had been since she'd stayed in bed until noon.

Afridi greeted her with a stern nod, and for once he came right to the point.

'Yesterday, when the Sikorsky lost all communication and avionics,' he said, 'that wasn't an accident, or human error, or some flaw in the manufacturing or design. It was a deliberate act. Someone compromised the computer systems on that helicopter. Thirty minutes after you took off from Delhi, this person keyed in an access code that is changed once a week. Using that code, along with a separate password, a specialist in Eggleston, Ohio, deployed a digital kill switch that caused a software failure.' Afridi paused for a moment, focusing on Anna's face. 'It's fortunate the engines didn't turn off as well and the pilot had the presence of mind to get you onto the ground as quickly as he did.'

'Are you sure?'

'Yes. Peregrine designs and programs the kill switch used in the Sikorsky. It's part of a highly classified project funded by the CIA. Virtually every major weapons system or aircraft that the United States sells to other countries incorporates this embedded technology. It's completely invisible and seldom activated but ensures that those armaments won't be used against the United States. Most buyers don't even know it's there. America's closest allies accept it as part of the price. The Israelis have spent millions of dollars trying to decipher the codes and override the kill switch, but they haven't succeeded.'

'So you're telling me the Americans can shut down any weapon or military vehicle they sell abroad?'

'Exactly,' said Afridi. 'Think about it. It's the perfect strategy for controlling conflict around the world. If Egypt suddenly orders its tanks to enter the Sinai, you switch them off and they won't even start. Their guidance systems go blank, and their artillery won't fire. It neutralizes any threat to peace. If the South Koreans decide to launch missiles across the demilitarized zone, you can stop the strike before it happens. Why do you think the Americans had such an easy time entering Iraq? All those vehicles disabled on the highway from Kuwait to Baghdad didn't just run out of fuel.'

'And Pakistan?' Anna said.

'Exactly,' Afridi said. 'A squadron of F-16s, stationed outside Lahore, can be disabled before their pilots have scrambled into the cockpits. They won't get off the ground, like pigeons whose wings have been clipped.'

'And Guldaar has access to this through Peregrine?'

'With the complicity of certain people in the CIA. Day after tomorrow, Guldaar himself is coming to Delhi, offering to sell our generals this capability. It's a tempting proposition. Half of

Pakistan's hardware immobilized. A perfect opportunity to take back disputed areas of Kashmir. The heavy guns on one side of Siachen Glacier would suddenly go silent, and India could capture Skardu within twelve hours.'

'Nobody in Delhi would seriously consider an offer like that.'

'Don't be so sure,' said Afridi. 'He'll be meeting with the defense secretary at noon, and there's a special briefing for the army chief right after that.'

'But it's absurd to think that India would go to war simply because we have an overwhelming strategic advantage. The truth is, we already have the capability to wipe out Pakistan, if we wanted.'

Afridi shook his head.

'It doesn't really matter if India entertains his offer. He's more interested in blackmailing Pakistan. Their generals and the ISI would be equally interested in controlling those codes, to keep their weapons functioning. First he speaks to Delhi, then he uses it to leverage his options in Islamabad.'

'Why can't the Americans just change the codes or disable the kill switch?'

'Well, for one thing, it's not that easy. Activating the kill switch is relatively simple, but dismantling the system involves a much more elaborate process. The other problem, of course, is that the United States doesn't want to acknowledge this technology.'

'Naturally,' said Anna. 'Because there would be far fewer customers for their products. Am I correct in assuming that Guldaar is blackmailing the CIA as well as Pakistan?'

Afridi looked at her and shrugged.

'I can't speculate.... Either way, it's a dangerous situation. If the Pakistanis feel they are cornered, they might panic and launch a preemptive nuclear strike. It's the worst-case scenario but totally within the realm of possibility.'

After a pause, Anna asked, 'Has Daphne been able to identify him in any of the photographs?'

'No, nothing,' said Afridi.

'What are we going to do?' Anna asked.

'I need you to go to Delhi immediately,' he said. 'Can you be ready in half an hour? The chopper will take you.'

'Of course,' said Anna.

'We have an extremely tight window of opportunity.'

'Yes, sir,' said Anna.

'I've spoken with Shinde, and he's approved your involvement—unofficially, of course. Anna, I want to make it clear that you are absolutely free to refuse this assignment. It's an extremely dangerous mission with a number of unpredictable risks. You'll be operating entirely outside standard procedures. Complete autonomy. Total exposure.'

'I'll have to speak with Manav first,' she said. 'He wasn't happy with what happened in America. I'm sure he thinks I overstepped my brief.'

'Unfortunately, Shinde isn't going to take your calls right now,' said Afridi. 'The situation is too sensitive.'

'Last evening, he specifically told me to keep him informed.'

'Everything changed this morning,' said Afridi. 'The day after tomorrow, there's a bilateral conference on reducing hostilities in Siachen. The minister of state for defense is meeting with his Pakistani counterpart, who flies into Delhi this evening. Guldaar will use this opportunity to broker a deal between Peregrine and our government as well as the Pakistanis. He's selling drones, but the kill switch option is also on the table, probably as a bargaining chip. We don't know how long he's going to be in Delhi, though he's likely to stay for only a few hours. Within that time frame, we need to isolate him and take him captive. Or, as a second option, eliminate him altogether.'

'Dead or alive,' said Anna with a reluctant smile.

'Exactly.'

'But if he's meeting the secretary and the generals,' said Anna. 'You aren't suggesting they're involved.'

'Not that we know,' said Afridi. 'But, frankly, at this point we don't trust anyone.'

'Which is why you're circumventing any chain of command.'

'Yes. That's why Manav has stepped out of the picture, though I can assure you he has given his consent. He will do whatever he can in Delhi to protect us. Nevertheless, if we fail, or if things go wrong, then you and I could be accused of treason or at the very least subverting national interests. Which is why you must decide if you want to accept the risks.'

'So, you're asking me to either kidnap Guldaar or assassinate him, whichever is expedient?' Anna asked.

'No,' said Afridi. 'We have someone else to do that job. Your assignment will be to contact him and provide support.'

Anna let out her breath slowly, studying Afridi with a cautious eye. Until now, she had believed he was acting in the best interests of the nation and she trusted his judgment. But by circumventing the intelligence community and the military's chain of command, even if Manav gave an ambivalent nod, Afridi seemed to be taking his obsession with Guldaar to the level of a personal vendetta.

'And who's this person I'm supposed to contact in Delhi?' she asked.

'His alias is Harsh Advani, but his real name is Major Yaqub Hussein, an ISI officer operating undercover,' said Afridi. 'For once, we're going to use the Pakistanis to do our dirty work.'

Fifty-One

'These birds must be carefully trained. Houbara bustards are three times their size, but when a falcon plummets from the air, it's like a rocket. Remember the formula they taught in school? Momentum equals mass times velocity.' Guldaar turned his gaze away from the plate glass window as he spoke.

'I'm afraid I never paid attention in physics,' Luke said.

'Whatever it may be, the falcon kills swiftly and efficiently. All you see is a puff of feathers and the houbara is knocked to the ground, and then it struggles for a moment before the falcon tears out its throat.'

The training facility was at a wadi forty kilometers outside Dubai, in the desert. An air-conditioned complex of rooms, including an aviary for the birds, stood on a low escarpment above the dry wash, which funneled out of a shallow canyon. Though it appeared as if there was nothing on all sides, Luke had seen fences stretching to the horizon when they drove through the gates. Outside the temperature was 110 degrees Fahrenheit, but inside the viewing gallery the air was pleasantly cool. Two sheikhs sat together on one side of the room, smoking and drinking coffee, while the trainers prepared for a demonstration.

Guldaar explained to Luke that the sheikhs had come from Qatar to purchase falcons. Two of the trainers appeared to be European. The other was Mongolian. Lighting a cigarette himself, Guldaar spoke about the traditions of falconry.

'The Mongolians understand the wind and raptors like nobody else. It's in their blood,' he said. 'They have a mystical relationship with these birds.'

Standing off to one side, in the shade of the buildings, was a man with two dogs on leashes. They were white Salukis with tasseled ears and feathery tails.

'What are the dogs for?' Luke asked.

'They'll chase down a wounded bird, if necessary,' said Guldaar. 'Salukis are the only dogs that Arabs consider clean enough to fetch an animal. The saliva of any other breed is haram. They're beautiful to watch when they run, like greyhounds. With the breeze in their coats, they look as if they're flying over the desert.'

A waiter entered carrying glasses of *karkade* and *limon*, along with a tray of canapés. He offered these to the sheikhs, then brought them across to Luke and Guldaar.

'Try one of these,' said Guldaar. 'Houbara pâté.'

Luke hesitated, then took a cracker smeared with something that looked like foie gras. It had a strong, gamey flavor.

'Have another, it's supposed to enhance your manhood.'

Luke declined but took a glass of lemonade. Outside, the falconer had emerged with a bird on his arm. The sheikhs picked up their binoculars and focused intently on the demonstration. Both Luke and Guldaar fell silent as the fatal drama began. The falconer removed the hood, and Luke could see the young bird swiveling its head, keen eyes alert to any sign of prey, its beak like the barb on a fish hook. A few seconds later, one of the cages was opened and a bustard emerged, running awkwardly for a few steps before taking flight. It looked like a small stork. Through the binoculars, Luke could see where it landed, perfectly camouflaged among the rocks and sand.

The falconer undid the leather jesses and released the raptor from his wrist. It was a shaheen falcon, and Luke could see its wings slicing through the air as it gained height. The wadi shimmered in the mid-morning sun, mirages creating pools of warped light, turning sand into liquid shapes.

'He's spotted it!' said Guldaar.

Luke watched the falcon hover, as its wings quivered against the sky. The bird seemed suspended on an invisible thread that was suddenly cut, and it plunged to the ground. All of this happened in silence—the only sound was the soft exhalation of air-conditioning. One of the sheikhs spoke, and the other laughed. Luke had lost sight of the houbara, but as he scanned the dry contours of the wadi with his binoculars, he finally spotted a wing flapping helplessly, feathers rustling in the throes of death. The falconer had gone forward now and seconds later, the bird of prey returned to his arm and was rewarded with a morsel of flesh. By this time, the dogs had been released and Luke watched them bounding across the sand, racing each other.

'Where do you get the houbaras?' Luke asked. 'I thought they were extinct in this part of the world.'

'We trap them in Pakistan and ship them here, alive. There's no other way to train the falcons. The birds have to recognize their prey.'

'And what will you do when there are no houbara left?' Luke asked. 'When they've all been hunted to extinction?'

Guldaar shrugged, glancing at his two clients across the room. 'By then the oil will also run out and this place will disappear back into the sand.'

By now, the dogs had returned, one of them with the dead bustard in his mouth. The handler took it gently and held the limp bird up for all to see. Instead of appreciating the triumph of the hunt, the beauty of the falcon and the dogs, Luke felt an empathy for the houbara, sacrificed for the pleasure of the sheikhs, knowing that he shared its fate.

Lighting another cigarette and shading his eyes from the glare outside, Guldaar put a hand on Luke's shoulder.

'I'll be traveling for the next few days,' he said.

'Where?' Luke asked. 'Back to Pakistan?'

'No,' Guldaar replied, breathing out a stream of smoke. 'Somewhere else. But I've got three more stories for you to write. I'll have the files delivered this afternoon.'

Fifty-Two

'It's kind of you to let me out of jail like this,' Daphne said.

'You're not a prisoner,' Afridi protested.

'Still, it felt a bit like house arrest.'

'Only for your protection.'

Against the advice of the NSG commander and ignoring security protocols that he himself had approved, Afridi had invited Daphne to dinner at his home. She was driven across with an armed escort and Black Cat commandoes were posted around the cottage. Once indoors, however, they had some privacy. Afridi had lit a fire in the fireplace and his cook was preparing their meal in the kitchen.

'What if I decide to walk out the gate and take my chances?' she asked.

'We'd have no choice but to stop you, I'm afraid. Until we know that Guldaar is no longer a threat, you'll have to accept our security arrangements,' he said, then wheeled himself toward the bar. 'What may I offer you to drink?'

'What are you having?' she asked.

'Scotch.'

'Then I'll have the same, if you don't mind drowning it in soda,' she said. 'I know some people think that's sacrilege.'

'I take soda with my whisky too.'

As he poured their drinks, she studied the climbing memorabilia on the walls, the ice axes crossed above the fireplace, and photographs taken on different Himalayan summits. But the picture that caught her eye was a watercolor painting of an alpine valley with a snow peak shaped like an ax-blade at the center.

'Which mountain is that?' she asked.

'Kolahoi, in Kashmir,' he said, glancing over his shoulder.

'Who painted it?'

'A friend of mine, many years ago. She was an artist who used to live on a houseboat in Srinagar,' said Afridi.

'An old girlfriend?' Daphne asked, as he handed her a drink.

'I suppose you could describe her as that,' he said. 'But she was a free spirit, and it would never have worked out.'

'Cheers,' said Daphne. They touched glasses before each of them took a sip.

'I hope your drink's all right?' he asked.

'It's stronger than I usually take it,' she said. 'You're going to get me drunk.'

'I can add more soda.'

'No thanks.'

Daphne had settled into a wingback chair opposite him, her drink beside her on the coffee table, next to a bowl of cashews and almonds.

'Where's Anna?' she asked.

'Gone to Delhi,' Afridi said.

'Preparing for Jimmy's arrival?'

He nodded.

'All right. Let's not talk about him,' she said, taking a cashew. 'Tell me about this house, instead. How long have you lived here?'

'I bought it just over twenty years ago,' said Afridi, 'but it took a while to renovate. The place had been neglected. I had to redo everything completely.'

'It's lovely,' she said. 'A bachelor's pad but tastefully done.'

For a while they talked about Ivanhoe, which was 170 years old. He explained that in the 1840s, when it was built, many of the houses in Mussoorie were named after the titles of books by Sir Walter Scott, or the settings of his novels and poems—Waverley, Woodstock, Rokeby, Alyndale.

'His books were bestsellers back then,' Afridi said. 'Walter Scott was the Jeffrey Archer of his day.'

'Have you read any of them?' she asked.

'I've tried, but they're heavy going, especially the poetry,' he said.

Glancing around her at the bookshelves, Daphne remarked, 'You must read a lot.'

'Not as much as I would like,' said Afridi, 'but I have a bookseller in town who gets me whatever I want. Strangely, though, more and more, I find myself going back to my old books nowadays. Rereading a novel after a gap of twenty or thirty years has a special pleasure, like traveling back in time.'

'It's funny you say that,' said Daphne. 'I'm the same as you. Before, I kept waiting for the latest book by an author I liked, but in the past fifteen years, since I moved to America, all I wanted to read was books I remembered from when I was young. Fortunately, I had the college library nearby, and I could find almost any title.'

She paused for a moment and sipped her scotch before continuing. 'The odd thing is that the books themselves are exactly the same, word for word, but you realize that you've become a different reader.'

Afridi laughed. 'How do you mean?'

'There are novels that I remember inspired me as a girl and excited my imagination, but now, when I go back to them, they ignite completely different feelings, sometimes sadness or regret…it's as if I understand things in a different way. The story hasn't changed, but I'm a different person and somehow that alters the book.'

'Do you ever wish you could start all over again?' Afridi asked.

She thought for a moment then shook her head. 'No. I'd probably end up making the same mistakes the second time round. There are many things I wish I could change in retrospect, but there's no point in thinking about that.'

'You've had a difficult life,' said Afridi, softly.

She smiled. 'And it's not over yet.'

'Forgive me for asking,' he said, 'but you never thought of leaving him?'

'Often,' she said. 'I ran away a couple of times, but Jimmy always had a way of finding me. He wouldn't give me that choice. He's a jealous, possessive man, though he never had the decency to marry me.'

'He had other wives?' Afridi asked.

'Two I think, maybe more,' she said. 'But I was the only woman who gave him a child.'

There were tears in her eyes. Afridi reached over to take her glass and moved toward the bar. As he poured the scotch, he asked, 'Did he ever threaten to kill you?'

'More than once,' she said. 'Sometimes, he would accuse me of having an affair, for no reason except that I happened to mention another man's name. He would lose his temper and take out a pistol and point it at me, saying he knew I was unfaithful.'

'Were you?'

She accepted the glass from his hands and raised it to her lips before answering.

'Only with Jehangir.'

For several minutes both of them stared at the fire in silence before she collected herself with a choked sort of laugh. 'I'm sorry. I thought we weren't going to talk about him.'

Over dinner, they avoided the topic of Guldaar and spoke about Bombay instead. She said it was the only city where she felt at home. Afridi's cook had made dhansak, one of his specialties, the mutton simmered all day with lentils until the flavors of meat and pulses merged. Daphne ate very little. Still, she enjoyed the meal, especially a simple dish of spinach and turnips with hot phulkas that the cook brought straight from the stove to the table.

'This was one of the things I missed in America,' she said.

'Sometimes I'd cook a little dal and rice for myself. The closest Indian restaurant was in Cincinnati, and I wasn't going to drive all the way there just to eat limp naan and butter chicken that tastes like ketchup.'

'I usually eat very simply,' said Afridi. 'It's only when I have guests that Mela Ram gets to show off his recipes.'

'You don't mind living alone?' she asked.

'No. I'm used to the solitude and my routines,' he said.

'I know what you mean,' Daphne replied. 'People used to feel sorry for me in America, being on my own, but it becomes a habit after a while. I was a bit of a hermit there, shutting out the world as best I could. Of course, it helps when you read a lot.'

'Your son was in a hospital nearby?' Afridi asked.

'Yes,' she said, 'But Naseem never knew I was there. It was like being alone in a room, except that someone else is present, a shadow, a shape beneath the sheets. Does that make sense?'

'It must have been terrible to lose him like that,' said Afridi.

'Well, nothing's ever easy in life,' said Daphne. 'But you learn to cope with what you've lost, and it makes you appreciate what little remains.'

'I'm sorry,' said Afridi.

Daphne shook her head and smiled. 'Don't be,' she said. 'I've never wanted anyone to pity me. I'm sure you feel the same.'

Afridi watched her closely, admiring her bravery, as he took the napkin from his lap and folded it beside his plate. By this time, the cook had cleared their plates and served them crème caramel that Daphne ate in tiny bites, savoring the bittersweet flavor of burnt sugar.

After dinner, they returned to the fire, now reduced to embers. It was warm enough in the room, and Afridi didn't bother to add more wood.

'It's a beautiful fireplace,' said Daphne. 'I always wished I had a real one in Ohio, but my house was centrally heated and there was an electric grate, with an artificial log that burned every winter without ever turning to ash.'

'I rebuilt this fireplace when I bought the house. The true measure of a good fire is when it burns down to coals. If it's banked correctly, there's still some warmth the next morning, a few embers among the ashes,' Afridi said. 'Will you have another whiskey, or some cognac?'

'No, thank you,' she said, 'but please go ahead yourself.'

He got a fresh glass and this time drank the scotch neat, an inch of amber fluid catching the firelight like a liquid flame burning inside a crystal lens.

'May I ask you a personal question?' Daphne spoke softly.

'I suppose,' he said. 'After all, I've asked you more than I should have.'

Her smile made her eyes light up again. 'Did you ever think of getting married?'

He let the scotch numb his tongue for a moment before he answered.

'Earlier, yes. But after my accident I reconciled myself to a single life. I didn't want anyone to take care of me,' he said. 'I didn't want to be treated like an invalid.'

'You fell off a mountain?'

'In a manner of speaking,' he replied. 'Between the injuries and the frostbite, I lost the use of my legs. I suppose I could have let it destroy me. For a while, I drank too much…

He held the glass up to the light.

'But then I realized that I didn't want to end up being a pathetic old man in a wheelchair drooling into his scotch.'

Her eyes were moist but instead of sympathy in her gaze, he saw that she understood.

'You must miss the mountains,' she said. 'I mean, climbing.'

He set his drink down and put his hands together in a gesture of finality.

'Sometimes there's a sensation in my legs, as if I'm walking through deep snow. I can't feel anything, but I'm aware of the coldness coming up to my thighs, each time my foot sinks in, like I'm struggling to break a path across a white expanse of emptiness.' He spoke slowly, as if he could feel it now. 'Of course it's all in my imagination, nothing more than residual memories in my nerves.'

For a minute or more he looked lost, as he stared at the glowing coals.

'I should be going,' said Daphne, rising to her feet. He nodded. 'I hope I wasn't being maudlin.'

'Of course not. I'm grateful…' She stopped and left the sentence unfinished.

'For what?' he asked.

'You rescued me,' she said, with a laugh.

'May I ask you one last question, before you leave?' he said. Daphne shrugged and studied him with a pensive smile.

Afridi paused and picked up his drink, letting the whiskey moisten and burn his lips.

'Naseem. Your son,' he said. 'Was Guldaar really his father?'

Daphne looked away for a moment and then turned to face the remains of the fire, both palms held out as if she'd suddenly felt a chill.

'No,' she said, 'though Jimmy was convinced.'

'Jehangir?'

Afridi expected to see sadness on her face when she turned around, but Daphne looked contented, at peace with herself. She touched his shoulder with one hand and nodded, though he had already seen the confirmation in her eyes.

He wheeled himself across to the door and opened it for her. 'The guards will take you back to your room,' he said. 'Good night.'

Fifty-Three

The video clip was being shown repeatedly on every news channel while copies circulated online. The news segments began with a warning about graphic and disturbing content. Portions had been deliberately blurred to protect the sensibilities of viewers, but most online versions were unexpurgated. Anna picked it up as soon as she reached Delhi, from a Facebook post a friend had sent her. Usually, she didn't watch video links that people forwarded, ignoring most of her messages and updates, but this one came with the headline: AMERICAN HOSTAGE TORTURED. 24 HOUR DEADLINE FOR BEHEADING.

Only two minutes and thirty-eight seconds long, the video was shot on a cheap digital camera. The resolution was poor. No editing had been done, the stationary camera focused on a naked man seated in a chair, hands tied behind his back. His face was clearly visible, staring straight ahead with a look of fear and exhaustion. Two men wearing ski masks entered the frame, carrying a large battery and jumper cables. In the background was a bare concrete wall. One of the captors held up a copy of *Dawn*. It took a moment for the camera to focus on the date of the newspaper—it was this morning. Then they attached the clamps from the jumper cables to the man's genitals and connected the battery. The hostage threw his head back and screamed, convulsing with the shock. After five seconds, the battery was disconnected and one of the men spoke to the camera. Anna couldn't understand what he said, though it sounded like a dialect of Pushto. After delivering the brief message, he stepped aside and the hostage was shown again breathing heavily and leaning sideways, eyes glazed with pain. Once again the cables were attached, and sparks flew as the torture continued. The clip ended abruptly, when the camera was switched off.

Watching the video, Anna felt sick to her stomach, revolted by the crude violence of the scene and the victim's agony. Identified as Luke McKenzie, the hostage was an American journalist who had been kidnapped two weeks earlier by unknown militants in the mountains west of Chitral. Their demand was simple. The United States must stop all drone attacks in Afghanistan and Pakistan within twenty-four hours, or the hostage would be decapitated.

Checking the time on her phone, Anna saw it was already 8:00 p.m. It would take her half an hour to reach the restaurant where she was meeting Major Yaqub. Afridi had arranged everything, but she found it unsettling that Manav Shinde was avoiding her calls. Anna had tried both his numbers. Each rang without response. She felt isolated and vulnerable. Driving through the familiar streets of Delhi, it felt as though she were in a foreign city. Her recent visit to America was like a brief flashback, cut and pasted into her memory, of interstate highways and country roads. Anna was glad to be back in her own car, a BMW Roadster that took the roundabouts with ease and wove through Delhi traffic with a menacing snarl.

Afridi had warned her about the restaurant—'greasy Mughlai served with Punjabi kitsch'—but he explained that he had chosen anonymity over ambience and cuisine. Anna had been to the restaurants on Pandara Lane during her student days. 'Have More,' Afridi's choice, lay in the center of the block, between 'Chicken Inn' and 'Shahi Andaaz.' The parking lot was full by the time Anna arrived at Pandara Market, but seeing the red convertible, one of the attendants moved a couple of scooters aside and made room for her to pull in parallel to the curb.

The restaurant was packed with mostly middle-aged men who eyed her like toads watching a dragonfly sail past, just out of reach. A few families were seated in booths. Tables were loaded with food, each dish a different shade of red, from scarlet tandoori chickens to vermillion kebabs, saffron kormas, and crimson mutton tikka masala, glistening like nail polish. Just looking at it all gave Anna heartburn. She spotted the Pakistani right away, partly because he was the only person sitting by himself, but also because he met her eye with a look of immediate distrust.

Major Yaqub introduced himself as Harsh Advani.

'Annapurna,' said Anna, shaking hands and putting her backpack on the seat beside her.

With the din of conversations around them and the clatter of cutlery and porcelain, there was little chance that anyone would listen in on what they said. Despite the mirrors on every wall, it wasn't likely they were being watched. Anna wondered what the ISI playbook prescribed for situations like this, though she wasn't even sure what protocols RAW laid down for collaborating with an enemy agent. She remembered Afridi's words: 'You'll be operating outside standard procedures. Complete autonomy. Total exposure.'

She was carrying her FN 57, just in case.

'Did you see the news about the American hostage?' Anna asked, as she sat down.

'Yes,' he replied, studying her carefully, as if the question were meant as a challenge.

'Who's behind it?'

'How should I know?' he replied.

'Do you think the US will give in to their demands?'

'Initially, of course. They'll try to buy some time. But in the end it's anyone's guess what will happen.' He spoke without emotion, keeping his answers brief and noncommittal. She would have placed him as a math teacher or a fortnightly columnist, certainly not an ISI asset. He was probably thinking the same about her, wondering why RAW had chosen a woman for a job like this.

The waiter interrupted them and took their order. Yaqub smiled for the first time, when Anna asked for 'less oil' in her chicken tikka. He ordered mutton do piyaza. Once the waiter was gone, Anna put both hands on the table.

'So, we'll be working together,' Anna said, consciously controlling the conversation. 'Are you sure I can trust you?'

Yaqub met her eye with a look of disdain.

'Does it matter?' he said. 'We share the same objective…the same target.'

'Fine,' she said. 'Then we won't pretend that this is anything more than a matter of mutual self-interest. My job is to provide whatever support you need, but you're the one who pulls the trigger.'

Yaqub glanced aside, checking to see if anyone was listening. The four men at the table beside them were huddled over their food.

'According to my source, he's arriving the day after tomorrow and will probably come in on a commercial flight, though we have no idea when or from where. Two of his bodyguards will be with him, but tracing them among the passengers arriving in Delhi will be impossible. For that matter, he could be landing in Mumbai or some other city and coming to Delhi on a domestic flight…Then they're supposed to attend the Qawali performance at Humayun's tomb, beginning at sunset, at seven o'clock.'

'Are you sure Guldaar himself will be there?' Anna asked.

Yaqub nodded.

'Who's your source?'

'The defense attaché at our embassy,' said Yaqub, after a brief hesitation. 'He's scheduling all of the meetings during the minister's visit, both official and unofficial.'

'And you have no photographs of the target, no way of identifying him?'

'No, that's why we're depending on you,' said Yaqub.

'Colonel Afridi has someone who can identify him,' Anna said.

'Who is it?'

'We can't share that information.'

Yaqub's face contorted in a grimace of disgust.

'And you talk about trust,' he said.

A minute later, the food arrived, along with a basket of naan. They served themselves in silence.

'What sort of help do you need from me?' Anna asked, once Yaqub had taken his first bite. He chewed and swallowed before answering.

'I need an official pass for the Qawali concert, and I'll need a weapon once I get inside. A Zittara 5.56 mm, with a silencer and three extra magazines of thirty rounds each.'

Anna smiled and tasted her chicken. 'I wouldn't have thought you'd use an Indian gun.'

Yaqub didn't appear amused. 'We train on every kind of weapon. Besides, it's nothing but a copy of an Israeli X 95.'

'Also known as an MTR 21. The silencer is going to be the challenge, but I'll do my best. We have less than twenty-four hours.'

'We'll also need an escape route, preferably through the southwestern gate into Nizamuddin East or over the wall facing the railway station. There should be someone there with a ladder. I'm sure the gardeners keep one ready for pruning trees. I'll need a car in which to get away or a motorcycle. Something powerful but inconspicuous.'

'It sounds as if you've given up on the option of capturing him alive,' said Anna.

'If possible, I'll try, but it's suicidal.'

'And after you get away?' Anna said.

Yaqub smiled again. 'Book me a room in a nice hotel. The Oberoi is nearby, but probably too close. Why not the Imperial?

I'll need a new passport, either British or American, with the appropriate visas and entry stamps.'

'What name shall we use?'

'Something simple. Ramesh Gupta, perhaps.'

He tore a piece of naan and scooped up a mouthful of meat and onions.

'When will you go back home?' Anna asked.

Yaqub glanced across at her with a wary expression.

'I'm not sure,' he said. 'Even if I succeed, it may be too dangerous for me to return to Pakistan.'

'Then why don't we give you an Indian passport?' she said. 'You can stay here as long as you want.'

Yaqub's eyes filled with derision. 'Don't patronize me. I'm doing this for my country, not for yours.'

Fifty-Four

For the past three hours, Daphne had been watching CCTV tapes of passengers coming through the arrival gates at Indira Gandhi International Airport, until it gave her a headache. A couple of times she thought she spotted Jimmy. But when they went back and played the tape in slow motion, it was obviously someone else.

'Amazing that you can have billions of people in the world, and none of them look exactly alike,' she said.

Afridi suggested they take a break and walk around the garden at HRI. It was mid-morning, a bright day with only a few clouds.

'Of course, there are doppelgangers, identical twins, and body doubles,' he said. 'But in the end, I suppose there's something unique in each of us.'

'Do you really think he's coming to Delhi?' she asked.

'I'm sure he'll show up, but it's impossible to know how or when, exactly,' said Afridi. 'He'll definitely cover his tracks.'

'I wish I could give you a better description of him, but he doesn't have a distinctive face. A seventy-year-old, balding man with no facial hair, still good-looking in a rugged sort of way.' She shook her head, as they reached the rock garden. Afridi wheeled himself ahead to open the gate. 'But once you've looked into his eyes, you'll never forget him.'

'I know,' said Afridi, under his breath. 'We considered getting a forensic sketch artist to create a composite portrait, but I'm never convinced of the results. They tend to look like shoddy caricatures.'

'But if he comes to Humayun's tomb this evening, you're sure we'll see him?'

'Don't worry. The only entry point is the main arch, and everyone will be passing through metal detectors. We'll have four cameras to catch him from different angles.'

Daphne stepped around Afridi and went through the gate.

'A rock garden!' she exclaimed.

'I call this my climbing garden,' said Afridi. 'These are mostly high altitude species that I've collected over the years.'

'They need special care?'

'Some do,' he said. 'But most are hardy plants. I've got a greenhouse for the more delicate species. It's not the cold so much as the monsoon that causes damage. Too much rain. Many of these plants need very little water.'

'What are these?'

'Gentians. Six different varieties, from the smallest, the size of an earring, to this larger flower, *Gentiana kurroo*. Its roots are extremely bitter. They feed it to horses as a medication for stomach ailments. It's also used on human beings but now critically endangered because of herb poaching.'

'I had a small garden in America. It was one of the few things that gave me pleasure. My daffodils were starting to come out this year, before I left.'

The winding path was just wide enough for the wheelchair. Afridi followed her to a point where it circled back under a limestone crag. A few wild irises were still blooming, but he caught sight of another flower, which hadn't been there two days ago, when he last visited the garden.

'Look ahead of you, above the path. That's a blue poppy, the first of the season,' said Afridi. 'I had the seeds smuggled out from Tibet.'

The bright papery bloom was rustling in the breeze. Daphne stopped to admire it.

'Why are so many Himalayan flowers blue?' she asked.

'Because they grow close to the sky,' Afridi replied. 'That's the folktale. It probably has something to do with minerals in the soil and climatic conditions.'

Daphne reached across and took his hand in hers. 'You're a very strange man,' she said.

'Why do you say that?' he asked.

'I would never have expected you to be a gardener,' said Daphne.

'There's a pragmatic creativity to gardening,' he said. 'It's science, plain and simple, though it cultivates a thing of beauty.'

She remained silent for a while, looking out across the valley that fell away below them, toward the eastern range of hills beyond.

'I'm afraid,' she said, squeezing his hand lightly before letting go.

'Don't worry. You're safe up here.'

'Not for myself,' she said. 'But trying to imagine what he'll do if he's cornered.'

'Hopefully, once he realizes the game is up, he'll surrender without a fight.'

'Jimmy isn't like that. You can be sure he's got an exit strategy, and he doesn't have any concern for human life.'

'We'll kill him if we have to,' said Afridi, 'though he's worth more to us alive.'

'What about the Americans?' asked Daphne.

'Agent Holman is on her way back to Washington. Things seem to have been sorted out with the embassy. She was taken by air ambulance this morning.'

'They'll send someone else.'

'Hopefully, by that time it will all be over,' said Afridi.

Daphne looked out across the valley to the mountains beyond. 'I should get back to watching those tapes.'

Fifty-Five

Since last night Luke had been locked up in one of the cages where the birds were kept. The floor was caked with bustard shit and feathers. Unlike the aviary, where the falcons were housed and pampered, there was no air-conditioning and the temperature climbed above ninety during the day in the cages. His captors had given him back his clothes, though it took him an hour to dress himself. They had thrown him a bottle of water to drink. It did not quench his thirst.

The pain had diminished slightly, though the burns on his scrotum and the insides of his thighs stung whenever he moved. Several hours had passed since they had tortured him, yet he could still feel the jarring numbness of the shocks. Twelve volts wasn't a fatal dose of electricity but the amperage of the truck battery had caused agonizing burns, like being struck by lightning. They left his mind singed, as if the current had gone straight up his spine, scorching every nerve, then shooting into his skull like an explosion of burning confetti. He could still feel the residual sensation behind his eyes, so many tiny detonations in his brain. He wanted to die each time they attached the cables, but somehow he couldn't escape consciousness, the fierce ache of charged electrons shooting through his groin.

Disoriented and afraid, Luke replayed yesterday's events in his mind, wishing he could start all over again. After the falconry demonstration, Guldaar had driven back with the two Qatari sheikhs while Luke traveled in a separate vehicle, just him and the driver. It turned out the driver was from the hills of Pakistan, a small town called Nathiagalli. Luke had been there many times, for it was only thirty kilometers west of Murree. Speaking Urdu, as they drove back across the desert toward Dubai, Luke had asked the driver about his family and how he'd come to the Gulf. He seemed a simple, homesick man who was happy to talk about the apple orchards and evergreen forests near his home, which he could only dream of in this desolate wasteland. For the first time in several weeks, Luke felt as if he was no longer a captive. He wondered if the driver was armed. It seemed almost too easy, though his seatbelt held him back and the car was moving at 120 km per hour. On ahead, he could see the silhouette of the Burj al Khalifa rising above the city, its syringe-like tower topped by a needle that pierced the sky. Seeing the glistening spire from a distance, he tried to calculate how high the 133rd floor might be.

They were approaching the outskirts of the city, barren desert giving way to scattered developments, some sort of campus lined with date palms, a Mercedes dealership, two blocks of flats facing a park, like a narrow oasis between walls of concrete. As they approached the Burj al Khalifa, Luke kept chatting with the driver, telling him about his childhood in Murree, how they used to gather wild raspberries in summer.

The traffic was thicker now, and the car slowed down, under thirty kilometers per hour. On ahead he saw a green stoplight. As they approached the crossing it turned amber, then red. Eight or ten other vehicles had stopped ahead of them. Counting the seconds until he felt the light was about to change, Luke braced himself. In a single motion, he unclasped his seatbelt and threw open the door. The driver had no time to react as he jumped out and began to run. He had timed it well, for the light was now green and the vehicles behind them began to blow their horns. Running between the cars, Luke cut across to the opposite side of the road and headed for a multi-story building with a line of shops on the ground floor selling electronics and household goods. Traffic from the opposite direction had already begun to move, and he barely missed being hit by a Jaguar XE that swerved at the last minute. It was hot outside, and the sun blinded him. Another vehicle braked and stopped in the left-hand lane. Luke ran to the window and gestured for the driver to let him get in. The man shook his head with alarm. Pounding on the glass, Luke tried to signal his desperation, but the man behind the wheel let out the clutch and sped away.

He could see that Guldaar's driver had abandoned his car in the middle of the road. He was running after him, a phone to his ear. Luke raced up a set of steps to the front of the building and called for help, though nobody came outside. He knew that the driver would see where he was going. Instead of entering the shops, he decided to run to the far end of the complex and try to find someone who could help. Turning the corner, he found himself in a service lane between two buildings. At the far end was a parking garage.

Luke ducked inside the entrance ramp and ran toward a flight of stairs at the farthest corner of the garage. He hadn't realized it, but this building was under construction. As he dashed out of the stairwell, white starbursts from a welding torch made him stop abruptly. Half a dozen laborers in hard hats were hauling steel girders. They looked as if they might be Chinese. At the far end of the unfinished structure, a crane was lifting material to upper floors. The staircase ended here. He gestured frantically and asked the laborers for help, but they didn't seem to understand what he said and stared at him blankly. The noise from a cement mixer made it difficult to hear anything at all. Luke started to run in one direction, then turned and ran the other way, but as he reached a pile of steel shutters for pouring concrete, a bullet flew past his arm and struck the metal panels. Raising both hands, he stopped, knowing there was no escape. When he turned around, the driver was walking toward him, a pistol in his hand. Both he and Luke were breathing heavily from the run. They said nothing to each other, though the Pakistani hit him twice across the face and began to drag him toward the steps. None of the construction workers moved to help him.

By the time they got downstairs, two other cars had pulled up. Luke recognized one of Guldaar's bodyguards, who grabbed him by the arm and hustled him into a Land Cruiser. Ten minutes later they were in the Burj al Khalifa again. Though the elevator ascended rapidly, Luke felt as if he were falling through the air.

Guldaar spoke without emotion, though his eyes seemed to puncture any hope Luke might have had for a reprieve.

'I thought we had an understanding,' he said. 'Why would you try to run away?'

Luke didn't answer, staring at the carpet.

'That was a cowardly thing to do. What did you hope for? Nobody is going to save you here. And now you've offended me. I bought your freedom. I offered you my hospitality. I trusted you. I confided in you. But you've shown me no gratitude.'

The driver was standing two steps behind Luke, while the bodyguard held both of his arms. Guldaar gestured for the pistol, which was still in the driver's hand. Taking it, he pointed the gun at Luke's forehead.

'I'm sorry,' said Luke. 'I made a mistake.'

'Yes, you did,' said Guldaar. 'A stupid mistake.'

The pistol went off and, for a moment, Luke wondered if he'd been shot, then heard someone fall. The driver lay sprawled at their feet. With a look of disgust, Guldaar threw the gun on the floor beside the dead man.

'Take him away,' he said, this time in Pushto. Luke could hear the finality in his voice, a note of dismissal and disdain.

By nightfall, he was back at the falconry complex, tossed into this cell where the houbara had faced extinction before him.

Sometime during the night, he was taken to another cell, where two men with hidden faces stripped off his clothes and filmed his torture. Three times the cables had been attached and three times the current had shaken him violently. He didn't know if it was punishment or a warning of worse things to come. Staring into the eye of the camera, before the first jolt, he knew that others would see him suffer. He wished he were back in the empty cistern, with a thin beam of light streaming in, projecting a ray of hope on the wall.

Fifty-Six

Paradise, according to Persian tradition, contains four rivers, each of which flow from the cardinal points of heaven. Surrounding Humayun's tomb is the Charbagh garden, which replicates this celestial geography with four water channels that converge on the tomb and divide the lawns and flowerbeds into equal squares. The mystical geometry employed by Mughal builders and landscape designers places the marble dome at the center, on a raised sandstone plinth.

In the satellite image, the symmetry was clear. For once, the air over Delhi had cleared, and Afridi was able to look down on the mausoleum and admire its architecture. Near the main entrance of the garden, he could see two small figures walking toward the emperor's tomb. It being midmorning, their shadows followed behind them.

Anna was wearing a headset and answered his call on the second ring.

'Good morning, sir,' she said. 'We're at the site.'

'Yes, I can see you,' Afridi replied.

'We've checked the entry point. They're setting up metal detectors. It seems secure enough, and I've got technicians positioning the cameras. We'll test them at noon and do a final check at 5:00 p.m.'

'Good. Now, make sure you have clear sightlines to the VIP enclosure. It should be to the center left of the stage.' As Afridi spoke, he could see them approaching the concert area directly in front of the mausoleum, where dozens of workers were erecting a raised platform and arranging rows of chairs. Others were hooking up speakers and wiring for the sound system. Seen from above, the workers looked like a colony of termites constructing a boudoir for their queen. Afridi gestured for his technician to move in closer. As the magnification increased, he recognized Anna as she pointed toward the main plinth of the tomb, which rose above the stage. The man with her walked forward another forty feet.

'How is our friend Major Yaqub?' Afridi asked. 'Not having second thoughts, is he?'

'No, sir,' said Anna. 'He seems very professional.'

'This evening, I want you to stay near him at all times. We'll keep an open line on your phone and if there's anything I need to communicate to him, I'll do that through you.'

'Understood,' said Anna.

'Make sure you check the perimeter of the garden for any recent construction or damage to the walls. We don't want Guldaar coming through an entrance we aren't watching.'

'We'll do that, sir. The National Security Guard is posting guards every thirty meters around the tomb. It will be impossible for anyone to enter undetected,' Anna reported.

'Yes, but it might make things complicated afterward,' said Afridi. 'NSG obviously doesn't know anything about this operation. They'll have orders to stop unauthorized individuals from leaving the venue, except through the main entrance and exit.'

'We've been discussing that,' said Anna. 'We can create a diversion to distract the guards, if necessary. On the eastern side of the garden, there's a small pavilion and a nursery, facing the railway tracks and the river. There's a boundary wall with a drop of about forty feet and a road below that cuts across to Nizamuddin Station. We'll have a car waiting at that point. From there Yaqub can take any one of three escape routes.'

'Does he seem capable to you?' Afridi asked.

'I believe so, sir. We've already got his weapon inside. I'll be armed as well.'

'But remember, Anna, I don't want you getting into a firefight,' said Afridi, as he saw Yaqub's figure disappear up the staircase to the main plinth of the tomb. 'You're there to provide liaison and communications. You may carry a concealed weapon for your own protection but nothing more than that. Yaqub will execute the mission on his own. Either he takes Guldaar captive or he kills him outright. You're not to get involved. Do you hear me?'

'Yes, sir. Understood.'

'Good. I'll speak with you again at 17:00 hours.'

Hearing the digital click of his phone switching off, Anna imagined Afridi sitting in front of the screens at HRI, watching every move she made. Instinctively, she shaded her eyes and looked up at the sky, where dozens of kites were wheeling in the air. She followed Yaqub and found him standing inside the mausoleum. Tourists were wandering about the main chamber where the marble tombstones lay. The monument would close early today, at 4:00 p.m. After that only invited guests for the concert would be admitted, once the garden had been swept and secured.

Inside the tomb it was at least five degrees cooler than outside. Anna removed her dark glasses and watched Yaqub standing in front of the western screen, facing Mecca. For a moment, she thought he might be praying and didn't disturb him, but he turned almost immediately and looked at her, with a guarded frown.

'The actual graves are down below in catacombs under the plinth,' Anna said.

'I know,' he said. 'You don't need to be my tour guide.'

'Okay,' she apologized, raising both hands. 'I was just wondering if any of the entrances to the burial chambers were open. Usually the archeological survey keeps them locked.'

'It might be useful if one or two of them were accessible in an emergency. It gives us additional options.'

'I'll see what we can do. They're full of bats,' Anna said.

He glanced at her abruptly, and she could see the alarm in his eyes.

'On second thought,' he said, 'let's not worry about opening those up.'

She laughed. 'You're scared of bats?'

'Terrified,' he confessed. For the first time since they'd met, Yaqub seemed to let down his guard. 'It's a phobia I've had since childhood.'

'Are you scared of anything else?' she asked teasingly.

'Nothing else that matters here,' he said.

Sensing that he was more willing to talk, Anna asked, 'What is it about Guldaar that makes you so determined to kill him?'

'I'm just following orders,' he said.

'Whose orders?' she asked. 'Afridi's or your handlers at ISI?'

'I don't take orders from Colonel Afridi.'

'This could cost you your career, perhaps even your life,' Anna said.

Yaqub waited for a couple of tourists to pass, staring up at the inside of the dome where pigeons were roosting in the niches. Anna thought she could see an expression of uncertainty beneath the confident mask.

'Why do you care?' said Yaqub. 'I'm doing your shit work for you. That's all that matters, isn't it?'

'If I'm going to back you up, I need to understand your motives,' Anna said.

'Guldaar is an evil man who is destroying my country,' said Yaqub. 'Isn't that reason enough?'

'I suppose,' said Anna. 'But I get a feeling it's personal.'

'So what?' said Yaqub, turning away from her toward the marble screen, which filtered the sunlight into a carpet of shadows on the floor.

'When I was training to become an intelligence officer,' said Anna, 'one of the first things they taught me was that you must ignore your emotions and approach each assignment with complete detachment, as if you were simply boiling an egg.'

Yaqub laughed, but she could tell he was not going to open up any further.

'Then let's get on with it and boil this egg,' he said, brushing past her and heading outside. 'We need to check the escape route.'

After the shadowy interior of the mausoleum, the glare outside was blinding. Both Anna and Yaqub put on sunglasses and headed toward the eastern edge of the plinth. Anna wondered if Afridi was still watching. To anyone else, they must have looked like a pair of tourists. When they reached the parapet wall, Anna pointed out the pavilion and the nursery.

'When this tomb was built, the Yamuna would have flowed past these walls, but now it's changed course and you can barely see the river from here,' she said.

They went down the steps and across the garden. Anna remembered how Afridi had met her here three weeks ago and laid out the plan, though she had never imagined it would all end at Humayun's tomb. When they reached the pavilion, a slow passenger train passed by, the rattle and click of its wheels on the tracks clearly audible.

'Where does this line go?' said Yaqub, as a faster freight train passed in the other direction.

'It crosses the Yamuna and connects to the main line into Punjab. Southward, it goes all the way to Mumbai.'

Yaqub scanned the terrain, a scrub jungle of acacia trees between the walls of the garden and the railway tracks. Just outside the northeast corner of the tomb stood a gurdwara. To the south was another Mughal tomb with the remnants of blue tiles on its dome. Further south he could see Nizamuddin railway station and the rooftops of the adjacent colony. Looking down, he studied the narrow road that ran along the base of the wall.

'We can have a rope or a ladder here, so you don't have to jump,' said Anna. 'A car will be waiting for you just over there to the right.'

'A rope should be fine,' said Yaqub. He seemed uninterested in the escape route.

'The only problem will be if you've got Guldaar with you. How are you going to get him down without a ladder?' Anna said.

Yaqub measured the drop with his eyes.

'You might as well know,' he said. 'I'm not planning on taking him out of here alive.'

Anna could see the conviction in his eyes. 'That makes things easier,' she said.

'He deserves to die,' said Yaqub. 'Guldaar killed my father because he wouldn't take a bribe.'

Anna held her breath for several seconds then asked, 'Was your father in the ISI?'

'He was decorated for his bravery in the 1971 war, when he was working as a junior intelligence officer in Chittagong. My father refused to surrender to the Indian army and kept radioing reports to Rawalpindi, even after General Niazi laid down his sword. Your soldiers tried to catch him, but he escaped into Burma and eventually made his way back to Pakistan. For almost a year, my mother thought he was dead.'

Another train went by but Anna barely heard the sound of its wheels as she listened to Yaqub's story.

'Ten years later, he was posted in Peshawar, when the Americans were supplying the mujahideen with weapons back in '82.' Yaqub spoke quietly, but anger underscored every word. 'Guldaar was working with the CIA, and he had become one of their main conduits. My father had contacts amongst the Pakhtun fighters, and he traveled into the tribal districts. There were complaints that many of the weapons weren't reaching the mujahideen, and middlemen were selling off some of the guns and ammunition to people who were supporting the Russians. The Americans didn't seem concerned, but my father wrote a confidential report that was circulated within the ISI, saying it was undermining morale and eroding Pakistan's support for the mujahideen. He was a man of principle and didn't care whose feathers got ruffled. Though the report was supposed to be secret, Guldaar got hold of it. He sent one of his men to meet my father and offered him twenty lakhs to retract his report and say nothing more. My father sent the man back with an empty rifle cartridge and the message that once a bullet is fired it cannot be retrieved, not for any price.'

Yaqub's words were punctuated by the sudden wail of a whistle as an express train roared by on a through line, its carriages shooting past, the clatter of wheels like prolonged applause.

'What was Guldaar's response?' Anna asked.

'He tried once more, offering thirty lakhs this time. My father told him to go fuck himself. He then wrote another report, describing the attempted bribe. All of this, I learned much later, when I was able to read his reports. They were suppressed by his superiors, but one of his colleagues kept a carbon copy, neatly typed on a foolscap sheet of paper. Back then, I was only five years old. My mother had taken me to Karachi to visit her parents. My father was alone in Peshawar. One day, after work, he went out in the evening, walking our dog near Garrison Park. Two men on a motorcycle came by and gunned him down, along with our golden retriever. He had five bullets in his chest, but it took him three days to die. He's buried in Peshawar, and I swore on his grave that someday I would take my revenge.'

Turning his back on the railway tracks, Yaqub set off toward the entrance of Humayun's tomb. Anna followed at a distance. As she watched his figure moving ahead of her in the bright sunlight, he looked like a shadow of himself. She didn't try to stop him, knowing that he would return in the evening to keep his promise.

Before she left the garden, Anna stopped to check where the weapon had been cached in a locked shed near the nursery. After hearing Yaqub's story, she realized how personal the operation was for him. For both Yaqub and Afridi, this was obviously more than just boiling an egg.

As she left the main entrance and walked toward the outer gate, which led to Isa Khan's tomb and the parking lots beyond, Anna could see more tourists arriving, a large group of Japanese and several Europeans. One man was standing to the side of the path with his camera focused on Humayun's tomb, though Anna felt as if he were zeroing in on her with his zoom lens. She was immediately aware of being watched. Approaching the tourist, Anna kept him in her peripheral vision, though she stared straight ahead. The lens was definitely pointed at her. A gaggle of Japanese came past him, and she deliberately slowed down as they approached and went by, talking and laughing among themselves.

As Anna came abreast of the man, he lowered his camera and she saw who it was. In the bright sunlight, the tinted lenses on his glasses had darkened to the point where she could not see his eyes. Carlton Fletcher smiled as she recognized him. His face was flushed with the heat, and the blood vessels in his pitted cheeks and nose were a virulent red.

'Good morning, Miss Khanna,' he said. 'Or is it Miss Tagore?'

Fifty-Seven

PAK DELEGATION ARRIVES TODAY

BILATERAL TALKS FOR DEMILITARIZATION OF SIACHEN GLACIER

Afridi glanced at the headline without bothering to read the story and passed the newspaper across his desk to Daphne.

'Virtually meaningless, at least on a strategic level. Two or three years back there were secretary level talks that failed completely, though they put a positive spin on it to say the deliberations resulted in an 'enhanced understanding of each other's position,' he said.

They were sitting in Afridi's office, after having listened to dozens of audio surveillance tapes, hoping that Daphne would recognize Guldaar's voice. So far, she hadn't been able to identify any images of him from the CCTV videos or photographs, and all of the phone tappings and other recordings produced no result. It was like trying to find a ghost.

Daphne skimmed the story about the negotiations between India and Pakistan.

'It seems so pointless,' she said. 'Soldiers fighting over a wasteland of ice.'

'The last time they had these talks,' said Afridi, 'Pakistan handed over a so-called 'non-paper', unofficially outlining their demands, and India agreed to study this document. But nothing has changed on the ground. It was all a bureaucratic charade. This time around, it's been booted up to the level of junior ministers, who will be talking to each other, shaking hands for the cameras, and attending a Qawali performance, after issuing a joint press statement that says nothing except that they agree to keep on talking. Essentially, both sides are intent on maintaining the status quo.'

'While soldiers keep dying for a line in the snow,' said Daphne.

'I suppose it's better than not talking to each other at all,' said Afridi, 'but I'm cynical about these kinds of meetings because it's all posturing and public relations.'

'Why would Jimmy want to be a part of it?' said Daphne.

'That's the other side of the game,' Afridi replied. 'What happens away from the cameras in the back rooms of the conference center. That's where commerce takes over from politics and diplomacy.'

'What do you mean?'

'Ever since India and Pakistan joined the nuclear club, the standoff between them has generated a huge amount of business for third parties. The United States gives Pakistan a hundred million dollars to protect its nuclear processing facilities from falling into the hands of terrorists. At the same time, American arms manufacturers are eagerly selling missile shield defense systems and early warning capabilities to India. It's all about deterrence, which was the driving force behind the US and Soviet economies during the Cold War. Now that same scenario is playing out in South Asia. There's nothing like the threat of mutual annihilation to get a country to increase its military budget. The people who benefit are the arms manufacturers and contractors, what used to be called the 'military-industrial complex.' It's a competition, and most of the negotiations are conducted by middlemen like Guldaar, who operate outside the maze of policy restrictions and international conventions. Basically, he manages the corruption that is part of every arms deal.'

'But if the talks between the two ministers end in a stalemate, how does he benefit?'

'Guldaar represents Peregrine, in which he owns a controlling interest. His holdings may be hidden behind layers of phantom investors, but essentially he's taken over the company in the past six months. When Guldaar came to see you three weeks ago, he flew into their testing facility in Eggleston. He met with Roger Fleischmann and several of their top executives, though they would be the first to deny it.'

'He didn't say anything about it to me,' Daphne admitted.

'Of course not. There's no official link between him and Peregrine, but he must control the board of directors, and the new acting CEO is probably his man. He also has his contacts in Washington and Langley, and nobody plays that network better than Guldaar.'

Afridi paused for a moment.

'Both India and Pakistan are very keen to acquire drones from Peregrine, because they can carry nuclear warheads. Unlike cruise missiles and bombs, these are light and maneuverable, relatively easy to operate, and difficult to detect. Nuclear weapons systems are no longer huge unwieldy rockets pointing at the sky. They can be operated by one or two technicians using remote control like a video game. Peregrine has two variations of the same system, UMA VII and VIII, known as Kestral and Merlin. These drones are under five feet long, with a range of five hundred kilometers. They can carry a warhead that will deliver the explosive force of the bombs that were dropped on Hiroshima. Half a dozen drones could decimate Islamabad or Delhi. NATO has been using them extensively with conventional warheads, targeting Taliban assets in the tribal areas. They are extremely accurate and virtually invisible, even with the most sophisticated radar. These are the ultimate birds of prey.'

'So, Jimmy's going to sell them to India?'

'Not just to India, but to Pakistan as well. That's the beauty of deterrence. In order to maintain a delicate balance, both countries want to acquire identical capabilities, and this doubles the demand and escalates sales.'

'But do they know that he's selling the same kind of drone to the other side?'

'Yes. It's what free trade and competition is all about. A number of other countries produce drones, some of which are extremely sophisticated—France, the UK, Brazil, Canada. Peregrine has a significant edge over all of them. The US government restricts Peregrine from selling their most recent technology, which is reserved for the US military, but even the second generation is highly effective. Of course, Peregrine's drones are also the most expensive. Each one costs millions of dollars. Out of that, Guldaar takes his percentage and pays off government officials and their political parties.'

'And all of this is going on behind the scenes at the Siachen conference?'

'As we speak,' said Afridi. 'Both customers are in the same building. Neither of them wants to end up at a disadvantage. And nobody wants to miss out on the kickbacks. Altogether, the contract for each country is worth a couple of billion dollars.'

'So, Jimmy's here to close the deal.'

'Ordinarily, he would never have come himself, but since he shot Jehangir, he lost one of the few people he trusted. At the same time, his top three representatives in Delhi have been arrested in connection with a heroin smuggling operation that was uncovered last week. And Roger Fleischmann is dead. Guldaar didn't have much choice but to come here himself. The stakes are too high.'

'But why would the United States permit Peregrine to sell drones that can carry nuclear warheads?'

'On paper, according to the specs, they don't have the

capability,' Afridi replied. 'But it doesn't take much to modify a Kestral or Merlin. The company probably sells the kit separately, for an extra fee, like apps for a cellphone.'

'It seems odd that both countries would have identical weapons.'

"They won't be exactly the same. India will probably buy the Kestral and Pakistan the Merlin, or vice versa. There's barely any difference in the specifications, but the Merlin is assembled by Peregrine's subsidiary in the Philippines. That way, each country can claim they've got an exclusive weapon system.'

'So what's going to happen today?'

'By five o'clock the meetings will conclude. A short press conference will be held, at which both countries will announce that they have agreed to keep talking. Journalists will demand to know if a peace agreement has been drafted, and they'll dodge the question with platitudes. Nothing will be resolved. Meanwhile, the agreements with Peregrine will have been concluded. Each of the junior ministers will have negotiated his cut, and they will adjourn to Humayun's tomb for a cultural evening of bilateral bonhomie and sufi music, which will put everyone in a cheerful mood.

'At the same time, Guldaar communicates with his people at Peregrine and preliminary contracts will be exchanged in the evening. 7:00 p.m. in Delhi is 3:30 p.m. in Luxembourg and Geneva. Banks are still open. As soon as Guldaar sends a green signal, the first installment of the incentive payments will be wired to personal accounts of the respective ministers, and anyone else who requires consideration. The balance will be paid in installments, once the final orders are placed and delivery is made to each country.'

'Why couldn't the whole deal be done over the phone, or by email?' Daphne asked.

'Because at this point in the process, the transaction is

conducted on trust. Each party has to look the other in the eye and be convinced that the deal is going through.'

'And if it doesn't? What if the Indian army decides they want a French drone instead?'

'Of course, it's happened. One minister overrules another, but that's where Guldaar's reputation precedes him. He's not just a salesman but an enforcer as well. It's what makes him so dangerous, and so difficult to track, because nobody wants to antagonize him. If they betray his trust, they can be sure he'll hunt them down.'

Daphne leaned back and closed her eyes.

'You don't have to tell me. I know that feeling,' she said.

Fifty-Eight

By 16:00 hours, Humayun's Tomb and the surrounding gardens were closed to visitors, and any remaining tourists had been ushered out of the gate. Several government agencies were handling arrangements for the event, including the Indian Council for Cultural Relations, who were sponsoring the musicians, and the Archeological Survey of India, which was responsible for the protection and maintenance of the monument. The Ministry of Defense and Ministry of External Affairs were coordinating the bilateral conference and the Pakistani delegation's visit. Security had been put in the hands of the National Security Guard. Anna was in contact with the commanding officer regarding camera surveillance. He did not ask too many questions, and it was clear that Afridi had made sure he would extend all cooperation and assistance.

Four cameras had been set up at the entrance and another four covering the VIP area in front of the concert stage. An additional two cameras with night vision lenses were positioned on either side of the tomb, encompassing the lawns and escape routes. All of the cameras had microphones and were carefully concealed. HRI technicians had tested each of them discreetly to make sure they were functioning properly.

By this time the stage and sound system had been set up, with the Mughal monument as a backdrop. While the sound checks were going on, Anna could hear a voice testing the microphones and amplifiers. NSG commandoes patrolled the perimeter of the garden with a couple of Labradors and an Alsatian, bomb-sniffing dogs, who circled the walls, their noses diligently lowered to the ground. At this hour of the day it was still hot, and the sun reflected off the marble dome with dazzling brilliance. Anna stood in the shade of a ficus tree waiting for Major Yaqub to arrive.

She was not a fan of sufi music any more than she appreciated Sanskrit poetry. It was all the same to her, a lot of pent-up emotions released through song and verse. Knowing the uncertainties of what might happen tonight, her mind was fixed on details. She wondered when Guldaar would actually appear. She and Yaqub were to stand near the entrance, so they could mark him when Daphne made the identification as he came in. There was bound to be confusion around the security screening area, with a lot of impatient VIPs trying to push their way through. The organizers anticipated an audience of at least a thousand, not counting the two delegations. The Qawali performers were some of the best from India and Pakistan, and most of Delhi's glitterati would be attending: political leaders, industrialists, diplomats, and socialites.

When her phone rang, Anna was surprised to see that Manav was calling.

'Greetings, my dear,' he said in an avuncular tone. 'I hope all's well.'

'Where have you been?' she demanded.

'Busy, extremely busy,' he said. 'I just wanted to make sure that all of the arrangements were in place for this evening. I'm looking forward to the concert.'

'So, you'll be here?'

'Purely for the music,' he said. 'I'm a great Qawali fan.'

'Did you hear that our American friend showed up?' she asked. 'Yes. In fact, I've been speaking to him. Things have grown complicated, I'm afraid,' he said with a vagueness in his voice that Anna recognized as meaning someone else was with him and he couldn't speak openly.

'A change of plan?' she said.

'No, not really,' Manav said. 'But we're going to have to avoid any unpleasantness.'

'You mean, you don't want Guldaar killed?' she asked.

'Exactly. Our American friends want to have a conversation with him. So do we.'

'He isn't likely to give up that easily,' said Anna, 'and Major Yaqub is fully prepared to terminate his target.'

'You'll have to persuade him against it,' said Manav. 'This must be a simple extraction and arrest. No fatalities.'

'Yaqub's made it clear that he isn't taking orders from us,' she said. 'Not even from Afridi. He's got personal history with Guldaar.'

'That's unfortunate, but you'll have to make him understand.'

'I'll try my best,' she said. 'But why are we suddenly cooperating with the Americans? Does Afridi know about this?'

'There comes a point when everyone must compromise,' Manav replied. She could tell he wanted to get off the phone. 'I'll see you this evening.'

A short while later, Afridi called to say that they would begin surveillance in half an hour, at 18:00 hours, when the first guests began arriving. Anna decided not to mention her conversation with Manav. She had enough to worry about already without getting caught up in conflicting agendas. As she ended the call, Anna could see Yaqub entering and passing through a metal detector. One of the NSG guards checked his pass and opened his bag, then waved him inside.

Yaqub had changed his clothes. Instead of jeans and a bush shirt, he was wearing a dark blue linen suit and a white shirt with the top two buttons open. Slung over one shoulder was a small backpack, designed to carry a laptop. He looked as if he was headed for the club after a day at the office, instead of preparing for a kidnapping or assassination. When they retrieved their weapons, Yaqub checked his Zittara and the extra clips of ammunition before putting them into his backpack. The compact assault rifle fit neatly inside. Anna had a similar bag and she slipped her FN 57 into the outer pocket.

Until now, they had hardly spoken, a brittle silence between them.

'Are you all right?' Anna asked.

'Of course,' he said.

'I had a call from my associate director,' she said. 'They want Guldaar taken alive.'

He looked at her with a flash of defiance.

'That's not possible,' he said.

'They're insisting.'

Yaqub laughed and gave her a condescending look.

'I don't think you realize who we're dealing with,' he said. 'This is not someone who puts his hands in the air the minute he sees a gun.'

'But he won't be armed,' said Anna.

'Are you sure of that?' Yaqub asked. 'He's likely to have bodyguards with him. They'll certainly be carrying weapons.'

Just then, they heard the sound of a train's whistle in the distance. The first group of musicians had arrived and were organizing themselves on the stage, positioning a harmonium and drums, moving the microphones about.

'We need to get in position,' said Anna.

By now, the sun was descending toward the western wall of the garden and a flock of mynahs were squabbling in the ficus trees. Parakeets sailed overhead. A pair of palm squirrels chased each other along a branch. Adjusting her earpiece, Anna felt the familiar sense of intensity she always did when something dangerous and important was about to begin, an anxious itch of anticipation.

Fifty-Nine

'The first song is always a *Hamd*, in praise of Allah. That's followed by a *Naat*, commemorating the prophet.' As they waited, Daphne had asked Afridi to explain the music playing over the speakers, a chorus of male voices echoing the lamentations of the lead singer. 'This group is from Lahore, singing mostly in Punjabi.'

'To me it always sounds like they're gargling and clearing their throats,' said Daphne. 'Jimmy used to listen to Qawali, but I'm afraid the voices grate on my ear.'

The Pakistani delegation had just arrived at Humayun's tomb, half an hour late, led by the junior minister of defense. On one of the screens, Afridi could see them being greeted by their Indian counterparts with hearty embraces and ingratiating smiles.

While the singers picked up the tempo, Daphne remained focused on the array of monitors that relayed images from the entrance. So far, there had been no sign of Guldaar, and she was beginning to get worried. Maybe she had missed him, or perhaps he wasn't coming after all. One of the cameras picked up Anna standing to the left of the metal detectors beside a young man in a well-cut suit. The lights were bright, and the music was so loud it was impossible to hear any of the conversations as the guests arrived. A trio of women, wearing embroidered saris with backless cholis, were entering now. Each of them carried a Gucci clutch, and Daphne could see their emeralds sparkling in the light.

Accompanying them were three men wearing achkan jackets

buttoned up to their necks. Daphne guessed they were sweating underneath. One of them mopped his face with a yellow silk hankie. They looked pale and unhealthy in the stark glare of electricity. The NSG commandoes in their black uniforms were restless shadows, checking passes and bags. Meanwhile, the singer was reaching a climax, his voice trilling in a high-pitched ululation. The latecomers had been held back to let the Pakistanis through, but now a crowd had assembled in an impatient queue behind the security barrier.

Daphne could see Afridi's fingers tapping on the armrest of his wheelchair. She wondered whether it was nervousness or an appreciation for the music.

'This song is in praise of Bulleh Shah,' said Afridi, speaking quietly, as the singer paused to explain the lyrics, offering commentary even as the harmonium and other instruments continued playing. Almost immediately, he picked up the refrain, leading the other vocalists in a wave of sound that swelled to an ecstatic crescendo.

'There he is.' Daphne spoke so softly Afridi didn't hear her at first. 'There!' she said, a little louder.

'Which one?' he asked, leaning forward.

'In the queue behind the Sikh with the pink turban. You'll see him in a moment when he turns…there! Yes, it's him.' Her voice broke.

Afridi could see an elderly, nondescript face, his hair combed back from a prominent forehead. He was looking away from the cameras, as if distracted. When his turn came, he handed his pass to the guard and glanced up. For just a second, his eyes looked straight into the camera, and Afridi recognized him too. Though he had aged and put on weight, it was definitely the same man he had interrogated years ago. Guldaar's shoulders were stooped. He looked older than seventy; his face was creased and tired, as if he'd been traveling for days.

'Jimmy…' Daphne whispered, as Afridi reached for his phone.

'Anna, can you hear me? We've got a positive ID,' Afridi said. 'He's coming through the metal detector right now, wearing a dark shirt. Have you seen him? Yes…He isn't carrying anything.'

Daphne could faintly hear Anna's voice on the phone.

'Okay, don't lose him.' Afridi's voice betrayed his excitement.

Putting aside the phone, he caught his breath before turning toward Daphne.

'We've got him,' he said, putting his hand on her arm.

He could feel her trembling, and when she glanced at him there were tears in her eyes.

~

Anna could see that Yaqub was watching every slow step Guldaar took down the aisle toward the VIP enclosure. He was alone, moving through the crowd with assured detachment, as if nobody else was there. The music had trailed away into silence followed by loud applause. By the time Guldaar reached the VIP seats, the Qawali singer had begun a ghazal with a slow alaap, his rough tenor testing the notes, full of pain and anguish. None of the dignitaries seemed to recognize the anonymous guest as he moved quietly forward to the front row, where a seat had been kept empty for him between the two ministers. Guldaar greeted them with a simple handshake before sitting down. Drums, both tabla and dholak, were now pulsing like an arrhythmic heartbeat. Moths flittered through the fluorescent aura surrounding the stage. The massive dome of Humayun's tomb was lit up with spotlights, glowing as bright as a bulbous moon.

~

Afridi spotted Manav Shinde seated in the third row from the front. Beside him was the American, Carlton Fletcher. They seemed to be listening to the music intently, though Afridi knew

Manav was tone deaf. On the other two screens was the front row of VIPs, with Guldaar in the middle. On Afridi's instructions, the HRI technicians had already grabbed two or three headshots from the video feed and sent these to Anna. Studying the face on the screen, Afridi felt as if the anonymous features had finally been unmasked.

'What are they doing?' Daphne asked.

'None of them are listening to the music, that's for sure,' said Afridi. 'They're checking messages on their phones.'

Both ministers were staring intently at the devices in their palms, as if waiting for a digital djinn to rise off the screen. After a few minutes, Guldaar leaned toward the Pakistani minister and spoke in his ear. He then turned to India's minister of state and gestured as if to say it would take another minute or two. They looked like three bored men deleting messages from their inboxes to pass the time. The generals on either side of them, with furled mustaches, ribbons, and medals, seemed oblivious to what was taking place, as did the rest of the entourage.

'Both parties have already signed letters of intent for the Peregrine contracts,' said Afridi. 'Now he's transferring the first payments to their accounts.'

'It looks as if they're playing video games,' said Daphne.

'Very expensive ones,' said Afridi. His fingers were still tapping out the rhythm of the music but with a lighter touch.

Guldaar held his phone up for the Pakistani minister to see what appeared on the screen. He then typed another command and waited. For a moment, he glanced over at the musicians and the dome of the tomb with a distracted expression, almost as if he knew that Daphne and Afridi were watching. On a separate screen Afridi could see the musicians, their gestures and features contorted with the emotions of the song. He recognized this ghazal, based on a poem by Faiz Ahmed Faiz, about the universal brotherhood of man.

'How long do you think he'll stay?' Daphne asked.

'Not long,' said Afridi, raising the phone to his ear. 'Anna, are you there?'

'Yes, sir.'

'Be prepared for Guldaar to leave any moment now. Is Major Yaqub ready?'

'Yes. He's right here beside me.'

'When he leaves, Yaqub should follow Guldaar out of the gate and apprehend him as soon as he's clear of the crowds. If he tries to escape, use force. And remember, Anna, I don't want you getting caught in the crossfire if shooting begins.'

'Yes, sir,' she said, leaning over to convey the message to Yaqub.

This time, Guldaar held up his phone for the Indian minister to see. They exchanged a few words, then the politician checked his own instrument and smiled briefly, nodding his head. The wire transfers had gone through. This entire process took no more than ten minutes, signals bouncing off satellites far above the earth and beamed to secure servers in European banks, encrypted messages relayed instantly from one device to another at the touch of a fingertip. Nobody in the audience, except those who knew, would have guessed that deals worth billions of dollars had been closed in as much time as it took for a moth to flit through the lights on the stage. While the musicians sang of divine love and beauty, the intoxication of spiritual desire, the security of their two nations had been compromised and the precarious balance of nuclear deterrence maintained.

Guldaar rose to his feet. The Pakistani minister stood up and kissed him on both cheeks. The Indian minister folded his hands, as if saying goodbye to an old and trusted friend, after which the elderly man excused himself and walked away. Seeing him on the screen, Afridi couldn't help but think how frail he looked, one leg dragging in an awkward limp. It was an old wound from a dozen years ago, when Guldaar had survived an attempt on his life. Glancing at Daphne, Afridi could see that she was thinking the same thing. He's just an ordinary man, as mortal as the rest of us. And yet, he was the embodiment of evil.

~

Yaqub was already in motion, cutting past the sound booth toward the exit. Anna hurried to keep up with him as she unzipped the outer pocket on her backpack. From the corner of her eye, she saw Manav watching them. He had acknowledged her when he arrived earlier, without them having spoken.

'We're moving, sir,' Anna said.

'I can see you,' Afridi replied. 'But as soon as you go through the gate, we'll lose all visual contact. Where is Guldaar?'

'He's just ahead of Yaqub. Ten steps. We're outside the security perimeter.'

She could see that Yaqub had shifted his backpack onto his right shoulder and loosened the strap so it hung near his waist. His hand was inside, gripping the Zittara, as he stalked his target. The area immediately beyond the gate was deserted. Everyone was focused on the concert. A broad, unpaved walk lined with ficus trees led from the entrance to the outer gate. As soon as Guldaar was outside, he stopped to light a cigarette. Anna watched him descend the steps slowly, one at a time, as Yaqub closed in. She was ten meters behind him and heard him speak in Urdu, telling Guldaar to stop. Her pistol was out as well as she slipped into the shadows of a flanking arch to cover Yaqub. He had grabbed Guldaar's arm and jammed the assault rifle into his ribs, although it looked as if he were helping the old man down the steps. Behind her, Anna could still hear the music, but a sudden silence seemed to close in around them. She could hear Afridi breathing into the phone.

'Target engaged,' she said, in a low whisper.

'What's happening?'

'He's not resisting.'

'Is anyone else around?'

'Not that I can see. Not yet.'

'Stay back, Anna.'

Guldaar seemed strangely passive, almost as if he were confused by what was happening. For a moment, Anna thought maybe they had got the wrong man. Maybe it was all a mistake. Perhaps Daphne had betrayed them. Everything was going too smoothly.

Then she heard the first gunshot, a popping sound, like a bursting balloon, followed by three more. Guldaar staggered as Yaqub held him. Anna pressed herself against the wall, her pistol raised. She knew that Yaqub hadn't fired, but it was impossible to know where the shots had come from or who had been hit. As the two men fell to the ground, she heard Yaqub shout, 'Back off, or I'll kill him.'

Guldaar himself now spoke, in a firm voice. 'Wait! No more!'

Anna saw a movement in the shadows under the trees that lined the walk. One of Guldaar's bodyguards was taking cover behind the trunk of the tree. She couldn't see a second man but guessed he was somewhere to her left. Seconds later, she watched the two men step forward.

'Put down your guns,' Yaqub cried in Urdu. His voice sounded weaker now. Anna could see a stream of blood on the ground beneath him and knew he was hit. There was barely any light, but her eyes had adjusted to the darkness and she could see both of Guldaar's men. They hadn't noticed her, or perhaps they thought she was an innocent bystander who had taken cover when the shots were fired.

'What's happening, Anna, talk to me?' Afridi's voice was in her ear, but she didn't have time to reply as she aimed and fired twice, following up with two more rounds. The FN 57 had no silencer, but with the volume of the concert, nobody inside heard the shots. The nearest NSG commandoes were posted at the outer gate, a hundred meters away. Both of the bodyguards fell where they stood. Turning, Anna saw that Yaqub was holding Guldaar face down, the Zittara's stubby barrel still tucked into his side. Anna kept her weapon ready as she checked both bodyguards to make sure they were dead, kicking their guns aside.

'Okay?' she said softly, kneeling beside Yaqub. 'You can let go now. Where are you hit?'

More blood was pooling beneath Yaqub, seeping into the dust on the path. He looked at her with a vacant expression, as if he didn't recognize who she was, then coughed up a froth of blood. Gently, Anna pried his fingers loose from Guldaar's arm, and she felt the old man move. Anna was afraid that Yaqub might fire, but he was already dead. When she pulled Guldaar aside, she could see two wounds in Yaqub's chest, his shirt stained red. The Zittara fell from a lifeless hand.

Her own pistol was pressed behind Guldaar's ear.

'Don't fucking move,' she said.

~

Afridi couldn't help but smile when he heard Anna's voice. Though he still didn't know what had happened, he felt sure she had the situation under control. Daphne sat beside him, her head lowered as the screens in front of them continued to transmit images from the concert. The musicians' voices subsided to a softer pitch, a melodic murmur accompanied by the soft flutter of fingers on the keys of the harmonium. Afridi waited a minute, not wanting to distract Anna with his questions. Over the phone he could hear indistinct voices. Finally, he asked her, 'Anna. Tell me. What's the situation?'

'We've got him,' she replied without emotion. 'Yaqub is dead, but Guldaar is alive.'

'Good work,' said Afridi, leaning back in relief.

'Sir, I'm switching off,' she said.

~

Fifteen minutes later, Carlton Fletcher sat in the front seat of a Tata Safari SUV, beside the driver. Turning around, he faced Anna and Manav, who had Guldaar between them in the back. The engine was running, and the air-conditioning was cold. They were in the parking lot in front of Humayun's tomb. Two NSG guards stood beside either door. Anna still held her pistol, but the other three men were unarmed. She could smell their sweat and cologne, as well as the stench of tobacco on Fletcher and Guldaar's breath. After the sudden violence, she felt a passing sense of nausea, the closeness of death. In her mind, she could still see the blood seeping out of Yaqub's wounds, soaking into the dirt. Guldaar was handcuffed, and his clothes were covered with dust. One of his sleeves was spattered with blood, but he was uninjured. Until now, he had said nothing. No questions had been asked. Close up, he looked like a tired old man, though Anna could see from his face that he would never surrender. The driver waited for instructions, staring straight ahead, both hands on the wheel. It seemed as if each of them was waiting for someone else to speak.

All at once, a phone began ringing, a rock 'n roll jingle that sounded like the soundtrack from a cartoon show. Eyes moved from one to the other. Fletcher reached into his pocket self-consciously and fumbled with the device. After answering, he listened for more than a minute, responding with grunts of displeasure. Twice he swore under his breath. Finally, he took the phone away from his ear and stared at it for a moment, eyes blinking behind the lenses of his glasses. He held the screen up for Manav and Anna to see.

The image was a live feed. Though small and indistinct, there was no mistaking what they were watching. A bearded man had been stripped to the waist. He was kneeling on a bare concrete floor, hands tied behind his back. Two other men, faces masked, stood on either side of the hostage. One of them was holding him by the hair, so that his head was raised, staring into the camera with a dazed expression. Anna recognized the American journalist from the earlier video. The second masked man was holding something in his hand, which was difficult to see at first, but when he raised it Anna could tell it was a bow saw.

'Where did this come from?' Manav asked.

'The link was forwarded from Langley. They got it a couple minutes ago. One of my people in Washington just sent it on to me.' Fletcher answered, as if he were ready to spit.

Guldaar finally spoke, moistening his lips with his tongue before the words came out of his mouth in a slow, deliberate monotone.

'If you don't release me in the next ten minutes, they will saw off his head.' He paused a moment, and Anna could see his eyes fixed on her pistol. 'But if you let me go, I will send a message, and they will set him free in half an hour.'

'Fuck you,' said Fletcher. 'Why should we trust you?'

'Because I work for your government,' said Guldaar. 'How do you think the CIA received this link? They know I'm not playing games.'

Guldaar glanced down at his watch, which was partly hidden under the handcuff.

'There isn't much time,' he said. 'It won't make any difference to me if you ignore my warning and let the journalist die. One way or the other, I'll be released. If not today, then tomorrow, for sure.'

'Let me remind you that you're in India, not Pakistan,' said Manav. 'Under our jurisdiction. We aren't going to let you go that easily.'

Guldaar let out his breath impatiently.

'Why? Because Colonel Afridi thinks he's got the upper hand?' said Guldaar. 'He's a clever man, but not clever enough.'

'We have plenty of evidence to lock you away for several lifetimes,' said Manav. 'Afridi has Daphne Shah with him. She's willing to talk.'

Guldaar's mouth twisted into a sneer. 'She's a cheap whore who killed her own son. What's she going to tell you?'

Anna was about to respond when another phone rang, an angry buzzing like a wasp trapped inside the car. This time it was Manav's cell. He seemed to recognize the caller, and Anna saw him stiffen.

'Yes, sir,' Manav said, then listened.

The tableau on Fletcher's phone remained, though one of the captors let go of the prisoner's hair and he fell forward. Anna glanced over at Manav as he switched off his phone.

'We don't have a choice, do we?' said Fletcher.

Manav shook his head, exhaling with disgust.

~

The remote control struck the flat screen monitor, which shattered into fragments of glass and microcircuitry. For a moment, it looked as if Afridi was going to stand up out of his wheelchair and smash the rest of the monitors, which continued to display scenes from Humayun's tomb. He seldom lost his temper, but when he did his rage was legendary, and the technicians knew they should leave the room. Only Daphne stayed with him, her eyes fixed on his face with a look of resignation and fear. Though Afridi had said nothing after the phone call, Daphne knew what had happened. The wail of the Qawali singer sounded like a tortured howl.

Sixty

They dropped Guldaar at the main roundabout near Hazrat Nizamuddin Auliya's dargah, less than half a kilometer from Humayun's tomb. The city was a swarm of lights against shadows of deepest black. Destitute pilgrims and street dwellers were preparing to make their beds on the pavement, while autorickshaws jockeyed for position near the entrance to the busy colony. Inside the narrow lanes and byways, crowds of men gathered at eating places and guesthouses surrounding the saint's tomb. It was a busy neighborhood, full of hawkers and touts, teashops and a cluttered bazaar, the perfect place for a man to disappear. Anna stepped down from the SUV to let Guldaar get out. She watched him walk away without looking back. After their first exchange, Guldaar had said nothing more to Fletcher or Manav, though he made a call and spoke to someone about the hostage, telling them to hold off on the execution.

As soon as Guldaar vanished into the shadows, Anna turned to look at Manav. He shook his head in frustration.

'There's nothing we could do,' he said. 'Orders straight from the top.'

Fletcher added. 'Even if we'd locked him up they would have sprung him loose by tomorrow. He's got more fucking clout than anyone I know.'

'It's absurd,' said Anna. 'We had him…and now he's gone.'

She began to get back into the vehicle, then stopped and looked behind her. Impulsively, she slammed the door and set off in pursuit. Manav's shouted warning followed Anna into the crowds, but she ignored him. When she reached the autorickshaw stand, the drivers eyed her with suspicion and curiosity, the only woman in their midst.

'An old man just left from here,' she said. 'Where did he go?'

The drivers shook their heads, leering at her.

'He was here a minute ago. Tell me where he went,' Anna insisted.

A bearded man with rheumy eyes finally answered, 'To the railway station.'

'Are you sure?'

'Yes, he was in a hurry. He said he had to catch a train.'

'Take me there,' said Anna, pushing her way into the rickshaw. The other drivers began to protest, but she shouted, 'Go!'

The autorickshaw started with a grinding roar, and they set off, dodging traffic and weaving through the steady stream of headlights. The driver sensed her urgency and whipped around a bus with inches to spare, the hot diesel exhaust in her face. Nizamuddin Station was only ten minutes from the dargah, but they made it there in five. Anna handed over a hundred rupee note before jumping out, her backpack slung over one shoulder.

Scanning the throng of passengers leaving and entering the station, she searched for Guldaar. Two policemen were posted at the entrance, beside a metal detector. Avoiding them, Anna pushed her way through the exit line. Porters were carrying suitcases and bags on their heads. Families were trying not to lose their children. Unintelligible announcements were broadcast over the sound system. She could hear the whistle of departing trains. Reaching for her phone, Anna switched it on and called Afridi.

He answered on the first ring. 'I'm going after him,' she said.

'Manav told me,' he replied. 'Anna, you're disobeying direct orders.'

'I don't have time to think about that,' she said. 'We can't let him get away.'

'Where are you?' Afridi demanded.

'Nizamuddin Railway Station. I'm standing in front of a board that lists all of the arrivals and departures,' she said, looking up at the screen above her. Someone brushed past her arm. Two men were running up a staircase toward an overhead walkway that led to other platforms.

'Which train is he on?' Afridi asked.

'I don't know,' said Anna. 'There's no sign of him, but I'm sure he's here.'

'What trains are listed?' Afridi asked, his voice crackling in her ear.

She began to read the names. 'Jabalpur-Jammu Tawi Express. Nizamuddin Indore Inter-City Express. Dakshin SF Express.' Half a dozen trains were leaving in the next hour, for destinations all across India—Mumbai…Chennai…Trivandrum. 'Golden Temple Mail.'

'When does that leave?' Afridi interrupted her.

'Eight-fifty. Ten minutes from now,' she said. 'It's running three hours late. Platform One.'

'He'll be on that train,' said Afridi.

'How do you know?' she asked, looking around anxiously as more and more passengers streamed by, an endless procession of humanity, laden with baggage.

'Trust me,' he said with assurance in his voice. 'He'll be heading for the border. The Golden Temple Mail used to be called the Frontier Mail, when it ran all the way to Peshawar. Now it goes only as far as Amritsar, but he'll find his way across from there into Pakistan.'

'Okay,' she said. 'I'll do my best.'

'I know you will,' Afridi replied. 'But be careful, please.'

Platform One was directly in front of her, and she could

see the placard on the side of a carriage: GOLDEN TEMPLE MAIL in English, Hindi, Urdu, and Gurmukhi. Second-class passengers were peering out of barred windows while others were pushing their way onto the train. Anna scanned the platform for any sign of Guldaar, but he was nowhere in sight. Positioning herself behind one of the pillars, she kept an eye out in both directions in case he got on or off the train. Several minutes later, the loudspeaker overhead announced the departure of train number 12903, the Golden Temple Mail, followed by the recorded phrase: 'We sincerely apologize for the delay. Inconvenience is deeply regretted.'

A minute later, the carriages began to move. Anna trusted Afridi's judgment, but she couldn't help but wonder if Guldaar would actually choose this train or any one of the others leaving tonight. Hesitating, she looked around one last time, then ran to climb on board a II AC Sleeper. By this time the train was picking up speed, and she had to jump and grab the bars to swing herself inside.

Other passengers were waiting in the vestibule, but they made room for her, and a familiar smell enveloped Anna, the combined fug of too many human beings packed into an unventilated space. Though Anna hadn't been on a train for several years, the shake and rattle of departure gave her a sense of leaving everything behind.

Almost immediately, she began to search for Guldaar, working her way down the aisle and peering into each of the compartments, where passengers were settling in for the night. Even if he was on this train, it seemed impossible that she would find him. The Frontier Mail made its way slowly out of Delhi but picked up speed after crossing the Yamuna, heading north. Anna searched everywhere, from first class air-conditioned coupes to the three-tier unreserved carriages with sitting room only. Each time she peered into a compartment, passengers stared back at her with blank and baleful eyes. While checking one of the toilets she locked the door and reloaded her pistol. Later on, a conductor stopped her, and she bought a second-class ticket, though she had no reservation. He charged her a penalty and demanded a bribe, both of which she paid without complaint.

Two hours later, almost everyone on the train was asleep. They had already passed through Meerut and Muzaffarnagar stations, where she stepped out onto the platform to make sure Guldaar didn't get off. Several times, she checked the photos on her phone to remind herself of his face, though his features were etched in her memory. As she pushed her way through the moving train from one carriage to the next, the couplings jostled against each other. Warm night air flew past in a murmuring rush of shadows. Anna began to give up hope. Most of the curtains had been drawn, and travelers lay like corpses, shrouded in sheets. In the upper-class carriages, doors had been bolted and locked. Even the conductors and attendants had gone to sleep.

As the train snaked its way across the Gangetic Plain, before turning northwest into the Punjab, Anna felt a strange sense of loneliness and despair, the click and stammer of the train, the passing lights outside, and the rocking of each carriage as they sped toward an uncertain destination. Manav had tried to contact her several times, but she ignored his calls. Twice she spoke to Afridi, reporting no sign of Guldaar. He told her to keep looking, insisting he must be on board.

'Why would he take a train?' she said, in frustration. 'If he has a private plane waiting for him at the airport?'

'He won't risk the chance of being stopped again,' said Afridi. 'Remember, his anonymity is what protects him. He's safest when nobody knows who he is.'

'But he could have hired a car, or taken any other train.'

'Yes, but he's a man who's superstitious about history. His instincts will have guided him to the Frontier Mail. Once he reaches Amritsar he'll bribe his way across the border at Wagah.'

'When do we reach Amritsar?' Anna asked.

'The scheduled time is 5:00 a.m. but you're running late. It will be 8:00 in the morning.'

'I'll have to find him before then. Once he's off the train, I'll lose him,' she said.

'Patience, Anna. Just keep looking.'

It was midnight by the time she completed a third search of the train from one end to the other. Anna was now back where she'd started, in the II AC Sleeper. Even if she wanted to lie down, she had no berth. Muffled snoring came from the attendant's bunk, which was tucked behind the air-conditioning unit. Leaning down, Anna peered out the window. She saw dark fields outside, the glimmer of villages passing by, and the headlights of a tractor at a level crossing. Saharanpur was the next station, twenty minutes on ahead.

One more time, she told herself. *Once more!* Stepping past the bathrooms and onto the swaying metal gangway, she entered the adjoining carriage, a first-class AC Sleeper. It was cleaner than the others with a door opening off the vestibule that sealed cold air inside. Opening it, she made her way down the narrow corridor, illuminated by blue night lamps. Curtains on the windows swayed back and forth. The doors to each compartment were locked. Nobody would open them at this hour of the night unless they were going to use the bathrooms. The train was moving at full speed, and Anna put up a hand to steady herself as she came to the door at the other end. As soon as she opened it, a warm gust of air greeted her, along with the smell of a freshly lit cigarette.

Instinctively, Anna unzipped her backpack and took out her FN 57. Moving carefully, she could tell that someone had opened the outside door of the carriage. As she stepped forward, she saw a man standing with his back to her, facing out into the passing night. She recognized him from his clothes. His one hand was braced against the metal door, which had been wedged open. In the other, he held a cigarette, smoke trailing over his shoulder as he exhaled. Anna took her stance, the pistol level with his back.

'Jimmy!' she said, loud enough for her words to carry over the rumbling of the train.

He turned as soon as he heard her voice. Anna could see that Guldaar had no idea she had followed him onto the train. It took him a moment to compose himself, as he tossed the half-smoked cigarette out the door.

'You're making a huge mistake,' he said.

'I don't think so,' Anna replied.

'What do you want?' he said. 'I can arrange—'

'Shut up,' she said.

'Everyone has a price. Name yours. Whatever you say.'

Anna smiled at his audacity, seeing the weary, anxious look in his eyes.

'There's nothing you could offer me that would make me spare your life,' she said.

'Do you think it will make a difference if you kill me? What will you accomplish? They're all corrupt, every one of them. Kill me and someone else will take my place.'

She shook her head, feeling his hypnotic gaze boring through her like an awl. The swaying carriage jostled them, but Anna had both feet planted firmly on the floor.

'Major Yaqub didn't share your cynicism,' she said. 'He sacrificed his life because he believed that you were destroying his country.'

'Who is this Yaqub? A minor player—nothing but a Pakistani pawn.'

'At least he believed in something,' Anna said.

The old man was five feet away from her, no more than twelve inches from the open door. When he lunged at Anna, both his hands reached out to try and knock the pistol from her grasp, but she was ready for him. Anna squeezed the trigger twice.

The first bullet caught him between the ribs. For a brief second, Guldaar raised his head with an arrogant look of disdain, as if he didn't believe that he was hit. The second bullet, with a muzzle velocity of 650 meters per second, threw him backward on his heels. His left arm struck the metal doorframe and he seemed to grab for it. But the full force of the 5.7 mm slug, puncturing his chest and then mushrooming into his lungs and heart, hurled him backward through the door.

Lowering her pistol, Anna took a step forward and pushed the heavy door shut. She then sank to the floor and let the Frontier Mail carry her onward into the night.

Sixty-One

Two days after Guldaar's body was recovered beside the railway tracks south of Saharanpur, Afridi and Daphne had dinner at Ivanhoe again. This time Afridi had dismissed his servant and cooked a cheese soufflé and prepared a watermelon and mint salad himself. The NSG commandoes remained on guard but there was no longer any threat. Afridi opened a bottle of Casale Del Giglio Cabernet Sauvignon, given to him by an Italian mountaineer. At Daphne's request, they listened to Sting and Annie Lennox, though Afridi insisted on playing a few tracks of Stephane Grappelli and Django Reinhardt. By mutual consent they did not speak about Guldaar, but after the first glass of wine they drank a toast to Jehangir Daruwalla's memory.

After they sat down to eat, Afridi explained that the American hostage, Luke McKenzie, had been found wandering along a desert highway northwest of Dubai. In the aftermath of Guldaar's death, the Americans, or at least Fletcher's branch of the NSA, and Manav Shinde seemed to have found common cause. Though the Peregrine contracts would undoubtedly be canceled, there was talk of collaboration. The minister of state for defense had tendered his resignation. Anna was let off with a bureaucratic scolding, even as a confidential commendation was added to her file. She had spoken with Afridi this morning and reported that Yaqub's body had been returned to Pakistan. He was now buried beside his father in Peshawar. Sounding tired and depressed,

Anna admitted that she needed some time off. Fortunately, a friend had invited to her to visit him in Goa, where she was planning to spend a couple of weeks. She asked Afridi to pass on her greetings to Daphne.

The soufflé turned out successfully, though Afridi had been worried it might collapse when he took it out of the oven. Daphne even asked for a second helping.

'What kind of cheese is it made from?' she asked.

'Yak,' said Afridi. 'There's a company in Nepal that makes it.'

'A Himalayan soufflé,' she said, teasing him. 'I suppose that's appropriate. You continue to surprise me. Gardening. Espionage. Cooking. A man of many talents, Colonel.'

She raised the wine glass to her lips.

'Please call me Imtiaz,' he said.

'Imtiaz,' she repeated after him. 'What does it mean?'

'It's difficult to translate from Arabic,' said Afridi, looking down at his plate self-consciously, 'but essentially it means "distinguished."'

'That's appropriate,' she said.

'It can also mean "antique,"' he added.

She laughed.

For dessert, a sticky toffee pudding had been ordered in from a restaurant nearby. They shared it with two spoons and continued to avoid talking about the events of the past few weeks. Instead they spoke about their memories of Bombay. Afridi had lived there briefly in the late sixties, while Daphne recalled when she'd first gone there more than a decade later. Both felt it was a much more interesting city than Delhi. No less corrupt and far more chaotic, but without the insidious cynicism that lay at the heart of India's capital, the smug politics and intrigue.

'Do you think you might go back to Bombay?'

'I suppose I could. I've still got a flat there, in Bandra. Jimmy bought it for me years ago and put it in my name. But I've lost touch with most people there and it would probably feel very strange, without Jehangir…or Naseem.'

For a few seconds her face subsided into sadness, and Afridi could see a lost expression in her eyes.

'Or you could go back to your hometown of Mughal Sarai?' he suggested, half-joking.

She shook her head, and her smile returned. 'I don't have family there anymore. In fact, I don't have anyone at all.'

'You're welcome to stay here as long as you wish,' he offered.

'Thank you. Let's see,' she said. 'You'll be tired of me within a week.'

They sat in silence for a while. Then Daphne pushed back her chair and picked up their plates and took them to the kitchen. Afridi helped her clear the table. Afterwards, he poured her the last of the wine and got a scotch for himself. They avoided saying anything more about the future but talked about books and music, as well as films. It was the kind of relaxed, meandering conversation in which the intimacy in the tone of their voices mattered more than the meaning of their words. They were at ease in each other's company like old friends meeting after a long separation. Eventually, Daphne shook her head in disbelief, startled by a thought.

'What is it?' Afridi asked.

'Isn't it odd, but I feel as if we've known each other for years,' she said, 'though it's hardly been a week. Maybe we met in a previous life.'

'I wouldn't know anything about that,' he replied. 'Though sometimes it isn't the length of time you've known someone but the circumstances that bring you together that create a bond.'

Instead of answering him, Daphne stood up and came across to his chair and placed her hands on the armrests. Leaning forward, she put her lips to his mouth, a slow, lingering kiss, as if surrendering unspoken words. Afridi responded, reaching up to brush a hand through her hair and across her cheek. After almost a minute, she drew back and looked at him with an expression no camera could have captured.

'I'll see you tomorrow,' she said. 'Thank you. I'll let myself out.'

Knowing the guards would escort her safely back to her suite, Afridi remained motionless by the dwindling fire.

ALSO FROM SPEAKING TIGER

THE SHAH OF CHICAGO

Nate Rabe

'Rabe-sahib has told a story as fresh as today's headlines, but as unexpected as a twist in the very best of Hindi films—Shah is not a hero, either of Chicago or of Chandni Chowk—but he is real and full of exquisite flaws... Be surprised, be sucked in, be seduced.' —Tom Alter

When he gets out of jail for the seventh time, Yaqub Shah aka Jack King—from Chicago—vows never to go back again. Fed up of running small-time scams for other people, he convinces his law-abiding guardian, Uncle Jalal, that he wants to sort out his life and return to Pakistan. What he really has in mind is to set up a blockbuster heroin deal—sourcing product from the motherland, and supplying to the Midwest in America—and retire as the 'King of Chicago.'

Heading back to the place of a painful past—his dear mother long gone and an estranged father only interested in growing his business empire—Jack is determined to stay no longer than necessary. Pakistan, however, finds a way of getting under his skin—he falls in love with the beautiful Afroz, who reminds him of the futility of running away from home; he gets into a drunken scuffle with Mushtaq Gill, who happens to be the head of the National Intelligence Agency; and when things really start heating up, he must confront himself and the life he truly desires.

A thrilling caper, hedonistic romp and a poignant homecoming story, *The Shah of Chicago* is a high-octane, swashbuckling adventure.

ALSO FROM SPEAKING TIGER

THE INVISIBLE MAN FROM SALEM

Christoffer Carlsson

'This unique Nordic thriller of enthralling suspense takes a sickening dive into the murky corners of Stockholm and its suburbs … a new and inspiring example.' —*Le Figaro Magazine*

'An unnerving, unsettling, and intelligent crime novel.' —*Dagens Nyheter*

'Carlsson's *The Invisible Man from Salem* is something different in the current wave of Nordic crime: ambitious, idiosyncratic and dripping with noir atmosphere. […] Leo Junker is a memorable creation.' —Barry Forshaw, author of *The Rough Guide to Crime Fiction*

In the final days of summer, a young woman is shot dead in her apartment. Three floors above, the blue lights of the police cars awaken disgraced ex-officer Leo Junker. Though suspended from the force, he can't stay away for long. Bluffing his way onto the crime scene, he examines the dead woman and sees that she is clasping a cheap necklace—a necklace he instantly recognizes.

As Leo sets out on a rogue investigation to catch the killer, a series of frightening connections emerge, linking the murder to his own troubled youth in Salem—a suburb of Stockholm where social and racial tensions run high—and forcing him to confront a long ago incident that changed his life forever.

Now, in backstreets, shadowed alleyways, and decaying suburbs ruled by Stockholm's criminal underground, the search for the young woman's killer—and the truth about Leo's past—begins.